Praise for #1 *New York Times* bestselling author Debbie Macomber

"A sweet holiday treat from Macomber has become an annual staple for many readers."
—*RT Book Reviews* on *The Perfect Christmas*

"An entertaining holiday story that will surely touch the heart… Best of all, readers will rediscover the magic of Christmas."
—*Bookreporter.com* on *Call Me Mrs. Miracle*

"Macomber's latest charming contemporary Christmas romance is a sweetly satisfying, gently humorous story that celebrates the joy and love of the holiday season."
—*Booklist* on *Christmas Letters*

"Another tale of romance in the lives of ordinary people, with a message that life is like a fruitcake: full of unexpected delights."
—*Publishers Weekly* on *There's Something About Christmas*

"It's just not Christmas without a Debbie Macomber story."
—*Armchair Interviews*

Praise for Lee Tobin McClain

"Will tug at the readers' heartstrings… Demonstrates that it is possible for one to keep their faith through life's struggles."
—*RT Book Reviews* on *Engaged to the Single Mom*

DEBBIE MACOMBER

The Gift of Christmas

mira

mira

ISBN-13: 978-0-7783-0864-5

The Gift of Christmas

Recycling programs
for this product may
not exist in your area.

Midnight Sons

Alaska Skies
  (*Brides for Brothers* and
  The Marriage Risk)
Alaska Nights
  (*Daddy's Little Helper* and
  Because of the Baby)
Alaska Home
  (*Falling for Him,*
  Ending in Marriage and
  Midnight Sons and Daughters)

This Matter of Marriage
Montana
Thursdays at Eight
Between Friends
Changing Habits
Married in Seattle
  (*First Comes Marriage* and
  Wanted: Perfect Partner)
Right Next Door
  (*Father's Day* and
  The Courtship of Carol Sommars)
Wyoming Brides
  (*Denim and Diamonds* and
  The Wyoming Kid)
Fairy Tale Weddings
  (*Cindy and the Prince* and
  Some Kind of Wonderful)
The Man You'll Marry
  (*The First Man You Meet* and
  The Man You'll Marry)
Orchard Valley Grooms
  (*Valerie* and *Stephanie*)
Orchard Valley Brides
  (*Norah* and *Lone Star Lovin'*)
The Sooner the Better
An Engagement in Seattle
  (*Groom Wanted* and
  Bride Wanted)
Out of the Rain
  (*Marriage Wanted* and
  Laughter in the Rain)
Learning to Love
  (*Sugar and Spice* and
  Love by Degree)

You…Again
  (*Baby Blessed* and
  Yesterday Once More)
The Unexpected Husband
  (*Jury of His Peers* and
  Any Sunday)
Three Brides, No Groom
Love in Plain Sight
  (*Love 'n' Marriage* and
  Almost an Angel)
I Left My Heart
  (*A Friend or Two* and
  No Competition)
Marriage Between Friends
  (*White Lace and Promises* and
  Friends—And Then Some)
A Man's Heart
  (*The Way to a Man's Heart*
  and *Hasty Wedding*)
North to Alaska
  (*That Wintry Feeling* and
  Borrowed Dreams)
On a Clear Day
  (*Starlight* and
  Promise Me Forever)
To Love and Protect
  (*Shadow Chasing* and
  For All My Tomorrows)
Home in Seattle
  (*The Playboy and the Widow*
  and *Fallen Angel*)
Together Again
  (*The Trouble with Caasi* and
  Reflections of Yesterday)
The Reluctant Groom
  (*All Things Considered*
  and *Almost Paradise*)
A Real Prince
  (*The Bachelor Prince*
  and *Yesterday's Hero*)
Private Paradise
  (in *That Summer Place*)

Debbie Macomber's
  Cedar Cove Cookbook
Debbie Macomber's
  Christmas Cookbook

CONTENTS

THE GIFT OF CHRISTMAS

Debbie Macomber

To Rachel Hauck, Roxanne St. Claire,
Virelle Kidder and Martha Powers,
my Florida sisters.

One

Ashley Robbins clenched her hands together as she sat in a plush velvet chair ten stories up in a Seattle high-rise. The cashier's check to Cooper Masters was in her purse. Rather than mail him the money, Ashley had impulsively decided to deliver it herself.

People moved about her, in and out of doors, as she thoughtfully watched their actions. Curious glances darted her way. She had never been one to blend into the background. Over the years she'd wondered if it was the striking ash blond hair that attracted attention, or her outrageous choice of clothes. Today, however, since she was meeting Cooper, she'd dressed conservatively. Never shy, she was a hit in the classroom, using techniques that had others shaking their heads in wonder. But no one doubted that she was the most popular teacher at John Knox Christian High School. Cooper had made that possible. No one knew he had loaned her the money to complete her studies. Not even Claudia, her best friend and Cooper's niece.

Ashley and Cooper were the godparents to John, Claudia's older boy. Being linked to Cooper had pleased Ashley more than her friend suspected. She'd been secretly in love with him since she was sixteen. It amazed her that no one had guessed during those ten years, least of all Cooper.

"Mr. Masters will see you now," his receptionist informed her.

Ashley smiled her appreciation and followed the attractive woman through the heavy oak door.

"Ashley." Cooper stood and strode to the front of his desk. "What a pleasant surprise."

"Hello, Cooper." He'd changed over the last six months since she'd seen him. Streaks of silver ran through his hair, and tiny lines fanned out from his eyes. But it would take more than years to disguise his strongly marked features. He wasn't a compellingly handsome man, not in the traditional sense, but seeing him again stirred familiar feelings of admiration and appreciation for all he'd done for her.

"Sit down, please." He indicated a chair not unlike the one she'd recently vacated. "What can I do for you? Any problems?"

She responded with a slight shake of her head. He had always been generous with her. Deep down, she doubted that there was anything she couldn't ask of this man, although she didn't expect any more favors, and he was probably aware of that.

"Everything's fine." She didn't meet his eyes as she opened the clasp of her purse and took out the check. "I wanted to personally give you this." Extending her arm, she handed him the check. "I owe you so much, it seemed almost rude to put it in the mail." The satisfaction of paying off the loan was secondary to the opportunity of seeing Cooper again. If she'd been honest with herself, she would have admitted she was hungry for the sight of him. After all these months she'd been looking for an excuse.

He glanced at the check and seemed to notice the amount. Two dark brows arched with surprise. "This satisfies the loan," he said thoughtfully. Half turning, he placed the check in the center of the large wooden desk. "Your mother tells me you've taken a second job?" The intonation in his voice made the statement a question.

"You see her more often than I do," she said in an attempt to evade the question. Her mother had been the Masters' cook and housekeeper from the time Ashley was a child.

He regarded her steadily, and although she could read no emotion in his eyes, she felt his irritation. "Was it necessary to pay this off as quickly as possible?"

"Fast? I've owed you this money for over four years." She laughed lightly. Someone had once told her that her laugh was one of the most appealing things about her. Sweet, gentle, melodic. She chanced a look at Cooper, whose cool dark eyes revealed nothing.

"I didn't care if you ever paid me back. I certainly didn't expect you'd half kill yourself to return it."

The displeasure in his voice surprised her. Taken aback, she watched as he stalked to the far corner of the office, putting as much distance between them as possible. Was it pride that had driven her to pay him back as quickly as possible? Maybe, but she doubted it. The loan to finish her schooling had been the answer to long, difficult prayers. From the time she'd been accepted into the University of Washington, she had attended on faith. Faith that God would supply the money for books and tuition. Faith that if God wanted her to obtain her teaching degree, then He would meet her needs. And He had. In the beginning things had worked well. She roomed with Claudia and managed two part-time jobs. But when Claudia and Seth got married, she was forced to find other accommodations, which quickly drained her funds. Cooper's offer had been completely unexpected. The loan had come at a time when she'd been hopeless and had been preparing to withdraw from classes. They'd never discussed terms, but surely he'd known she intended to repay him.

A tentative smile brushed her lips. She'd thought he would be pleased. His reaction amazed her. She attempted to keep her voice level as she assured him, "It was the honorable thing to do."

"But it wasn't necessary," he answered, turning back to her.

Again she experienced the familiar twinge of awareness that only Cooper Masters was capable of stirring within her.

"It was for me," she countered quickly.

"It wasn't necessary," he repeated in a flat tone.

Ashley released a slow breath. "We could go on like this all day. I didn't mean to offend you, I only came here today because I wanted to show my appreciation."

He stared back at her, then slowly nodded. "I understand."

Silence stretched between them.

"Have you heard from Claudia and Seth?" he asked after a while.

Ashley smiled. They had so little in common that whenever they were together that the conversation invariably centered around Claudia and their godson. "The last I heard she said something about coming down for Christmas."

"I hope they do." His intercom buzzed, and he leaned over and pressed a button on the phone. "Yes, Gloria?"

"Mr. Benson is here."

"Thank you."

Taking her cue, Ashley stood. "I won't keep you." Her fingers brushed her wool skirt. She'd been hoping he would notice the new outfit and comment. He hadn't. "Thank you again. I guess you know that I wouldn't have been able to finish school without your help."

"I was wondering..." Cooper moved to her side, his look slightly uneasy, as if he was unsure of himself. "I mean, I can understand if you'd rather not."

"Rather not what?" She couldn't remember him ever acting with anything but supreme confidence. In control of himself and every situation.

"Have dinner with me. A small celebration for paying off the loan."

"I'd like that very much. Anytime." Her heart soared at the suggestion; she wasn't sure how she managed to keep her voice level.

"Tonight at seven?"

"Wonderful. Should I wear something...formal?" It wouldn't hurt to ask, and he hadn't mentioned where he intended they dine.

"Dress comfortably."

"Great."

An hour later Ashley's heart still refused to beat at a normal pace. This was the first time Cooper had asked her out or given any indication he would like to see her socially. The man was difficult to understand, always had been. Even Claudia didn't fully know him; she saw him as dignified, predictable and overly concerned with re-

spectability. In some ways he was, but through the years
Ashley had seen past that facade. He might be refined,
and sometimes overly proper, but he was a man who'd
been forced to take on heavy responsibility at an early
age. There had been little time for fun or frivolity in his
life. Ashley wanted to be the one to change that. She
loved him. Her mother claimed that opposites attract,
and after meeting Cooper, Ashley had never doubted the
truth of that statement.

Ashley chose to wear her finest designer jeans, knowing she looked good. At five foot nine, she was all legs.
Her pink sweatshirt contained a starburst of sequins that
extended to the ends of the full length sleeves. Her hair
was styled in a casual perm, and soft curls reached her
shoulders. Her perfume was a fragrance Cooper had
given her the previous Christmas. Although not imagina-
tive, the gift had pleased her immeasurably, even though
he hadn't given it to her personally, but to her mother,
who'd passed it on. When she'd phoned to thank him,
his response had been clipped and vaguely ill-at-ease.
Politely, he'd assured her that it was his duty, since they
were John's godparents. He'd also told her he'd sent the
same fragrance to Claudia. Ashley had hung up the phone
feeling deflated. The next time she'd seen him had been
in June, when her mother had gone to the hospital for sur-
gery. Cooper had come for a visit at the same time Ashley had arrived. Standing on opposite sides of the bed,
her sleeping mother between them, Ashley had hungrily
drunk in the sight of him. Their short conversation had
been carried on in hushed tones, and after a while they
hadn't spoken at all. Afterward he'd had coffee out of a
machine, and she'd sipped fruit juice as they sat talking

in the waiting area at the end of the corridor. She hadn't seen him again until today.

Over the months she had dated several men, and she'd recently been seeing Dennis Webb, another teacher, on a steady basis. But no one had ever attracted her the way Cooper did. Whenever a pensive mood overtook her, she recognized how pointless that attraction was. Whole universes stretched between them, both social and economic. For Ashley, loving Cooper Masters was as impossible as understanding income tax forms.

The doorbell chimed precisely at seven. Claudia had claimed that she could set her watch by Cooper. If he said seven, he would arrive exactly at seven.

A sense of panic filled Ashley as she glanced at her wristwatch. It couldn't possibly be that time already, could it? With one red cowboy boot on and the other lying on the carpet, she looked around frantically. The laundry still hadn't been put away. Quickly she hobbled across the floor and shoved the basket full of folded clean clothes into the entryway closet, then closed the door with her back as she conducted a sweeping inspection of the apartment. Expelling a calming sigh, she forced herself to smile casually as she opened the door.

He greeted her with a warm look, that gradually faded as he handed her a florist's box.

To Cooper, apparently informal meant a three-piece suit and flowers. Glancing down at her jeans and sweatshirt, one cowboy boot on, the other missing, she smiled weakly and felt wretched. "Thank you." She took the small white box. "Sit down, please." Hurrying ahead of him, she fluffed up the pillows at the end of the sofa, then hugged one to her stomach. "I'm running a little late tonight. If you'll give me a few minutes I'll change clothes."

"You look fine just the way you are," he murmured, glancing at his watch.

What he was really saying, she realized, was that they would be late for their reservation if she took the time to change clothes. After glancing down at the hot pink sweatshirt, she raised her gaze to meet his. "You're sure? It'll only take a minute."

His nod seemed determined. Self-conscious, embarrassed and angry with herself, Ashley sat at the opposite end of the sofa and slipped her foot into the other boot. After tucking in her denim pant leg, she sat up and reached for the florist's box. A lovely white orchid was nestled in a bed of sheer green paper. A gasp of pleasure escaped her.

"Oh, Cooper," she murmured, feeling close to tears. No one had ever given her an orchid. "Thank you."

"Since I didn't know the color of your dress…" He paused to correct himself. "…your outfit…this seemed appropriate." He remained standing, studying her. "It's the type women wear on their wrist."

As Ashley lifted the orchid from the box, its gentle fragrance drifted pleasantly to her. "I'm always having to thank you, Cooper. You've been very good to me."

He dismissed her appreciation with a hard shake of his head. "Nonsense."

She knew that further discussion would only embarrass them both. Standing, she glanced at the closet door, knowing nothing would induce her to open it and expose her folded underwear to Cooper. "I'll get my purse and we can go."

"You might want to wear a coat," he suggested. "I heard something about the possibility of snow over the radio this afternoon."

"Yes, of course." If he remained standing exactly as he was, she might be able to open the door just enough to slip her hand in and jerk her faux fur jacket off the hanger. Somehow she managed it. Turning, she noted that Cooper was regarding her curiously. Rather than fabricate a wild excuse about why she couldn't open the closet all the way, she decided to say nothing.

He took the coat from her grasp, holding it open for her to slip her arms into the sleeves. It seemed as if his hands lingered longer than necessary on her shoulders, but it could have been her imagination. He had never been one to display affection openly.

"Where are we going?" she asked, and her voice trembled slightly, affected by even the most impersonal touch.

"I chose an Italian restaurant not far from here. I hope that suits you."

"Sounds delicious. I love Italian food." Her tastes in food were wide and varied, but it wouldn't have mattered. If he had suggested hot dogs, she would have been thrilled. The idea of Cooper eating anything with his fingers produced a quivering smile. If he noticed it, he said nothing.

Cooper parked outside the small, family-owned restaurant and came around to her side of the car, opening the door for her. It was apparent when they were seated that he had never been there before. The thought flashed through her mind that he didn't want to be seen with her where he might be recognized. But she quickly dismissed the idea. If he didn't want to be with her, then he wouldn't have asked her out. Those thoughts were unworthy of Cooper, who had always been good to her.

"Is everything all right?" As he stared across the table at her, a frown drew his brows together.

"Yes, of course." She looked down at her menu, guiltily forcing a smile on her face. "I wonder how long it'll be before we know if Claudia will be coming for Christmas," she said, hoping to resume the even flow of conversation.

"Time's getting close. I imagine we'll know soon."

Thanksgiving was the following weekend, but Christmas displays were already up in stores; some had shown up as early as Halloween. Doubtless Seth and Claudia would let them know by the end of next week. The prospect of sharing the holiday with her friend—and therefore Cooper—produced a glow of happiness inside Ashley.

The waiter took their order, then promptly delivered their fresh green salads.

"It's been exceptionally chilly for this time of the year," Cooper commented, lifting his fork, his gaze centered on his plate.

Ashley thought it was a sad commentary that their only common ground consisted of Claudia and the weather. "Yes, it has." She looked up to note that a veiled look had come over his features. Perhaps he was thinking the same thing.

The conversation during dinner seemed stiff and strained to her. Cooper asked her about school and politely inquired if she liked teaching. In return she asked him about the business supply operation he owned and was surprised to learn how much it had grown over the past few years. The knowledge should have pleased her, but instead it only served to remind her that he was a rich man and she was still struggling financially.

When they stepped out of the restaurant, she was pleased to discover that it was snowing.

"Oh, Cooper, look!" she cried with delight. "I love it when it snows. Let's go for a walk." She couldn't keep the excitement out of her voice. "There's something magical about walking in the falling snow."

"Are you sure that's what you want?" He glanced at the thin layer of white powder that covered the ground, then he looked up, his expression odd as his eyes searched hers.

"I'd forgotten, you'll have to drive back in this stuff. Maybe it wouldn't be such a good idea," she commented, unable to hide her disappointment.

His hand cupped her elbow, bringing her near, and when she slipped on the slick sidewalk he quickly placed his arm around her waist, preventing her from falling. He left his arm there, holding her protectively close to his side. Her spirits soared at being linked this way with Cooper.

"Where would you like to walk?" An indiscernible expression clouded his eyes.

"There's a marina a couple of blocks from here, and I love to watch the snow fall on the water, but if you'd rather not, I understand."

"By all means, let's go to the marina." The smile he gave her was the first genuine one she'd witnessed the entire evening.

"Doesn't this make you want to sing?" she asked, and started to hum "White Christmas" even before he could answer.

"No," he said, and chuckled. "It makes me want to sit in front of a roaring fireplace with a warm drink."

She clucked and pressed her lips together to keep from laughing.

"What was that all about?"

"What?" she asked, feigning ignorance.

"That silly little noise you just made."

"If you must know, I don't think you've done anything impulsive or daring in your entire life, Cooper Masters." She said it all in one giant breath, then watched as a shocked look came over his face.

"Of course I have," he insisted righteously.

"Then I dare you to do something right now."

"What?" He looked unsure.

"Make a snowball and throw it at me," she demanded. Breaking from his hold, she ran a few steps ahead of him. "Bet you can't do it," she taunted, and waved her hands at him.

With marked determination, Cooper stuffed his hands inside his coat pockets. "This is silly."

"It's supposed to be crazy, remember?" she chided him softly.

"But it's not right for a man to throw snowballs at a woman."

"Will this make things easier for you?" she shouted, bending over to scoop up a handful of snow. With an accuracy that astonished her, she threw a snowball that hit him directly in the middle of his chest. If she was surprised, the horrified look on Cooper's face sent her into peals of laughter. Losing her balance on the ice-slickened sidewalk, she went sprawling to the cement with an undignified plop.

"That's what you get for hurling snow at courteous gentlemen," Cooper called once he was sure she wasn't hurt. As he advanced toward her, he shifted a tightly packed snowball from one hand to the other.

"Cooper, you wouldn't—would you?" She gave him her most defenseless look, batting her eyelashes. "Here, help me up." She extended a hand to him, which he ignored.

A wicked gleam flashed from the dark depths of his eyes. "I thought you said I never did anything crazy or daring?"

"You wouldn't!" Her voice trembled with laughter as she struggled to stand up.

"You're right, I wouldn't," he murmured, dropping the snowball and reaching for her. Surprise rocked her as he pulled her into his arms. He hesitated momentarily, as if expecting her to protest. When she didn't, he gently brushed the hair from her temple and just as softly pressed his mouth over hers. The kiss should have been tender, but the moment their lips met it became hungry and needy. The effect was jarring, as if a bolt of awareness were flashing through them. They broke apart, shocked and breathless. The oxygen was trapped in her lungs, making it impossible to breathe.

"Did I hurt you?" he asked, his voice thick with concern.

A shake of her head was all she could manage. "Cooper?" Her voice was a mere whisper. "Would you mind doing that again?"

"Now?"

She nodded.

"Here?"

Again she nodded.

He pulled her back into his embrace, his eyes drinking deeply from hers. This time the kiss was gentle, as if he, too, needed to test these sensations. Lost in the swirling awareness, Ashley felt as if he had touched the deep inner part of her being. For years she had dreamed of this moment, wondered what effect his touch would have on her. Now she knew. She felt a free-flowing happiness steal over her. He had taken her heart and touched her spirit. When he entwined his fingers in the curling length of her hair, she pressed her head against his shoulder and breathed in deeply. A soft smile lifted her lips at the sound of his furiously pounding heart.

"This is crazy," he murmured hoarsely.

"No," she swiftly countered. "This is wonderful."

Carefully he relaxed his hold, easing her from his embrace. His features were unnaturally pale as he smoothed the hair at the side of his head with an impatient movement. "I'm too old for you." His mouth had thinned, and his look was remote.

Her bubble of happy contentment burst; he regretted kissing her. What had been so wonderful for her was a source of embarrassment for him. "I dared you to do something impulsive, remember?" she said with forced gaiety. "It doesn't mean anything. I've been kissed before. It happens all the time."

"I'm sure it does," he replied stiffly. His gaze moved pointedly to his watch. "I think it would be best if I took you home now. Perhaps we could see the marina another time."

"Sure."

His touch was impersonal as they strolled purposefully back toward the restaurant parking lot. To hide her discomfort, Ashley began to hum Christmas music again.

"Rushing the season a bit, aren't you?"

She concentrated on moving one foot in front of the other. "I suppose. But the snow makes it feel like Christmas. Christ wouldn't mind if we celebrated His birth every day of the year."

"The shopping malls would love it if we did," he remarked cynically.

"You're speaking of the commercial aspect of the holiday, I'm talking about the spiritual one."

Cooper didn't comment. In fact, neither one of them spoke until he pulled up to the curb in front of her apartment building.

"Would you like to come in and warm up? It would only take a minute to heat up some cocoa." Although the offer was sincere, she knew he wouldn't accept.

"Perhaps another time."

There wouldn't be another time. He wouldn't ask her out again; the whole evening had been a fiasco. Cooper Masters was a powerful, influential man, whereas she was a high school English Lit teacher.

"You'll let me know if you hear anything from Seth and Claudia?"

"Of course."

He came around to her side of the car, opening the door. "You don't need to walk me all the way to my door," she mumbled miserably.

"There's every need." Although his voice was level, she could tell he was determined to live up to what he felt a gentleman should be.

She didn't argue when he took the keys out of her hand and opened the door of her first-floor apartment for her. "Thank you," she murmured. "The evening was…"

"Crazy," he finished for her.

Wonderful, her mind insisted in return. Afraid of what her eyes would reveal, she lowered her head and her blond curls fell forward, wreathing her face. "Crazy," she repeated.

A finger placed under her chin lifted her eyes to his. His were dark and unreadable, hers soft and shining. Slowly his hand moved to caress the soft, smooth skin of her cheek. The gentle caress sent the blood pulsing through her veins, flushing her face with telltale color.

"If ever you're in trouble or need someone, I want you to contact me."

Although he had never verbally said as much, she had always been aware that she could go to him if ever she needed help.

"I will." Her voice sounded irritatingly weak.

"I want you to promise me." He unbuttoned his coat pocket and took out a business card. Using the door as a support, he wrote down a phone number. "You can reach me here any time of the day."

"I'm not going to trouble you with—"

"Promise me, Ashley."

He was so serious, his look demanding. "Okay," she agreed, accepting the card. "But why?"

A long moment passed before he answered her. "I have a vested interest in you," he said, and shrugged, the indifferent gesture contradicting his words. "Besides, I'd hate to have anything happen to Johnny's godmother."

"Nothing's going to happen to me."

"In case it does, I want you to know I'll always be there."

The business card seemed to sear her hand. In his own way, Cooper cared about her. "Thank you." Impulsively, she raised two fingers to her lips, then brushed them across his mouth. His hand stopped hers, gripping her wrist; his look branded her. Slowly he lowered his mouth to hers in a gentle, sweet kiss.

"Good night, Ashley."

"Good night." Standing in the open doorway, she watched until he drove into the dark night. A solitary figure illuminated by the falling snow.

Expelling her breath in a long quivering sigh, she tucked the card in her purse. Why did she have to love Cooper Masters? Why couldn't she feel for Webb what she did for Cooper? Webb was nice and almost as unpredictable as she was. Maybe that was why they got along so well. Yet it was Cooper who occupied her thoughts. Cooper who made her heart sing. Cooper who filled her dreams. The time had come to wake up and face reality. She was at the age when she should start thinking about marriage and a family, because she definitely wanted children. Cooper wasn't going to be interested in someone like her. He might care about her, even feel some affection for her, but she wasn't the type of woman he would ever ask to be his wife.

Troubled and confused, Ashley made herself a cup of cocoa and sat on the sofa, her feet tucked under the cushion next to her. Things had been so easy for her friends, even Claudia. They met someone, fell in love, got married and started a family. Maybe God had decided He didn't want her to marry. The thought seemed intolerable, but she had learned long ago not to second-guess her heavenly Father. She'd given Him her life, her will, even Cooper's safekeeping. Now she had to learn to trust.

She rinsed out the cup, placed it in the kitchen sink and turned out the lights. Her eyes fell on her purse, hanging on the closet doorknob. She wondered if the day might come when she would need to use the card, not that she intended to.

That same thought ran through her mind several days later when the police officer directed her to the phone. She didn't want to contact Cooper, so she'd tried phoning her family first, hoping she would catch her father at home. But there had been no answer.

"Is there anyone else, Miss?" the tall, uniformed man asked.

"Yes," she answered tightly, opening her purse and taking out the card. Her fingers actually trembled as she dialed the number.

"Cooper Masters."

As she suspected, he'd given her his private cell number. "Oh, hi…it's Ashley."

"Ashley." His voice carried clearly over the line. "What's wrong?"

"It isn't an emergency or anything," she began, feeling incredibly silly. "I mean, I don't think they'll keep me."

"Ashley," he heaved her name on an angry sigh. "What's going on?"

"It's a long story."

"All right, tell me where you are. I'll come to you, and then we'll straighten everything out."

She hesitated, swallowing past the lump forming in her throat. "I'm in jail."

Two

"Jail!" Cooper's voice boomed over the line. "I'll be there in ten minutes."

"But, Cooper, Kent's a good thirty minutes from downtown Seattle."

"Kent?" The anger in his voice was barely controlled.

"If you're going to get so mad…" Ashley let the rest of the sentence fade, realizing that the phone line had already been disconnected.

Casting a glance at the police officer beside her, she gave him a wary smile. "A friend's coming."

A smile quivered at one corner of the older man's mouth. "I heard." Looking away, he asked, "Would you like a cup of coffee while you wait?"

"No thanks."

Ashley heard Cooper's voice several minutes before she saw him. By the time he was brought into the area where she was waiting, there wasn't a person in the entire police station who hadn't heard him. She had always known him to be a calm, discreet person. That he would react this way to a minor misunderstanding shocked her. Although…a lot of things about Cooper had surprised her lately. She was standing, her face devoid of color, when he was escorted into the room.

"Can you tell me what's going on here?" he demanded.

His look did little to encourage confidences; she swallowed tightly and waved her hand helplessly. "Well, apparently someone took the license plate off Milligan."

"Who the heck…?" He paused and took a deep, calming breath. "Who's Milligan?"

"Not who," she corrected, "but what. Milligan's my moped. I parked it outside the Mexican restaurant where I work odd hours, and someone apparently took off with my license plate."

"That isn't any reason to arrest you!" he shouted.

"They haven't arrested me!" she yelled in return, and was humiliated when her voice cracked and wavered. "And if you won't quit shouting at me, then you can just leave."

Raking his fingers roughly through his hair, Cooper stalked to the other side of the room. His mouth was tightly pinched, and he said nothing for several long moments. "All right, let's try this again," he replied in a deceivingly soft tone. "Start at the beginning, and tell me everything."

"There's not much to tell. Someone took the license plate, and, since I don't have the registration on me, the police need some evidence that I own the bike. I haven't been arrested or anything. In fact, they've been very nice." In nervous reaction she looped a long strand of curly hair around her ear. "All I need for you to do is go to my apartment and bring back the registration for Milligan. Then I'll be free to leave." She opened her purse and took out her key ring, then extracted the key to the apartment. "Here," she said, handing it to him. "The registration's in the kitchen, in the silverware drawer, stuck under the aluminum foil. I keep all my important papers there."

If he thought her record storage system was a bit unusual, he said nothing.

"There's a lawyer on his way here, I'll leave word at the front desk for him." Without another word, he turned and left the room.

Within twenty minutes she heard him talking to the officer who had offered her the coffee. A few moments later they both entered the waiting area.

"You're free to go," the policeman explained. "Although I'm afraid we can't let you drive the moped until you have a new license plate."

Before she could protest Cooper inserted, "No need to worry. I've already made arrangements for the bike to be picked up." He turned and directed his words to Ashley. "It'll be delivered to your place sometime tomorrow afternoon."

Rather than argue, Ashley mutely agreed.

"If you're ready, I'll take you home," Cooper said.

Shoving her knit cap onto her head, she stood and swung her backpack over her shoulder, then gave the kind officer a polite smile. She wasn't pleased with the way things were working out. If she didn't have Milligan, she would have to take a series of busses to and from work, with a long trek between stops. Surely something could be done to enable her to ride her moped until she could replace the plate. One look from Cooper discouraged her from asking.

His hand cupped her elbow as they walked to the parking lot. Her attention was centered on the scenery outside the car window as they crossed the Green River and connected with the freeway. Wordlessly, he took the first exit and a couple of minutes later pulled into the parking lot to her apartment building.

He turned off the engine, then called his office. "Gloria, cancel the rest of my appointments for today," he said stiffly, his voice clipped and abrupt. Without waiting for a confirmation, he promptly ended the call, and then turned to Ashley. "Invite me in for coffee."

Her heart lodged someplace near her throat. "Yes, of course." She didn't wait for him to come around to her side of the car and let herself out. He gave her a disapproving look as they met in front of the vehicle. He opened the apartment door and returned the key to her. She placed it back on the key ring and took off her jacket, carelessly tossing it across the top of the sofa. He removed his black overcoat and neatly folded it over the back of the chair opposite the sofa.

"I'll put on the coffee." She moved into the kitchen, pouring water into the small, five-cup pot. She could hear Cooper agitatedly pacing the floor behind her.

"Why are you so angry with me?" she asked. She couldn't look at him, not when he was so obviously furious with her. "I couldn't help it if someone stole my license plate. I never should have phoned you, I'm sorry I did."

"I'm not mad at you," he stormed. "I'm angry that you were put through that ordeal, that you were treated like a criminal, that..." He left the rest unsaid.

"It's not the policeman's fault. He was only doing his job," she tried to explain, still not facing him. Her fingers trembled as she added the grounds to the pot, placed the lid on top and set it to brew.

A large masculine hand landed on her shoulder, and

she had to fight not to lay her cheek on it. A subtle pressure turned her around. With both hands behind her, she gripped the oven door for support. Slowly she raised her eyes to meet his. She was surprised at the tenderness she saw in the dark depths of his gaze, which seemed to be centered on her mouth. Nervously she moistened her dry lips with the tip of her tongue. She hadn't meant to be provocative, but when Cooper softly groaned she realized what she'd done. When he reached for her, she went willingly into his embrace.

He held her against him, breathing in deeply as he buried his face in the curve of her neck. His hands roamed her back, arching her as close as humanly possible. Ashley molded herself to him, savoring the light scent of musk and man; she longed for him to kiss her. She silently pleaded with him to throw common sense to the wind and crush his mouth over hers. Just being held by him was more happiness than she'd ever hoped to experience. Happiness and torment all rolled into one. An embrace, a light caress, a longing look, could never satisfy her, not when she wanted so much more. Gently he kissed the crown of her head and released her. She wanted to cry with disappointment.

The coffee had begun to perk, and to disguise her emotions, Ashley turned and reached for two cups, waiting for the pot to finish before pouring.

While she dealt with the coffee, Cooper sat in the living room waiting for her. He stood when she entered, taking one cup from her hand.

"I'm sorry, Ashley," he said, his eyes probing hers.

He didn't need to elaborate. He was sorry for his anger, sorry he'd overreacted in the police station, but mostly he regretted throwing aside his self-control and taking her in his arms.

Unable to verbally acknowledge his apology she simply shook her head, letting him know that she understood what he was saying.

"So you work at a Mexican restaurant?" he asked, after taking a sip from the steaming cup.

She wasn't fooled by the veiled interest. He'd commented on the fact she'd taken a second job once before, and he hadn't been pleased then.

"I only work odd hours, less now that I've paid off the loan," she answered, her finger making lazy loops around the rim of her cup.

He pinched his mouth tightly shut, and she recognized that he was biting back words. She wondered how he managed in business confrontations when she found him so easy to read.

Taking another sip of coffee, he stood and moved into the kitchen to put the half-full cup into the sink. "I should go."

She followed his movements. "I haven't thanked you. I...I don't know what I would have done if you hadn't come."

Her appreciation seemed to embarrass him, because his mouth thinned. He lifted his coat off the back of the chair. "I said I wanted you to call me if you needed help. I'm glad you did."

She walked him to the door. "How'd you get to Kent so fast?" Asking him questions helped delay the time when he would leave.

"I was already in the car when you phoned. It was simply a matter of heading in the right direction."

"Oh," she said in a small voice. "I apologize if I inconvenienced you."

"You didn't," he returned gruffly. His eyes met hers then, and again she found herself drowning in those dark depths.

Clenching her hands at her sides, she gave him a falsely cheerful smile. "Thanks again, Cooper. God go with you."

He turned. "And you," he murmured, surprising her.

"Have a nice Thanksgiving."

"I'm sure I will. Are you spending the day with your family?"

"Yes, Mom's making her famous turkey stuffing, and Jeff and his wife, Marsha, are coming." Jeff was her younger brother. John, the youngest Robbins, was working in Spokane and had decided not to make the long drive over the Cascade Mountains in uncertain weather.

Cooper didn't elaborate on his own plans for the holiday, and she didn't ask. "Goodbye, and thanks again."

"Goodbye, Ashley."

As she watched him walk away, she had the strongest desire to blow him a kiss. Immediately she quelled the impulse, but she couldn't help feeling disappointed and frustrated. Closing the front door, she leaned against it and breathed in deeply. She was filling her head with fanciful dreams if she dared to hope Cooper would ever come to love her. Wasting her time and her life. But her heart refused to listen.

As Cooper promised, her moped was delivered safely to her apartment the following afternoon. Webb drove her home from school, and once she dropped off her things, he took her to the Department of Motor Vehicles, where she applied for new license plates. Granted a temporary plate, she was relieved to learn she could now ride Milligan. The moped might not be much, but it got her where she needed to go in the most economical way.

Webb was tall and thin, his facial features almost gaunt, but he was one of the nicest people Ashley had ever known. When he dropped her off at her apartment, she invited him inside. He accepted with a smile.

"Got plans for the weekend?" he asked over a cup of cocoa.

She shrugged. "Not really. I wanted to do some Christmas shopping, but I dread fighting the crowds."

"Want to go skiing Saturday afternoon? I understand the slopes are open."

"I didn't know you skied?" Ashley questioned, her eyes twinkling.

"I don't," Webb confirmed. "I thought you'd teach me."

"Forget that, buddy. You can take lessons like everyone else, then we'll talk about skiing," she said with a laugh. "You could invite me to dinner instead," she suggested hopefully.

"Fine, what are you cooking?"

"Leftovers."

"I'll bring the egg nog," he said with a sly grin.

"Honestly, Webb, how do you do it?" she asked, laughing.

"Do what?"

"Invite me out to dinner, and I end up cooking?"

"It's all in the wrist, all in the wrist," he told her, flexing his hand, looking smug.

Thinking about their conversation later, she couldn't help laughing. Webb was a fun person, but what she felt for Cooper was exciting and intense and couldn't compare with the friendship she shared with her co-worker.

With Cooper she felt vulnerable in a way that couldn't be explained. But then she was in love with Cooper Masters, and that was simply pointless.

Disturbed by her thoughts, she went to change clothes. As part of her preparation for the coming holidays and the extra calories she would consume, she had started to work out. Following the instructions on the DVD she'd purchased, she practiced a routine that used Christian music for an aerobic dancercise program. Dressed in purple satin shorts, pink leg-warmers and a gray T-shirt, she placed her hands on her hips in the middle of the living room and waited for the warm-up instructions. Just as she completed the first round of exercises, the doorbell rang.

She paused, and with her breath deep and ragged, she turned off the player and checked the peep hole in the door. She wasn't expecting anyone. To her horror, she saw it was Cooper.

The doorbell buzzed again, and for a fleeting second she was tempted to let him think she wasn't home, but overriding her embarrassment at having him see her dressed in shorts and a T-shirt was her desire to know why he'd come.

"Hello," she said as she opened the door.

He walked into the apartment, his brow marred by a puzzled frown as he glanced at her. "Maybe I should come back later."

"Nonsense," she mumbled, dismissing the suggestion. She grabbed a towel to wipe the perspiration from her face. "I was just doing some aerobics. Care to join me?"

"No thanks." The corners of his mouth formed deep

grooves as he suppressed a smile. "But don't let me stop you."

His attempt at humor amazed her. It was the first time she could remember him bantering with her—or anyone. "I think I'll skip the rest of the program," she said and laughed.

"Is that coffee I smell?" he asked as he sat on the edge of the sofa.

"No, cocoa. Want some? If you want coffee, though, it'd only take me a minute to brew a pot."

He shook his head.

Looping the towel around her neck, she sat cross-legged opposite him. Her face was glowing and red from the exertion, and she noted the way Cooper couldn't keep his eyes off her. Her heart was pounding fiercely, but she wasn't sure if it was the effects of seeing him again or the aerobics.

For a long moment silence filled the room. "Did you get Mádigan back?" he eventually asked.

"Milligan," she corrected.

"How'd you happen to name a moped Milligan?"

"It was the salesman's name. We went out a couple of times afterward, and I couldn't think of the bike without thinking of Milligan, so I started calling it by his name."

Cooper's mouth narrowed slightly. "What do you do when it rains?"

"Wear rain gear," she returned casually. "It's a bit of a hassle, but I don't mind." Why was he so curious about Milligan? Certainly he'd known—or at least known of—someone who rode a moped before now?

"They're not the safest thing around, are they?"

"I suppose not, but I'm careful." This line of questioning was beginning to rankle. "Why all the curiosity?"

Leaning forward, he rested his elbows on his knees, then quickly shifted position, placing his ankle across one knee as if to give a casual impression. "The more I thought about you riding that moped, the more concerned I became. In checking statistics I discovered—"

"Statistics?" she interrupted him. "Honestly, Cooper, I'm perfectly safe."

He closed his eyes for a moment in apparent frustration, then opened them again. "I knew this wasn't going to be easy. You're as stubborn as Claudia," he said, and expelled his breath slowly. "I'm going to worry about you riding around on that silly bit of chrome and rubber."

"I've had Milligan for almost two years," she inserted, feeling the color drain from her face.

"Ashley," he said, his gaze lingering on her. "I want you to accept these and promise me you'll use them." He took a set of keys from his pocket and held them out to her.

"What are they?" Her voice trembled slightly.

"The keys to a new car. If you don't like the color we can—"

"The keys to a new car?" she echoed in shocked disbelief. "You don't honestly expect me to accept that, do you?"

"No," he acknowledged with a heavy sigh, "knowing you, I didn't think you would. If you insist on paying me—"

"Paying you!" she cried, leaping to her feet. "I just cleared one loan—I'm not about to take on another." Her arms cradling her waist, she paced the floor directly in front of him. "Don't you realize how many enchiladas I had to serve to pay off the last loan? I can't understand you. I can't understand why you'd do something like this."

He inhaled deeply, his look full of trepidation. "I don't want you riding around on a stupid moped and getting yourself killed."

"You know, Cooper, you're beginning to sound like my father. I don't need another parent. I'm a capable twenty-six-year-old woman, not a half-wit teenager. What I ride to work is my prerogative."

"I'm only trying to…"

"I know what you're trying to do," she stormed. "Run my life! I have to admit, I was fooled." Her hand flew to her face and she wiped a thin layer of moisture from her brow. "You gave me your phone number and told me to call, but you didn't tell me there were strings attached."

"You're overreacting!" Although he appeared outwardly calm, she knew he was as unsettled as she was. Bright red color was creeping up his neck, but she doubted that he would vent his emotions in front of her.

"I'm not overreacting!" she exclaimed at fever pitch. "You think that because I phoned you, it gives you the right to step into my life. Keep the car, because I assure you I don't need it."

"As you wish," he murmured, his voice tight and controlled. Standing, he returned the keys to his pocket, his expression a stoic mask. "If you'll excuse me, I have an appointment."

"I hope the car isn't in the apartment parking lot, because the manager will have it towed away." The minute the words were out, she regretted having said them.

"It's not," he assured her coldly. Brushing past her, he let himself out, leaving her feeling deflated and depressed. The nerve of the man… He seemed to think…

Her thoughts faded as she felt a hard knot form in her stomach. Now she'd done it, really done it.

"Happy Thanksgiving, Mom." Ashley laid the freshly baked pie on the kitchen countertop and leaned over to kiss her mother on the cheek.

"Hello, sweetheart." Sarah Robbins placed an arm around Ashley's waist and hugged her close. "I'm glad you're early, dear, would you mind peeling the potatoes?"

"Sure, Mom," she agreed, pulling open the kitchen drawer and taking out the peeler. Ashley had hoped for some time to talk to her mother privately. "How's work?" she asked in what she hoped was a casual tone. "Is Mr. Masters cracking the whip?" Her mother would have thought it disrespectful if she'd called Cooper anything but Mr. Masters, but the formal title nearly stuck in her throat.

"Oh, hardly." Sarah wiped the back of her hand across her apron. "He's always been wonderful to work for. I must say, he certainly loves those nephews of his. There are pictures of John and Scott all over that house, and I swear the only reason he moved out of the condominium was so those boys would have a decent yard to play in when they came to visit. That's all he ever talks about." Opening the oven door, she pulled out the rack to baste the turkey with a giblet broth simmering on the top of the stove. "Have you heard from Claudia and Seth?"

Ashley was chewing on a stalk of celery, and she waited until she'd swallowed before answering. "We chat all the time. I'm hoping she'll be here for Christmas."

"That'll please Mr. Masters. I think he needs a bit of cheering up. He's been in the blackest mood the last couple of days."

"He has?" She hoped to disguise her attentiveness. Her family, especially her mother, wouldn't approve of her interest in Cooper. Her feelings for her mother's employer had never been discussed, but she had sensed her mother's subtle disapproval of even their shared role as godparents more than once. In some ways Sarah Robbins and Cooper Masters were a lot alike. Her mother would view it as inappropriate for Ashley to be interested in an important man like Cooper.

"Did you cook a turkey for him this year?"

"No, he said he'd fix himself something, said he didn't want me fussing, when I had a family to tend to," she said on a soft sigh. "He really is the nicest man."

"I think he's wonderful," Ashley agreed absently, without thinking, and colored slightly when she turned to find her mother staring at her with questioning eyes. She was saved from answering any embarrassing questions by her sister-in-law, Marsha, who breezed through the door full of the joy of the season. She was grateful that she and her mother were never alone after that, and soon the meal was on the table.

Everything was delicious, as all her mother's cooking was. As they sat around the table, Ashley's father asked the blessing, then opened the Bible to Psalms and read several praises aloud. After a moment's silence he asked each family member to verbally state one of the blessings they were most thankful for this year. Tears shimmered in Marsha's eyes as she announced that she and Jeff were going to have a baby. The news brought shouts of delight from Ashley's parents. When it came to her turn she thanked God for the rich Christian heritage she had received from her parents and also that she was going to be an aunt at last.

Later, as she helped with the dishes, Ashley's thoughts again drifted to Cooper. Here she was, with a loving family surrounding her, and he was probably alone in his large house. No, she told herself, most likely he was sharing the day with friends or business associates. But she wasn't convinced.

Hounded by constant self-recrimination since their last meeting, she had berated her quick temper a hundred times. He had only been concerned about her safety, and she'd acted as if he'd accosted her.

"Mom," she said and swallowed tightly. "Would you mind if I took a plate of food over to a friend who has to spend the day alone?"

"Of course not, dear, but why didn't you say something earlier? You could have invited them to dinner."

"I wish I'd thought of it," she said.

When she was all set with a large cooler overflowing with turkey and all the extras, Ashley's father loaned her the family car.

Her heartbeat raced frantically as she pulled into Cooper's driveway in the exclusive Redondo area of south Seattle. She wouldn't blame him if he closed the door on her. He'd purchased the house with the surrounding two acres of prime view property shortly after Claudia had given birth to John. Ashley had never seen the house although her mother had told her about it several times.

Now the large, two-story brick structure loomed before her, elegant and impressive. Adjusting her red beret, she rang the doorbell and waited. Several minutes passed before Cooper answered. He wore a suit, and she couldn't recall ever seeing him look more distinguished.

"Happy Thanksgiving, Cooper," she said with a trembling smile. If he didn't invite her inside, she was afraid she would burst into tears and humiliate them both.

"Ashley." He sounded shocked to see her. "Come in. For heaven's sake you didn't ride that deathtrap moped over here, did you?"

"No." She smiled and cast a glance over her shoulder to the older model car parked in the driveway. "Dad loaned me his car."

"Come in, it's cold, and it looks like rain," he offered again. He held out his hand, gesturing her inside.

Ashley didn't need a second invitation. "Here." She handed him the cooler. "I didn't know if you…" She hesitated. "Mom sent this along." Might as well jump in with both feet. Being underhanded about anything went against her inherent streak of honesty, but if her mother questioned her later, she would explain then.

Cooper took the cooler into the kitchen. She followed close behind, awestruck by every nook of the impressive home. The kitchen was a study in polished chrome and marble. It looked as clean as a hospital, yet welcoming. That was her mother's gift, she realized.

"Let me fix you something to drink. Coffee okay?" His eyes pinned hers, and she nodded.

After he poured her a mug, she followed him into a room with a fireplace and book-lined walls. His den, she decided. Two dark leather chairs with matching ottomans sat obliquely in front of the fireplace. He took her hat and red wool coat, hung them in a closet and motioned for her to sit in the chair opposite him.

Centering her attention on the steaming coffee, Ashley paused before speaking again. "I came to apologize."

A movement out of the corner of her eye attracted

her gaze, and she watched as Cooper relaxed against the back of the chair.

"Apologize? Whatever for?" he asked.

Her head shot up, and she swallowed the bitter taste in her mouth. He wasn't going to make this easy for her. "I was unforgivably rude the other day, and I have no excuse. You were being thoughtful, and…"

He didn't allow her to finish. Instead he gestured with his hand, dismissing her regret. "Nonsense."

Scooting to the very edge of her cushion, she inhaled a quivering breath. "Will you please stop waving at me as though you find my apology amusing?" she said, fighting to keep a grip on her rising irritation. She bolted to her feet and walked to the far side of the room, pretending to examine his collection of books while struggling to keep her composure. Without turning around she mumbled miserably, "I'm sorry, I didn't mean that."

His soft chuckle sounded remarkably close, and when she turned she discovered that only a few inches separated them.

"Oh, Cooper." Her eyes drank in the heady sight of him. "I've felt wretched all week. Please forgive me for the way I acted the other day."

"Have you decided to accept my offer?" The laughter drained from his eyes.

Sadly she shook her head. "Please understand why I can't."

He raked his hands through his hair, ruining the well-groomed effect.

Ashley's finger itched to smooth down the sides, to follow the proud line of his jaw, to touch him. Of its own volition her hand rose halfway to his face before she realized what she was doing.

Their eyes holding one another, Cooper captured her hand and held her motionless. Even his touch had the power to shoot sparks of awareness up her spine. When he raised her fingers to his mouth, his lips gently caressed her knuckles. Trapped in a whirlpool of sensation, she swayed toward him.

Her movement seemed to snap something within him, and he roughly pulled her into his embrace.

"Cooper." His name was a bittersweet sigh that was muffled as his mouth crushed hers. His hold was so tight that for a moment it was difficult to breathe, not that it mattered when she was in his arms.

Automatically, she raised her hands and linked them behind his neck as their mouths strained against one another. It was as if they couldn't get close enough, couldn't give enough. Ashley's lithe frame was flooded with a warm excitement, a glowing happiness that stole over her. A soft, whispering sigh escaped as he moved his face against her hair, brushing against her like a cat seeking contentment.

"Why is it you bring out the—"

The phone interrupted him, the sharp ringing shattering the tender moment. With a low, protesting groan he kissed the tip of her nose and moved across the room to answer the insistent call.

Ashley watched him, her heart swelling with pride and love. Their eyes met, and she noticed a warm light she had never seen in him before.

"Yes," he answered abruptly, then stiffened. "Claudia, this is a surprise."

Three

"Wonderful." Cooper continued speaking into the receiver, his eyes avoiding Ashley's. "Of course you're welcome, you know that. Plan to stay as long as you like."

The conversation lasted several more minutes, but it didn't take Ashley long to realize that Cooper wasn't going to let her friend know she was with him. She couldn't help wondering if she was a source of embarrassment to him. How could he hold her and kiss her one minute, then pretend that she wasn't even there with him the next? The promise of happiness she had savored so briefly in his arms left a bitter aftertaste. He must have sensed her confusion, because he turned away as the conversation with Claudia continued and kept his back to her until it ended a few minutes later.

"That was Claudia and Seth," he told her unnecessarily. "He's got a conference coming up in Seattle the second week of December. They've decided to fly down for that, then stay for the holidays."

He sounded so genuinely pleased that Ashley quickly quelled the spark of hurt. She didn't know why he'd chosen to ignore her, but she was going to put it out of her mind, and she certainly wouldn't ask.

"That's great."

"It is, isn't it?" He moved back to her side, gently easing her into his arms. "This is going to be a wonderful Christmas," he murmured against the softness of her hair.

His voice was like that of an eager child, and it rang a chord of compassion within her. He had taken over his brother's business when he was barely into his twenties. Over the years he had built up the supply operation that extended into ten western states. Claudia had once told her that his goal was to have the business go nationwide. But at what price? she wondered. His health? His personal life? What drove a man like Cooper Masters? she wondered. Could it be the desire for wealth? He was already richer than anyone she knew. Recognition? Yet he was careful to keep a low profile, and from what her mother and Claudia told her, he seemed to jealously guard his privacy. The man was a mystery she might never understand, a puzzle she might never solve.

What did it matter, as long as he held her like this? she asked herself. Her arms around his waist, she laid her head against his solid, muscular chest. The steady beat of his heart sounded in her ear, and she smiled with contentment.

"I feel like doing something crazy," he said, and tipped his head back, laughter dancing in his eyes. "Usually that means taking you in my arms and kissing you like there's no tomorrow."

"I'm game." The urge to wrap her arms around his neck and abandon her pride was almost overwhelming. What pride? her mind echoed. That had been lost long ago where Cooper was concerned.

"Let's go for a walk," he suggested.

Ashley stifled a protest. "It's raining," she warned. A torrential downpour would have been a more accurate description of the turn the weather had taken. She moistened her lips. For once she would have been content to sit in front of the fireplace.

"I'll get us an umbrella," he said, a smile softening the sharp, angular lines of his face.

When he returned, he'd changed clothes and shoes, and was wearing a dark overcoat. A black umbrella dangled from his forearm.

"Ready?" he asked, regarding her expectantly.

He took her red beret and matching wool coat from the closet. He held the coat open for her to slip her arms into the silk-lined sleeves. As he pulled the coat to her shoulders, he paused to gently kiss the slim column of her neck from behind. The tiny kiss shot a tingling awareness over her skin, and she sighed.

"Doesn't this make you want to sing," he teased as they stepped outside. Rain pelted the earth in an angry outburst.

"No." She laughed. "It makes me want to sit in front of a warm fireplace and drink something warm."

Cooper tipped back his head and howled with laughter. She was only echoing his words to her the night it had snowed. It hadn't been that funny. She watched him sheepishly, trying to recall a time she had ever heard him really laugh.

One arm tucked around her waist, he brought her close to his side. "Why is it when I'm with you I want to laugh and sing and behave totally irrationally?"

Wrapping her arm around his waist, she looked up

into his sparkling eyes. "I seem to bring out that quality in a lot of people."

He chuckled and opened the umbrella, which protected them from the worst of the downpour. He led her along a cement walkway that meandered around the property, finally ending at a chain link fence that was built at the top of a bluff that fell sharply into Puget Sound. The night view was spectacular. Ashley could only imagine how much more beautiful it would be during the day. An array of distant lights illuminated the sky and cast their reflective glow into the dark waters of the Sound.

"That must be Vashon Island," she said without realizing she had spoken out loud.

"Yes, and over there's Commencement Bay in Tacoma." He pointed to another section of lights. But his gaze wasn't on the city. Instead she felt it lingering, gently caressing her. When she turned her head, their eyes locked and time came to a screeching halt. Later she wouldn't remember who moved first. But suddenly she was tightly held in his arms, the umbrella carelessly tossed aside as they wrapped one another in a feverish embrace. The kiss that followed was the most beautiful she had ever received, filled with some unnamable emotion, deep, tender, sweet, and all-consuming.

Rain bombarded them, drenching her hair until it hung in wet ringlets. He looked down at her, his breathing uneven and hoarse. Gently he smiled, wiping the moisture from her face. With a laugh, he tugged her hand, and together they ran back to the safety and warmth of the house.

It was the memory of his kiss and that night that sustained Ashley through the long, silent days that followed.

Every night she hurried home from work hoping Cooper would contact her in some way. Each day led to bitter disillusionment. When her mother phoned Wednesday afternoon, Ashley already knew what she was going to say.

"Mr. Masters thanked me for the Thanksgiving dinner you brought him. Why didn't you say he was the friend you were going to see?" Her tone hinted of disapproval.

"Because I knew what you would have said if I did," Ashley countered honestly.

"I had no idea you've been seeing Mr. Masters."

"We've only gone out once."

A short, stilted silence followed. "He's too old for you, dear. He's forty, you know."

Closing her eyes, Ashley successfully controlled the desire to argue. "I don't think you need to worry, Mother," she said soothingly. "I doubt that I'll be seeing him again."

"I just don't want to see you get hurt," her mother added on a gentler note.

"I know you don't."

They chatted for a few minutes longer and ended the conversation on a happy note, talking about Marsha and the coming baby, her mother's first grandchild.

Replacing the phone, Ashley released a long, slow breath. Cooper's image returned to trouble her again. Everything about him only served as a confirmation of her mother's unspoken warning. He wore expensively tailored suits, his hair was professionally styled, and he seemed to be stamped with an unmistakable look of refinement. Something she would never have. And he was almost fourteen years older than she was, but why should that bother him or her parents when it had never mattered to her? At least she didn't need an explanation for why he

hadn't contacted her. After talking to her mother, he had
undoubtedly been reminded of their differences. Once
again he would shut himself off from her, and who knew
how long it would be before she could break through the
thick wall of his pride?

Sunday morning during church the pastor lit the first
candle of the Advent wreath. Ashley listened attentively
as the man of God explained that the first candle repre-
sented prophecy. Then he read Scripture from the Old
Testament that foretold the birth of a Savior.

Ashley left church feeling more uplifted than she had
the entire week. How could she be depressed and miserable at the happiest time of the year? Claudia, Seth and the
boys were coming, and Cooper wouldn't be able to avoid
seeing her. Perhaps then she could find a way to prove
that their obvious differences weren't all that significant.

An email from Claudia was waiting for her after work
Monday afternoon. It read:

Ashley,
    I'm sorry it's taken me so long to write. I can't
believe how busy my boys manage to keep me.
I've got some wonderful news! No, I'm not pregnant again, although I don't think Seth would mind.
Cooper either, for that matter. He's surprised both
of us the way he loves the boys. The good news is
that we'll be arriving at Sea/Tac Airport, Saturday,
December 12th at 10 A.M. and plan to stay with
Cooper through to the first of the year. That first
week Seth will be involved in a series of meetings,
but the remainder of the time will be the vacation
we didn't get the chance to take this summer.
    I can't tell you how excited I am to be seeing

you again. I've missed you so much. You've always been closer to me than any sister. You'll hardly recognize John. At three, he's taller than most four-year-olds, but then what can we expect, with Seth being almost six-six? There's so much I want to tell you that it seems impossible to put in an email or speak about over the phone. Promise to block out the holidays on your calendar, because I'm dying to see you again. The Lord's been good to me, and I have so much to tell you.

Scotty just woke from his nap and he never has been one to wake in a happy mood. Take care. I'm counting the days until the 12th.
Love,
Claudia, Seth, John and Scott

Ashley read the message several times. Of course, Claudia didn't realize that she already knew they were coming. Again the hurt washed over her that Cooper had pretended she wasn't there when Claudia had phoned on Thanksgiving Day.

She circled the day on her calendar and stepped back wistfully. When Scott had been born that spring, Cooper had flown up to Nome to spend time with Claudia, Seth and John. Ashley had yet to see the newest Lessinger. Cooper had said it earlier, and now Ashley added her own affirmation. This was going to be the most wonderful Christmas yet.

Ashley's alarm buzzed early the morning of the twelfth. She groaned defiantly until she remembered that she would have to hurry and shower if she was going to meet Claudia's plane as she intended.

A little while later, wearing jeans and a red cable knit sweater, she tucked her pant legs into her boots. Thank goodness it wasn't raining.

She parked Milligan in the multistory circular parking garage, then hurried down to baggage claim, her heels clicking against the tiled surface.

Cooper was already waiting when she arrived. He didn't notice her, and for a moment she enjoyed just watching him. He looked fresh and vital. It hardly seemed like more than two weeks since she'd last seen him, and yet they'd been the longest weeks of her life.

The morning sunlight filtered unrestrained through the large plate glass windows, glinting on his dark hair. He was tall and broad shouldered. Seeing him again allowed all her pent-up feelings to spill over. It took more restraint than she cared to admit not to run into his arms. Instead she adjusted her purse strap over her shoulder, stuffed her hands in her pockets and approached him with a dignified air.

"Good morning, Cooper." She gave him a bright smile, although the muscles at the corners of her mouth trembled with the effort. "It's a beautiful day, isn't it?"

If he was surprised to see her, he hid the shock well. "Ashley," he said, and stood. "Did you bring Madigan with you?" Concern laced his voice.

"Milligan," she corrected and laughed. "You never give up, do you?"

"Not if I can help it." He seemed to struggle with himself for a moment. "How have you been?"

"Sick," she lied unmercifully. "I was in the hospital for several days, doctors said I could have died. But I'm fine now. How about you?" she asked with a flippant air.

"Don't taunt me, Ashley," he warned thickly.

She was deliberately provoking him, but she didn't care. "For all you know it could be true. It's been more than two weeks since I've heard from you."

Turning his gaze to the window, he stood stiffly, watching the sky. "It seems longer," he murmured so low she had to strain to hear.

"Why?" she challenged, standing directly beside him, her own gaze cast toward the heavens.

"How's Webber?" He answered her question with one of his own.

"Webber?" she repeated, her face twisted into a puzzled frown. "You mean Webb?"

"Whoever." He shrugged.

"How do you know about Webb? Oh, wait. Mom." She answered her own question before he had the chance. "Webb and I are friends, nothing more." So this was the way her mother had handled the situation. For a moment fiery resentment burned in her eyes. She loved her mother, but there were times when Sarah Robbins's actions incensed her.

"Your mother mentioned that you and he see a lot of one another." His words were spoken without emotion, as if the subject bored him.

"Friends often do," she returned defensively. "But then, I doubt you'd know that."

She could feel the anger exude from him as he bristled.

"I'm sorry," she whispered, her tone contrite. "I didn't mean that the way it sounded." When she turned her head to look at him, she saw the cold fury leave his eyes. She placed her hand gently on his forearm, drawing his attention to her. "I don't want to argue. Seth and Claudia will know something's wrong, we won't be able to hide it."

He placed his hand on top of hers and squeezed it momentarily. "I don't want to argue, either," he finished. "According to the notice board, their flight has landed."

Ashley's heart fluttered with excitement. "Cooper," she mouthed softly. "My school is having a Christmas party next weekend. Would you…" Her tongue stumbled over the words. "I mean, could you…would you consider going with me?"

His shocked look cut through her hopes. "Next weekend?"

"The nineteenth…it's a Friday night. A dinner party, I don't think it'll be all that formal, just a faculty get together. It's the last day of school, and the dinner is a small celebration."

"Will you be wearing your red cowboy boots?"

"No, I was going to borrow Dad's fishing rubbers," she shot back, then immediately relented. "All right, for you, I'll wear a dress, pantyhose, the whole bit."

Unbuttoning his coat, Cooper took out his cell phone from inside his suit pocket. He punched a few buttons. A frown brought thick brows together. "It seems I've already got plans that night."

Disappointment settled over Ashley. Somehow she'd known he wouldn't accept, that he would find an excuse not to attend.

"I understand," she murmured, but her voice wobbled dangerously.

The silence between them lasted until she saw Claudia, Seth and the boys descending the escalator. As soon as they reached the bottom John broke loose from his father's hand and ran into Cooper's waiting arms.

"Uncle Coop, Uncle Coop!" he cried with childish delight and looped his arms around Cooper's neck. John didn't seem to remember Ashley at first until she offered him a bright smile. "Auntie Ash?" he questioned, holding out his arms to her.

She held out her own arms, and Cooper handed the boy to her. Immediately John spread moist kisses over her cheek. When she glanced over she noticed that Seth and Cooper were enthusiastically shaking hands.

"Ashley," Claudia chimed happily. "I didn't know whether you'd make it to the airport or not. I love your hair."

"So does Webb," she laughed, and had the satisfaction of seeing Cooper's eyes narrow angrily. "And this little angel must be Scott." With John's legs wrapped around her waist, Ashley leaned over to examine the eight-month-old baby in Claudia's arms. "And I bet John's a wonderful big brother, aren't you, John?"

The boy's head bobbed up and down. Both of the Lessinger boys had Seth's dark looks, but their eyes were as blue as a cloudless sky. Claudia's eyes.

Ashley didn't get a chance to talk to her friend until later that afternoon. Both boys were down for a nap, Seth and Cooper were concentrating on a game of chess in Cooper's den, while Ashley and Claudia sat enjoying the view from a bay window in the formal dining room.

"I can't get over how good you look," Claudia said, blowing into a steaming coffee mug. "Your hair really is great."

"The easiest style I've ever had." Ashley ran her fingers through the bouncing curls and shook her head, and her blond locks fell naturally into place.

"Do you see much of Cooper?" Claudia delivered the question with deceptive casualness.

"Hardly at all," Ashley replied truthfully. "Why do you ask?"

"I don't know. You two were giving one another odd looks at the airport. I could tell he wasn't pleased with your riding that moped. I thought maybe something was going on between the two of you."

Ashley dismissed Claudia's words with a short shake of her hand. "I'm sure you're mistaken. Can you imagine Cooper Masters being interested in anyone like me?"

"In some ways I can," Claudia insisted. "You two balance one another. He takes everything so seriously, while you finagle your way in and out of anything. I know one thing," she said. "He thinks very highly of you. He has for years."

"You're kidding!"

"I'm not. I don't know that he would have been as happy about me marrying Seth if it hadn't been for you."

"Nonsense," Ashley countered quickly. "I knew you and Seth were right for one another from the first moment I saw you with him. I don't know of any couple who belong together more than you two. And it shows, Claudia, it shows. Your face is radiant. That kind of inner happiness only comes with the deep love of a man."

Claudia's face flushed with color. "I know it sounds crazy, but I'm more in love with Seth now than when I married him four years ago. I never thought that would be possible. I don't understand how I could have doubted our love and that God wanted us together. My priorities are so different now."

"What about your degree? Do you think you'll ever go back to school?"

"I don't know. Maybe someday, but my life is so full now with the boys I can't imagine squeezing another thing in. I wouldn't want to. John and Scott need me. I suppose when they're older and in school full time I might think about finishing my doctorate, but that's years down the road. I do know that Seth will do whatever he can to help me if I decide to go ahead and get my degree." Pausing, she took another drink from her mug. "What about you? Any man in your life?"

"Several," Ashley teased, without looking at her friend. "None I'm serious about, though."

"What about Webb? You've written about him."

Before Ashley could assure Claudia her relationship with Webb didn't extend beyond a convenient friendship, a dark shadow fell into the room, diverting their attention to the two men who had just entered.

Seth's smile rested on his wife as he crossed the room and placed a loving arm across her shoulders. Cooper remained framed in the archway.

"As usual, Cooper beat the socks off me. I don't know why I bother to play. I can't recall ever beating him."

"What about you, Claudia?" Cooper asked. "You used to play a mean, if a bit unorthodox, game of chess."

Standing, Claudia looped her arm around her husband's waist. "Not me, I'm too tired to concentrate. If everyone will excuse me, I think I'll join the boys and take a nap."

Clenching her mug with both hands, Ashley stood. "I'd better rev up Milligan and get home before the weather—"

"No," Claudia interrupted. "You play Cooper, Ash. You always were a better chess player than me."

Ashley threw a speculative glance toward Cooper, awaiting his reaction. He arched his thick brows in challenge. "Would you care for a game, Miss Robbins?" he asked formally.

Wickedly fluttering her eyelashes, she placed both

hands over her heart. "Just what are you suggesting, Mr. Masters?"

Claudia giggled. "You know, suddenly I'm not the least bit tired."

"Yes, you are," Seth murmured, tightening his grip on his wife's waist. "You and I are going to rest and leave these two to a game of chess."

Claudia didn't object when Seth led her from the room.

"Shall we?" Cooper asked, long strides carrying him to her side. He extended his elbow, and when Ashley placed her arm in his, he gave her a curt nod.

The thought of playing chess with Cooper was an opportunity too good to miss. She was an excellent player and had been the assistant coach for the school's team the year before.

The two leather chairs were pushed opposite one another with a mahogany table standing between. An inlaid board with ivory figures sat atop the table.

"I would like to suggest a friendly wager." The words were offered as a clear challenge.

"Just what are you suggesting?" she asked.

"I'm saying that if I win the match, then you'll accept the new car."

"Honestly, Cooper, you don't give up, do you?"

"Accept the car without any obligation to reimburse me," he continued undaunted, "plus the promise that you'll faithfully drive it to and from work daily."

"And just what do I get if *I* win?" she countered.

"That's up to you."

She released a weary sigh. "I don't think you can give me what I want," she mumbled, lowering her gaze to her hands, laced tightly together in her lap.

"I think I can."

"All right," she added, straightening slightly. "If I win, you must promise never to speak derogatorily of Milligan again, or in any way insinuate that riding my moped is unsafe." He opened and closed his mouth in mute protest. "And in addition I would ask that a generous donation be made to the school's scholarship fund. Agreed?" She could tell he wasn't pleased.

"Agreed." The teasing light left his eyes as he viewed the chess board with a serious look. Taking both a black and a white pawn, he placed them behind his back, then extended his clenched fists for her to choose.

She mumbled a silent prayer, knowing she would have the advantage if she were lucky enough to pick white. Lightly, she tapped his right hand.

Cooper relaxed his fist and revealed the white pawn.

Her spirits soared. He would now be on the defensive.

Neither spoke as they positioned the pieces on the board. A strained, tense air filled the den, and the only sound was the occasional crackle from the fireplace.

Her first move was a standard opening, pawn to king four, which he countered with an identical play. She immediately responded with a gambit, pawn to king's bishop four.

It didn't take her long to impress him with her ability. A smug smile lightly brushed her mouth as she viewed his shock as she gained momentum and dominated the game.

Bending forward, he rubbed a hand across his forehead and then his eyes. Ashley was forced to restrain another smile when he glanced up at her.

"Claudia was right, you *are* a good player."

"Thank you," she responded, hoping to hide the pleasure his acknowledgement gave her.

He made his next move, and she paused to study the board.

"Claudia was right about something else, too," he said softly.

"What's that?" she asked absently, pinching her bottom lip between her thumb and index finger, her concentration centered on the chess board.

"I don't think I've ever told you what an attractive woman you are."

His husky tone seemed to reach out and wrap itself around her. "What'd you say?" Her concentration faltered, and she lifted her gaze to his.

His eyes were narrowed on her mouth. "I said you're beautiful."

The current of awareness between them was so strong that she would gladly have surrendered the game right then and there. She felt close to Cooper, closer than she had to any other person. They had so little in common, and yet they shared the most basic, the strongest, emotion of all. If he had moved or in any way indicated that he wanted her, she would have tossed the chess game aside and wrapped herself in his arms. As it was, her will to win, the determination to prove herself, was quickly lost in the power of his gaze.

"It's your move."

Her eyes darkened with anger as she seethed inwardly. He was playing another game with her, a psychological game in which he had proved to be the clear winner with the first move. Using the attraction she felt for him, he'd hope to derail her concentration. His game read Cooper one, Ashley zilch.

She jumped to her feet and jogged around the room.

Pausing to take a series of deep breaths, she took in his cynical look with amusement.

"I hate to appear ignorant here, but just what are you doing?"

"What does it look like?" she countered sarcastically.

"Either you're training for the Olympics or you're sorely testing my limited patience."

"Guess again," she returned impudently, beginning a series of jumping jacks.

"I thought we were playing chess, not twenty questions."

Hands resting challengingly on her hips, she paused and tossed him a brazen glare. "It was either vent my anger physically or punch you out, Cooper Masters."

"Punch me out?" he echoed in disbelief. "What did I do?"

"You know, so don't try to deny it." The anger had dissipated from her blue eyes as she returned to her chair and resumed her study of the board. As the blood pounded in her ears, she knew she'd made a mistake the minute she lifted her hand from the pawn. But would Cooper recognize her error and gain the advantage?

"Cooper?" she whispered.

"Hmm," he answered absently.

"Do you remember the last time I was here?"

He lifted his gaze to hers. "I'm not likely to forget it. After the cold I caught, I coughed for a week."

"Sometimes doing something crazy and irrational has a price." She leaned forward, her chin supported by the palm of her hand.

"Not this time, Ashley Robbins," he gloated, making the one move that would cost her the game. "Check."

Four

Ashley stared at the chess board with a sense of unreality. There was only one move she could make, and she knew what would happen when she took it.

"Checkmate."

She stared at him for a long moment, unable to speak or move. Cooper stood and crossed the room to a huge oak desk that dominated one corner. She watched as he opened a drawer and took out some papers. When he returned to her side, he gave her the car keys.

Her hand was shaking so badly she nearly dropped them.

"This is the registration," he told her, handing her a piece of paper. "After what happened not so long ago, I suggest you keep it in the glove compartment."

Unable to respond with anything more than a nod, she avoided his eyes, which were sure to be sparkling with triumph.

"These are the insurance forms, made out in your name. I believe there's a space for you to sign at the bottom of the policy." He pointed to the large "X" marking the spot, then handed her a pen.

Mutely Ashley complied, but her signature was barely recognizable. She returned the pen.

"I believe that's everything."

"No," she protested, unable to recognize the thin, high voice as her own. "I insist upon paying for the car."

"That wasn't part of our agreement."

"Nonetheless, I insist." She had to struggle to speak clearly.

"No, Ashley," he insisted, "the car is yours."

"But I can't accept something so valuable, not over a silly chess game." She raised her eyes to meet his. Their gazes held, his proud and determined, hers wary and unsure. A muscle moved convulsively at the side of his jaw, and she realized she had lost.

"The car is a gift from me to you. There isn't any way on this earth that I'll accept payment. You were aware of the terms before you agreed to the game."

A painful lump filled her throat, and when she spoke her voice was hoarse. "You have so much," she murmured, her voice cracking. "Must you take my pride, too?" Tears shimmered in the clear depths of her eyes. Wordlessly she left the den, took her coat and walked out the front door. Without a backward glance she climbed aboard Milligan and rode home.

Her mood hadn't improved the next morning as she dressed for church. The sky was dark and threatening, mirroring her temper. How could she love someone as headstrong and narrow minded as Cooper Masters? No wonder his business had grown and prospered over the years. He was ruthless, determined and obstinate.

After tucking her Bible into her backpack, she stepped outside to lock her apartment door. A patch of red in the parking lot caught her attention and she noted that a shiny new car was parked beside Milligan in front of her apartment. As she seethed inwardly, it took great restraint not to vent her anger by kicking the gleaming new car.

The first drops of rain fell lazily to the ground. Even God seemed to be on Cooper's side, she thought, as she heaved a troubled sigh. Either she had to change into her rain gear or drive the car. She chose the latter. Pulling out of the parking lot, she was forced to admit the car handled like a dream. Ashley was prepared to hate the car, but it didn't even take the full five miles to church for her to acknowledge she was going to love this car. Just as much as she loved the man who had given it to her.

As the Sunday School teacher for the three-year-olds, she was excited that John Lessinger would be in her class.

Claudia dropped him off at the classroom, Scotty resting on her hip, the diaper bag dangling from her arm.

"Morning." Ashley beamed warmly. "How's Johnny?" She directed her attention to the small boy who hid behind Claudia's skirts.

"He's playing shy today," Claudia warned.

"I don't blame him," Ashley whispered in return. "A lot's happened in the last couple of days."

"I'll drop Scotty off at the nursery and come back to see how John does."

"He'll be fine," Ashley assured her. "Did you see the playdough, Johnny?" she asked, directing his attention to the low table where several other children were busy playing. "Come over here and I'll introduce you to some of my friends."

John's look was unsure, and he glanced over his shoulder at his retreating mother. His lower lip began to quiver as tears welled in his blue eyes. Kneeling down to his level, Ashley placed her hands on his small shoulders. "Johnny, it's Auntie Ash. You remember me, don't you? There's nothing to frighten you here. Come over and meet Joseph and Matthew. You can tell them all about Alaska."

John was playing nicely with the other children when Claudia returned. She sighed in relief. "Now I can relax," she whispered. "I don't know what it is about men and Sunday mornings, but it takes Seth twice as long as me to get ready. Then I'm left to carry Scott, steer John, haul the diaper bag, the Bibles and my purse, while Seth can't manage anything more than his car keys."

Ashley stifled a giggle. She allowed the children to play for several more minutes, chatting with Claudia, who insisted on staying for the first part of Sunday school to be sure John was really all right.

Ashley gathered the children in a circle and had them sit on the patch of carpet in the middle of the floor. As she sat cross-legged on the floor with them, one of the shyer children came over and seated herself in Ashley's lap. "I'm glad we're all together, together, together," the little girl sang in a sweet, melodious voice. "Because Jesus is here, and teacher's here, and—"

"Cooper's here," Claudia chimed in softly.

The song died on the girl's lips as everyone looked over at the tall, compelling figure standing in the open door. His attention was centered on Ashley and the little girl in her lap. For a moment he seemed to go pale, and the muscles in his jaw jerked, and Ashley wondered what she had done now to anger him. Without a word, he pivoted and left the room.

"I'd better see what he wanted," Claudia said, following him out of the room.

Ashley didn't see either of them again until it was

time for the morning worship service. The four adults sat together, Claudia between her and Cooper. A hundred questions whirled in her mind. How had Claudia gotten Cooper to attend church? It wasn't all that long ago that he had scoffed at her friend's newfound faith. She wondered if Seth had some influence on Cooper's decision to attend church. More than likely John had said something, and Cooper had been unable to refuse.

Just as the pastor stepped in front of the congregation to light the third candle of the Advent wreath, a loud cry came from the nursery.

Claudia emitted a low groan. "Scotty." She leaned over and whispered to Ashley, "I wasn't sure I'd be able to leave him this long." She stood and made her way out of the pew. Cooper closed the space separating them.

Never had Ashley been more aware of a man's presence. As his thigh lightly touched hers, she closed her eyes at the potency of the contact. Nervously she scooted away, putting some space between them. When he turned and looked at her an unfamiliar quality had entered his eyes. He smiled, one of those rare smiles that came from his heart and nearly stopped hers. Its overwhelming force left her exposed and completely vulnerable. Undoubtedly he would be able to read the effect he had on her and know her thoughts. Quickly turning her face away, she squeezed her eyes closed, and then the pastor, the service, everything, everyone, was lost as Cooper closed his hand firmly over hers.

In all the years she had loved Cooper, Ashley had never dared to dream that he would sit beside her in church or share her strong faith. The intense sensations of having him near touched her so dramatically that for a moment she was sure her heart would burst with unrestrained happiness.

His grip remained tight and firm until Claudia returned to the pew and sat beside Seth. Immediately Cooper released Ashley's hand. The happiness that had filled her so briefly was gone. He seemed content to hold her hand only as long as no one knew. The minute someone came, he let her go.

Once again she was forcefully reminded of the huge differences that separated them. He was a corporate manager, a powerful, wealthy man. She was a financially struggling schoolteacher. In some ways she was certain he cared for her, but not enough to admit it openly. She sometimes feared she was an embarrassment to him, a fear that had dogged her from the beginning.

"Did you win the Irish Sweepstakes?" Webb asked Ashley as she pulled into the school parking lot and climbed out of the shining new car.

"No," she said and sighed unhappily. "I lost a chess game."

He gave her a funny look. "Let me make certain I've got this straight. You *lost* the chess game and won the car?"

"You got it."

Rubbing the side of his chin with one hand, he stared at her with confused eyes. "I know there's logic in this someplace, but for the moment it's escaped me."

"I wouldn't doubt it," she said, and nodded a friendly greeting to the school secretary as she walked through the door.

"What would you have gotten if you'd *won?*" Webb asked as he followed on her heels.

"Milligan and my pride."

"That's another one of those answers that seems to have gone right over my head." He waved his hand over the top of his blond head in illustration. Confusion clouded his eyes. "All I really want to know is whether this person likes chess and plays often? It wouldn't be hard for me to lose. I don't even like the game."

"You wouldn't want to play this person," she mumbled under her breath, heading toward the faculty room.

"Don't be hasty, Ashley," he countered quickly. "Let me be the judge of that."

Tossing him a look she usually reserved for rowdy students was enough to quell his curiosity.

"We're going to the Christmas party Friday night, aren't we?" he asked, steering clear of the former topic of discussion.

Releasing a slow breath, Ashley cupped a coffee mug with both hands. Her enthusiasm for the party had disappeared with Cooper's excuse not to attend. Probably because she believed that the previous appointment he claimed to have was merely a pretext to avoid refusing her outright.

"I don't know, I have a friend visiting from Alaska," she said before sipping. "We may be doing something that night."

"Sure, no problem," he said with a smile. "Let me know if you change your mind."

No pleading, no hesitation, no regrets. The least he could do was show some remorse over her missing the party. As she watched him saunter out of the faculty room, she threw imaginary daggers at his back. Unhappy and more than a little depressed, she finished her coffee and went to her homeroom.

* * *

"Is there something drastically wrong with me?" Ashley asked Claudia later that afternoon. She'd stopped by after school for a short visit with Claudia and the boys before Cooper returned from his office.

When Claudia looked up from bouncing Scotty on her knee, her eyes showed surprise. "Heavens, no. What makes you ask?"

"I mean, you'd tell me if I had bad breath or something, wouldn't you?"

"You know me well enough to answer that."

As Johnny weaved a toy truck around the chair legs, then pushed it under the table to the far side of the room, Ashley's eyes followed the movement of her godson. Lowering her face, she took a deep breath, afraid she might do something stupid like cry. "I want to get married and have children. I'm twenty-six and not getting any younger."

"I'm sure there are plenty of men out there who'd be interested. Only yesterday Seth was saying how pretty you've gotten. Surely there's someone—"

"That's just it," Ashley interrupted, knowing she couldn't mention Cooper. "There isn't, and I found a gray hair the other day. I'm getting scared."

"You and Cooper both. Have you noticed how he's getting gray along his sideburns? It really makes him look distinguished, doesn't it?"

Ashley agreed with a smile, but her eyes refused to meet her friend's, afraid she wouldn't be able to disguise her feelings for Cooper.

"Oh, before I forget, Seth and I have been invited to a dinner party this Friday night, and we were wondering if you could watch the boys. If you have plans just say so, because I think your mother might be able to do it."

Some devilish impulse made her ask, "What about Cooper?"

"He's got some appointment he can't get out of."

For a startled second the oxygen seemed trapped in Ashley's lungs. He had been telling the truth. He *did* have an appointment. In that brief second the sun took on a brighter intensity; it was as if the birds began to chirp.

"I'd love to stay with John and Scott," she returned enthusiastically. "We'll have a wonderful time, won't we, boys?" Neither one looked especially pleased. Glancing at her watch, Ashley quickly stood. "I've gotta scoot, I'll see you Friday. What time do you want me?"

"Is six too early? I'll try to get the boys fed and dressed."

"Don't do that," Ashley admonished with a laugh. "It'll be good practice for me. I need to learn all this motherhood stuff, you know."

"Don't rush off," Claudia said. "Cooper will be home any minute."

"I can't stay. Tell him I said hello—no, don't," she added abruptly. He might have been telling the truth about being busy Friday night, but it didn't lessen the hurt of his rejection. "Mid-year reports go home this Friday, and I want to get a head start."

Claudia regarded her quizzically as she walked her to the door. "Thanks again for Friday. I don't like to leave the boys with strangers. It's bad enough for them to be away from home."

"Happy to help," Ashley said sincerely. Giving a tiny wave to both boys, she smiled when Scotty raised his chubby hand to her. Johnny ran to the front window to look out, and Ashley played peek-a-boo with him. The small head had just bobbed out from behind the drapes when Cooper spoke from behind her.

"Hello, Ashley."

She stiffened at the sound of his voice, her heartbeat racing double time. Last Sunday at church had been the last time she'd seen him.

"Hello." Her voice was devoid of any warmth or welcome. He looked dignified in his suit and silk tie. Childishly she was upset at him all the more for it.

"Is something the matter?" he asked in a quiet voice.

"No," she answered, her gaze stern and unyielding. "I'm just surprised that you'd taint your image by being seen with me."

"What are you talking about?"

"If you don't know, then I'm not going to tell you."

His gaze narrowed. "What's wrong? Obviously something's troubling you."

"The man's a genius," she replied flippantly. "Now, if you'll excuse me, I'll be on my way."

Cooper's eyes contained a hard gleam she had never seen. His hand shot out and gripped her upper arm. "Tell me what's going on in that unpredictable mind of yours."

Defiance flared from her as she stared pointedly at his hand until he relaxed his hold. Breaking free, she took a few steps in retreat, creating the breathing space she needed to vent her frustration. "I'll have you know, Cooper Masters, I'm not the least bit ashamed of who or what I am. My mother may be your housekeeper, but she has served you well all these years. My father's a skilled sheet metal worker, and I'm proud of them both. I don't have a thing to be ashamed about. Not in front of you or anyone." Having finished her tirade, she avoided looking at him and walked straight to her car.

She never made it. A strong hand on her shoulder swung her around, pinning her against the side of the car. "What are you implying?" The tone of his voice made Ashley shudder. His nostrils flared with barely restrained fury.

Tears shimmered in her eyes until his face was swimming before her. She bit her bottom lip. Suddenly she could feel the anger drain out of him.

"What's the matter with us?" he demanded hoarsely, then expelled an impatient breath.

"Everything!" she cried, her voice trembling. "Everything," she repeated. When she struggled, he released her and didn't try to stop her again. He stepped back as she climbed inside the car, revved the engine, and drove away.

If Ashley was miserable then, it was nothing compared to the way she felt later. To soothe away her emotional turmoil and frustration, she filled the bathtub with hot water and bubble bath, and soaked in it until the water became tepid. In an attempt to pray, she tried the conversational approach that had come so naturally to her in the past, but even that was impossible in her present state of mind.

Sleep was a long time coming that night. She couldn't seem to find a comfortable position, and when she did drift off she found herself trapped in a dream of hopelessness. Waking early the next morning, she rose before the alarm sounded, put on the coffee and sat in the dark, shadow-filled room waiting for the first light.

Lackadaisically, she reached for her devotional and

discovered the suggested reading for the day was the famous love chapter in First Corinthians, Chapter Thirteen. *Love is very patient and kind*, verse four stated.

Had she been patient? Ten years seemed a long time to her, and that was how long it had been since she first realized she'd loved Cooper. Since the tender age of sixteen. Glancing back to her Bible, she continued reading. *Love doesn't demand its own way. It isn't irritable or touchy. It doesn't hold grudges and will hardly notice when others do wrong.... If you love someone you will always believe in him, always expect the best of him, and always stand your ground in defending him.*

Closing her Bible, Ashley released an uneven breath. It looked as though she had a long way to go to achieve the standards God had set.

When it came time for her to pray, she got down on her knees, meditating first on the words she had read. Ever since Sunday she'd expected the worst from Cooper, thought the worst of him. She'd wanted to explain how hurt she was, but it sounded so petty to accuse him of being ashamed of her because he'd quit holding her hand. In voicing her thoughts, the whole incident sounded ludicrous. It seemed she was building things in her own mind because she was insecure. The same thoughts had come to her the night he'd taken her to the Italian restaurant, and the night Claudia had phoned from Alaska. She'd never thought of herself as someone with low self-esteem before Cooper.

"Oh, ye of little faith," she said aloud. *No*, her heart countered, *ye of little love.*

Ashley hummed cheerfully as she pulled into the school parking lot. She was proud of the fact that she had worked things out in her own mind—with God's help, of course. The next time she saw Cooper, she would apologize for her behavior and ask that they start again. Poor man, he wouldn't know what to think. One minute she was ranting and raving, and the next she was apologizing.

Today was a special day for her Senior Literature class. They'd been reading and studying the Western classic *The Oxbow Incident* by Walter Van Tilburg Clark. As part of her preparation for their final exam, Ashley dressed up as one of the characters in the book. Portraying the part as believably as possible, she was usually able to draw out heated discussions and points that might otherwise have been glossed over.

Today she was dressing as Donald Martin, one of the three men accused of cattle rustling in the powerful narrative. This was always Ashley's favorite part of the quarter, and her classroom antics were well known.

Her afternoon students were buzzing with speculation when the bell rang. She waited until everyone was seated before she came through the door to be greeted by laughter and cheers. She was wearing a ten gallon hat. Her cowboy boots had silver spurs, and her long, slim legs were disguised by leather chaps. Two toy six-shooters were holstered at her hips. With her hair tucked under the hat, she'd made a token attempt toward realism by smearing dirt over her creamy smooth cheeks and pasting a long black mustache across her upper lip.

The class loved it, and immediate speculation arose about what character she was portraying.

"I'm here today to talk about mob justice," she began, sitting on the corner of her desk and dangling one foot over the edge.

"She's Gil," one of the boys in the back row called out.

"Good guess, David," she said, pointing to him. "But I'm no drifter. I own my own spread at Pike's Hole. Me and the Missus are building up our herd."

"It's Mex," someone else shouted.

"No way," Diana Crosby corrected. "Mex wasn't married."

"Good girl, Diana." She twirled both six-shooters around a couple of times and by pure luck happened to place them in the holsters right side up. When her class applauded she bowed, her hat falling off her head. As she bent to pick it up she noticed a face staring at her from the small glass portion of the class door. The face was lovingly familiar. Cooper.

"If you'll excuse me a minute, I have to check my horse," she said, quickly making up a pretense to escape into the hallway.

"What are you doing here?" she demanded in a low tone.

A smile danced in his eyes as he attempted to hide his grin by rubbing his thumb across the angular line of his jaw. "Butch Cassidy, I presume."

"Cooper, I'm in the middle of class," she muttered with an exaggerated sigh, both hands gripping his arms. "But I'm so glad to see you. I feel terrible about the way I acted yesterday. I was wrong, terribly wrong."

The laughter faded from his features as he regarded her seriously. "I had no idea the dinner party meant so much to you."

"What dinner party?" He was talking in riddles.

"The one you asked me to attend with you. I assumed that was what upset you yesterday."

She shook her head in wry dismay. "No…that wasn't it."

"Then what was?"

Casting an apprehensive glare over her shoulder, she turned pleading eyes to him. "I can't talk now."

He rubbed a weary hand over his face. "Ashley, I rearranged my schedule. I'll be happy to take you to the school Christmas party."

She groaned softly. "But I can't go now."

"What do you mean, you can't go?" His dark, steely eyes narrowed.

He didn't need to say another word for her to know how much it had inconvenienced him to readjust his schedule.

"Cooper, I'm sorry, but I…"

"Invited someone else," he finished for her, his eyes as cold as a blast of arctic wind. "That Webber fellow, I imagine."

"I haven't got time to stand in the hall and argue with you. My class is waiting."

"And so, I imagine, is Webber."

Fury blazed in her eyes as she slashed him a cutting look. "You do that on purpose."

"Do what?" His voice was barely civil.

"Call Webb 'Webber,' the same way you call Milligan 'Madigan.' I find the whole denial thing rather childish," she snapped resentfully. By now she was too incensed to care if she was making sense.

"I find that statement unworthy of comment."

"You would." She spun away and stalked back into the classroom, restraining the impulse to slam the door.

Claudia was dressed in a mauve-colored chiffon evening gown that was a stunning complement to her auburn hair and cream coloring. Seth, too, looked remarkably attractive in his suit and tie.

"Okay, I showed you where everything is in the bedroom, and here's the phone number of the restaurant." Claudia laid the pad near the phone in the kitchen. "I've left a baby bottle in the refrigerator, but I've already nursed Scotty, so he probably won't need it."

"Okay," Ashley said, following Claudia out of the kitchen.

"Both boys are dressed for bed, and don't let either of them stay up past eight-thirty. You may need to rock Scotty to sleep."

"No problem, I got my degree in rocking chair."

Checking her reflection in the hallway mirror, Claudia tucked a stray hair back into her coiled French coiffure. "You didn't happen to have an argument with Cooper, did you?" The question came out of the blue.

Ashley could feel the blood rush from her face, then just as quickly flood back. "What makes you ask?"

"Seth and I have hardly seen him the last couple of days, and he's been in the foulest mood. It's not like him to behave like this. I can't understand it."

"What makes you think I have anything to do with it?" she asked, doing her best to conceal her reaction.

"I know it sounds crazy, and I wouldn't want to offend you, Ash, but I still think something's stirring between you two. I may be an old married fuddy-duddy, but I recognize the looks he's been giving you. What I can't understand is why the two of you work so hard at hiding it. As far as I'm concerned, you're perfect for one another."

"Ha," Ashley said harshly. "We can't spend two minutes together lately without going for each other's jugular."

Seth took Claudia's wrap from the hall closet and placed it over her shoulders. "Sounds like the way it was with us a few times, doesn't it, Honey?" he asked, and tenderly kissed the creamy smooth slope of Claudia's neck.

"Call if you have any problems, won't you?" Claudia said, suddenly sounding worried. "Scotty will cry the first few minutes after we've left, but he should quiet down in a little bit, so don't panic."

"I never panic," Ashley assured her with a cheeky grin.

True to his mother's word, Scott gave a hearty cry the minute the door was closed.

"It's all right. Look, here's your teddy."

Scotty took the stuffed animal, threw it across the room and cried all the louder.

Ten minutes passed and nothing seemed to calm his frantic cries. Even John looked as if he was ready to give way and start howling.

"Come on, sweetie, not you, too."

"I want my mommy."

"Let's pretend I'm your mommy," Ashley offered, "and then you can tell me how to make Scotty happy."

"Will you hold me like my mommy?" Johnny asked, a tear running down his pale face.

"Sure, join the crowd," Ashley laughed, lifting him so that she had a baby on each hip. Johnny cried in small whimpering sounds and Scott in large howling sobs.

Pacing the floor, she glanced up to find Cooper standing in the entryway watching her, a stunned look on his face.

Five

"Look, Johnny, Scott," Ashley said cheerfully. "Uncle Cooper's here."

Both boys cried harder. Scotty buried his face in her neck, his stubby hands tangled in her blond hair. When he pulled a long strand, she cried out involuntarily, "Ouch."

The small protest spurred Cooper into action. He hung his overcoat in the hall closet and entered the living room, taking John from Ashley.

"What's the matter, fella?" he asked in a reassuring tone.

"I want my mommy!" John wailed.

"They went out for the evening," Ashley explained, both hands supporting Scott as she paced the floor, making cooing sounds in his ear. But nothing seemed to comfort the baby, who continued to cry pitifully.

"What about Webber and your party?" Cooper asked stiffly.

"I tried to tell you that I wasn't going," she explained, and breathed in deeply. "I didn't say a thing about attending the party with Webb. You assumed I was."

"Are you telling me the reason you didn't go tonight is because you'd promised to baby-sit John and Scotty?"

Ashley silently confirmed the statement with a weak nod. His dark eyes narrowed with self-directed anger.

"Why do you put up with me?" he asked.

She didn't get the opportunity to answer, because Scotty began bellowing even louder.

A troubled frown broke across Cooper's expression. "Is he sick? I've never heard him cry like that."

"No, just unhappy. Claudia said she'd left a bottle for him. Maybe we should heat it up."

All four moved into the kitchen. With Scotty balanced on her hip, Ashley took the baby bottle out of the refrigerator. "It needs to be heated." She held it out to him.

"If you say so," he said, shrugging his broad shoulders. "How does your mommy do it?" he asked Johnny, who seemed more secure now that his uncle had arrived.

"She nurses Scotty."

Slowly Cooper's dark eyes met hers, amusement flickering across his face. She giggled, and soon they were both laughing. Scotty cried all the harder, clinging to Ashley.

The humor broke the terrible tension that had existed between them for days.

Cooper smiled warmly into her eyes, trying to hold back his laughter. He walked across the room and took a large pan out of the bottom cupboard, then filled it with hot water. "I don't want to chance the microwave. What if I melt the bottle? It's plastic, after all." By the time he'd set the pan on the stove and turned on the burner, he'd regained his composure.

Ashley placed the baby bottle in the water. "Is it supposed to float?"

"I don't know." He shook his head briefly, the look in his eyes unbelievably tender.

"Oh well, we'll experiment, won't we, boys?"

"What's an experiment?" Johnny asked. He was sitting on top of the counter, his short legs dangling over the edge.

"It's a process by which we examine the validity of a hypothesis and determine the nature of something as yet unknown."

"Cooper…" Ashley laughed at the way the three-year-old's mouth and eyes rounded as he tried to understand what Cooper was saying. "Honestly! Let me explain." She turned to Johnny. "An experiment is trying something you've never done before."

"Oh!" Johnny's clouded expression brightened, and he eagerly shook his head. "Mommy does that a lot with dinner."

"That's right." Ashley beamed.

"Smart aleck," Cooper whispered under his breath, his gaze lingering on her for a heart-stopping moment.

Ashley found herself drowning in the dark depths of his eyes and quickly averted her head. The water in the pan was coming to a boil, the baby bottle tossing back and forth in the bubbling liquid.

"It must be ready by now," she commented as she turned off the burner.

Cooper went out to the back porch and returned with a huge pair of barbeque tongs. He quickly lifted the bottle from the hot water, setting it upright on the counter.

"Nicely done," she commented, and waited a few minutes before testing the milk's temperature. Once she was sure it wouldn't burn Scotty's tender mouth, she led the way into the living room.

Remembering what Claudia had said about rocking the baby, Ashley sat in the polished wooden rocker and gently tipped back and forth. Scotty reached for the bottle and held it himself, sucking greedily. Her eyes filled with tenderness. She brushed the fine hair from his face and cupped his ear. The room was blissfully silent as John and Cooper sat across from her.

Johnny crawled into Cooper's lap and handed him a book that he wanted read. Cooper complied, his voice and face expressive as he turned page after page, reading quietly.

Ashley found her attention drawn again and again to the man and the young boy. A surge of love filled her, so strong and overpowering that tears formed in her eyes. Hurriedly she looked away, batting her eyelashes to forestall the moisture.

Losing interest in the bottle, Scotty began chewing the nipple and watching Ashley. His round eyes held a fascinated expression as he studied her hair and reached out to grab her blond curls.

Carefully, she brushed her hair back. As she did her eyes met Cooper's. His gaze had centered on her mouth with a disturbing intensity. The power he had over her produced an aching tightness in her throat.

"You'll make a good mother someday." His voice was low and husky.

"I was just thinking the same thing about you," she murmured, then realizing what she'd said and hastened to correct herself. "I mean a good father."

"I know what you meant."

"Uncle Cooper." Johnny tugged at Cooper's arm. "You're supposed to be reading."

"So I am," he agreed in a lazy drawl. "So I am."

Finished now, Scotty tossed the bottle aside, then struggled to sit up. "I know I should burp him," Ashley said, "but I'm not sure of the best way to hold him."

Cooper stood. "Claudia left a baby book lying around here somewhere. Maybe it would be best to look it up."

The small party moved into Cooper's den. Ashley carried Scotty on her hip. He didn't make a sound, having apparently become accustomed to her, and that pleased her.

Cooper found the book and set it on his desk, flipping the pages. As soon as Ashley bent over next to him to read a paragraph, Scotty burped loudly.

"Well I guess that answers that, doesn't it?" she said, laughing.

"Uncle Coop, can I have a piggy back ride?" Johnny climbed onto the chair and held out his hands entreatingly.

Cooper looked unsure for a moment but agreed with a good-natured nod. "Okay, partner."

Johnny climbed onto Cooper's back, looped his legs around his uncle's waist and clung tightly with his chubby arms. "Gitty-up, horsey," he commanded happily.

Cooper grinned. "How come this is called a piggy-back ride and you say 'Gitty-up, horsey'?"

Johnny chuckled. "It's an experiment."

"He's got you there." Ashley flashed him a cheeky grin.

Cooper mumbled something unintelligible and trotted into the next room.

Ashley followed, enjoying the sight of Cooper looking so relaxed. Scotty clapped his hands gleefully, and Ashley trotted after the others.

After a moment Cooper paused. "I smell something."

"Not…" She didn't finish.

"I think it must be."

Three pairs of eyes centered on the baby. Dramatically, Johnny plugged his nose. "Scotty has a messy diaper," he announced with the formality of a judge.

"Well, he's still a baby, and they're expected to do that sort of thing. Isn't that right, Scotty?"

Unconcerned, Scotty cooed happily, chewing on his pajama sleeve.

"Claudia showed me where everything is, this shouldn't take long."

"Ashley." Cooper stopped her, his face tight. "I think I should probably be the one to change him."

"You? Why? Are you saying it's the proper thing to do, since he's a boy?"

"I'm saying it's not a lot of fun and I've done it before, so…"

Unsuccessfully disguising a grateful smile, she handed him the baby. Scotty protested loudly as Cooper supported him with his hands under the baby's armpits, holding him as far away as possible.

"Call me if you need help."

Johnny led the way up the stairs, the large wooden steps almost more than he could manage. Cooper glanced down, his brow marred by a frown, then followed his nephew down the hall.

Ashley waited at the foot of the stairs, one shoe positioned on the bottom step, in case Cooper called.

"Auntie Ash." Johnny came running down the wide hallway and stopped at the top of the stairs. "Uncle Cooper says he needs you."

A tiny smile formed lines at the edges of her mouth. Somehow the words sounded exceedingly beautiful. She yearned to hear them from Cooper himself, though not exactly in this context.

She entered the bedroom and saw that his frown had deepened. He extended a hand to stop her as she entered the nursery. "I need a washcloth or something...you can give it to John."

Ashley ran the water in the bathroom sink until it was warm and soaked the washcloth in it. After wringing out most of the moisture, she handed it to Johnny, who ran full speed into the bedroom.

Loitering outside the room, Ashley impatiently stuck her head inside the door. "Cooper, this is silly."

"I'm almost finished," he mumbled. "This was just a little...more than I'm used to dealing with." His expensive silk tie was loosened, and the long sleeves of his crisp business shirt had been rolled up to his elbows.

Ashley watched from the doorway, highly amused.

"Voilà," he said, pleased with himself, as he stood Scotty up on the table.

Ashley dissolved into fits of laughter. The disposable diaper stuck out at odd angles in every direction. Had he really done this before, or had he just been trying to spare her an unpleasant task? As she was giggling, the diaper began to slide down Scotty's legs, stopping at knee level. She laughed so hard that her shoulders shook.

"Here, let me try," she insisted after a moment, swallowing her amusement as best she could.

Cooper looked almost grateful when she took the baby and laid him back onto the changing table. She did the best she could, but her efforts weren't much better than Cooper's. He was kind enough not to comment.

When she had finished, she paused to look around the room for the first time. Claudia had told her about the bedroom Cooper had decorated for the boys, but she hadn't had a chance to take it all in earlier. Now she could stand back and marvel. The walls were painted blue, with cotton candy clouds floating past and a huge multicolored rainbow with a pot of gold.

Johnny, who had apparently noticed her appreciation, tugged at her hand. "Come look."

Obligingly, Ashley followed.

He closed the door, and flipped the light switch, casting the room into darkness. "See," he said, pointing to the ceiling.

Ashley looked up and noticed a hundred glittering stars illuminated on the huge ceiling. What had been an attractive, whimsical room with the light on became a land of fantasy with the light off.

"It's great," she murmured, her voice slightly thick. Over and over again Claudia had commented on how much Cooper loved the boys. Ashley had seen it herself. He wasn't lofty or untouchable when he was with John and Scott. His affinity for children showed he could be human and vulnerable. He was so warm and loving with the boys that it was all she could do to keep from running into his arms.

Cooper made a show of checking his wristwatch. "Isn't it about time for you boys to go to bed?"

"Can I wear your watch again?" Johnny asked eagerly.

Cooper didn't hesitate, slipping the gold band from his wrist and placing it on his godson's arm.

Ashley couldn't help but wonder at the ease with which Cooper relinquished a timepiece that must have cost thousands of dollars.

Scotty cried when she placed him in the crib. She stayed for several minutes, attempting to comfort him, but to no avail. She would just get him to lie down and tuck him under the blanket when he would pull himself upright, hold onto the bars and look at her with those pleading blue eyes. She couldn't refuse, and finally gave in and lifted him out of the crib.

"Claudia said something about rocking him to sleep."

"No problem," Cooper said with a sly grin. He left and returned a minute later with the wooden rocker from downstairs.

"Will you pray with me, Uncle Cooper?" Johnny— who was also still wide awake—requested, kneeling at his bedside.

Cooper joined the little boy on the plush navy blue carpet.

For the second time that night Ashley was emotionally stirred by the sight of this man with a child.

"God bless Mommy, Daddy and Scotty," John prayed, his head bowed reverently, his small hands folded. "And God bless Uncle Cooper, Auntie Ash and all the angels. And I love you, Jesus, and amen."

"Amen," Cooper echoed softly.

Scotty had his eyes closed as he lay securely in Ashley's arms. Gently she stood to lay him in the crib, but both eyes flew open anxiously and he struggled to sit up. With a short sigh of acquiescence, she sat back down and began to rock again. Content, Scotty watched her, but with every minute his eyes closed a little more. She wouldn't make the mistake of getting up too early a second time. Gently, she brushed the wisps of hair from his brow.

Cooper was sitting on the mattress beside Johnny, who was playing with the wristwatch, his gaze fixed on the lighted digits. Cooper pushed a variety of buttons, which delighted the boy. After a few minutes, Cooper tucked Johnny between the sheets and leaned over to kiss his brow.

"Night, night, Auntie Ash," Johnny whispered.

She blew him a kiss. Johnny pretended to catch it, then tucked his stuffed animal under his arm and rolled over.

The moment was serene and peaceful. Finally sure that Scotty was asleep, she stood and gently put him into the crib. Cooper came to stand at her side, a hand cupping her shoulder as they looked down on the sleeping baby.

Neither spoke, afraid of destroying the tranquility. When they finally stepped back, he removed his hand. Immediately, Ashley missed the warmth of his touch as they headed back downstairs.

He paused at the bottom of the stairs, a step ahead of her. He turned, halting her descent.

"Ashley," he whispered on a soft trembling breath, his look dark and troubled.

A tremor ran through her at the perplexing expression she saw in his eyes. Spontaneously she slipped her arms around his neck without even being aware of what she was doing.

"Ashley," he repeated, the husky sound a gentle caress. He crushed her to him, his arms hugging her waist as his lips sought hers. The kiss was like it had always been between them. That jolt of awareness so strong it seemed to catch them both off guard. When his mouth broke from hers, she could hear his labored breathing and the heavy thud of his heart.

He loosened his hold, bringing his hands up to her neck, weaving long fingers through her hair. His lips soothed her chin and temple, and she gloried in the tingling sensations that spread through her. She continued to lean against him, needing his support, because her legs felt weak and wobbly.

"I'm sorry about the party tonight," he murmured, and she couldn't doubt the sincerity in his voice.

"No, I'm the one who should be sorry. I said so many terrible things to you." Tipping her head back so she could gaze into his impassioned eyes, she spoke again. "I'm amazed you put up with me." Lovingly, she traced the proud line of his jaw, a finger paused to investigate the tiny cleft in his chin. Unable to resist, she kissed him there and loved the sound of his groan.

"Ashley," he warned, "please, it's hard enough keeping my hands off you."

"It is? Really? Oh, Cooper, really?"

"Yes, so don't tease."

"I think that's the nicest thing you've ever said to me."

His hand curved around her waist as he brought her down the last step. "Have you eaten dinner?"

"No, I didn't have time. You?"

"I'm starved. Maybe we can dig up something in the kitchen."

She couldn't see why they needed to look for anything. Her mother did the cooking for him, and there were bound to be leftovers. "Mom—"

"I gave her the rest of the month off," he explained before she could finish.

"Well, in that case, I vote for pizza."

"Pizza?" He glanced at her, aghast.

"All right, you choose." She placed an arm around him and smiled deeply into his dark eyes.

"Let's look." Together they rounded the corner that led to the kitchen. He checked the refrigerator and turned, shaking his head. "I don't know how we'd manage to make pizza from any of this."

"Not make," she corrected. "Order. All we need to do is phone and wait for the delivery guy."

"Amazing." He tilted his head at an inquiring angle. "Is this something you and this Webber fellow do often?"

A denial rose automatically to her lips, but she successfully swallowed it back. "Sometimes. And his name is Dennis Webb."

The corner of his mouth lifted in a half-smile. "Sorry." But he didn't look the least bit repentant.

"Do you want me to order?"

He straightened and leaned against the kitchen counter. "Sure, whatever you want."

"Canadian bacon, pineapple and olives."

His dark eyes widened questioningly, but he nodded his agreement.

She couldn't help laughing. "It tastes great, trust me."

"I'm afraid I'll have to."

She used the phone in the kitchen. Cooper regarded her suspiciously when she punched in the number without looking it up in the directory.

"You know the number by heart? Just how often do you do this?"

"I'm good with numbers."

After placing their order, she turned and smiled seductively. "Shall we play a game of chess while we're waiting?"

His look was faintly mocking. "I have a feeling I'd better not."

"Why?" she asked, batting her long lashes.

"If I say yes, then no wagers," he insisted.

"You take all the fun out of it," she said, and feigned a pout. "But I'll manage to whip you anyway."

He chuckled and took her hand, leading them into his den.

While she set up the game board, Cooper lit the logs in the fireplace. Within minutes flickering shadows played across the walls.

His eyes were serious as he sat down opposite her. As before, each move was measured and thought-filled. At mid-game the advantage was Ashley's. Then the doorbell chimed, interrupting their concentration.

Cooper answered and returned with a huge flat box, his look slightly abashed. "You ordered enough for a family of five," he chastised her.

"You said you were hungry," she argued, not lifting her gaze from the game. Her eyes brightened as she moved and captured his knight, lifting it from the board.

"How'd you do that?" His expression turned serious as he set the pizza on the hearth to keep warm. "I don't want to stop now. We can eat later."

"I'm hungry," she insisted slyly.

He waved her away with the flick of his hand, his attention centered on the board. "You go ahead and eat, then."

She left the room and returned a minute later with a plate and napkin, sitting on the floor in front of the fire. The aroma of melted cheese and Canadian bacon filled the room when she lifted the lid. "Yumm, this is delicious," she said after swallowing her first bite.

A frown drove three wide creases into his brow as he glanced up. "You're eating in here," he said, as if noticing her for the first time.

"I'm not supposed to?" Color invaded her face until

her cheeks felt hot. She was always doing something she shouldn't where Cooper was concerned. Her actions had probably shocked him. No doubt he had never in his entire life eaten any place but on a table with a linen cloth. Pizza on the floor made her look childish and gauche.

His expression softened. "It's fine, I'm sure. It's just that I never have."

"Oh." She felt ridiculously close to tears and bowed her head. The pizza suddenly tasted like glue. She closed the lid, then set her plate aside. "The carpet is probably worth a fortune. I wouldn't want to ruin it," she said with total sincerity.

He put a finger under her chin and raised her eyes to his. "Shh," he whispered, and gently laid his mouth over hers.

His kiss had been unexpected, catching her off guard, but quickly she became a willing victim.

"You're right," Cooper murmured, then chuckled. "The pizza does taste good." He lowered himself onto the floor beside her and helped himself to a piece. "Delicious," he agreed, his eyes smiling.

"Can I have a taste?" she asked, a faint smile curving her mouth.

He held out the triangular wedge. She leaned forward and carefully took a bite.

"Thank you," she told him seriously.

With slow, deliberate movements, he placed the pizza box, plates and napkins aside, and reached for her.

Ashley moved willingly into his arms. Sliding her hands around his neck, she raised her face, eager for his attention. Her mouth was trembling in anticipation when he claimed it. A feeling of warmth wove its way through her and seemed to touch Cooper as the kiss deepened.

Somewhere, a long way in the distance, a bell began to chime. Fleetingly, she wondered why it had taken so long to hear bells when Cooper kissed her.

Abruptly, he broke away, grumbling something unintelligible. He briefly touched his mouth to her cheek before he stood and answered the phone.

Six

"It's Claudia," Cooper said, holding out the receiver.

Ashley stood, her movements awkward as the lingering effects of Cooper's kiss continued to stir her senses. "Hello."

"Ash, I'm sorry," Claudia began. "I didn't know Cooper was going to show up. Is everything okay?"

"Wonderful."

"You two aren't arguing, are you?"

"Quite the contrary," Ashley murmured, closing her eyes as Cooper cupped her cheek with his hand. A kaleidoscope of emotions rippled through her.

"Are the boys down?" Claudia inquired.

"The boys?" Ashley jerked her eyes open and straightened. "Yes, they're both asleep."

"Seth and I may be several hours yet. If everything's peaceful, then don't feel like you need to stay. I'm sure Cooper can handle things if the boys wake up. But they probably won't."

"Okay," she agreed. "I'll talk to you later. Don't worry about anything."

The sound of Claudia's soft laugh came over the line. "I don't think I need to. Take care."

"Bye," Ashley said, and replaced the phone. "That was Claudia checking on the boys," she explained unnecessarily.

"I thought it might be," he said, and nuzzled the top of her head. "Let's finish our dinner," he suggested, taking her by the hand and leading her back to the fireplace.

They ate in contented silence. His look was thoughtful as he paused once to ask, "Do you pray?"

The question was completely unexpected.

"Yes," she responded simply. "What makes you ask?"

He shrugged indifferently, and she had the impression he was far more interested than he wanted to admit. "This is the first time I've eaten pizza on the floor with a beautiful woman."

"Beautiful woman?" she teased. "Where?"

His eyes were more serious than she had ever seen them. "You," he answered, and looked away. The steady tone of his voice revealed how sincere he was.

"There are a lot of things I haven't done in my life. Prayer is one of them. Tonight when Johnny had me get down on my knees with him…" He let the rest of what he was going to say fade. "It felt right." He glanced back at her. "Do you kneel down, too, or is that just something for children?"

"I do on occasion, but it certainly isn't necessary."

Cooper straightened, leaning back against the ottoman. "How do you pray?"

Ashley was surprised by the directness of his question. "Whole books have been written on the subject. I don't know if I'm qualified to answer."

"I didn't ask about anyone else, only you," he countered.

"Well," she began, unsure on how best to answer him. "I don't know that anyone else does it like me."

"I've noted on several occasions that you're a free spirit," he muttered, doing his best to hide his amusement. "Okay, let's go at this from a different angle. When do you pray?"

Answering questions was easier for her. "Mostly in the morning, but any time throughout the day. I pray for little things, parking places at the grocery store, and before I pay bills, and over the mail, and also for the big ones, like everyone in my life staying healthy and happy."

"Why mostly in the morning?" He regarded her steadily.

"That's when I do my devotions," she explained patiently.

"What are devotions?"

"Bible reading and praying," she told him. "My private time with the Lord. My day goes better when I've had a chance to discuss things with Jesus."

"You talk to Him as if He were a regular person?"

"He is," she said, more forcefully than she intended.

He paused and appeared to consider her words thoughtfully. "Do you speak to Him conversationally, then?"

"Yes and no."

"You don't like talking about this, do you?"

"It isn't that," she tried to explain, a soft catch in her voice. "If I tell you…I guess I'm afraid you'll think it's silly."

"I won't." The wealth of tenderness in his voice assured her he wouldn't.

"Usually I set aside a formal time for reading my Bible, other devotional books and praying. After I do my Bible reading, I get down on my knees, close my eyes and picture myself on a beautiful beach." She glanced up hesitantly, and Cooper nodded. The warmth in his look seemed to caress her, and she continued. "The scene is perfectly set in my mind. The waves are crashing against the sandy shore and easing back into the sea. I envision the tiny bubbles popping against the sand as the water ebbs out. This is where I meet Christ."

"Does He talk to you?"

"Not with words." She looked away uneasily. "I don't know how to explain this part. I know He hears me, and I know He answers my prayers. I see the evidence of that every day. But as for Him verbally speaking to me, I'd have to say no, though I hear His voice in other ways."

"I don't understand."

"I'm not sure I can explain, I just *do*."

Cooper seemed to accept that. "Then all you do is talk. You make it sound too easy." He seemed unsure, and she hastened to arrest his doubts.

"No, I spend part of the time thanking Him or…praising Him would be a better description, I guess. Another part is spent going over the previous day and asking His forgiveness for any wrongs I've done."

"That shouldn't take a lot of time," he teased.

"Longer than I care to admit," she informed him sheepishly and mentally added that the time had increased since she'd been seeing Cooper. "I also keep a list of requests that I pray about regularly and go down each one."

"Am I on your list?" The question was asked so softly that she wasn't sure he'd even spoken.

"Yes," she answered. "I pray for you every day," she admitted, her voice gaining intensity. She didn't add that all the people she loved were on her list. To avoid other questions she continued speaking. "For a while I wrote out my prayers. That was years ago, and it became a journal of God's faithfulness. But I can't write as fast as I can think, so I found that often I'd lose my train of thought. But I've saved those journals and sometimes read over them. When I do, I'm amazed again at God's goodness to me."

A baby's frantic cry broke into their conversation. "Scotty," Ashley said, bounding to her feet. "I'll go see what's wrong."

Scotty was standing in the crib, holding onto the sides. His crying grew louder and more desperate as she hurried into the room.

"What's wrong, Scotty?" she asked soothingly. Soft light from the hallway illuminated the dark recess of the bedroom. She lifted him out of the crib and hugged him close. Checking his diaper, she noted that he didn't seem to be wet. Probably he'd been frightened by a nightmare. Settling him in her arms, she sat in the rocking chair and rocked until she was sure he was back to sleep. With a kiss on the top of his head, she placed him back in his crib.

Cooper was waiting for her at the bottom of the stairs.

"He's asleep again," she whispered.

"I made coffee, would you like a cup?"

She smiled her appreciation. He curved an arm around her narrow waist, bringing her close to his side as he led her back into the den. A silver tea service was set on his desk. She saw that the remains of their dinner had been cleared away, along with their chess game. Biting into her bottom lip to contain her amusement, she decided not to comment on what a neat-freak he was.

He poured the steaming liquid into the china cups, then offered her one. Her hand shook momentarily as she accepted it. Dainty pieces of delicate china made her nervous, and she would have much preferred a ceramic mug.

"This set is lovely," she said, holding the cup in one hand. Tiny pink rosebuds, faded with age, decorated the teacup. She balanced the matching saucer in the palm of her other hand.

"It was my grandmother's," he said proudly. "There are only a few of the original pieces left."

"Oh." Her index finger tightened around the porcelain handle. In her nervousness, her hand wobbled and the boiling hot coffee sloshed over the side onto her hand and her lap, immediately soaking through her thin corduroy jeans. With a gasp of pain, she jumped to her feet. The saucer flew out of her lap and smashed against the leg of the desk, shattering into a thousand pieces.

"Ashley, are you all right?" Cooper bounded to his feet beside her.

Stunned, she couldn't move, her eyes fixed on the broken china as despair filled her. "I'm so sorry," she mumbled. Her voice cracked, and she swallowed past the huge lump building in her throat.

"Forget the china," he said, and took the teacup out of her hand. "It doesn't matter, none of it matters."

"It does matter!" she cried, her voice wobbling uncontrollably. "It matters very much."

"You've got to get that hand in ice water. What about your leg? Is it badly burned?" He tugged at her elbow, almost dragging her into the kitchen. He brought her to the sink and stuck her hand under the cold water. She looked down to see an angry red patch on the back of her left hand, where the coffee had spilled. Funny, she didn't feel any pain. Nothing. Only a horrible deep regret.

"Cooper, please, listen to me. I'm so sorry…your grandmother's china is ruined because of me."

"Keep that hand under the water," he said, ignoring her words. Then he went to get ice from the automatic dispenser on the refrigerator door.

Ashley looked away rather than face him. She heard the water splash as he dumped the ice into the sink.

"What about your leg?" he demanded.

"It's fine." She tilted her chin upward and closed her eyes to forestall the tears. The burns didn't hurt; if anything, her hand was growing numb with cold. How could she have been so stupid? His grandmother's china…only a few pieces left. His earlier words echoed in her ears until they were nearly deafening.

"Ashley," he whispered, a hand on her shoulder. "Are you all right? You've gone pale. Is the pain very bad? Should I take you to a doctor?"

Talking was impossible, because her throat felt raw and painful, so she shook her head. "Your grandmother's china," she said at last, her voice barely above a tortured whisper.

"Would you quit acting like it's some great tragedy? You've been burned, and that's far more important than some stupid china."

"Do you know what my mother uses for fancy dinners?" she asked in a hoarse voice, then didn't wait for him to answer. "Dishes she picked up at the grocery store. With every ten dollar purchase she could buy another plate at a discount price."

"What has that go to do with anything?" he demanded irritably.

"Nothing. Everything. I swear I'll replace the saucer. I'll contact an antique dealer, I promise..."

"Ashley, stop." His firm hands squeezed her shoulders. "Stop right now. I don't care about a stupid saucer. But I do care about you." His grip tightened. "The saucer means nothing. Nothing," he repeated. "Do you understand?"

Her throat muscles had constricted so that she couldn't speak. Miserably, she hung her head, and her soft curls fell forward, wreathing her face.

She started to tremble, and with a muted groan Cooper hauled her into his arms.

"Honey, it doesn't matter. Please believe me when I tell you that."

She held on to him hard, because only the warmth of his touch was capable of easing the cold that pierced her heart. A lone tear squeezed past her lashes. She loved Cooper Masters so much it had become a physical pain. Never before had she realized how wrong she was for him. He needed someone who...

She wasn't allowed to complete the thought as Cooper's hand touched her face, turning her to meet his gaze. Her tortured eyes tried to avoid him, but he held her steady.

"Ashley, look at me." He sounded gruff, impatient.

But she was determined, and she shook herself loose, then swayed against him, her fingers spread against his shirt. He found her lips and kissed her with a desperation she hadn't experienced from him. It was as if he needed to confirm what he was saying, to comfort her, reassure her. She knew she shouldn't accept any of it. But one minute in Cooper's arms and it didn't matter. All she could do was feel.

His hands roamed her back as he buried his face in the hair at the side of her face. "Let's sit down."

He took her into the living room and set her down in the soft comfort of the large sofa. Next he opened the drapes and revealed the same view of Puget Sound that they'd enjoyed on Thanksgiving Day, when they'd walked on his property in the rain.

Hands in his pockets, he paused to admire the beauty. "Sometimes in the evening I sit here, staring into the sky, counting the stars." He spoke absently, standing at the far corner of the window, gazing into the still night. "Looking at all that magnificence makes me feel small and very insignificant. One man, alone." His back was to her. "It's times like this that make me regret not having a wife and family. I've worked hard, and what do I have to show for it? An expensive home and no one to share it with." He stopped and turned, their eyes meeting. For a breathless moment they stared at one another. Then he dropped his gaze and turned slowly back to the window.

Confused for a moment, she watched as he turned away from her, as if trying to block her out of his mind. His action troubled her. He stood alone, across the room, a solitary figure silhouetted against the night. What was he telling her? She didn't understand, but she did realize that he had revealed a part of himself others didn't see.

Unfolding her long legs from the sofa, she joined him at the window. Standing at his side, she slipped an arm around his waist as if she'd done it a thousand times.

He smiled at her then, and she couldn't remember ever seeing anything transform a face more. His dark eyes seemed to spark with something she couldn't define. Happiness? Contentment? Pleasure? His smile widened as he looped his arm over her shoulders, and then he brushed her temple with a light kiss.

"Do you have your Christmas tree up yet?"

"No," she whispered, afraid talking normally would destroy the wonderful mood. "I thought I'd put it up tomorrow."

"Would you like some help?"

The offer shocked her. "I'd...I'd love some."

"What time?"

"Probably afternoon." Her sigh was filled with a sense of dread. "I've got to get some shopping done. There are only a few days left, and I've hardly started."

"Me either, and I still need to get something for the boys."

"I'm afraid I haven't had the chance to shop. The last days of school were so hectic. I hate leaving everything to the last minute like this."

"Why don't we make a day of it?" he suggested. "I'll pick you up, say around ten. We can do the shopping, go for lunch and decorate your tree afterward."

"That sounds wonderful. I'd like that. I'd like it very much."

"And, Ashley..." Cooper said, looking away uncomfortably.

"Yes?"

"I was thinking about buying myself a pair of cowboy boots and wanted to ask your advice about the best place to go."

"I know just the store, in the Pavilion near South-center. But be warned, they're expensive." As soon as the words were out, she regretted them. Cooper didn't need to worry about money.

He chuckled and gave her a tiny squeeze. "I wish other people were as reluctant to spend my money."

"We'll see how reluctant I am tomorrow," she murmured with a small laugh.

Seven

Ashley changed clothes three times before the doorbell chimed, announcing Cooper's arrival. Her final choice had been a soft gray wool skirt and a white bouclé-knit sweater. The outfit, with knee-high black leather boots, was one she usually reserved for church, but she wanted everything to be perfect for Cooper.

A warm smile lit up her face as she opened the door. "Morning, you're right on…" She didn't finish; the words died on her lips. Cooper in jeans! Levis so new and stiff they looked as if they would stand up on their own. Her lashes fluttered downward to disguise her shock.

"Morning. You look as beautiful as ever."

"Thank you," she whispered, somewhat bewildered. "Do you want a cup of coffee or something before we go?"

"No, I think we'd better get started before the crowds get too bad."

She lounged back in her seat, content to let him drive. He flipped a switch, and immediately the interior was filled with classical music. She savored the gentle sounds of the string section and glanced up, surprised when the music abruptly changed to a top forty station.

"Why'd you do that?" she asked, her blue gaze sweeping toward him, searching his profile.

"I thought this would probably be more to your liking." His gaze remained on the freeway, the traffic surprisingly heavy for early morning.

"It's not," she murmured, a little of her earlier happiness dissipating with the thought that Cooper assumed she preferred more popular music to the classics. *But don't you?* her mind countered.

They took the exit for Southcenter, a huge shopping complex south of Seattle, but didn't stop there. The area's largest toy store was situated nearby, and they had decided earlier that it would be the best place to start.

The parking lot was already full, so Cooper had to drive around a couple of times before locating a spot at the far end.

His hand cupped her elbow as they hurried inside. Only a few shopping carts were left, and she glanced around, doing her best to squelch a growing sense of panic. The store had barely opened, and already there was hardly room to move through the aisles.

"My goodness," she murmured impatiently. They were forced to wait to move past the throng of shoppers entering the first aisle. "Do you want to come back later?" she asked, glancing at him anxiously.

"I don't think it's going to get any better," he muttered darkly.

"I don't think it will, either. Maybe we should decide now what we want to buy the boys. That would at least streamline the process. We're going together, aren't we?"

At Cooper's questioning glance, she added, "I mean, we'll split the cost."

"I'll pay," he insisted.

"Cooper," she groaned. "Either we divide the cost or forget it."

His mouth thinned slightly. "All right, I should know better. You and that pride of yours."

He looked as if he wanted to add something more, but the crowd moved, and she pushed the cart forward.

"Okay, what should we get Johnny?" Her eyes followed the floor-to-ceiling display of computer games. On the other side of the aisle were more traditional games and puzzles.

"I've thought of something perfect," Cooper announced proudly. "I'm sure you'll agree."

"What?"

"A computer chess game. I saw one advertised the other day."

"He's too young for that," Ashley declared. She hated to stifle Cooper's enthusiasm, but Johnny wasn't interested in chess.

"He's not," Cooper shot back. "I've been teaching him a few moves. It's the perfect gift—educational, too."

"Good," she said emphatically. "Then you get him that, but I want to buy him something he'll enjoy."

Cooper's soft chuckle caught her unaware. "What's so funny?" she asked.

"You." He paused and looked around before lightly kissing her cheek. "I can't think of a thing in the world that you and I will ever agree on. Our tastes are too different." His gaze seemed to be fixed on her softly parted lips. "Do men often have to restrain themselves from kissing you?"

A happy light shimmered from her deep blue eyes. "Hundreds," she teased. Immediately she realized it had been the wrong thing to say. She could almost visualize the wall that was going up between them.

He straightened and pretended an interest in one of the displays.

"Cooper," she whispered, and laid her hand across his forearm. "That was a dumb joke."

"I imagine it was closer to the truth than you realize."

"Oh, hardly," she denied with a light laugh.

An hour and a half later, their packages stored in the booth beside them, Ashley exhaled a long sigh.

"Coffee," Cooper told the waitress, who quickly returned and filled their mugs.

"I can't remember a time when I needed this more," Ashley murmured and took an appreciative sip.

"Me, either. Could you believe that checkout line?"

"But Johnny's going to love his fire truck and hat."

"And his computer chess game."

"Of course," she agreed, grinning.

"At least we agreed on Scotty's gift. That wasn't so difficult, was it?"

Ashley's gaze skipped from Cooper to the stuffed animal beside him, and she burst into peals of laughter. "Oh, Cooper, if only your friends could see you now with that gorilla next to you."

"Yes, I guess that would be cause for amusement."

Digging through her purse, Ashley brought out her Bible, flipping through the worn pages.

"What are you doing now?" he asked in a hushed whisper.

"Don't worry, I'm not going to stand on the seat and start a crusade. I want to find something."

"What?"

"A verse." She paused, a finger marking the place. "Here it is. First Peter 1:4."

"Honestly, you've got to be the only woman in the world who whips out her Bible in a restaurant."

Unaffected by his teasing tone, she laid the book open on the tabletop, turned it sideways and pointed to the passage she wanted him to read. "After what we just went through, I decided I wanted to be sure heaven has reserved seating. It does, look." Aloud she read a portion of the text. "'To obtain an inheritance which is reserved in heaven for you.'"

A hint of a smile quivered at the edges of his mouth. "You're serious, aren't you?"

"Sure I am. I've seen pictures of riots that looked more organized than that mess we were in."

He laughed loudly then, attracting the curious glances of others. "Ashley Robbins, I find you delightful."

Pleased, she beamed and placed the small Bible back inside her purse.

"Where do you want to go next?" he asked as he glanced at his wristwatch.

"Do you need to be back for something?"

He raised his eyes to meet hers. "No," he said, and shook his head to emphasize his denial.

"If you feel like you could brave the maddening crowd a second time, we could tackle the mall."

He looked unsure for a moment. She couldn't blame him. The thought of facing thousands of last-minute shoppers wasn't an appealing one, but she did still have gifts to buy—and he wanted those boots.

"Sure, why not?" he agreed.

Ashley could think of forty thousand hectic reasons why not, but she didn't voice a single one, content simply being with Cooper.

"However, I hope you don't object if we store Tarzan's friend in the trunk of the car," he added, and glanced wryly at the stuffed animal.

The crowds at the mall proved to be even worse than the toy store, but a couple of hours later, their arms loaded with packages, they finally retreated to the car.

Even Cooper, who was normally so calm and reserved, looked a bit ashen after fighting the chaos. They hadn't even stopped for lunch, eating caramel apples instead as they walked from one end of the mall to the other.

"Do you think Claudia will like the necklace?" he asked as he joined her in the front seat and inserted the key into the ignition.

"Of course." Ashley had picked out the turquoise necklace and knew her friend would love it, but he was still skeptical. "Trust me."

"There's something about that phrase that makes me nervous."

"But you didn't buy two. Now I'm curious," she ventured, not paying attention to what he'd said.

"Two? Two what?"

"Necklaces." She gave him an impatient look. Sometimes they seemed to be speaking at complete cross purposes.

"Do you think Claudia would want two?" He gave her a curious glance.

"Of course not," she said with a sigh. "But you always buy me the same thing as Claudia." She didn't add that it had been perfume for the past three Christmases.

"Not this year."

"Really?" Her interested piqued, she asked, "What are you getting me?"

"Like John and Scott, you'll have to wait until Christmas morning."

She was more pleased than she dared show. Not that she would be forced to wait until Christmas, but that she'd moved beyond the same safe category as Claudia. It thrilled her to know that their relationship had evolved to the point that he wanted to get her something different this year.

Cooper played with the radio until he found some Christmas music.

Again Ashley could feel the comforting music float around her, soothing her tattered nerves. "Doesn't that make you want to sing?"

"Every time you say that we have a storm," he complained.

"Killjoy," she muttered under her breath.

A large hand reached over and squeezed hers. "Ready to decorate the tree?"

"More than ready," she agreed. Much of her shopping remained to be done, but she'd promised Claudia that they would head out early Monday morning so there would be plenty of time to finish.

The remainder of the short drive to her apartment was accomplished in a companionable silence. Her mind wandered to the first time Cooper had asked her to dinner after she'd paid off the loan. At the time she would have doubted she could ever sit at his side without being nervous. Now she felt relaxed, content.

Although nothing had ever been openly stated, their relationship had come a long way in the past couple of months. She could only pray that this budding rapport would continue after Claudia, Seth and the boys returned to Alaska.

Ever the gentleman, Cooper took the apartment key away from her and unlocked the door. Men didn't usually do that sort of thing for her, but then again, she probably wouldn't have let anyone but Cooper.

"I put the tree on the lanai until it was time to decorate," she told him, and took his coat, hanging it with hers in the closet. When she turned around Cooper was helping himself to a handful of popcorn.

"I wouldn't eat that if I were you, it's a week old."

He dropped the kernels back into the bowl and wrinkled his nose.

"Quit giving me funny looks like I'm a terrible housekeeper. You're supposed to leave the popcorn out to get stale. It strings easier that way."

"Strings?"

"For the tree."

"Of course, for the tree," he echoed.

She had the uneasy sensation that he didn't know what she meant. Lightly, she shrugged her shoulders. He would learn soon enough.

"Are you hungry?" she asked on her way into the kitchen. "I can make us pastrami sandwiches with dill pickles and potato chips."

"That sounds good, except I'll have my potato chips on the side."

"Cute," she murmured, sticking her head around the corner.

"With you I never know," he complained with a full smile.

While she made lunch, Cooper brought the Christmas tree inside. Since it was already in the stand, all he had to do was find a place to set it in the living room. When he'd finished he joined her in the compact kitchen.

Working contentedly with her back to him, she hummed softly and cut thin slices of pickle.

"You can have one of the chocolates I bought if you like," she told him, as she spread a thick layer of mustard across the bread.

"I thought you said chocolates weren't meant to be shared."

She laughed softly. "I was only teasing."

"Ashley..."

Just the way he spoke her name caused her to pause and turn around.

"I think we should do this before we eat."

"Do what?" Her heart was chugging like a locomotive at the look he was giving her.

"This." He took the knife out of her hand and laid it on the counter. His gaze centered on her mouth.

She gave a soft welcoming moan as his lips fit over hers. All day she'd yearned for his touch. It was torture to be so close to him and maintain the friendly facade, when in her heart all she wanted was to be held and loved by him.

When he dragged his mouth from hers, she knew he felt as unsatisfied as she did. Kissing was quickly becoming insufficient to satisfy either of them. His hands roamed possessively over her back, arching her closer. Again his mouth dipped to drink from the sweetness of hers. With a shuddering breath he released her.

Sensation after sensation swirled through her. These feelings he stirred within her were what God had intended her to feel toward the man she loved, and she couldn't doubt the rightness of them. But what was *he* feeling? Certainly he wasn't immune to all this.

His smile was gentle when he asked, "Did you say something about lunch?"

"Lunch," she repeated like a robot, then lightly shook her head, irritated that she was reacting like a lovesick teenager. No, she mused, Cooper couldn't help but be aware of the powerful physical attraction between them. He was simply much more in control of himself than she was.

A few minutes later she carried their meal into the living room on a tray. He was sorting through her ornaments and looked up. A frown was creasing his brow.

"What's wrong?" she asked, setting their plates on the coffee table and glancing over at him.

"There's something written across these glass ornaments."

"I know," she answered simply.

"But what is it and why?"

A soft smile touched her mouth as she lifted half of her sandwich and prepared to take the first bite. "Remember how I mentioned that I dated the man who sold me Milligan a couple of times?"

"I remember."

The tightness in his voice sent her searching gaze to him a second time. "Unfortunately, Jim was decidedly not a Christian. We saw one another a couple of times in December, and he couldn't understand why I didn't want to do certain things."

"What things?" Cooper's tone had taken on an arctic chill.

"It doesn't matter," she said, and smiled, dismissing

his curiosity. The past was over, and she didn't want to review it with him. "But one thing I *am* grateful for is the fact Jim told me the Christmas tree is a pagan custom. He found it interesting that I professed this deep faith in Christ yet chose to allow a pagan ritual to desecrate my home." She set the sandwich aside and knelt beside Cooper on the carpet. "You know, he's right. I was shocked, so I decided to make my Christmas tree Christ centered."

"But how?"

"It wasn't that difficult. The tree is an evergreen, constant, never changing, just as my faith in Christ is meant to be. And Christ died upon a tree. The lights were the easiest part. Jesus asks that each one of us be the light of the world. But when it came to the ornaments, I had to be a little inventive, so I took glitter glue—"

"Glitter glue?" he interrupted.

"Glue that has glitter already in it. It's much easier to write out the fruits of the Holy Spirit that way."

"Hold on, you've lost me."

"Here." She stood and retrieved her Bible from the oak end table. Flipping the pages, she located the verses she wanted. "Paul wrote in his epistle to the Galatians about the fruits of the Christian life."

"Love, joy, peace," he read from each of the pink glass ornaments. "I get it now."

"Exactly," she stated excitedly.

"Clever girl." His thick brows arched expressively.

"Thank you."

"I'm very curious now about how you tie in the popcorn."

"Yes, well…" Frantically, her mind searched for a plausible reason. She hadn't thought about the decorative strings she added each year.

"I've got it," he said. "White and spotless like the Christ child."

"Very good," she congratulated him.

There was a disconcerted look in his eyes as they met hers. "Your commitment to Christ is important to you, isn't it?"

"Vital," she confirmed. "One's relationship with God is a personal thing. But Christ is the most important person in my life. He has been for several years."

"You stopped seeing Madigan because he didn't have the same belief system as you."

"More or less. In some ways we hit it off immediately. I liked Jim, I still do. But our relationship was headed for a dead end, so I cut it off before either one of us got serious."

"Because he didn't believe the same way as you? Isn't that narrow minded?"

"To me it isn't, and that wasn't the only reason. Cooper..." She paused and held her breath when she saw his troubled look. "Why all the questions? Do you think I'm wrong in the way I believe?"

"It doesn't matter what I think."

"Of course, it matters." *Because you do,* she added silently.

He rose and walked to the far side of the room. "I don't believe the same way you do. Oh, I acknowledge there's a God. I couldn't look at the heavens and examine our world and not believe in a Supreme Being. I accept that Christ was born, but I never have understood salvation, justification and all the rest of it. Everyone talks about the free gift, but—"

A loud knock on her door interrupted him.

She glanced at him and shrugged. She wasn't expecting anyone. She got to her feet, crossed the room and checked the peephole.

"It's Webb," she told Cooper before opening the door.

"Hello, Sweet Thing. How's your day been?" He sauntered into the room whistling "White Christmas" and paused long enough to brush his lips across her cheek. The song died on his lips when he spotted Cooper.

"Webb," Ashley said stiffly, folding her hands tightly together in front of her. "This is Cooper Masters. I believe I've mentioned him."

She watched as the two men exchanged handshakes. "Cooper, this is Dennis Webb."

Ashley wanted to shout at her friend. Webb couldn't have picked a worse time to pop in for one of his spontaneous visits.

"No, I can't say that I recall you mentioning him," Webb announced as he glanced back to Ashley.

She seethed silently and somehow managed a weak smile.

"I can't say the same about you," Cooper muttered in the stiff, formal tone she'd come to hate.

"Would you like to sit down, Webb?" She motioned toward the sofa and glared at him, desperately hoping he would get the message and leave.

"Thanks." He plopped down on the couch and crossed his legs. "You missed a great party last night. Hardly seemed right without you there, Ash. Next time I won't take no for an answer."

Cooper lowered himself onto the far end of the sofa. His back remained rigid.

"I'll make coffee," Ashley volunteered as she left the room, thinking the atmosphere back there was so thick she could taste it.

"I'll see if I can help in the kitchen," she heard Webb say, and a second later he was at her side.

"Who is this guy?" he hissed.

"What do you mean?" she demanded in a hushed whisper, then didn't wait for an answer. "He's my best friend's uncle, and what do you mean I've never mentioned him? I talk about him all the time."

"You haven't," Webb insisted. "Unless he's the one you played chess with and lost?"

"That's him." Her fingers refused to work properly, and coffee grounds spilled across the counter. "Darn, darn, darn."

"I don't care who he is, if he calls me Webber one more time, I'm going to punch him."

"Webb," she expelled her breath and noticed that Cooper was watching her intently from the doorway. She stopped talking and forced a beguiling smile onto her face. Her teeth were clenched so tight her jaw hurt. "Can't you see it's not a good time?" she hissed beneath her breath.

"Are you saying you want me to leave?"

"Yes." She nearly shouted the one word.

Cooper stepped closer. "Is everything all right, Ashley?" he asked in a formal tone, but his burning gaze was focused on Webb.

The look was searing. She had never seen such disapproval illuminated so clearly on anyone's features. Cooper's mouth was pinched, his eyes narrowed. For a crazy second she wanted to laugh. The two men were eyeing one another like bears who had encroached on each other's territory.

"I'm fine. Webb was just saying that he has to go."

"I do?" he said. "Oh, yes, I guess I do." He walked out

of the kitchen with Ashley on his heels. "I'll talk to you soon," he told her, his gaze full of meaning.

"Right." She held open the door for him. "Sorry you have to leave so soon."

The look Webb gave her nearly sent her into peals of laughter. "I'll phone you soon," she promised.

"Nice meeting you, Cooper," Webb said graciously. "Now that I recall, Ash *has* mentioned you. I understand you play a mean game of chess."

"I play," Cooper admitted with a look of indifference.

"I dabble in the game myself," Webb said, tossing Ashley a teasing glance.

"See you later, Webb," she said firmly, and closed the door. The lock clicked shut, and she paused, her eyes closed, and released a long, slow, breath.

"Nice fellow, Webber," Cooper said from behind her.

"He's a friend." She had to be certain Cooper understood that her relationship with Webb didn't go any further than that of congenial co-workers.

"I imagine he's the kind of Christian who fits right into that cozy picture you have built in your mind." His tone was almost harsh.

Ashley did her best to ignore it. "Webb's a wonderful Christian man."

"You probably should marry someone like him," he stated with a sharp edge. His gaze narrowed on her. It wasn't difficult to tell that he was angry, but she didn't know why.

"You're upset, aren't you?" she asked, confronting him. Her back was against the door, her hands clenched at her side.

Cooper's long strides carried him to the far side of the room. He tried to ram his hands in his pockets, apparently forgetting he was wearing jeans. That seemed to irritate him all the more.

"We never did eat our lunch," she said shakily.

He glared at the thick sandwich and then back to her. "I'm not hungry."

"Let's decorate the tree, then." She hugged her middle to ward off the cold she felt beginning to surround her. Cooper was freezing her out, and she didn't know what to say or do to prevent him from doing that.

He stared at her blankly, as if he hadn't heard a word she'd said. Helplessly, she watched as he opened the closet door and took out his coat.

"Cooper?" she whispered, but he didn't hesitate, slipping his arms into the sleeves and starting on the buttons.

She was still standing in front of the door, and she decided she wouldn't move, wouldn't let him walk out as if she wasn't there. What had happened? Everything had been so beautiful last night and today, and now, for no apparent reason, he was pushing her away. She felt as if their relationship had taken a giant step backward.

His drawn expression didn't alter as he came to stand directly in front of her. His hand brushed a blond curl off her face and lingered a second to trace a finger across her cheek.

"You really should marry someone like Webber."

"No." The sound was barely audible. "I won't." How could she marry Webb when she loved Cooper?

"Funny how we never seem to do the things we should," he muttered cryptically.

"Cooper?" Her voice throbbed with a feeling she couldn't identify. Agony? Need? Desperation? "What's wrong?" she tried again.

"Other than the fact you and I are as different as night and day?"

"We've always been different, why should it matter now?"

"I don't know," he told her honestly.

"I had a wonderful time today," she whispered, and hung her head to avoid his searching look. Her lashes fluttered wearily. She knew she was losing, but not why. "I don't want it to end like this. I didn't know Webb was coming."

"It isn't Webber," Cooper admitted harshly. "It's everything." An ominous silence followed his announcement. "I like to pretend with you."

"Pretend?" She lifted her gaze, uncertain of what he was admitting.

"You're warm and alive, and you make me yearn for things that were never meant to be."

"Now you're talking in riddles. And I hate riddles, because I can never understand them. I don't understand *you*."

"No," he murmured, and rubbed a hand across his face. "I don't suppose that's possible."

Ashley didn't know what directed her, perhaps instinct. Of their own volition her arms slipped around his neck. At first he held himself stiff and unyielding against her, but she refused to be deterred. Her exploring fingers toyed with the dark hair at the back of his head. She applied a gentle pressure, urging his mouth to hers. His resistance grew stronger, forcing her to stand on her tip toes and mold herself to him. Gradually, she eased her mouth over his.

He didn't want her kiss, but she could feel the part of him that unwillingly reached out to her.

Abruptly he broke the contact and pulled himself away. Both hands cupped her face, tilting it up at an angle. A smoldering light of something she couldn't decipher burned in his eyes.

"Ashley." The husky tone of his voice betrayed his desire, yet she marveled at his control.

"Hmm?" she answered with a contented whisper.

"Next time I start acting like a jerk, promise me you'll bring me out of my ill temper just like this."

She gave a glad cry and kissed him again. "I promise," she said after a long while.

Eight

"Was Cooper with you Saturday?" Claudia asked as she laid the menu aside.

Most of Monday morning and half the afternoon had been spent finishing up their Christmas shopping. For the past two hours Ashley had dragged Claudia to every antique store she could find.

Her index finger made a lazy circle around the rim of her water glass. "What makes you ask?" A peculiar pain knotted her stomach. It happened every time she suspected Cooper didn't want anyone to know they were seeing one another. She had spent the entire day with him. After decorating the tree they'd gone out to dinner and a movie. It was midnight before he kissed her good night. Yet he hadn't told Claudia anything.

"What makes me ask?" Claudia repeated incredulously. "You mean besides the fact that he mysteriously disappeared for the entire day? Then he saunters in about midnight with a sheepish look. Gets up early Sunday morning whistling. Cooper. Whistling. He even went to church with us again, which surprised both Seth and me."

"What makes you think I had anything to do with it?"

"What is it with you two? You'd think you were ashamed to be seen with one another."

"You're being ridiculous."

"I'm not. Look at how elusive you're being. Were you or were you not with Cooper Sunday?"

"Yes, I was with him."

"Just part of the time?"

"No," she admitted and breathed in heavily. "All day."

"Ash?" Claudia hesitated as if searching for the right words. "I know you're probably going to say this is none of my business, but I've never seen you act like this."

"Act like what?" she returned defensively.

"All our lives you were the fearless one. There didn't seem to be anything you weren't willing to try. I've never seen you so reticent."

Ashley shrugged one shoulder slightly.

"You're in love with Cooper, aren't you?"

A small smile played over Ashley's mouth. "Yes." It felt good to finally verbalize her feelings. "Very much."

Claudia's eyes glinted with an inner glow of happiness. "Who would ever have guessed you'd fall in love with Cooper?"

"I don't know. Probably no one."

"Has he told you he loves you yet?" Claudia asked, obviously doing her best to contain her excitement.

"No, but then I'm not exactly an 'uptown girl,' am I?" The words slipped out more flippantly than she'd intended.

"Ashley," Claudia snapped, "I can't believe you'd say something like this. You're closer to me than any sister could ever—"

"It's not you," Ashley interrupted, lowering her gaze

to her half-full water glass. "Cooper's ashamed to be seen with me."

"That's pure nonsense," Claudia insisted.

"I wish it was," Ashley said in a serious tone.

Any additional discussion was interrupted by the waitress, who arrived to take their order.

"Promise me one thing," Claudia asked as soon as the woman was gone, her eyes pleading.

"What?"

"That you won't drag me to any more antique shops. Cooper doesn't care about that saucer, so I don't see why you should."

"But I do," Ashley said forcefully. "I'm going to replace it if I have to look for the rest of my life."

"Honestly, Ash, it's not that big a deal. Cooper would feel terrible if he knew the trouble you're putting yourself through."

"Don't you dare tell him."

Their Cobb salads arrived, and the flow of conversation came to a halt as they began to eat.

"You're planning to come with us Wednesday, aren't you?" Claudia asked, looking up from her salad.

"Is that the day you're taking the boys to Seattle Center Enchanted Forest?" Every Christmas the Food Circus inside the Center created a fantasyland for young children. The large open area was filled with tall trees and a train that enthralled the youngsters. Clowns performed and handed out balloons. "That's Christmas Eve day."

"Brilliant deduction," Claudia teased. "Cooper's going," she added, as if Ashley needed an inducement.

Ashley's blond curls bounced as she laughed. "I'd be excited about it even if Cooper wasn't coming along.

We're going to have a wonderful time. The boys will love it."

"Cooper's been asking Seth a lot of questions," Claudia announced unexpectedly.

"Questions? About what?"

"The Bible." Claudia placed her fork beside her plate. "They spent almost the entire afternoon on Sunday discussing things. When I talked to Seth about it later, he told me that he felt inadequate because some of Cooper's questions were so complicated. Personally, I don't know where Cooper stands with the Lord, but he seems to be having a difficult time with some of the basic concepts." She paused, then added, "He can't seem to accept that salvation is not something we can earn with donations or good works."

"I can understand that," Ashley defended him. "Cooper has worked hard all his life. Nothing's been free. I can see that the concept would be more difficult for him to accept than for others."

Claudia lounged back, a smile twinkling in her eyes. "You really *do* love him, don't you?"

"I'll tell you something else that'll shock you." Ashley nervously smoothed her pant leg. "I've loved him from the time I was sixteen. It's just been...harder to hide lately."

Claudia's expression softened knowingly. "I think I guessed how you felt almost as soon as I saw the two of you together at the airport when Seth and I arrived with the boys. And then, when I thought back, I realized how long it had been going on, at least for you."

"How did you know?" Ashley's eyes narrowed thoughtfully.

"From the time we were teens, it was you who defended Cooper when he did something to irritate me. You were always ready to leap to his defense."

"Was I so obvious?"

"Not at all," Claudia assured her. "Now, are you ready for something else?" She didn't wait for a response. "Cooper's been in love with you since before I married Seth."

"That I don't believe," Ashley argued. She picked up her fork and put it back down twice before finally setting it aside.

"Think about it," Claudia challenged, a determined lift to her chin. "Seth asked me to marry him, and I was so undecided. I knew I loved him, but moving to Alaska, leaving school and all my dreams of becoming a doctor, made the decision difficult. You were telling me to follow my heart, and at the same time Cooper was unconditionally opposed to the whole idea."

"I remember how miserable you were."

"I was more than miserable. I was at the airport wanting to die, I loved him so much, yet I felt it would never work for Seth and me. You told me if I loved him to go after him." Her blue eyes glimmered with the memory, and a soft smile played at the corners of her mouth. "Still, I was undecided, and I looked to Cooper, wanting him to make up my mind for me. It's funny how clearly I can recall that scene now. Cooper glanced from me to you. At the time I didn't recognize the look in his eyes, but I do now. After so many bitter arguments, Cooper looked at you and told me the decision was mine."

"I think you've blown the whole thing out of proportion." Ashley felt safer in denying what her friend thought than placing any faith in it.

"Don't you see?" Claudia persisted. "Cooper changed

his mind because, for the first time in his life, he knew what it was to be in love with someone."

"I wish it were true," Ashley murmured sadly, "but if he felt that way four years ago, why didn't he make an effort to go out with me?"

A wayward lock of auburn hair fell across Claudia's cheek. "Knowing Cooper, that isn't so difficult to understand."

"I wish I could believe it, I really do."

Claudia reached across the small table and squeezed Ashley's forearm. "I've been waiting four years to give you the kind of advice you gave me. Go for him, Ash. Cooper needs you."

Ashley's eyes were filled with determination. "I have no intention of letting him go."

Claudia's laugh was almost musical. "In some ways I almost pity my uncle."

Ashley was sitting on the floor with Scott on her lap when Johnny crawled in beside him. "Can we play a game, Auntie Ash?"

Ashley looked into his round blue eyes, unsure. She'd told Claudia she'd watch the boys while her friends wrapped Christmas presents, and she didn't want to get Johnny all wound up.

"What kind of game?"

"Horsey. Uncle Cooper let me ride him, and Scotty and Daddy were the other horsey."

The picture that flashed into her mind produced a warm smile. "But I wouldn't be a good horse for both you *and* Scotty," she told him gently.

A disappointed look clouded his expressive face, but

he accepted her decision. "Can you read?" he asked next, and handed her a book.

"Sure." With her natural flair for theatrics, she began to read from the *Bible Story Book*.

"How many days until Jesus's birthday?" Johnny asked when she'd finished.

"Only a few now. Are you excited to open all your presents?"

Eagerly he shook his head. "If Jesus hadn't been born, would we have Christmas?" He cocked his head at a curious angle so he could look at her.

"No. We wouldn't have any churches or Sunday School, either."

"What else wouldn't we have?"

"If Jesus hadn't come, our world would be a very sad place. Because Jesus wouldn't live in people's hearts, and they wouldn't love one another the way they should."

"We wouldn't have a Christmas tree," Johnny added.

"Or presents, or Easter."

The young boy's eyes grew wide. "Not even Easter?"

"Nope."

Johnny sat quietly for a minute. "Then the best gift of all at Christmas is Jesus."

A rush of tenderness warmed Ashley's heart. "You said it beautifully."

Scotty squirmed out of her arms and onto the thick carpet, crawling with all his might toward the Christmas tree. Ashley hurriedly intercepted him and, with a laugh, swept him from the carpet and into the air high above her head.

Scotty gurgled with delight. "You like this funny looking tree, don't you?" she asked him, laughing. "I bet if you got the opportunity, every present here would be torn to shreds."

The front door closed, and she turned with Scotty in her arms to find Cooper shaking the rain from his hat.

"Hi."

He didn't see her immediately, and as he turned a surprised look crossed his dark features. Almost as quickly the look was replaced with one of welcome that sent her heart beating at an erratic pace.

"Claudia and Seth left you to the mercies of these two again?"

"No, they're wrapping presents. My duty is to keep the boys out of trouble."

He hung his coat in the hall closet and joined her, lifting Johnny into his arms. The boy squeezed Cooper's neck and gave him a moist kiss on the cheek.

"You know what Auntie Ash said?" John leaned back to look at his uncle.

"I can only guess," Cooper replied, his eyes brightening with a smile. Lovingly he searched her face.

"She said if Jesus hadn't been born, we wouldn't have Christmas."

"No, we wouldn't," Cooper agreed.

"I know something else we wouldn't have," she murmured and moistened her lips.

Johnny's gaze followed hers, and he shouted excitedly, "Mistletoe."

Cooper's eyes hadn't left hers, although his narrowed slightly as if he couldn't take them off her.

"Mistletoe," she repeated, her invitation blatant.

Motionless, Cooper held her look, but gave her no indication of what he was thinking.

Two quick strides carried him to her side. Her senses

whirled as he placed Johnny on the ground and gathered her in his arms. Half of her pleasure came from the fact that he didn't look around to see if anyone was watching.

Cooper's gaze skidded to the baby she was still holding between them, and he let out a long exaggerated sigh. "No help for this. I can't kiss you properly while you're holding the baby."

"I'll take a rain check," she teased.

"But I won't," he announced, then removed Scotty from her arms and gently set him on the floor.

Ashley started to protest, but before she could utter a sound, Cooper's mouth was over hers. Winding her arms around his neck, she reveled in the feel of him as his hands gripped her narrow waist.

The sound of someone clearing their throat had barely registered with her when he abruptly broke off the kiss and breathed in deeply.

"You two forget something?" Claudia demanded, hands on her hips as she watched them with a teasing smile.

"Forget?" Ashley was still caught in the rapture; clear thinking was almost impossible. Cooper's warm breath continued to caress her cheek, and she knew he was as affected as she was.

"Like Scotty and John?"

"Oh." Ashley gasped and looked around, remembering how the baby had been enthralled with the Christmas tree.

Seth had lifted the baby by the seat of his pants and was holding him several inches off the ground.

"I think we've been found out," Ashley whispered to Cooper.

"Looks that way," he said releasing her.

Seth handed his wife the baby, who cooed happily, and the two men left the room.

"I've been meaning to ask you all day what you're wearing tomorrow," Claudia said, tucking her son close to her side.

"Wearing tomorrow?" Ashley echoed. "I don't understand?"

"To the party." Claudia looked at her as if she had suddenly developed amnesia.

"The party?"

"Cooper's dinner party tomorrow night, of course," Claudia said, laughing lightly.

The world suddenly seemed to come to an abrupt stop. Ashley's heart pounded frantically; the blood rushed to her face. In that instant she knew what it must feel like to be hit in the stomach. Claudia continued to elaborate, giving her the details of the formal dinner party. But Ashley was only half listening; the words drifted off into nothingness. The only sound that penetrated the cloud of hurt and disappointment were the words *family...friends*. She was neither. She was the cook's daughter, nothing more.

She heard footsteps, and her breathing became actively painful as her gaze shifted to meet Cooper's eyes. Standing there, Ashley prayed she would find something in his look that could explain why she had been excluded from the party. But all she saw was regret. He hadn't wanted her to know.

"Ashley, are those tears?" Claudia asked in a shocked whisper. "What did I say? What's wrong?"

In a haze, Ashley looked beyond the concerned face of her friend. Seth was standing with Johnny at his side, a troubled look on his face. Everyone she loved was there to witness her humiliation. Without a word, she turned and walked out of the house.

"Ashley." There was a pleading quality in Cooper's voice as he followed her out of the house. She quickened her pace, ignoring his demand that she wait. By the time he reached her, she was inside her car, the key in the ignition.

"Will you stop?" he shouted, his mouth tight. "At least give me the chance to explain."

Nothing was worth her staying and listening; he'd said everything without having uttered a word. She wanted to tell him that, but it was all she could do to swallow back the tears.

When she started the engine, Cooper tried to yank open the car door, but she was quicker and hit the lock. Jerking the car into reverse, she pulled out of the driveway. One last glance in Cooper's direction showed him standing alone, watching her leave. His shoulders were hunched in defeat.

Her cell phone was ringing even before she reached her small apartment. She knew without looking that it was Cooper. She also knew he would refuse to give up, so finally, in exasperation, she answered.

"Yes," she snapped.

A slight pause followed. "Miss Robbins?"

"Yes?" Some of the impatience left her voice.

"This is Larry Marshall, of Marshall's Antiques. You talked to me this morning about that china saucer you were looking for."

"Did you find one?"

"A friend of mine has the piece you're looking for," he told her.

"How soon can I pick it up?"

"Tomorrow, if you like. There's only one problem," he continued.

"What's that?"

"My friend's shop is in Victoria, Canada."

Ashley wouldn't have cared if it was in Alaska. Replacing Cooper's china saucer was of the utmost importance. He need never know it had come from her. She could give it to Claudia. After writing down the dealer's name and address, she thanked the man and told him she would put a check in the mail to cover his finder's fee.

Immediately after she replaced the receiver, the phone rang again. She stared at it dumbfounded, unable to move as Cooper's name came up on the screen. She stared at it for a long moment, unwilling to deal with him. After several rings she muted the phone and stuck it back inside her purse.

Silence followed, and she exhaled, unaware until then that she'd been holding her breath. Her palms hurt, and she turned her hand over and saw that her long nails had made deep indentations in the sensitive skin of her palm.

For weeks she'd tried to convince herself that Cooper wasn't ashamed to be seen with her, but the love she felt had blinded her to the truth. Even what Claudia had explained to her over lunch couldn't refute the fact that he hadn't invited her to the dinner party.

Twenty minutes later the doorbell chimed.

"Ashley!" Cooper shouted and pounded on the door. "At least let me explain."

What could he possibly say that hadn't already been said more clearly by his action?

Her heart was crying out, demanding that she listen, but she'd been foolish in the past and had learned from her mistakes. She'd been too easily swayed by her love, but not again.

"Please don't do this," he said.

Her resolve weakened. Cooper had never sounded more sincere. She jerked open the hall closet door and whipped her faux fur jacket off the hanger, put it on and zipped it up all the way to her neck. Then she threw open the front door, crossed her arms and stared at a shocked Cooper with defiance flashing from her blue eyes.

"You have three minutes." Unable to look at him, she held up her wrist and pretended an acute interest in her watch.

"Where are you going?" he demanded.

"Two minutes and fifty seconds," she answered stiffly. "But if you must know, I'm going to see Webber. He happens to like me. It doesn't matter to him that my mother's some rich man's cook, or that my father's a laborer."

"It's Webb."

"Dear heaven," she said, and laughed almost hysterically. "You've got me doing it now."

"Ashley," he said, his voice softening. "It doesn't matter to me who your mother is or where your father works. I'm sorry about the party. I wouldn't want to hurt you for the world."

She bit into the soft skin of her inner lip to keep from letting herself be affected by his words. Her back rigid, she glared at the face of the watch, her body frozen. "Two minutes even," she murmured.

"I didn't think you'd want to come," he began again. "Mostly it's business associates—"

"Don't make excuses. I understand, believe me," she interrupted.

"I'm sure you don't," he countered sharply.

"But I do. I'm the kind of girl who enjoys pizza on the floor in front of a fireplace. I wouldn't fit in, that's what you're saying isn't it? It would be terribly embarrassing for all involved if I showed up wearing red cowboy boots. I might even break a piece of china or, worse yet, use the wrong spoon. No, I understand. I understand all too well." Her eyes and throat burned with the effort of suppressing tears. "Your time's up. Now, if you'll excuse me…" She stepped outside and closed the door.

"I want you to be there tomorrow night," he told her as she turned her key in the lock.

"I don't see any reason to make an issue over it. I couldn't have come anyway, I'm working tomorrow night."

"That's not true," he said harshly.

"You don't stop, do you? Does it give you pleasure to say these things to me…to call me a liar?" she whispered. "I suppose I should have learned how stubborn you are when I was forced to accept the car." She turned her stricken eyes to his. "I'm not lying."

"You told me school's out," he said with calculated anger.

"It is," she said. "This is my second job, the menial one. I'm a waitress, remember?"

Frustration marked his features as he followed her into the parking lot. "Ashley…"

"I'd like to stay and chat, but I have to be on my way." She paused and laughed mirthlessly. "I appreciate what you're trying to do, but you're the last person on God's green earth I ever want to see again. Goodbye, Cooper."

"Try to understand." The glimpse of pain she witnessed in his eyes couldn't be disguised. Despite what he'd done, she hadn't meant to hurt him, but in her own anguish she had lashed back at him. It was better that she leave now, before they said more hurtful things to one another.

A tight smile lingered on her mouth as she stared into his hard features. "I do understand," she whispered in defeat.

"I doubt that," he mumbled, as he opened the car door for her and stepped back.

She could see him in the side mirror, standing stiff and proud, his look angry, arrogant. He almost fooled her, until he lifted a hand and wiped it across his face. When he dropped his arm, she noted the pain and frustration that glittered from his eyes. The sight made her ache inside, but she wouldn't let herself be influenced, not after what he'd done.

Ashley pulled out of the parking lot, intent on doing as she'd said. Webb would know what to say to comfort her. He was her friend, and she needed him. Tears blinded her vision, and she had to wipe them aside at every traffic signal. Tears would shock Webb; he'd never seen her cry.

Webb's car was in the driveway as she pulled in. He must have seen her arrive, because he opened the front door before she'd had time to ring the bell.

"Ashley." He sounded surprised, but his amazement quickly turned to apprehension. "Are you all right? You look upset. You're not crying, are you?"

All she could do was nod. "Oh, Webb," she sobbed, and walked into his arms.

He hugged her and patted her back like a comforting big brother, which was just what she needed. "I don't suppose this has anything to do with that Cooper character, does it?"

Miserably, she nodded. "How'd you know?"

He led her into the house and closed the door. "Because he just pulled up and parked across the street."

Ashley's head snapped up. "You're kidding! You mean he followed me here?" She took a tissue from her purse and blew her nose. "He probably followed me to find out if I was telling the truth."

"The truth?"

"I told him I was coming to see you. Do you mind?" She glanced up at him anxiously.

"Of course I don't mind." Webb's enthusiasm sounded forced. "Cooper's only four inches taller than I am and outweighs me by fifty pounds. Do you think he'll give me a choice of weapons?"

"You're being silly." She laughed, and then, to her supreme embarrassment, she hiccupped.

"Hang on," he said, and disappeared into the kitchen. A moment later he was back. "Here, drink this." He handed her a bottle of water.

She accepted because it gave her something to do with her hands. Tipping her head back, she took a large swallow.

"You're in love with him, aren't you?"

"Don't be ridiculous. I thoroughly dislike the man," she countered quickly.

"Now that's a sure sign. I wasn't positive before, but that clinched it."

"Webb, don't tease," she pleaded.

"Who's joking?" He led her to a chair, then sat across the room from her. "I've seen it coming on for the last couple of weeks. Other than the fact that he thinks I'm his arch rival and can't seem to get my name right, I like your Cooper."

"He's not mine," she said, more forcefully than she'd meant to.

"Okay, I won't argue. But if you love each other and really want things to work out, then whatever's wrong can be cleared up. If it doesn't, then you have to believe God has other plans for you."

Ashley closed her eyes for a long moment, then opened them and released a weary sigh. "You know, one of the worst things about you is that you're so darn logical. I can't stand it. I've always said an organized desk is the sign of a sick mind."

"And that, my friend, is one of the nicest things you've ever said to me."

They talked for a bit longer, and Webb did his best to raise her spirits. He joked with her, coaxing her to smile. Later they ordered pizza and played a game of Scrabble. He won royally and refused to discount the fact that her mind wasn't on the game. When he walked her to the car, he kissed her lightly and waved as she backed out of the driveway.

Ashley slept fitfully, her heart heavy. The alarm went off at four-thirty, and she doubted that she'd gotten any rest. Cold water took the sleep out of her eyes, but she looked wan and felt worse. Connecting with the early ferry still meant a five-hour ride across Puget Sound to Victoria, British Columbia. The schedule gave her an hour to locate the antique shop, buy the saucer and connect with the ferry home. The trip would be tiring, and she would barely have enough time to shower and change clothes before leaving for her job at Lindo's Mexican Restaurant.

She had visited the Victorian seaport many times, and

its beauty had never failed to enthrall her. Usually she came in summer when the Butchart Gardens were in full bloom. She found it amazing how a city tucked in the corner of the Pacific Northwest could have the feel, the flavor and the flair of England. Even the accent was decidedly British.

Without difficulty she located the small antique shop off one of the many side streets that catered to the tourists. When Larry Marshall phoned she'd been so pleased to have found the saucer that she'd forgotten to ask about the price. She paled visibly when the proprietor cheerfully informed her how fortunate she was to have found this rare piece and she read the sticker. Her mind balked, but her pride made two hundred dollars for one small saucer sound like a bargain.

On the return trip, she stood at the rail. A demon wind whipped her hair across her face and numbed her with its cold. But she didn't leave, her eyes following the narrow strip of land until it gradually disappeared. Only when a freezing rain began to pelt the deck did she move inside. Surprisingly, she fell asleep until the foghorn blast of the ferry woke her as they eased into the dock in Seattle.

An hour later she smiled at Manuel, Lindo's manager, as she stepped in the back door. After hanging her coat on a hook in the kitchen, she paused long enough to tie an apron around her waist.

"There's someone to see you," Manuel told her in a heavy Spanish accent.

She looked up, perplexed.

"Out front," he added.

She peered around the corner to see a stern-faced Cooper sitting alone at a table. His steel-hard eyes met and trapped her as effectively as a vice.

Nine

Carrying ice water and the menu, Ashley approached Cooper. What was he doing here? What about the party?

Dark, angry sparks flashed from his gaze, and a muscle twitched along the side of his jaw as his eyes followed her. "Where have you been all day?" he asked coldly.

Ashley ignored the question. "The daily special is chili verde." She pointed it out on the menu with the tip of her pencil. "I'll be back to take your order in a few minutes." Her voice contained a breathless tremor that betrayed what seeing him was doing to her. She hated herself for the weakness.

"Don't walk away from me," he warned. The lack of emotion in his voice was almost frightening.

"Are you ready to order now?" She took out the small pad from the apron pocket. Her fingers trembled slightly as she paused, ready to write down his choice.

"Ashley." His look was tight and grim. "Where were you?"

"I could say I was with Webb," she said, and swallowed tightly at the implication she was trying to give.

"Then you'd be lying," he added flatly.

"Yes, I would."

"Okay, we'll do this your way. It doesn't matter where you were or what sick game you've been playing with me…"

"Sick game?" she echoed, remarkably calm. A sad smile touched her mouth as she averted her gaze.

"I didn't mean that," he muttered.

"It doesn't matter." She lowered her chin. "You'd think by now that we could accept the fact that we're wrong for one another. Forcing the issue is only going to hurt us." She paused and swallowed past the growing tightness in her throat. "I'm not willing to be hurt anymore."

His narrowed eyes searched hers. "I want you to come to the party with me."

Sadly, she hung her head. "No."

"I've already talked to the manager. He says he doesn't think tonight's going to be all that busy anyway."

"I won't go," she repeated insistently.

"Then I'm not leaving. I'll sit here all night if that's what it takes." The tight set of his mouth convinced her the threat wasn't idle.

"But you can't, your guests…" She stopped, angry at how easily she'd fallen into his plan. "I won't be blackmailed, Cooper. Sit here all night if you like." Her pulse raced wildly.

"All right." His head shifted slightly to one side as he studied the menu. "I'll take a plate of nachos and the special you mentioned."

Furiously, she wrote down the order.

"You stay?" Manuel asked after she called Cooper's order into the kitchen. "I already call my cousin to come in and work for you. You can go to this important party."

"I'm here to work, Manuel," she explained in a patient

tone. "I'm sure there will be enough work for both your cousin and me."

Nothing seemed to be going right. Cooper watched her every action like a hawk studying its prey before the kill. By seven o'clock Manuel's cousin had served nearly every customer. Only two customers were seated in her section. Ashley was convinced Cooper had somehow arranged that. She wanted to cry in frustration.

"Cooper," she pleaded, "won't you please leave? It's almost seven."

"I won't go without you," he told her calmly.

"Talk about sick games," she lashed back, and to her consternation a sensuous smile curved his mouth.

"I'm not playing games," he stated firmly.

"Then if you miss your own party it's your problem." She tried to sound nonchalant.

By seven-fifteen she was pacing the floor, her resolve weakening. Cooper couldn't offend his associates this way. It could hurt him and his business.

Using the need to refill his coffee cup as an excuse, she avoided his gaze as she said, "I don't have anything to wear."

"Cowboy boots are fine. I'll wear mine, if you like." Her hand was suddenly captured between his. "Nothing in the world means more to me than having you at my side tonight."

"Oh, Cooper," she moaned. "I don't know. I don't belong there."

He studied her slowly, his eyes focused on her soft mouth. "You belong with me."

She felt the determination to defy him drain out of her. "All right," she whispered in defeat.

"Thank God." As he hurried out of the booth he added, "I'll meet you at your place."

Numbly she nodded. As it worked out, he pulled into the apartment parking lot directly behind her.

"While you change, I'll phone Claudia."

Ashley wanted to kick herself for being so weak. Examining the contents of her closet, she pulled out a wool blend dress with a Victorian flair. The antique lace inserts around the neck, bodice and cuffs gave the white dress a formal look. The glittering gold belt matched the high heels she chose.

Her fingers shook as she applied a light layer of makeup. After a moment of hurried effort, she gripped the edge of the small bathroom sink as she stopped to pray. It wasn't the first time today that she'd turned to God. She'd tried to pray standing on the deck of the ferry, the wind whipping at her, but somehow the words wouldn't come. The pain of Cooper's rejection had been too sharp to voice, even to God. Now, having finished, she lifted her head and released a shuddering breath. More confident, she added a dab of perfume to the pulse points at her wrists and neck, and stepped out to meet Cooper.

He turned around as she entered the room. A shocked look entered his eyes. "You're beautiful."

"Don't sound so surprised. I can dress up every now and then."

"You're a little pale. Come here, I can change that." Before she was aware of what he was doing, he pulled her into his arms and kissed her. The demand of his mouth tilted her head back. His hand pressed against her back, arching her against him.

Ashley's breath caught in her lungs at the unexpectedness of his action. Her hands were poised on the broad expanse of his chest, his heartbeat hammering against her palm.

"There." He tilted his face to study her. "Plenty of color now." Releasing her, he held her coat open so she could easily slip her arms inside. "I'm afraid we're going to make something of a grand entrance. Everyone's arrived. Claudia sounded frantic. She said the hors d'oeuvres ran out fifteen minutes ago."

"Is my mother…?" She let the rest of the question fade, sure Cooper would know what she was asking.

"No, it's being catered." With a hand at the back of her waist, he urged her out the door.

"Oh, Cooper." She hurried back inside. "I almost forgot." Her heels made funny little noises against the floor as she rushed into her bedroom and came out with the wrapped package. "Here." She gave it to him.

"Do I have to wait for Christmas?"

"No. It's a replacement for the saucer I broke, the one from your grandmother's service."

"I can't believe… Where did you ever find it?"

"Don't ask."

"Ashley…" He set his hands on her shoulders and turned her around so she was facing him. "Is this what you were up to today?"

She nodded silently.

His mouth thinned as his look became distant. "I think I went a little crazy looking for you." He slipped an arm around her waist. "We'll talk about that later. If we keep Claudia waiting another minute, she's likely to disown us both."

The street and driveway outside Cooper's house

looked like a high performance car showroom. Ashley felt her nerves tense as she clenched her hands in her lap.

"Ashley, stop."

"Stop?"

"I can feel you tightening up like a coiled spring. Every man here is going to be envious of me. Just be yourself."

The front door flew open before they were halfway up the walk. Claudia stood there like an avenging warlord, waving her arms and glaring at them.

"Thank goodness you're here!" she exclaimed forcefully. "If you ever do this to me again, I swear I'll…" Her voice drifted away. "Don't stand out here listening to me, get inside. Everyone's waiting." Her gaze narrowed on Cooper. "And I do mean everyone."

Ashley didn't need to be reminded that some of the most important people in Seattle would be there.

Claudia gave her an encouraging smile, winked and took her coat.

His hand at her elbow, Cooper led Ashley into the living room. The low conversational hum rose as a few guests called out his name. Apparently the champagne had been flowing freely, because no one seemed to mind that Cooper was late to his own party.

He introduced her to several couples, though she knew she couldn't hope to remember all the names. After twenty minutes the smile felt frozen on her face. Someone handed her a glass of what she assumed was wine, but she didn't drink it. Tonight she would need to keep her wits about her in a room full of intimidating people. There was hardly room to maneuver, and she felt as if the walls were closing in around her.

"Is this the little lady who kept us waiting?" A distinguished, middle-aged man with silver streaks at his temples asked Cooper for an introduction.

"I am," she admitted with a weak smile. "I hope you'll forgive me."

"I find it very easy to forgive someone as pretty as you. Maybe we could get together later, so I can listen to your excuse."

"Whoa, Tom," Cooper teased, but his voice contained an underlying warning. "The lady's with me."

With a good-natured chuckle, Tom slapped him across the shoulder. "Anything you say."

Ashley spotted Claudia at the far side of the room. "If you'll both excuse me a minute...?" she whispered.

Claudia caught her eye and arched her delicate brows.

"Boy, am I glad to see a familiar face," Ashley said, and released a slow sigh as she leaned against the wall for support.

"What took you two so long?" Claudia demanded. "I was frantic. You wouldn't believe some of the excuses I gave. Dear heavens, Ash, where were you today? I thought Cooper was going to go mad."

"Canada."

"Canada?" Claudia shot back. "Well, I must admit, that was one place he didn't look. Have you talked to your mother yet? I don't know what he said to her, but he was closed up in his den for an hour afterward. Believe me, he didn't look happy. No one, not even the boys, could get near him."

"I know he feels miserable about the whole thing, but I understand better than he realizes. I wouldn't have invited me to this party, either. Look at me. I stick out like a sore thumb."

"If you do, it's because you're the prettiest woman here."

Ashley's light laugh was forced. "You're a better friend than I thought."

"I *am* your friend, but don't underestimate yourself." A hush came over the room as someone in a caterer's apron made the announcement that dinner was ready. "I don't know why Cooper wouldn't invite you tonight. He wasn't overly pleased with me for letting the cat out of the bag, I can tell you that."

"No, I imagine he wasn't." How much simpler things would have been if she'd stayed innocently unaware. "But I'm glad you did," she murmured, and hung her head. "Very glad." When she glanced up she saw the object of their conversation weaving his way toward her. Progress was slow, as people stopped to chat or ask him a question. Although he smiled and chatted, his probing gaze didn't leave her for more than a moment.

"I don't want you hiding in a corner," he muttered when he finally got to her, and gripped her elbow, then led her toward the huge dining room.

"I'm not hiding," she defended herself. "I just wanted to talk to Claudia for a minute."

"It was far longer than a minute," he said between clenched teeth.

"Honestly, Cooper, are you going to start an argument now? I'm here under protest as it is."

"You're here because I want you here. It's where you belong." His control over his temper seemed fragile.

Rather than say anything she would regret later, Ashley pinched her mouth tightly closed.

The dining room table had been extended to accommodate forty guests. Ashley looked at the china and sparkling crystal, and the fir and candle centerpiece that extended the full length of the table. Everything was exquisite, and she was filled with a sense of awe. She didn't belong here. What was she doing fooling herself?

Cooper sat at the head of the table, with Ashley at his right side. Under normal circumstances she would have enjoyed the meal. The caterers had also supplied four waitresses, and she found herself watching their movements instead of involving herself in idle conversation with Cooper or the white-haired man on her right. Once the salad plates were removed, they were served prime rib, fresh green beans and new potatoes. Every bite and swallow was calculated, measured, to be sure she would do nothing that would call attention to herself. For dessert a cake in the shape of a yule log was carried into the room. She only took one bite, afraid she would end up spilling frosting on her white dress. Once, when she glanced up, she found Cooper watching her, his look both foreboding and thoughtful. If this was a test, she was certain she was failing miserably, and his look did nothing to boost her confidence.

When the meal was finished, she couldn't recall ever being more relieved.

Cooper's hand was pressed to her waist, keeping her at his side, as they moved into the living room. She didn't join the conversation, only smiled and nodded at the appropriate times. An hour later, her face felt frozen into a permanent smile.

A few people started to leave. Grateful for the opportunity to slip away, she murmured a friendly farewell and left Cooper to deal with his guests.

"I don't know how much more of this I can take," she whispered to Claudia.

"Don't worry, you're doing great. Not much longer now."

"Where's Seth?"

"Checking the boys. He's not much for this kind of thing, either. Haven't you noticed the way he keeps loosening his tie? By the time the evening's over, the whole thing will be missing."

"What time is it?" Ashley muttered.

"Just after eleven."

"How much longer?"

"I don't know. Don't look now, but Cooper's headed our way."

His stern expression hadn't relaxed. He was obviously displeased about something. "I want to talk to you in my den when everyone's gone." His look was ominous as he turned and left.

Primly, Ashley clasped her hands together in front of her. "Heavens, what did I do now?" she asked Claudia.

Claudia shrugged. "I don't know, but for heaven's sake, humor him. Another day like today, and Seth and I are packing our bags and finding a hotel."

By the time the last couple had left, Ashley's stomach was coiled into a hard lump.

The caterers were clearing away glasses and the last of the dishes from the living room when Cooper found her in the corner talking to Seth and Claudia. As Claudia had predicted, Seth's tie had mysteriously disappeared. His arm was draped across his wife's shoulders.

Seth looked over to Cooper. "You don't mind if we head upstairs, do you?"

"No, no, go ahead." Cooper's answer sounded preoccupied. He gestured toward his den. "We'll be more comfortable in there," he said to Ashley.

She tossed Claudia a puzzled look. Cooper didn't look upset anymore, and she didn't know what to think. His face was tight and drawn, but not with anger. She couldn't recall ever seeing him quite like this.

"Oh!" Claudia paused halfway up the stairs and turned around. "Don't forget tomorrow morning. We'll pick you up around ten. The boys are looking forward to it."

"I am, too," Ashley replied.

They entered the familiar den, and he closed the door, leaning against the heavy wood momentarily. He gestured toward a chair, and she sat down, her back straight.

Again he paused. He rubbed the back of his neck, and when he glanced up, it struck Ashley couldn't remember ever having seen him look more tired.

"Cooper, are you feeling all right? You're not sick, are you?"

"Sick?" he repeated slowly. "No."

"What's wrong, then? You look like you've lost your best friend."

"In some ways, I think I have." He moved across the room to his desk, rearranging the few items that littered the top.

Impatiently, Ashley watched him. He'd said he wanted to talk to her, yet he seemed hesitant.

"How do you feel about the way things went tonight?" he asked finally.

"What do you mean? Was the food good? It was excellent. Do I like your friends? I found them to be cordial, if a bit overwhelming. Cooper, you have to remember I'm just an ordinary schoolteacher."

The pencil he'd just picked up snapped in two. "You know, I think I'm sick of hearing how ordinary you are."

"What do you mean?" She watched as his mouth formed a brittle line.

"You ran to a corner to hide every chance you got. You wouldn't so much as lift a fork until you'd examined the way three other people were holding theirs to be sure you did it the same way."

"Is that so bad?" she flared. "I felt safe in a corner."

"And not with me?"

"No!"

"I think that tells me everything I want to know."

"You forced me into coming tonight," she accused him.

"It was a no-win situation. You understand that, don't you?"

She stood and moved to the far side of the room. Cooper was talking down to her as if she was a disobedient child, and she hated it. "No, I don't. But there's very little I understand about you anymore."

"I didn't invite you tonight for a reason!" he shouted.

"Do you think I don't already know that?" she flashed bitterly. "I don't fit in with this crowd."

"That's not why," he insisted loudly.

"If you raise your voice to me one more time, I'm leaving." Tears welled in her eyes. How she hated to cry. Her eyes stung, and her throat ached. "It's not the first time, either, is it?"

"What are you talking about?" He tossed her a puzzled look.

"For a while I thought it was just my overactive imagination. That I was thinking like an insecure schoolgirl. But it's true."

"What are you talking about?" What little patience he had was quickly evaporating.

"The first time we went out, you chose a small Italian restaurant, and I thought you didn't want to be seen with me."

"You can't honestly believe that?" His eyes filled with disbelief.

"Then Claudia phoned on Thanksgiving Day and I was there, but you didn't say a word." She paused long enough to swallow back a sob. "I knew you didn't want Claudia or Seth or anyone else to know I was with you. Even in church when you held my hand, it was done secretively and only when there wasn't a possibility of anyone seeing us."

A tense silence enclosed them.

"You've thought that all this time?" The dark, troubled look was back on his face.

She nodded. "I don't know about you, but I'm tired. I want to go home."

His dark eyes searched her face. She noted the weariness that wrinkled his brow and the indomitable pride in his stern jaw.

He opened the door wordlessly and retrieved her coat. He didn't say a word until he pulled up in front of her apartment building. "I find it amazing that you could think all those things, yet continue to see me."

"Now that you mention it, so do I," she returned bitterly.

His mouth thinned, but he didn't retaliate.

She handed him her apartment key, and he unlocked the door. She held out her hand, waiting for him to return the key. He didn't seem to notice, his look a thousand miles away.

When he did glance up, their eyes met and held. The troubled look remained, but with flecks of something she couldn't quite decipher. A softness entered as he lowered his gaze to her soft mouth. "It's not true, Ashley, none of it." With that he turned and left.

Stunned, she stood watching him until he was out of sight.

Her room was dark and still when she turned out the light. She hadn't behaved well tonight. That was what had originally upset Cooper. But she'd been frightened, out of her element. Those people were important, and she was nothing. The four walls surrounding her seemed to close in. Why had he left that way? For once, couldn't he have stayed and explained himself? Tomorrow she would make sure everything was cleared up between them. No more misunderstandings, her heart couldn't take it.

"Are you ready, Auntie Ash?" Johnny asked as he bounded into her apartment excitedly the next morning.

"You bet." She bent over to give her godson a big hug.

"You should hurry, 'cause Daddy's driving Uncle Cooper's car," John added.

Ashley straightened. "Where's Cooper?"

"He decided at the last minute not to come. What happened with you two last night?" Claudia asked.

"Why?"

Claudia glanced at her son, who was impatiently pacing the floor. "We'll talk about it later."

"Uncle Cooper bought the car seat just for Scotty," Johnny told her proudly when she climbed in the back seat. "He said I was a big boy and could use a special one with a real seat belt. Watch." He pulled the belt across his small body, and after several tries the lock clicked into place. "See? I can do it all by myself."

"Good for you." Ashley looped an arm around his shoulders.

"You should put yours on, too," Johnny insisted. "Uncle Cooper does."

"I think you're right," she agreed with a wry smile.

It was all Ashley could do not to quiz her friend about Cooper's absence as Seth maneuvered in and out of the heavy traffic.

"Christmas Eve Day," Johnny said as he looked around eagerly. "It's Jesus's birthday tomorrow, and we get to open all our gifts. Scotty's never opened presents."

"I don't think he'll have any problem getting the hang of it," Seth teased from the front seat.

"You're coming tonight, aren't you, Ash?" Claudia half turned to glance into the rear seat.

"I don't know," Ashley said, trying to ignore the heaviness that weighted her heart.

"But I thought it was already settled. Christmas Eve with us and Christmas with your parents."

Ashley pretended an inordinate amount of interest in the scenery flashing past outside her window. "I thought it was, too." Cooper was saying several things with his absence today. One of them was crystal clear. "Maybe I'll come for a little while. I want to see the boys open the presents from Cooper and me."

"Do I get to open a present tonight?" Johnny demanded.

Claudia threw Ashley a disgruntled look. "We'll see," she answered her son.

The downtown Seattle area was crowded with last minute shoppers. Amazingly, Seth found a parking place on the street. While Ashley and Claudia dug through the bottoms of their purses for the correct change for the meter, Seth opened the trunk and retrieved the stroller for Scotty.

"Can I put the money in?" Johnny wanted to know.

Ashley handed him the coins and lifted him up so he could insert them into the slot.

"Good boy," Ashley said, and he beamed proudly.

"Now tell me what happened," Claudia insisted in a low voice. "I'm dying to know."

"Nothing, really. He wasn't pleased with the way the party turned out. Mainly, he was disappointed in me."

"In *you*?" Claudia looked surprised. "What did you do? I thought you were fine."

"I don't understand him, Claudia." She couldn't conceal a sigh of regret. "First, he pointedly doesn't invite me and openly admits he didn't want me there. Then he forcefully insists that I attend. And to make matters worse, he doesn't approve of the way I acted."

"If you ask me, I think he's got a lot of nerve," Claudia admitted. "I hardly spoke to him this morning. But something's wrong. He's miserable. He loves you, I'd bet my life on it. It would be a terrible shame if you two didn't get together."

"I suppose."

"You suppose?" Claudia drawled the word slowly. "If you love one another, then nothing should keep you apart."

"Spoken like a true optimist. But I'm not right for Cooper," Ashley announced sadly. "He needs someone with a little more—I hate to use this word, but…finesse."

"And you need someone more easy-going and fun-loving. Like Webb," Claudia finished for her.

"No, not at all." Ashley's cool blue eyes turned questioningly toward her friend. "I'm surprised you'd even suggest that. Webb's a friend, nothing more."

Clearly pleased, Claudia shook her head knowingly. "I don't think you realize that you bring out the best in Cooper, or that he does the same for you. I don't think I've seen a couple who belong together more than you two."

"Oh, Claudia, I hope we do, because I love him so much."

"Have you ever thought about letting *him* know that?"

A blustery wind whipped Ashley's coat around her, preventing her from answering.

"I think we should catch the monorail," Seth suggested. "It's getting windy out here. Agreed?"

The two women had been so caught up in their conversation they'd hardly noticed.

"Fine." Ashley shook her head.

"Sure," Claudia said, looking a little guilty as Seth handled both boys so she could talk.

For a nominal fee they were able to catch the transport that had been built as part of the Seattle World's Fair in 1962. The rail delivered them to the heart of the Seattle Center, only a few blocks from the Food Circus.

The boys squealed with delight the minute they spied the Enchanted Forest. Scotty clapped his hands gleefully and pointed to the kiddy size train that traveled between artificial trees.

"Are you hungry?" Seth wanted to know.

"Not me." Ashley's thoughts were on other things.

"I wouldn't object to cotton candy," Claudia confessed.

"I had to ask," Seth teased, and lovingly brushed his lips over his wife's cheek.

Ashley viewed the tender scene with building despair. Someday, she wanted Cooper to look at her like that.

More than anything else, she wanted to share her life with him, have his children.

"Ash, are you all right?" Claudia asked.

Quickly, she shook her head. "Of course. What made you ask?"

"You looked so sad."

"I am, I…"

"My goodness, Ash, look, Cooper's here."

"Cooper?" Her spirits soared. "Where?"

"Across the room." Claudia pointed, then waved when he saw them.

His level gaze crossed the crowded room to hold Ashley's, his look discouraging.

"I'm going to do it," Ashley said, straightening. Claudia gave her a funny look, but didn't question her as she started toward him.

They met halfway. He looked tired, but just as determined as she felt.

"Ashley."

"I want to talk to you," she said sternly.

"I want to talk to *you*, too."

"Wonderful. Let me go first."

He looked at her blankly. "All right," he agreed.

"You asked me last night why I continued to see you if I believed all those things I confessed. I'll tell you why. Simply. Honestly. I love you, Cooper Masters, and if you don't love me, I think I'll die."

Ten

"That's not the kind of thing you say to a man in a public place." He studied her face for a tantalizing moment, gradually softening.

"I know, and I apologize, but I couldn't hold it in any longer."

"Why couldn't you have told me that last night?"

Oblivious to the crowds milling around, they stared at one another with only a small space separating them.

"Because I was afraid, and you were so..."

Cooper rubbed a hand across his eyes. "Don't say it. I know how I was."

"When you weren't with Claudia this morning, I didn't know what to think."

"I couldn't come. Not when you believed that I didn't want to be seen with you—that I was ashamed of you. You've carried that inside all these weeks, and not once did you question me."

Her teeth bit tightly into her lower lip. "I was afraid. Sounds silly, doesn't it?" She didn't wait for him to answer. "Afraid if I brought my fears into the open and forced you to admit it, that I wouldn't see you again. I couldn't face the truth if it meant losing you."

"The day you started ranting about your mother being my cook and your father being a steelworker... Was that the reason?"

She looked away and nodded.

Slowly he shook his head. "I can understand how you came to that conclusion, but you couldn't be more wrong. I love you, Ashley, I—"

"Cooper, oh, Cooper," she cried excitedly and threw her arms around him, spreading happy kisses over his face.

His mouth intercepted her as he hungrily devoured her lips. Although she could hear the people around them, she wouldn't have cared if they were in New York City at Grand Central Station. Cooper loved her. She'd prayed to hear those words, and nothing, not even a Christmas crowd in a public place, was going to ruin her pleasure.

When he dragged his mouth from hers, his husky voice breathed against her ear, "Do you promise to do that every time I admit I love you?"

"Yes, oh, yes," she said with a joyous smile.

He cleared his throat self-consciously. "In case you hadn't noticed, we have an audience."

She was too contented to care. A searing happiness was bubbling within her. "I want the whole world to know how I feel."

"You seem to have gotten a good start," he teased with an easy laugh, and kissed the top of her head. "Don't look now, but Claudia and company are headed our way."

Reluctantly, Ashley dropped her arms and stepped back. Cooper pulled her close to his side, cradling her waist.

"Is everything okay with you two, or do you need more time?" Claudia's gaze went from one of them to the other. "If that embrace was anything to go by, I'd say things are looking much better."

"You could say that," Cooper agreed, his eyes holding Ashley's. The look he gave her was so warm and loving that it seemed to burst free and touch her heart and soul.

"But there are several things we need to discuss," Cooper continued. "If you don't mind, I'm going to take Ashley with me. We'll all meet back at the house later."

Claudia and Seth exchanged knowing looks. "We don't mind," Seth answered for them.

"But...Seth has your car," Ashley said, confused. "How will we...?"

He smiled. "I have a second car, since I can't afford to be without transportation. We'll be fine."

"Do I still get to open a present tonight? Because Auntie Ash said we could," Johnny quizzed anxiously, not the least bit interested in the logistics of the grownups' plans.

Cooper's eyes met Claudia's, and she shrugged.

"I think that will be fine, if that's what your Auntie Ash said," Seth interrupted.

"Uncle Cooper?" John's head tilted up at an inquiring angle.

"Yes?" He squatted down so that he was eye level with his godson.

"Is there mistletoe here, too?"

Briefly Cooper scanned the interior of the huge building. "I don't see any, why?"

"'Cause you were kissing Auntie Ash again."

"Sometime I like to kiss her even when there isn't any reason."

"You mean like Daddy and Mommy?"

"Exactly," he said, and smiled as his eyes caught Ashley's.

"I think it's time we left and let these two talk. We'll meet you later," Seth announced. Claudia lifted Johnny into her arms and turned around, then looked back and winked.

"Are you hungry?" Cooper asked.

She hadn't eaten all day. "Starved. I hardly touched dinner last night."

"I noticed." His tone was dry.

She ignored it. "And then this morning I was too miserable to think about food. But now I could eat a cow."

"We're at the right place. Choose what you want, and while you find us a table, I'll go get it."

The Food Circus had a large variety of booths that sold every imaginable cuisine. The toughest decision was making a choice from everything that was available.

They hardly spoke as they ate their chicken. Ashley licked her fingers. Cooper carefully unfolded one of the moistened towelettes that had been provided with their meal and carefully cleaned his own hands.

He glanced up and found her watching him. A tiny smile twitched at the corner of her mouth. "What's so funny?" he asked.

"Us." She opened her own towelette and followed his example. "Claudia told me she didn't know any two people more meant for one another."

Cooper acknowledged the statement with a curt nod. "I know I love you, whether we're right or wrong for one another doesn't seem to be the question." He reached across the table and captured her hand. "But then, you're an easy person to love. You're warm and alive, and so unique you make my heart sing just watching you."

"And you're so calm and dignified. Nothing rattles you, and so many times I've wished I could be like that."

"We balance one another." His eyes searched hers in a room that seemed filled with only them.

A burst of applause diverted Cooper's attention to the antics of a clown. "Let's get out of here."

Ashley happily agreed.

They stood, dumped their garbage in the proper receptacles, and linked their arms around one another's waists as they strolled outside.

A chill raced over her forearms, and she shivered.

Cooper brought her closer to his side. "Cold?"

"Only when you close me out," she whispered truthfully. "If you hadn't admitted to loving me, I don't know that I could have withstood the cold."

He drank deeply from her eyes, perhaps realizing for the first time how strong her emotions rang. "We need to talk," he murmured, and quickened his pace.

A half hour later he pulled into the driveway of his home.

"Coffee?" he suggested as he hung her coat in the hall closet.

"Yes." She nodded eagerly. "But, Cooper, could I have it in a mug? I'd feel safer."

His mouth thinned slightly, and she knew her request had troubled him. "I'm not the dainty teacup type," she said more forcefully than she wanted to. "What I mean is…"

"I know what you mean." Lightly he pressed a kiss on her cheek, then against the hollow of her throat. "Do you have any idea how difficult it's been this week to keep my hands off you?"

"Not half as difficult as it's been not to encourage

you to touch me," she admitted, and felt color suffuse her cheeks.

A few minutes later he carried two ceramic mugs into the den on a silver platter.

A soft smile danced from Ashley's eyes. "Compromise?"

"Compromise," he agreed, handing her one of the mugs.

She held it with both hands and stared into its depths. "I have a feeling I know what you're going to say."

"I doubt that very much, but go ahead."

"No." She shook her head, then nervously tugged a strand of hair around her ear. "I've put my foot in my mouth so many times that for once I'm content to let you do the talking."

"We seem to have a penchant for saying the wrong things to each other, don't we?" His gaze searched hers, and the silence was broken only by an occasional snap and pop from the logs in the fireplace.

His look was thoughtful as he straightened in his chair. Nervously, she glanced around the den she had come to love—the books and desk, the chess set. One of the most ostentatious rooms in the house and, strangely, the one in which she felt the most comfortable. Maybe it was because this was the room Cooper used most often.

"I think it's important to clear away any misunderstandings, especially about the party. Ashley, when I saw how hurt you were to be excluded, well...I can't remember ever feeling worse. Believe this, because it's the truth. I wanted you there from the first. But I felt you would be uncomfortable. Those people are a lot like me."

"But I love you," she said, keeping her gaze on her coffee.

"I didn't know that at the time. I didn't want to do anything that was going to make you feel ill-at-ease. Thrusting you into my world could have destroyed our promising relationship, and that was far more important to me. Now I realize what a terrible mistake that was."

"And the other things?" She had to know, had to clear away any reasons for doubt.

"Thinking over everything you've told me, your point of view makes perfect sense." He set his cup aside and sat on the ottoman in front of her chair. Holding her face with both hands, he tilted her gaze to meet his. Ashley couldn't doubt the sincerity of his look. "I did those things because I thought you wouldn't want to be associated with me. I didn't let Claudia know you were here on Thanksgiving when she phoned to protect you from speculation and embarrassing questions. The same with what happened in church."

"Oh, Cooper…" She groaned at her own stupidity. "I was so miserable. I know it was stupid not to say anything, but I was afraid of the truth."

His kiss was sweet and filled with the awe of the discovery of her love. "Things being what they are, maybe you should open your Christmas gift now."

"Oh, could I?"

"I think you'd better." He opened the closet and brought out a large, beautifully wrapped box.

Much bigger than an engagement ring, Ashley mused thoughtfully, fighting to overcome her disappointment. Cowboy boots? She'd tried on a couple of pairs when they'd bought his, but she'd decided against them because of the expense. But if her present was cowboy boots, why would Cooper feel it was important to give it to her now?

He placed it on her lap, and she untied the red velvet

bow, then hesitated. "My gift to you is at home." It was important that he know he'd meant enough to her to buy him something special. "But I'm making you wait until Christmas."

"Maybe I should make *you* wait, too," he teased, ready to take back the gaily wrapped present.

"No you don't," she objected, and gripped the package tightly.

"Actually," he said, and the teasing light left his eyes, "it's important that you open this now." He smiled huskily and kissed her. His lips were a light caress across her brow.

Ashley's fingers shook as she pulled back the paper and lifted the lid of the box. Inside, nestled in white tissue, was a large family Bible. Her heart was thumping so loudly she could barely hear Cooper speaking above the hammering beat.

"A Bible," she murmured and looked up at him, her gaze probing his.

"I've thought about what you said about your relationship with Christ, and how important it was to you. I wanted to have a strong faith for you, because of my love. But that wasn't good enough. There were so many things I didn't understand. If Christ paid the price for my salvation with His life, then how can my faith be of value if all I have to do is ask for it?" He stood and walked across the room, pausing once to run his hand through his hair. "I talked to Seth about it several times. He always had the answers, but I wasn't convinced. Last Sunday I was in church, sitting in the sanctuary waiting for the service to begin, and I asked God to help me. On the way out of church after the service I saw the car I had given you in the parking lot. Suddenly I knew."

Ashley had been at church, but she had taught Sunday

School and then helped in the nursery during the worship service. She had talked only briefly to Claudia and hadn't seen Cooper at all.

"My car? How did my car help?"

"It sounds crazy, I know," he admitted wryly. "But I gave it to you because I love you. Freely, without seeking reimbursement, knowing that you couldn't afford a car. It was my gift to you, because I love you. It suddenly occurred to me that was exactly why Christ died for me. He paid the price because I couldn't."

Unabashed tears of happiness clouded her eyes as her hands lovingly traced the gilded print on the cover of the Bible.

"I've made my commitment to Christ," he told her, his voice rich and vibrant. "He's my Savior."

"Oh, Cooper." She wiped a tear from her cheek and smiled up at him.

"That's not all."

An overwhelming happiness stole through her. She couldn't imagine anything more wonderful than what he'd just finished explaining.

"Do you recall the first Sunday Claudia and Seth arrived?"

Ashley nodded.

"I stepped into your Sunday school class." He looked away as a glossy shine came over his dark eyes. "You were on the floor with a little girl sitting in your lap."

"I remember. You turned around and walked out. I thought I'd done something to upset you."

"Upset me?" he repeated incredulously. "No. Never that. You looked up, and your blue eyes softened, and in that moment I imagined you holding another child. Ours. Never have I felt an emotion so strong. It nearly choked me, I could hardly think. If I hadn't turned around and walked away, I don't know what I would have done."

Ashley thought her heart would burst with unrestrained joy. "Our child."

"Yes." Cooper knelt on the floor beside her, took the Bible out of its box and set the box on the floor. Reverently, he opened the first pages of the holy book. "I got this one for a reason. I've written our names here, and I'm asking that we fill the rest out together."

Ashley looked down at the page, which had been set aside to record a family history. Both their names were entered under "Marriage," the date left blank.

"Will you marry me, Ashley?" he asked, an unfamiliar humble quality in his voice.

The lump of joy in her throat prevented her from doing anything but nodding her head. "Yes," she finally managed. "Yes, Cooper, yes." She flung her arms around his neck and spread kisses over his face. She laughed with breathless joy as the tears slid down her cheeks.

His arms went around her as he pulled her closer. His mouth found hers in a lingering kiss that cast away all doubts and misgivings.

She lovingly caressed the side of his face. "I don't know how you can love me. I always seem to think the worst of you."

"Not anymore you won't," he whispered against her temple as he continued to stroke her back. "I won't ever give you reason to doubt again. I love you, Ashley."

She linked her hands behind his neck and smiled contentedly into his eyes. "I do want children. Just being with Johnny and Scott has shown me how much I want babies of my own."

"We'll fill the house. I can't wait to tuck them into bed at night and listen to their prayers."

"What about horsey rides?"

"Those too."

"Cooper…" She paused and swallowed tightly. "Why were you so angry with me after the party?" She wanted everything to be right and needed to know what she'd done to displease him.

Some of the happiness left his face. "I love you so much, Ashley. It hurt me to see you so uncomfortable, afraid to make a move. Your fun-loving, outgoing nature had been completely squelched. I wanted you to be yourself. Later—" He sat on the ottoman and took both her hands in his. "—I had already gotten the Bible with the hope of asking you to marry me, and you listed off all the things I had done to make you believe I was ashamed to be seen with you. I don't mind telling you that it shook me up. I was on the verge of asking you to be my wife, and you didn't even know how much I loved you."

"I won't have that problem again," she told him softly.

"I know you won't, because you'll never have reason to doubt again. I promise you that, my love."

The sound of footsteps in the hall brought their attention to the world outside the door.

Cooper stood, and extended a hand toward her. "I don't think either Claudia or Seth will be surprised by our announcement. Or your family, for that matter."

"My family?"

"I talked to your mother and father yesterday. They've given us their blessing. I was determined to have you, Ash. I wouldn't want to live my life without you now." He hugged her tightly and curved an arm around her waist. "Christmas. It's almost too wonderful to believe. God gave His Son in love. And now He's given me you."

* * * * *

SECRET CHRISTMAS TWINS

Lee Tobin McClain

One

Detective Jason Stephanidis steered his truck down the narrow, icy road, feeling better than anytime since being placed on administrative leave. He'd checked on several elderly neighbors near Holly Creek Farm and promised to plow them out after the storm ended. Now he was headed back to the farm to spend some much-needed time with his grandfather.

It wasn't that he was feeling the Christmas spirit, not exactly. Being useful was how he tamed the wolves inside him.

Slowly, cautiously, he guided the truck around a bend. Amid the rapidly falling snow, something flashed. Headlights? In the middle of the road?

What was a little passenger car doing out on a night like this? This part of Pennsylvania definitely required all-wheel drive and heavy snow tires in winter.

He swerved right to avoid hitting the small vehicle. Perilously close to the edge of the gulch, he stopped his truck, positioning it to provide a barrier against the other car going over the edge.

There. The car should be able to pass him now, safely on the side away from the ledge.

Rather than slowing down gradually, though, the other driver hit the brakes hard. The little car spun and careened into an icy snowdrift, stopping with a resounding thump.

Jason put on his flashers, leaped from his truck and ran toward the vehicle. He couldn't see through the fogged-up window on the driver's side, so he carefully tried the door. The moment he opened it, he heard a baby's cry.

Oh no.

"The babies. My babies! Are they okay?" The driver clicked open her seat belt and twisted toward the back seat. "Mikey! Teddy!"

There were two of them? "Sit still, ma'am. I'll check on your children." He eased open the back door and saw two car seats. A baby in each. One laughing, one crying, but they both looked uninjured, at least to his inexperienced eye.

Between the front seats, the driver's face appeared. "Oh, my sweet boys, are you okay?" There was an edge of hysteria in her voice.

"They seem fine, ma'am. You need to turn off your vehicle."

She looked at him as if he were speaking Greek, then reached a shaky hand toward the baby who was wailing. "It's okay, Mikey. You're okay." She patted and clucked in that way women seemed to naturally know how to do.

The baby's crying slowed down a little.

"Turn off your vehicle," he repeated.

"What?" She was still rubbing the crying baby's leg, making soothing sounds. It seemed to work; the baby took one more gasping breath, let it out in a hiccupy sigh and subsided into silence.

She fumbled around, found a pacifier and stuck it in the baby's mouth. Then she cooed at the nearer baby, found his pacifier pinned to his clothes and did the same.

Unhurt, quiet babies. Jason felt his shoulders relax a little. "Turn the car off. For safety. We don't want any engine fires."

"Engine fires?" She gasped, then spun and did as he'd instructed.

He straightened and closed the rear car door to keep the heat inside.

She got out, looked back in at the babies and closed the door. And then she collapsed against it, hands going to her face, breathing rapid.

"Are you all right?" He stepped closer and noticed a flowery scent. It seemed to come from her masses of long red hair.

"Just a little shaky. Delayed reaction." Her voice was surprisingly husky.

"How old are your babies?"

She hesitated just a little bit. "They're twins. Fifteen months."

He focused on her lightweight leather jacket, the non-waterproof sneakers she wore. *Not* on her long legs nicely showcased by slim-fitting jeans. "Ma'am, you shouldn't be out on a night like this. If I hadn't come along—"

"If you hadn't come along, I wouldn't have gone off the road!"

"Yes, you would've. You can't slam on your brakes in the snow."

"How was I supposed to know that?"

"Ma'am, any teenager would know not to…" He trailed off. No point rubbing in how foolish she'd been.

She bit her lip and held up a hand. "Actually, you're right that I shouldn't be out. I was slipping and sliding all over the place." Walking up to the front end of the car, she studied it, frowning. "Wonder if I can just back out?"

Jason knelt and checked for damage, but fortunately, the car looked okay. Good and stuck, though. "You probably can't, but I can tow you." As he walked around the car to study the rear bumper in preparation for towing, he noticed the Arizona plates.

So that was why she didn't know how to drive in the snow.

He set up some flares, just in case another vehicle came their way, and then made short order of connecting the tow rope and pulling her out of the drift.

He turned off his truck, jumped out and walked over to her. Snow still fell around them, blanketing the forest with quiet.

"Thank you so much." She held out a hand to shake his.

He felt the strangest urge to wrap her cold fingers in his palm, to warm them. To comfort her, which would shock the daylights out of his ex-fiancée, who'd rightly assessed him as cold and heartless. He was bad at relationships and family life, but at least now he knew it. "You should wear gloves," he said sternly instead of holding on to that small, delicate hand.

For just the briefest second he thought she rolled her eyes. "Cold hands are the least of my problems."

Really? "It didn't look like your children are dressed warmly enough, either."

She turned her back to him, opened her car door and

grabbed a woven, Southwestern-looking purse. "Can I pay you for your help?"

"*Pay* me? Ma'am, that's not how we do things around here."

She arched an eyebrow. "Look, I'd love to hang out and discuss local customs, but I need to get my boys to shelter. Since, as you've pointed out so helpfully, they're inadequately dressed."

"I'll lead you back to a road that's straighter, cleared off better," he said. "Where were you headed?"

"Holly Creek Farm."

Jason stared at her.

"It's supposed to be just a few miles down this road, I think. I should be fine."

"Are you sure that's the name of the place? There's a lot of Holly-this and Holly-that around here, especially since the closest town is Holly Springs."

"I know where I'm going!" She crossed her arms, tucking her hands close to her sides. "It's a farm owned by the Stephanidis family. The grandparents...er, an older couple lives there." A frown creased her forehead, and she fingered her necklace, a distinctive silver cross embedded with rose quartz and turquoise.

A chill ran down Jason's spine. The necklace was familiar. He leaned closer. "That looks like a cross my sister used to wear." Sadness flooded him as he remembered the older sister who'd once been like a mother to him, warm and loving, protecting him from their parents' whims.

Before she'd gone underground, out of sight.

"A friend gave it to me."

Surely Kimmie hadn't ended up back in Arizona, where they'd spent their early childhood. An odd thrum-

ming started in his head. "Why did you say you were
going to the Holly Creek Farm?"

"I didn't say." She cocked her head, looking at him
strangely. "The twins...um, my boys and I are going there
to live for a while. Our friend Kimmie Stephanidis gave
us permission, since it's her family home. What did you
say your name is?"

"I didn't say." He echoed her words through a dry
throat. "But I'm Jason. Jason Stephanidis."

She gasped and her hand flew to her mouth. She went
pale and leaned back against her car.

Jason didn't feel so steady himself. What had this red-
headed stranger been to Kimmie? And was she seriously
thinking of staying at the farm—with babies—when she
obviously knew nothing about managing a country winter? "Look, do you want to bring your kids and come sit
in my truck? I have bottled water in there, and it's warm.
You're not looking so good."

She ignored the suggestion. "You're Jason Stephanidis?
Oh, wow." She didn't sound happy as she glanced at the
babies in the back seat of her car.

"And your name is…"

"Erica. Erica Lindholm."

"Well, Erica, we need to talk." He needed to pump
her for information and then send her on her way. The
farm was no place for her and her boys, not at this time
of year. And Jason's grandfather didn't need the stress.

On the other hand, given the rusty appearance of her
small car, a model popular at least ten years ago, she
probably didn't have a lot of money for a hotel. If she
could even get to one at this time of night, in this storm.

She straightened her back and gave him a steady look
that suggested she had courage, at least. "If you're Kim-

mie's brother, we do need to talk. She needs help, if you're willing. But for now, I need to get the boys to shelter. If you could just point me toward the farm—"

He made a snap decision to take her there, at least for tonight. "I'll clear the road and you can follow me there." She'd obviously been close to Kimmie. Maybe a fellow addict who needed a place to stay, dry out.

If he caught one whiff of drug use around those babies, though, he'd have her arrested so fast she wouldn't know what had hit her.

"I don't want to put you out." Her voice sounded tight, shaky. "I'm sure you have somewhere to go."

"It's no trouble to lead you there," he said, "since I live at Holly Creek Farm."

The detective in him couldn't help but notice that his announcement made the pretty redhead very, very uncomfortable.

Erica Lindholm clutched the steering wheel and squinted through the heavily falling snow, her eyes on the red taillights in front of her.

Jason Stephanidis *lived* there. In the place Kimmie had said belonged to her grandparents. What nightmare was this?

How could she take care of the babies here? Kimmie's brother, being a detective, was sure to find out she'd taken them and run with no official guardianship papers. That had to be a crime.

And he might—probably would—attempt to take them away from her.

She couldn't let him—that was all. Which meant she couldn't let him know that the boys were actually Kimmie's sons.

Somewhere on the long road trip, caring for the twins and worrying about them, comforting them and feeding them, she'd come to love them with pure maternal fierceness. She'd protect them with her life.

Including protecting them from Kimmie's rigid, controlling brother, if need be. She'd promised Kimmie that.

In just ten minutes, which somehow felt all too soon, they turned off the main road. The truck ahead slowed down, and a moment later she realized Jason had lowered the plow on the front of his truck and was clearing the small road that curved up a little hill and over a quaint-looking bridge.

A moment later they pulled up to a white farmhouse, its front door light revealing a wraparound front porch, the stuff of a million farm movies.

Behind her, Teddy started to fuss. From the smell of things, one or both of the boys needed a diaper change.

Jason had emerged from the truck and was coming back toward her, and she got out of her car to meet him. He looked as big as a mountain: giant, stubbly and dangerous.

Erica's heart beat faster. "Thank you for all you've done for us tonight," she said. "I understand there's a cabin on the property. We can go directly there, if you'll point the way."

"No, you can't."

"Why not?"

"That cabin hasn't been opened up in a couple of years. The heat's off, water's off, who knows what critters have been living there…" He shook his head. "I don't know what you were thinking, bringing those babies out in this storm."

Guilt surged up in her. He was right.

"For now, you'll have to stay at the farmhouse with me."

Whoa. No *way*. "That's not safe or appropriate. I don't know you from—"

The front door burst open. "There you are! I was ready to call the rescue squad. Who'd you bring with you?"

All she could see of the man in the doorway was a tall blur, backlit by a golden, homey light that looked mercifully warm.

"Open up the guest room, would you, Papa? We've got Kimmie's friend here, and she has babies."

"Babies! Get them inside. I'll put on the soup pot and pull out the crib." The front door closed.

Jason looked at Erica, and for the first time, she saw a trace of humor in his eyes. "My grandfather's house. He'll keep you and the twins safe from me and anything else."

Behind her, through the car's closed windows, she could hear both twins crying. She didn't have another solution, at least not tonight. "All right. Thank you."

Moments later they were inside a large, well-heated farmhouse kitchen. Erica spread a blanket and changed the twins' diapers while Jason's grandfather took a dishrag to an ancient-looking high chair. "There you go," he said, giving the chair's wooden tray a final polish. "One of 'em can sit there. You'll have to hold the other for now." He extended a weathered hand. "Andrew Stephanidis. You can call me Papa Andy."

"Thank you." She shook his hand and then lifted Teddy into the high chair. "This is Teddy, and—" she bent down and picked up Mikey "—this is Mikey, and I'm Erica. Erica Lindholm." *Who might be wanted by the police right about now.* "I'm very grateful to you for taking us in."

"Always room for the little ones. That's what Mama

used to say." The old man looked away for a moment, then turned back to face Erica. "Sorry we're not decorated for Christmas. Used to have holly and evergreens and tinsel to the roof, but…seems like I just don't have the heart for it this year."

Jason carried in the last of her boxes and set it on the table. "I put your suitcases up in the guest room, but this box looks like food." He was removing his enormous boots as he spoke. "Sorry about the mess, Papa. I'll clean it up."

The old man waved a hand. "Later. Sit down and have some soup."

Erica's head was spinning. How had Kimmie gotten it so wrong, telling her the mean brother never came to the farm? And it sure seemed like Kimmie's grandmother, the "Mama" Papa Andy had spoken of, had passed on. Obviously, Kimmie had completely lost touch with her own family.

In front of Erica, a steaming bowl of vegetable soup sent up amazing smells, pushing aside her questions. She'd been so focused on feeding and caring for the twins during four long days of travel that she'd barely managed to eat. The occasional drive-through burger and the packets of cheese and crackers in the cheap motels where they'd crashed each night couldn't compare to the deliciousness in front of her.

"Go ahead. Dig in. I'll hold the little one." Papa Andy lifted Mikey from her lap and sat down, bouncing him on his knee with a practiced movement.

Erica held her breath. With the twins' developmental delays came some fussiness, and she wanted to avoid questions she wouldn't know how to answer. Wanted to avoid a tantrum, too.

But Mikey seemed content with Papa Andy's bouncing, while Teddy plucked cereal from the wooden high chair tray and looked around, wide-eyed. The babies cared for, Erica scooped up soup and ate two big pieces of buttered corn bread, matching Jason bite for bite even though he was twice her size.

When her hunger was sated, she studied him from under her eyelashes and tried to quell her own fear. Kimmie had been afraid of her brother's wrath if he discovered that she'd gone back to drugs and gotten pregnant out of wedlock. And she'd feared disappointing her grandparents. That was why she'd become estranged from the family. She hadn't said it outright, but Erica had gotten the feeling that Kimmie might have stolen money from some of them, as well.

None of that was the twins' fault, and if Kimmie's family history were the only barrier, Erica wouldn't hesitate to let Jason and Papa Andy know that the twins were their own relatives. She wasn't foolish enough to think she could raise them herself with no help, and having a caring uncle and great-grandfather and more resources on their side would be only to their benefit.

But Kimmie had said Jason would try to get custody of the twins, and seeing how authoritative he seemed to be, Erica didn't doubt it.

Kimmie hadn't wanted her brother to have them. She'd insisted there were good reasons for it.

Erica wished she could call and ask, but Kimmie wasn't answering her phone. In fact, she'd left a teary message two days ago, saying she was moving into a rehab center. She'd assured Erica that she was getting good care, but might not be reachable by phone.

Now that Erica was sitting still, for the moment not

worried about her and the twins' survival, sadness washed over her. For Kimmie, for the twins and for herself. With all her flaws, Kimmie had been a loving friend, and they'd spent almost every moment of the past month together. Like a vivid movie, she remembered when Kimmie—addicted, terminally ill and in trouble with the law—had begged her to take the twins.

"I know it's a lot to ask. You're so young. You'll find a husband and have babies of your own…"

"No, I won't," Erica had responded. "But that's not what's important now."

"You have time. You can get over your past." Kimmie had pulled a lock of hair out of Erica's ponytail. "You could be beautiful if you'd stop hiding it. And you need to realize that there are a few men out there worth trusting."

Remembering Kimmie's attempt at mothering, even at such a horrible moment, brought tears to Erica's eyes even now, in the bright farmhouse kitchen. Erica *wouldn't* get over her past, wouldn't have kids of her own, as Kimmie would have realized if she hadn't been so ill.

But Erica had these babies, and she'd protect them with her life. They were her family now.

The old black wall phone rang, and Papa answered it.

"Yes, he's here." She listened. "No, Heather Marie, he's not coming out again in the storm just because you forgot to buy nail polish or some such crazy thing!" He held the phone away from his ear and indistinguishable, agitated words buzzed out from it. "You saw a *what?* A *dog?*"

Jason took one more bite of corn bread, wiped his mouth and stood. He might have even looked relieved. "It's okay, Papa. I'll talk to her."

Papa narrowed his eyes at him. "You're an enabler."

Jason took the phone and moved into the hall, the long cord stretching to accommodate. Minutes later he came back in. "She thinks she saw a dog out wandering on Bear Creek Road, but she was afraid if she stopped she couldn't get going again. I'm going to run out there and see if I can find it."

"And visit her? Maybe get snowed in? Because that's what she wants."

Jason waved a dismissive hand. "I don't mind helping." Then he turned to Erica. "We have to talk, but I'm sure you're exhausted. We can figure all of this out tomorrow." He left the room, a giant in sock feet. Moments later, a chilly breeze blew through the kitchen, and then the front door slammed shut.

A chill remained in Erica's heart, though. She had the feeling that Kimmie's big brother would have plenty of questions for her when he returned. Questions she didn't dare to answer.

It was almost midnight by the time Jason arrived back at the house. Exhausted, cold and wet, he went around to the passenger side to get leverage enough to lift the large dog he'd finally found limping through the woods near Bear Creek.

He carried the dog to the house and fumbled with the door, trying to open it without putting down the dog.

Suddenly, it swung open, and there was Erica, her hair glowing like fire in the hallway's golden light. "Oh, wow, what can I do?" She hurried out to hold open the storm door for him, regardless of the cold. "Want me to grab towels? A blanket?"

"Both. Closet at the top of the stairs."

She ran up and came back down and into the front

room quickly, her green eyes full of concern. Her soft jeans had holes at the knees, and not the on-purpose kind teenagers wore.

After she'd spread the blankets on the floor in front of the gas fireplace, he carefully set the dog down and studied him. Dirty, yellow fur, a heavy build: probably a Lab-shepherd mix. The dog didn't try to move much but sighed and dropped his head to the floor as if relieved to have found a safe haven.

"Go take off your wet things," Erica ordered Jason. "I'll watch the dog."

"The twins are asleep?"

"Like logs."

Jason shed his jacket, boots and hat, got two bowls of water and a couple of thin dishrags, and came back into the warm room. It hadn't changed much since he was a kid. He half expected his grandmother to come around the corner, bringing cookies and hot chocolate.

But that wasn't happening, ever again.

"Was he in a fight?" Erica asked. She was gently plucking sticks and berries out of the dog's fur. "His leg seems awful tender."

"I'll try to clean it and wrap it. He's friendly, like he's had a good home, though maybe not for a while." He put the cold water down, and the dog lifted his big golden head and drank loud and long, spilling water all over the floor.

"He's skinny under his fur," Erica said. "And a mess. What are all these sticky berries on him?" She plucked a sprig from the dog's back, green with a few white berries.

"It's mistletoe." Made him think of Christmas parties full of music and laughter. Of happy, carefree times.

Erica didn't look at Jason as she pulled more debris

from the dog's fur. "Then that's what we'll call him. Mistletoe."

"You're *naming* the dog?"

"We have to call him something," she said reasonably. "You work on him. I'll be right back."

He puzzled over Erica as he carefully examined the dog's leg. She seemed kind and helpful and well-spoken. So how had Kimmie connected with her? Had Kimmie gotten her life together, started running with a better crowd? Was Erica some kind of emissary from his sister?

He breathed in and out and tried to focus on the present moment. This homey room, the quiet, the dog's warm brown eyes. Letting his thoughts run away with him was dangerous, was what had made him okay with administrative leave. The only crime he'd committed was trusting his partner, who'd turned out to be corrupt, taking bribes. With time, Jason knew he'd be exonerated of wrongdoing.

But still, he was all too aware that he'd lost perspective. He'd been working too hard and getting angrier and angrier, partly because of worrying about his sister's situation and wondering where she was. He'd had no life. Coming here, taking a break, was the right thing to do, especially given his grandmother's death earlier this year.

He should have come home more. He'd made so many mistakes as a brother, a son, a grandson. And a fiancé, according to what Renea had screamed as she'd stormed out for the last time. Funny how that was the weakness that bothered him the least.

Erica came back into the room and set a tray down on the end table beside the couch.

A familiar, delicious smell wafted toward him. *Déjà vu.* "You made hot chocolate?"

She looked worried. "Papa Andy showed me where to

find everything before he went to bed. I hope it's okay. You just looked so cold."

He took one of the two mugs and sipped, then drank. "Almost as good as Gran's."

Her face broke into a relieved smile, and if she'd been pretty before, her smile made her absolutely gorgeous. Wow.

"How's Mistletoe?" She set down the other mug and knelt by the dog.

He snorted out a laugh at the name. "He let me look at his leg. Whether he'll let me wash it remains to be seen." He put down the hot chocolate and dipped a rag into the warm water.

"Want me to hold his head?"

"No." Was she crazy? "If he bites anybody, it's going to be me, not you."

"I'm not afraid." She scooted over, gently lifted the dog's large head and crossed her legs beneath. "It's okay, boy," she said, stroking his face and ears. "Jason's going to fix it."

Jason parted the dog's fur. "Don't look—it's not pretty."

She ignored his instruction, leaning over to see. "Aw, ouch. Wonder what happened?"

"A fight, or clipped by a car. He's limping pretty bad, so I'm worried the bone is involved." As gently as possible, he squeezed water onto the wound and then wiped away as much dirt as he could. Once, the dog yelped, but Erica soothed him immediately and he relaxed back into her lap.

Smart dog.

Jason ripped strips of towel and wrapped the leg, aiming for gentle compression. "There you go, fella. We'll call the vet in the morning."

"That wasn't so bad, was it?" Erica eased out from under the dog's head, gave him a few more ear scratches and then moved to the couch, picking up her mug on the way. "I love hot chocolate, but in Phoenix, we didn't have much occasion to drink it."

Jason picked up his half-full cup and sat in the adjacent armchair. "How did you know Kimmie?"

The question was abrupt, and he meant it to be. People answered more honestly when they hadn't had a chance to relax and figure out what their interrogator wanted to hear.

She drew in a deep breath and blew it out. "Fair question. I met her at Canyon Lodge." She looked at him, but when he didn't react, she clarified. "It's a drug rehab center."

"You're an addict, too?"

"Noooo." She lifted an eyebrow at his assumption. "My mom was. I met Kimmie, wow, ten years ago, on visits to Mom. When they both got out, we stayed in touch."

And yet she hadn't turned to her mom when she'd needed a place to stay. "How's your mom doing?" he asked.

She looked away. "She didn't make it."

"I'm sorry."

"Thanks." She slid down off the couch to sit beside the dog again, petting him in long, gentle strokes.

"Where's Kimmie now? Is she in Phoenix?"

Erica hesitated.

"Look, we've been out of touch for years. But if she's

sober now…" He saw Erica's expression change. "*Is* she sober now?"

Erica looked down at the dog, into the fire, anywhere but at him.

Hope leaked out of him like air from a deflating tire. "She's not."

Finally, she blew out a breath and met his eyes. "I don't know how to answer that."

"What do you mean? She's straight or she's not."

Erica's face went tense, and he realized he'd spoken harshly. Not the way to gain trust and information. "Sorry. Let's start over. Why did she send you to Holly Creek Farm?"

Simple enough question, he'd thought. Apparently not.

"It's complicated," she said.

He ground his teeth to maintain patience. His superiors had been right; he was too much on the edge to be working the streets right now. For a fleeting, fearful moment, he wondered if he could ever do it again.

But interviewing someone about your own kin was different, obviously, than asking questions about a stranger.

"Kimmie isn't…well," she said finally.

Jason jerked to attention at her tone. "What's wrong?"

She opened her mouth to speak, but his cell phone buzzed. Wretched thing. And as a cop, even one on leave, he had to take it.

"It's late for a phone call." Then she waved a hand, looking embarrassed. "Not my business. Sorry."

A feeling of foreboding came over Jason as he looked at the unfamiliar number. "Area code 602. Phoenix, isn't it?"

She gasped, her hand going to her mouth. "Yes."

He clicked to answer. "Jason Stephanidis."

"Mr. Stephanidis." The voice on the other end was male, and there was background noise Jason couldn't identify. "Are you the brother of Kimberly Stephanidis?"

Jason closed his eyes. "Yes."

"Okay. This is Officer John Jiminez. Phoenix PD. You're a cop, too?"

"That's right."

"Good. My information's accurate. Do you know... Have you seen your sister recently?"

"No."

Silence. Then: "Look, I'm sorry to inform you that she's passed away. I've been assigned to locate her next of kin."

A chasm opened in his chest. "Drugs?"

"The coroner listed the cause of death as an overdose. But it also looks like she had advanced lung cancer."

Jason squeezed his eyes closed, tighter, as if that could block out the words he was hearing. What he wanted to do was to shout back: *No. No. No.*

Erica sat on the couch, her arms wrapped around herself. Trying to hold herself together.

Kimmie was gone.

The twins were motherless.

Grief warred with worry and fear, and she jumped up and paced the room.

After Jason had barked out the news, said that a lawyer would call back tomorrow with more information, he'd banged out of the house.

What had happened? Had Kimmie gone peacefully, with good care, or died alone and in pain? Or, given the mention of overdose, had she taken the low road one last time?

Erica sank her head into her hands and offered up wordless prayers. Finally, a little peace came to her as the truth she believed with all her heart sank in: Kimmie had gone home to a forgiving God, happy, all pain gone.

She paced over to the window and looked out. The snow had stopped, and as she watched, the moon came out from under a cloud, sending a cold, silvery light over the rolling farmland.

Off to the side, Jason shoveled a walkway, fast, furious, robotic.

Wanting air herself, wanting to see that moon better and remind herself that God had a plan, Erica found a heavy jacket in the hall closet and slipped outside.

Sharp cold took her breath away. A wide creek ran alongside the house, a little stone bridge arching over it. Snow blanketed hills and trees and barns.

And the moonlight! It reflected off snow and water, rendering the scene almost as bright as daytime, bright enough that a wooden fence and a line of tall pines cast shadows on the snow.

The only sound was the steady *chink-chink-chink* of Jason's shovel.

The newness, the majesty, the fearfulness of the scene made her tremble. God's creation, beautiful and dangerous. A Sunday school verse flashed through her mind: *"In His hand is the life of every creature and the breath of all mankind."*

The shovel stopped. Heavy boot steps came toward her.

"You should have contacted me!" Jason's voice was

loud, angry. "How long were you with her? Didn't you think her family might want to know?"

His accusatory tone stung. "She didn't want me to contact you!"

"You listened to an addict?"

"She said you told her you were through helping her."

"I didn't know she had cancer!" He sank down on the front step and let his head fall into his hands. "I would have helped." The last word came out choked.

Erica's desire to fight left her. He was Kimmie's brother, and he was hurting.

She sat down beside him. "She wasn't alone, until just a short while ago. I was with her."

He turned his head to face her. "I don't get it. On top of everything else she had to deal with, she took in you and your kids?"

She saw how it looked to him. But what was she supposed to say? Kimmie hadn't wanted her to tell Jason about the twins. She'd spoken of him bitterly. "I was a support to her, not a burden," she said. "You can believe that or not."

He leaned back on his elbows, staring out across the moon-bright countryside. "Tough love," he muttered. "Everyone says to use tough love."

Behind them, there was a scratching sound and then a mournful howl.

Jason stood and opened the door, and Mistletoe limped outside. He lifted his golden head and sniffed the air.

"Guess he got lonely." Jason sat back down.

Mistletoe shoved in between them and rested his head on Jason's lap.

They were silent for a few minutes. Erica was cold, especially where her thin jeans met the stone porch steps.

But she felt lonely, too. She didn't want to leave the dog. And strangely enough, she didn't want to leave Jason. Although he was obviously angry, and even blaming her, he was the only person in the world right now, besides her, who was grieving Kimmie's terribly early death.

"I just don't get your story," he burst out. "How'd you help her when you were trying to care for your babies, too? And why'd she send you and your kids here?"

Mistletoe nudged his head under Jason's hand, demanding attention.

"I want some answers, Erica."

Praying for the words to come to her, Erica spoke. "She said this was a good place, a safe place. She knew I...didn't have much."

He lifted a brow like he didn't believe her.

"She'd loved my mom." Which was true. "She was kind of like a big sister to me."

"She was a *real* big sister to me." Suddenly, Jason pounded a fist into his open hand. "I can't believe this. Can't believe she OD'd alone." He paused and drew in a ragged breath, then looked at Erica. "I'm going to find out more about you and what went on out there. I'm going to get some answers."

Erica looked away from his intensity. She didn't want him to see the fear in her eyes.

And she especially didn't want him to find one particular answer: that Kimmie was the biological mother of the twins sleeping upstairs.

Two

Sunday morning, just after sunrise, Jason followed the smell of coffee into the farmhouse kitchen. He poured himself a cup and strolled around, looking for his grandfather and listening to the morning sounds of Erica and the twins upstairs.

Yesterday had been rough. He'd called their mother overseas—the easier telling, strangely—and then he'd let Papa know about Kimmie. Papa hadn't cried; he'd just said, "I'm glad Mama wasn't alive to hear of this." Then he'd gone out to the barn all day, coming in only to eat a sandwich and go to bed.

Erica and the twins had stayed mostly in the guest room. Jason had made a trip to the vet to get Mistletoe looked over, and then rattled around the downstairs, alone and miserable, battling his own feelings of guilt and failure.

Tough love hadn't worked. His sister had died alone.

It was sadness times two, especially for his grandfather. And though the old man was healthy, an active farmer at age seventy-eight, Jason still worried about him.

Where was his grandfather now, anyway? Jason

looked out the windows and saw a trail broken through newly drifted snow. Papa had gone out to do morning chores without him.

A door opened upstairs, and he heard Erica talking to the twins. Maybe bringing them down for breakfast.

She was too pretty and he didn't trust her. Coward that he was, he poured his coffee into a travel cup and headed out, only stopping to lace his boots and zip his jacket when he'd closed the door behind him.

Jason approached the big red barn and saw Papa moving around inside. After taking a moment to admire the rosy morning sky crisscrossed by tree limbs, he went inside.

Somehow, Papa had pulled the old red sleigh out into the center of the barn and was cleaning off the cobwebs. In the stalls, the two horses they still kept stomped and snorted.

Papa gave him a half smile and nodded toward the horses. "They know what day it is."

"What day?"

"You've really been gone that long? It's Sleigh Bell Sunday."

"You don't plan on…" He trailed off, because Papa obviously did intend to hitch up the horses and drive the sleigh to church. It was tradition. The first Sunday in December, all the farm families that still kept horses came in by sleigh, if there was anything resembling enough snow to do it. There was a makeshift stable at the church and volunteers to tend the horses, and after church, all the town kids got sleigh rides. The church ladies served hot cider and cocoa and homemade doughnuts, and the choir sang carols.

It was a great event, but Papa already looked tired.

"We don't have to do it this year. Everyone would understand."

"It's important to the people in this community." Papa knelt to polish the sleigh's runner, adding in a muffled voice, "It was important to your grandmother."

Jason blew out a sigh, picked up a rag and started cleaning the inside of the old sleigh.

They fed and watered the horses. As they started to pull out the harnesses, Jason noticed the old sleigh bells he and Kimmie had always fought over, each of them wanting to be the one to pin them to the front of the sleigh.

Carefully, eyes watering a little, he hooked the bells in place.

"You know," Papa said, "this place belongs to you and Kimmie. We set it up so I'm a life tenant, but it's already yours."

Jason nodded. He knew about the provisions allowed to family farmers, made to ensure later generations like Jason and Kimmie wouldn't have to pay heavy inheritance taxes.

"I'm working the farm okay now. But you'll need to think about the future. There's gonna come a time when I'm not able."

"I'm thinking on it." They'd had this conversation soon after Gran had died, so Jason wondered where his grandfather was going with it.

"I imagine Kimmie left her half to you."

Oh. That was why. He coughed away the sudden roughness in his throat. "Lawyer's going to call back tomorrow and go through her will."

"That's fine, then." Papa went to the barn door. "Need

a break and some coffee. You finish hitching and pull it up." He paused, then added, "If you remember how."

The dig wasn't lost on Jason. It had been years since he'd driven horses or, for that matter, helped with the farm.

It wasn't like he'd been eating bonbons or walking on the beach. But he'd definitely let his family down. He had to do better.

By the time he'd figured out the hitches and pulled the sleigh up to the front door of the old white house, Papa was on the porch with a huge armload of blankets. "They'll be right out," he said.

"Who?"

"Erica and the babies."

"Those babies can't come! They're little!"

Papa waved a dismissive hand. "We've always taken the little ones. Safer than a car."

"But it's cold!" Even though it wasn't frostbite weather, the twins weren't used to Pennsylvania winters. "They're from Arizona!"

"So were you, up until you started elementary school." Papa chuckled. "Why, your parents brought you to visit at Christmas when you were only three months old, and Kimmie was, what, five? You both loved the ride, and no harm done."

And they'd continued to visit the farm and ride in the sleigh every Christmas after they'd moved back to the Pittsburgh area. Even when their parents had declined to go to church, Gran and Papa had insisted on taking them. Christmases on the farm had been one of the best parts of his childhood.

Maybe Kimmie had held on to some of those memories, too.

He fought down his emotions. "I don't trust Erica. There's something going on with her."

Papa didn't answer, and when Jason looked up, he saw that Erica had come out onto the porch. Papa just lifted an eyebrow and went to help her get the twins into the sleigh.

Had she heard what he'd said? But what did it matter if she had; she already knew he thought she was hiding something.

"This is amazing!" She stared at the sleigh and horses, round-eyed. "It's like a movie! Only better. Look, Mikey, horses!" She pointed toward the big furry-footed draft horses, their breath steaming in the cold, crisp air.

"Uuusss," Mikey said.

Erica's gloved hand—at least Papa had found her gloves—flew to her mouth. "That's his second word! Wow!"

"What did he say?" It had sounded like nonsense to Jason.

"He said *horse*. Didn't you, you smart boy?" Erica danced the twins around until they both giggled and yelled.

Papa lifted one of the babies from her arms and held him out to Jason. "Hold this one, will you?"

"But I..." He didn't have a choice, so he took the baby, even though he knew less than nothing about them. In his police work, whenever there'd been a baby to handle, he'd foisted it off on other officers who already had kids.

He put the baby on his knee, and the baby—was this Mikey?—gestured toward the horses and chortled. "Uuusss! Uuusss!"

Oh. Uuusss meant horse.

"I'll hold this one, and you climb in," Papa said to Erica. "Then I'll hand 'em to you one at a time, and you wrap 'em up in those blankets." Papa sounded like a pro at all of this, and given that he'd done it already for two generations, Jason guessed he was.

Once both twins were bundled, snug between Papa and Erica, Jason set the horses to trotting forward. The sun was up now, making millions of diamonds on the snow that stretched across the hills, far into the distance. He smelled pine, a sharp, resin-laden sweetness.

When he picked up the pace, the sleigh bells jingled.

"Real sleigh bells!" Erica said, and then, as they approached the white covered bridge, decorated with a simple wreath for Christmas, she gasped. "This is the most beautiful place I've ever seen."

Jason glanced back, unable to resist watching her fall in love with his home.

Papa was smiling for the first time since he'd learned of Kimmie's death. And as they crossed the bridge and trotted toward the church, converging with other horse-drawn sleighs, Jason felt a sense of rightness.

"Over here, Mr. S!" cried a couple of chest-high boys, and Jason pulled the sleigh over to their side of the temporary hitching post.

"I'll tie 'em up," Papa said, climbing out of the sleigh.

Mikey started babbling to Teddy, accompanied by gestures and much repetition of his new word, *uuusss*. Teddy tilted his head to one side and burst forth with his own stream of nonsense syllables, seeming to ask a question, batting Mikey on the arm. Mikey waved toward the horses and jabbered some more, as if he were explaining something important.

They were such personalities, even as little as they were. Jason couldn't help smiling as he watched them interact.

Once Papa had the reins set and the horses tied up, Jason jumped out of the sleigh and then turned to help Erica down. She handed him a twin. "Can you hold Mikey?"

He caught a whiff of baby powder and pulled the little one tight against his shoulder. Then he reached out to help Erica, and she took his hand to climb down, Teddy on her hip.

When he held her hand, something electric seemed to travel right to his heart. Involuntarily he squeezed and held on.

She drew in a sharp breath as she looked at him, some mixture of puzzlement and awareness in her eyes.

And then Teddy grabbed her hair and yanked, and Mikey struggled to get to her, and the connection was lost.

The next few minutes were a blur of greetings and "been too long" came from seemingly everyone in the congregation.

"Jason Stephanidis," said Mrs. Habler, a good-hearted pillar of the church whom he'd known since childhood. She'd held back until the other congregants had drifted toward the church, probably so she could probe for the latest news. "I didn't know you were in town."

He put an arm around her. "Good to see you, Mrs. Habler."

"And this must be your wife and boys. Isn't that sweet. Twins have always run in your family. You know, I don't think your mother ever got over losing her twin so young."

Mother had been a twin?

Erica cleared her throat. "We're actually just family friends, passing through. No relation to Jason."

The words sounded like she'd rehearsed them, not quite natural. And from Mrs. Habler's pursed lips and wrinkled brow, it looked like she felt the same.

What was Erica's secret?

And why hadn't he ever known his mother was a twin?

And wasn't it curious that, after all these years, there were twins in the farmhouse again?

When they returned to the farm, Erica's heart was both aching and full.

After dropping Jason, Erica and the twins in front of the farmhouse—along with the real Christmas tree they'd brought home—Papa insisted on taking the horses and sleigh to the barn himself, even though Erica saw the worried look on Jason's face.

"Is he going to be okay?" she asked as they hauled the twins' gear into the house in the midst of Mistletoe's excited barking.

Jason turned to watch his grandfather drive the sleigh into the barn. "He enjoyed the sleigh ride, but I think picking out a tree brought up too many memories. He'll spend a few hours in the barn, is my guess. That's his therapy."

"He's upset about Kimmie?"

"Yes. And on top of that, this is his first Christmas without my grandma."

Her face crinkled with sympathy. "How long were they married?"

"We had a fiftieth-anniversary party for them a couple of years ago," he said, thinking back. "So I think it was fifty-two years by the time she passed."

"Did Kimmie come?"

He barked out a disgusted-sounding laugh. "No."

Not wanting to get into any Kimmie-bashing, Erica changed the subject. "Could we do something to cheer him up?"

He looked thoughtful. "Gran always did a ton of decorating. I'd guess the stuff is up in the attic." He quirked his mouth. "I'm not very good at it. Neither is Papa. It's not a guy thing."

"Sexist," she scolded. "You don't need two X chromosomes to decorate."

"In this family you do. Will you... Would you mind helping me put up at least some of the decorations?" He sounded tentative, unsure of himself, and Erica could understand why. She wasn't sure if they had a truce or if he was still upset with her about the way she'd handled things with Kimmie.

But it was Christmastime, and an old man needed comfort. "Sure. I just need to put these guys down for a nap. Look at Mikey. He's about half-asleep already."

"I'll start bringing stuff down from the attic."

Erica carried the babies up the stairs, their large diaper bag slung across her shoulders. Man, she'd never realized how hard it was to single-parent twins.

Not that she'd give up a bit of it. They'd been so adorable wrapped up in their blankets in the sleigh, and everyone at church had made a fuss over them. One of the other mothers in the church, a woman named Sheila, had insisted on going to her truck and getting out a hand-me-down, Mikey-sized snowsuit right then and there. She'd promised to see if she could locate another spare one among her mom friends.

Erica saw, now, why Kimmie had sent her here. It was a beautiful community, aesthetically and heartwise, perfect for raising kids.

She'd love to stay. If only she wasn't terrified of having them taken from her by the man downstairs.

Kimmie had seemed to feel a mix of love and regret and anger toward her brother. Now that she'd met him, Erica could understand it better.

A free spirit, Kimmie had often been irresponsible, unwilling to do things by the book or follow rules. It was part of why she'd smoked cigarettes and done drugs and gotten in trouble with the police.

Jason seemed to be the exact opposite: responsible, concerned about his grandfather, an officer of the law.

Erica wished with all her heart that she could just reveal the truth to Jason and Papa. She hated this secrecy.

But she would hate even more for Jason to take the twins away from her. This last thing she could do for Kimmie, she'd do.

And it wasn't one-sided. Kimmie had actually done Erica a favor, offered her a huge blessing.

Erica rarely dated, didn't really understand the give-and-take of relationships. Certainly, her mother hadn't modeled anything healthy in that regard. So it was no big surprise that Erica wasn't attractive to men. She didn't want to be. She dressed purposefully in utilitarian clothes and didn't wear makeup. She just didn't trust men, not with her childhood. And men didn't like her, at least not romantically.

So the incredible gift that Kimmie had given her that she could never have gotten for herself was a family.

She put the twins down in their portable playpen, settling them on opposite sides, knowing they'd end up tangled together by the end of the nap. Mikey was out immediately, but Teddy needed some back rubbing and quiet talk before he relaxed into sleep.

Pretty soon, they'd need toddler beds. They'd need a lot of things. Including insurance and winter clothing and early intervention services for their developmental delays.

And just how was she going to manage that, when she didn't have a job, a savings account or a real right to parent the twins?

Teddy kicked and fussed a little, seeming to sense her tension. So she pushed aside her anxiety and prayed for peace and for the twins to be okay and for Papa to receive comfort.

And for Kimmie's soul.

When she got toward the bottom of the stairs, she paused. Jason was lying on the floor, pouring water into a green-and-red tree stand. Somehow, he'd gotten the tree they'd quickly chosen into the house by himself and set it upright, and it emitted a pungent, earthy scent that was worlds better than the pine room freshener her mother had sometimes sprayed around at Christmastime.

Jason had changed out of church clothes. He wore faded jeans and a sage-green T-shirt that clung to his impressive chest and arms.

Weight lifting was a part of being a cop, she supposed. And obviously, he'd excelled at it.

Her face heating at the direction of her own thoughts, she came the rest of the way down the stairs. "It smells so good! I never had a live tree before."

"Never?" He looked at her as if she must have been raised in a third world country. "What were your Christmases like?" He eased back from the tree and started opening boxes of decorations.

"Nothing like a TV Christmas movie, but who has that, really? Sometimes Mom would get me a present, and sometimes a Secret Santa or church program would leave something on our doorstep."

Jason looked at her with curiosity and something that might have been compassion, and she didn't want that kind of attention. "What about you? Did you and Kimmie and your parents come here for the holidays?"

"My parents loved to travel." He dug through a box and pulled out a set of green, heart-shaped ornaments. "See? From Ireland. They usually went on an overseas trip or a cruise at Christmas, and every year they brought back ornaments. We have 'em from every continent."

"Wow. Pretty." But it didn't sound very warm and family oriented. "Didn't they ever take you and Kimmie with them?"

"Nope. Dumped us here. But that was fine with us." He waved an arm around the high-ceilinged, sunlit room. "Imagine it all decorated, with a whole heap of presents under the tree. Snowball fights and gingerbread cookies and sleigh rides. For a kid, it couldn't get much better."

"For a grown-up, too," she murmured without thinking.

He nodded. "I'm glad to be here. For Papa and for me, too."

"Where are your parents now?"

"Dad passed about five years ago, and Mom's living on the French Riviera with her new husband. We exchange Christmas cards." He sounded blasé about it. But Erica knew how much emotion and hurt a blasé tone could cover.

They spent a couple of hours decorating the tree, spreading garland along the mantel and stringing lights. By the time Erica heard a cry from upstairs, indicating that the twins were waking up, they'd created a practically perfect farm-style Christmas environment.

"Do you need help with the babies?" Jason asked.

She would love to have help, but she knew she shouldn't start getting used to it. "It's fine. I'll get them."

"I'm going to check on Papa, then."

Erica's back was aching by the time she'd changed the twins' diapers and brought them downstairs, one on each hip. But the couple of hours they'd spent decorating were worth it. When Jason opened the door and Papa came in, his face lit up, even as his hands went to his hips. He shook his head. "You didn't have to do this. I wasn't..." He looked away and Erica realized he was choking up. "I wasn't going to put anything up this year. But seeing as how we have children in the house again..." He broke off.

Erica carried the twins into the front room. "Let's see how they like all the lights," she said, and both men seemed glad to have another focus than the losses they were facing.

She sat on the couch and put Mikey on the floor, then Teddy. She waved her hand toward the tree. "Pretty!" she said, and then her own throat tightened, remembering the silver foil tree she'd put up in Kimmie's apartment. They'd taken a lot of photographs in front of it, Kimmie in her wheelchair holding the twins. Erica had promised to show the twins when they were older, so they'd know how much their mother had loved them.

The boys' brown eyes grew round as they surveyed the sparkling lights and ornaments.

"Priiiiiy," Mikey said, cocking his head to one side.

Erica had no time to get excited about Mikey learning another new word because Teddy started to scoot toward the tree, then rocked forward into an awkward crawl.

"Whoa, little man," Jason said, intercepting him before he could reach the shining ornaments.

"Better put the ornaments higher up and anchor the tree to the wall," Papa said. "It's what we used to do for you and your sister. You were a terrible one for pulling things off the tree. One year, you even managed to climb it!"

Jason picked up Teddy and plunked him back down on the floor beside Mikey, but not before Erica had seen the red spots on the baby's knees. "I need to get them some long pants," she fretted. "Sturdy ones, if he's going to be mobile."

"Can you afford it?" Jason asked.

Erica thought of the stash of money Kimmie had given her. She'd spent more than half of it on the cross-country drive; even being as frugal as possible in terms of motels and meals, diapers didn't come cheap. "I can afford some."

Questions lurked in his eyes, but he didn't give them voice.

Teddy rocked back and forth and got himself on hands and knees again, then crawled—backward—toward Mistletoe, who lay by the gas fire. Quickly, Jason positioned himself to block the baby if needed.

Mistletoe nuzzled Teddy, then gave his face a couple of licks.

Teddy laughed and waved his arms.

"Not very sanitary," Papa commented.

"Oh, well," Erica and Jason said at the same time.

From the kitchen came a buzzing sound and Erica realized it was her phone. She went in and grabbed it. An Arizona number. She walked back into the front room's doorway and clicked to accept the call.

"Hello," came an unfamiliar voice. "Erica Lindholm?"

"That's me."

"This is Ryan Finnigan. An old friend of Kimmie Stephanidis. Do you have a moment to talk?"

She looked at the twins. "Can you watch the boys?" she asked the two men.

Jason looked a little daunted, but Papa nodded and waved a hand. "Go ahead. We'll be fine."

She headed through the kitchen to the dining room. "I'm here."

"I'm not only an old friend, but I'm Miss Stephanidis's attorney," the man said.

"Kimmie had an attorney?" Kimmie had barely been organized enough to buy groceries.

"Not exactly. The medical personnel who brought her to the hospital, after her overdose, happened to find one of my business cards and gave me a call. I went to see her, and we made a will right there in the hospital. None too soon, I'm afraid."

She was glad to know that Kimmie had had a friend near and that she'd been under medical care, and said so.

"I did what I could. I was...rather fond of her, at one time." He cleared his throat. "She let me know her wishes, and I was able to carry those out. But as for her estate...she's left you her half of the Holly Creek Farm."

"What?" Erica's voice rose up into a squeak and she felt for the nearest chair and sat down.

"She's left you half the farm her family owns. It's a small, working farm in Western Pennsylvania. The other half belongs to her brother."

"Half of Holly Creek Farm? And it's, like, legal?"

"It certainly is."

She sat a moment, trying to digest this news.

"I'm sure it's a lot to take in," the lawyer said after a moment. "Do you have any questions for me, off the top of your head?"

"Did Kimmie…" She trailed off, peeked through the kitchen into the front room to make sure no one could hear. "Look, is this confidential?"

"Absolutely."

"Did she leave any instructions about her children?"

"Her *children*?"

"I take it that's a no." *Oh, Kimmie, why would you provide for them with the farm, but not grant me guardianship?*

"If Kimmie did have children…the most important thing would be that they're safe, in an acceptable home."

"Right. That's right." She didn't want to admit to anything, but if he'd been fond of Kimmie at one time, as he'd mentioned, he would obviously be concerned.

He cleared his throat. "Just speaking hypothetically, if Kimmie had children and died without leaving any written instructions, they would become wards of the state."

Erica's heart sank.

"Unless…is there a father in the picture?"

"No," she said through an impossibly dry mouth. Kimmie had told her that after abandoning her and the twins, the babies' father had gone to prison with a life sentence, some drug-related theft gone bad.

"If there's no evidence that someone like you— hypothetically—had permission to take her children, no birth certificates, nothing, then any concerned party could make a phone call to Children and Youth Services."

"And they'd take the children?" She could hear the breathy fear in her voice.

"They might."

"But…this is hypothetical. You wouldn't—"

"Purely hypothetical. I'm not calling anyone. Now, even if the state has legal custody, if you have physical custody—and the children in question are doing well in your care—then the courts might decide it's in the best interest of the children for you to retain physical custody."

"I see." *It's not enough.*

"None of this might come up for a while, not until medical attention is needed or the children start school."

Or early intervention. Erica's heart sank even as she berated herself for not thinking it all through. "If it did come up…would there be some kind of hearing?"

"Yes, and at that time, any relative who had questions or concerns could raise them." He paused. "It seems Kimmie had very few personal effects, but whatever there is will be sent to her family as soon as possible."

Her hands were so sweaty she could barely keep a grip on the cell phone. "Thank you. This has been very helpful."

"Oh, one more thing," the lawyer said. "You'll be wanting to know the executor of Kimmie's will."

"It's not you?"

"No. I'm happy to help, of course, but if there's a capable family member, I usually recommend that individual."

Erica had a sinking feeling she knew where this was going. "Who is it?"

"It's her brother. Jason Stephanidis."

Three

The next morning, Jason padded down the stairs toward the warmth of coffee and the kitchen. Noticing a movement in the front room, he stopped to look in.

There was his grandfather, in his everyday flannel shirt and jeans, staring out the window while holding a ceramic angel they'd set on the mantel yesterday. As Jason watched, Papa set it down and moved over to a framed Christmas photo of Jason and Kimmie as young kids, visiting Santa. Papa looked at it, ran a finger over it, shook his head.

Jason's chest felt heavy, knowing there was precious little he could do to relieve his grandfather's suffering.

But whatever he could do, he would. He'd been a negligent grandson, but no more.

Mistletoe leaned against his leg and panted up at him.

He gave the dog a quick head rub and then walked into the room just as Papa set down the photograph he'd been studying and turned. His face lit up. "Just the man I want to see. Come get some coffee. Got an idea to run by you."

"Yeah?" Jason slung an arm around his grandfather's shoulders as they walked into the kitchen. He poured them both a fresh cup of coffee, black. "What've you got in mind?"

Papa pulled a chair up to the old wooden table and sat down. "Got someone coming over to do a little investigating about our guests."

"You, too?" Jason was relieved that he wasn't the only one who felt suspicious. In a corner of his mind, he'd worried that it was as Renea had said: he couldn't trust, couldn't be a family person. "I can't figure out why Kimmie left the farm to her. What were they to each other?" As executor of the estate, he needed to know.

The mere thought of there being an estate—of Kimmie being gone—racked his chest with a sudden ache so strong he had to sit down at the table to keep from falling apart.

"I'm thinking about those babies, for one thing," Papa said unexpectedly.

"What about them?"

"Something's not right about them, but I don't know what it is. So I've got Ruthie Delacroix coming over this morning. There's nobody knows as much about babies as Ruthie."

Jason remembered the woman, vaguely, from visits home; she'd always had a child on her hip at church, and he seemed to recall she ran a child care operation on the edge of town.

"And that's not all I'm wondering," Papa said darkly, "but first things first."

Jason grinned. Papa conniving and plotting was better than Papa grieving.

"I figure I have to take the lead on this, since you haven't shown a whole lot of sense about women. When you brought home that skinny thing—what was her

name? Renea?—and said you were going to marry her,
your grandmother had a fit."

Jason wasn't going to rise to that bait. And he wasn't
going to think about Renea. He got up and started wiping down the already-clean counters.

No sooner had his grandfather headed upstairs to his
bedroom than Jason heard the sound of babies babbling
and laughing, matched by Erica's melodic, soothing
voice. A moment later, she appeared, a baby in each arm.

Even without a trace of makeup, her fair skin seemed
to glow. Her hair wasn't styled, but clipped back, with
strands already escaping.

His heart rate picked up just looking at her.

As she nuzzled one of the baby's heads—was that
Mikey or Teddy?—he was drawn into her force field.
"Want me to hold one of them?"

And where did *that* come from? He never, but never,
offered to hold a baby.

"Um…sure!" She nodded toward the wigglier baby.
"Take Teddy. But keep a grip on him. He's a handful. I
just need to get them some breakfast." As she spoke, she
strapped Mikey into the old wooden high chair.

Jason sat down and held the baby on his knee, studying
him, wondering what Papa saw that made him worry. But
the kid looked healthy and lively to him as he waved his
arms and banged the table, trying to get Erica's attention.

Which seemed perfectly sensible to Jason. Even in
old jeans and a loose blue sweater, Erica was a knockout. Any male would want her attention.

Nostalgia pierced him. Erica moved around the room
easily, already comfortable, starting to know where
things were. It made him think of his grandfather sitting at this very table after a long day of farmwork, his

grandmother bustling around fixing food, declining all offers of help in the kingdom that was her kitchen.

Papa was grieving the loss of his wife now, but his life had been immeasurably enriched by his family. In fact, it was impossible to think of Papa without thinking of all those who loved him. And when Jason and Kimmie had needed some extra parenting, Papa and Gran had opened their arms without a second thought. They'd been the making of Jason's childhood.

Unfortunately, Kimmie had seen more neglect before Papa and Gran had stepped in. She'd never quite recovered from their parents' lack of real love.

"Would you like some oatmeal?" Erica asked a few minutes later, already dishing up four bowls, two big and two small. "I'm sorry, I should've asked rather than assuming. The twins love oatmeal, and so do I, and it's about the most economical breakfast you can find."

"That would be great." He shifted Teddy on his knee. "Put his down here and I'll try to feed him. No guarantees, though."

"You don't have to do that."

"It's no problem. You had the care of them all night. At least you ought to get a minute to eat a bowl of oatmeal yourself."

"That would be a treat." She placed a small bowl beside his larger one and handed him a bib and a spoon. "Go to it."

Trying to get spoonfuls of oatmeal into a curious baby proved a challenge, and as Erica expertly scooped the cereal into Mikey's mouth, she laughed at Jason's attempts. How she managed two, as a single mom, he couldn't fathom.

"Hey now," he said when Teddy blew a raspberry that

spattered oatmeal all over himself, the high chair and Jason. "Give me a break. I don't know what I'm doing here."

"Teddy! Behave yourself!" A smile tugged at Erica's face as she passed Jason a cloth. "When he spits like that, he's probably done. Just wipe his face and we'll let them crawl around a little."

Mistletoe had been weaving between their legs, licking up the bits of oatmeal and banana that hit the floor. Jason reached down to pat the dog at the same moment Erica did.

Their hands brushed—and Jason felt it to his core. "Nothing like a canine vacuum cleaner," he tried to joke. And kept his hand on the dog, hoping for another moment of contact with Erica.

"I know, right? We totally should have gotten them a dog back in Arizona."

And then her hand went still. When he looked up at her face, it had gone still, too.

"Who?" Jason asked. "You and their dad?"

"*I* should have gotten them a dog," she said, not looking at him. "I meant, *I* should have."

The detective in him stored away that remark as relevant. And it was a good reminder, he reflected as they both scarfed down the rest of their breakfast without more talk. He couldn't trust Erica, didn't know what she had been to Kimmie. Getting domestic with her would only cloud his judgment. More than likely, she'd been a bad influence, dragging Kimmie down.

Beyond that likelihood, he needed to remember that he was no good at family relationships. He was here, in part, to see if he could reset his values, and he'd vowed to himself that he wouldn't even try to start anything with a woman until he'd improved significantly in that regard. It wasn't fair to either him or the woman.

Just moments later, as Jason finished up the breakfast dishes, there was a pounding on the door. Mistletoe ran toward it, barking, as Papa came out of his room and trotted down the stairs to the entryway. Jason heard the door open and then his grandfather's hearty greeting.

Immediately, the noise level jumped up a notch. "Hey there, Andy! What's this I hear about babies in the place?"

An accompanying wail revealed that she'd brought at least one baby with her. Probably her grandson, whom she seemed to bring everywhere.

Jason walked into the front room, where Erica was sitting on the floor with the twins. "Ruth Delacroix," he said in answer to Erica's questioning expression. "She's a force of nature. Prepare yourself."

"Good morning, everyone!" Ruth cried as she came in, giving Jason a big hug and kiss around the baby she held on one hip. Then she spun toward Erica. "And you must be Erica. Andy was telling me about you, that you're here for a visit with some... Oh my, aren't they adorable!"

"Let's sit down," Papa suggested, "and Jason will bring us all out some coffee. Isn't that right?"

"Sure." Jason didn't mind playing host. He was glad to see his grandfather seeming a little peppier.

When he carried a tray with coffee cups, sugar and milk into the front room, the three babies were all on the floor, and Ruth and Erica were there with them. The pine scent from the Christmas tree was strong, and the sun sparkled bright through the windows, making the ornaments glisten. Papa had turned on the radio and Christmas music poured out.

"Mason! Stop that!" Ruth scrambled after her toddling grandbaby with more agility than Jason could muster up, most days, even though Ruth had to have thirty years on him. "He's a handful, ever since he started to walk."

Teddy, not to be outdone, started scooting toward the shiny tree, and Mikey observed with round eyes, legs straight out in front of him.

"Like I said," Ruth continued, "I'm down a kid, so I'd be glad to watch these little sweethearts anytime you need. A couple of my regular clients are off this week and kept their little ones at home."

"Thanks." Erica was dangling a toy in front of Mikey, who reached for it. "I'm not sure quite what I'll be doing, but knowing there's someone who could look after the twins for a few hours is wonderful. I really appreciate you thinking of it," she added to Papa Andy.

"No problem, sweetheart." Papa took a small ornament off the tree and held it out to Jason. "Remember this?"

"The lump!" Jason laughed at the misshapen clay blob. "Haven't seen that in years. That's my master-piece, right?"

"You were pretty proud of it. Insisted on hanging it in a place of honor every Christmas, at least until you turned into an embarrassed teenager. And so here it is right now."

Jason smiled as Papa reminisced, egged on by Ruth and Erica. This was important, and Jason was starting to realize it was what he wanted for himself. Traditions and family, carried on from generation to generation. Just because his own parents hadn't done a good job of making a true home for him and Kimmie, that didn't mean he had to follow their patterns. He wanted to be more like Papa.

He had some work to do on himself first.

While he reflected, he'd been absently watching Erica—she was easy on the eyes, for sure—so he noticed when her expression got guarded and he tuned back into the conversation.

"What are they, seven, eight months?" Ruth was saying. "They're big boys."

"They're fifteen months," Erica said.

"Oh." Ruth frowned, and then her face cleared. "Well, Mason, here, he's real advanced. Started walking at ten months."

"They have some delays." Erica picked up Mikey and held him high, then down, high, then down, jumping him until he chortled.

Teddy did his strange little scoot crawl in their direction. Jason noticed then that Ruth's grandson was indeed a lot more mobile than the twins, a real pro at pushing himself to his feet and toddling around.

"Why are they delayed?" Ruth asked. "Problems at birth?"

"You might say that." Erica swooped Mikey down in front of his brother, and the two laughed.

Teddy pointed at the tree. "Da-da-da-DA-da-da," he said, leaning forward to look at Mikey.

"Da-da-da-da-da!" Mikey waved a hand as if to agree with what his twin brother had said.

Teddy burst out with a short laugh, and that made Mikey laugh, too.

"Now, isn't that cute. Twin talk." Ruth went off into a story about some twins she'd known who had communicated together in a mysterious language all through elementary school.

As the women got deeper into conversation about babies, Papa gestured Jason into the kitchen. He pulled a baggie from a box and started spooning baking soda into it.

"What are you doing?"

"You'll see." He tossed the baggie onto the counter and then pulled out a couple of syringes. He grabbed a spoon from the silverware drawer.

Jason stared. "Where'd you get that stuff and what are you doing with it?"

"From your narco kit, and it's just a little test. You'll see."

"But you can't... That's not—"

"Come on, hide in the pantry!" Papa shoved Jason toward the small room just off the kitchen. "Hey, Erica, where did you put those baby snack puffs?" he called into the front room.

There was a little murmuring between the two women as Papa hastily stepped into the pantry and edged around Jason. "Watch for anything suspicious," he ordered.

Helpless to stop the plan Papa had set into motion, Jason watched as Erica came into the kitchen, opened a cupboard and pulled out some kind of baby treats. Behind her, Mistletoe sat, held up a paw and cocked his head.

Erica laughed down at him. "It's not treats for you, silly. It's for the babies." She squatted, petted the dog and then stood and reached toward the jar of dog treats on the counter. "All right, beggar, I'll get you just one..."

She froze. Stared at the pseudo drug supplies. Looked around the kitchen.

Then she leaned back against the counter, hand pressed against her mouth, eyes closed.

She drew in a breath, let it out in a big sigh and picked up the baggie between two fingers as if it were going to jump up and bite her. "Papa Andy," she called. "Could you come in here a minute?"

Papa nudged his way around Jason and went into the kitchen.

"I found this." Erica held up the bag. "What's going on here?"

Papa frowned, turned back toward the pantry and spoke to Jason. "She knows what it is. That's a bad sign."

Jason sighed and came out into the kitchen. "Actually, most people know what that is. If she were using, she'd have hidden the stuff, not called you in to look at it."

Erica stared at Papa, then slowly turned to Jason. There was an expression of betrayal on her face. "You guys were testing me?"

"Yes, ma'am," Papa said. "And if the expert here is right, you passed with flying colors."

"You thought I was a drug addict?" She looked from one to the other, then flung the bag onto the counter. "And so you set this up to test me, instead of asking me outright."

Jason waded in to defend his grandfather. "Papa just had to be sure. No addict would answer a question about being on drugs honestly, right?"

She rolled her eyes and crossed her arms, holding her elbows.

"And you know Kimmie well, obviously," he stumbled on. "She's struggled with addiction for years, as I'm sure you know, and it would make a lot of sense if you'd had a problem, too. But I've watched how addicts respond to drugs, and I can tell you're clean."

She straightened, her jaw set. "Yes, I am," she said, and stalked back into the front room.

Leaving Papa to look at Jason. "Guess that wasn't such

a good idea," he said. He turned and followed Erica back into the front room.

And Jason just leaned back against the counter, disgusted with himself. He should have somehow stopped that from happening. Now they'd not only hurt her but lost her trust.

A few minutes later, Erica came back into the kitchen and glared at Jason, then at Papa, who'd followed after her. "I don't appreciate that you tried to trick me. That you thought I was an addict." From all the free therapists she'd seen in the course of living with her mother, she knew she ought to say next: when you mistrust me, I feel hurt.

She *did* feel hurt. But she didn't trust them any more than they trusted her, and especially not with her feelings.

What could you expect from men, anyway?

The thing was, Jason had been so nice to her and the twins. It had seemed like they were getting to know each other, that they might become friends. And Papa Andy... He'd seemed so warm, so welcoming.

In reality, they'd been conspiring against her, plotting.

"I'm sorry. It was a bad idea and we shouldn't have done it." Jason crossed his arms and looked at the floor.

"We trust you *now*, honey," Papa Andy said.

"Hey, what's going on out there?" Ruth's merry voice broke in. "I could use a hand here!"

The men turned toward the front room.

As Erica followed, years of feeling unworthy came back to her, an emotional tsunami she always tried to tamp down when it arose. But it refused to stay in its usual closed mental container.

She'd always been known as the addict's kid. Never

any pretty clothes or new toys. Regular stints of home-lessness, of trying to stay clean by way of public rest-room sinks. The dread of Mom getting arrested, which meant another few months in a foster home.

Always moving somewhere unfamiliar, always the new girl in school. People didn't like her, didn't trust her, didn't want to be with her.

"Ma-ma." Mikey batted her ankle and reached up his arms.

Automatically she picked him up and cuddled him close, and the sensation of a warm baby in her arms grounded her. She couldn't give in to that old, familiar sense of worthlessness.

But she also couldn't stay in an environment where she was being tricked and treated badly. That was toxic.

"Hey, Ruth," she said to the older woman, who was sitting on the couch beside Papa, trying to encourage Teddy to pull up and cruise along it. "You said you could babysit for me. How about giving me an hour right now?"

"You're going somewhere?"

"That's right. I can pay you your usual hourly rate, whatever's fair." Her cache of money was going down at an alarming rate, and she had to deal with that. But first things first.

"Why, sure, honey. I don't have anyplace I have to be until later in the afternoon."

"And if she has to go, I'll look after the little guys." Papa's voice was soft.

Erica spun toward Jason, who still stood in the door-way between the front room and the kitchen. "Could you show me the cabin?"

"What?"

She walked over to stand in front of him, out of earshot of the elders, feeling stiff as a robot. "The cabin on this property. Where Kimmie originally told me to go. I'd like to see about fixing that up."

"You don't want to do that, Erica. It's cold. It's a mess—"

"I can go alone if you don't want to take me." She turned toward Papa. "Could you give me directions to—"

"I'll take you!" Jason interrupted.

After she'd made sure Ruth had what she needed for the twins, after Jason had insisted on outfitting her in boots, gloves and a warm hat, she followed him outside.

He looked back as if he wanted to say something, but she glared at him and he faced ahead and beckoned for her to follow.

The walking was easy when they started out toward the barn. A trail was broken like a gully, with two-foot-deep snow on either side.

The brisk air stung her eyes and nose. Sunshine glinted on the surrounding snow, and trees extended lacy branches into the bright blue sky. Low chirps and chatters sounded from a row of evergreens, and as Jason turned from the path into fresh snow, a bright red cardinal landed on a fence post beside them, chirping a *too-eee, too-eee*.

Jason moved steadily and methodically in front of her, breaking trail. Despite his doing most of the work, she stumbled and struggled her way and was soon plenty warm, panting in the chilly air.

Impossible to maintain anger in God's beautiful world. Her emotions settled into a resigned awareness: something about her, probably an attitude or set of mannerisms she didn't even know she had, made people suspicious of her. If it hadn't changed by now, it wasn't going to. And if she was going to be alone, raising the babies, she needed to find a safe, healthy place for them to grow and thrive. And she needed to be away from painful encounters like what had happened this morning. She had to take care of herself so she could take care of the twins.

Her foot caught in an icy lump of snow and she stumbled and pitched forward on one knee. She caught herself with her hands, didn't sprawl full facedown, but snow pushed up the wrists of her jacket and sent its chill through her thin jeans.

"We're almost—" Jason turned, saw that she'd fallen and made his way back to her. "What happened? Here, give me your hand."

It would be silly to refuse. She grasped his glove-clad hand and he pulled her upright easily, brushing snow from her arms and then retrieving her hat.

"You okay? Anything hurt?"

"Fine," she said, her breath coming out fast.

"You're sure?" He was looking into her eyes. Very direct. Very intense.

She turned away and nodded. "I'm fine. Snow's soft."

"We're almost there," he said.

After a few more minutes slogging through the snow, Jason gestured ahead. "There it is, in all its glory."

Erica looked to see a weathered log cabin, small, with a steep, slanting roof and a front porch topped by a snow-covered wooden awning. One of the small front windows was boarded up, and the other needed to be, its glass clearly broken.

Behind the cabin and on one side, pine trees, their branches heavy with snow, gave the area a deep quiet and privacy.

"You still want to see inside? It's pretty run-down."

"Yeah," she said, breaking off into fresh snow to check

out the sides of the cabin. It *was* run-down, but with work it could be cute.

For just a moment she flashed back on years of living in crowded, dirty cities. She'd always dreamed of a country getaway, a place that was safe, with privacy and no one to bother her. A place of her own—not just an apartment but a whole little house.

"Let me go in first." Jason tested the strength of the front porch boards before unlocking the door and going in.

Not much point locking it when someone had broken the windows out, but whatever.

"Come on in. It's just us and the chipmunks."

If he thought a few critters would scare her, he was sadly mistaken. She stepped over a broken stair and into the cabin's single room.

She'd feared it would be dark and gloomy, but it was bright, with side windows larger than those in front. A ladder led up to what must be a loft bedroom. The wood-plank walls looked sturdy, and a sink and stove lined one wall. No refrigerator, but that was easily obtained, and in the meantime, a gallon of milk would keep just fine in the snow.

A concrete floor showed through linoleum torn in one corner. That would have to be repaired, but for now, a thick rug would cover the ugliness. She walked to the back of the cabin and opened a door, discovering a storage area and bathroom.

She gave Jason a brisk nod. "It'll do. What would be the steps to getting the heat going? And I assume that once we turn on the water, the plumbing is okay?"

"Erica, you can't live like this. It's primitive and it's filthy." As if to punctuate his words, a small mouse raced across the floor, and he gestured toward it and looked at her.

"I grew up with an addict. I've lived in much dirtier places, with rats *and* scorpions." She tested the ladder, found it secure and started up to peek at the loft bedroom.

"Besides which, there's no heat per se—there's a wood-burning fireplace. Do you know anything at all about keeping that going so you and the kids won't freeze to death?"

"I'm a fast learner."

"You're not going to find someone to clean it during the holidays."

"I can clean it myself," she called down to him. The loft was even dirtier, if that was possible, littered with beer cans and newspapers and something that looked like a dead bird. Ugh.

Against one wall was a stained mattress that smelled bad even in the cold. Kids or hunters—or vagrants—must have taken refuge here.

For just a moment her courage failed as she relived dozens of dirty sleeping rooms she'd stayed in as a kid. Was she going backward in her life? Was filth and desolation her destiny?

She clenched her jaw. She was going to get rid of that mattress and clean this place to a shine. The twins wouldn't grow up as she had. She'd make sure the lock was sturdy and that the window got fixed. As a kid, she hadn't had a choice, but now she did. She would do better for her boys.

She climbed down the ladder. Now that she wasn't moving, she was getting cold, and she noticed Jason stamping his feet. Their breath made steam clouds in the cabin air, which she would've thought was cool if she'd been in a better mood.

"Look, Erica, I'm sorry. I was a jerk. I should have realized you weren't one to do drugs."

"I've never used in my life," she told him. "You don't make the same mistakes your parents made, though you might make different ones."

"You could be right about that." He rubbed his hands together. "But look, I'm sorry I was deceptive. That wasn't right."

His choice of words brought her to attention. Yes, Jason had been deceptive and it had made her angry. But his deception paled in comparison with the one she was trying to pull off, the fact that the twins were Kimmie's.

Certainly, her own deception was bigger. But she didn't know what he'd done to make Kimmie so mistrustful, only that he was rigid and judgmental, seeing everything in black-and-white. A perfectionist with a mean streak.

Not a person to raise kids.

Moreover, if Jason were sneaky and suspicious enough to attempt to trap her into revealing an addiction, he'd certainly be able to discover the truth about the twins, once his suspicions started to move in that direction.

And that couldn't happen, because he'd take the twins away. Kimmie hadn't wanted that. She'd wanted Erica to raise them.

Erica wanted that, too. They belonged to her and she loved them. In her heart, which was what mattered, she was their mother.

All the more reason to move out of Jason and Papa's house immediately.

"I can start cleaning the place tomorrow," she said,

"and if you'll give me the information, I can make calls about the water and heat today. The twins and I can move in within a few days."

"You can't live here!" Jason lifted his hands, obviously exasperated. "How are you going to manage the twins when there's a ladder to get to the bedroom? Are you going to leave one up there while you carry the other down? There's no railing. It's dangerous."

"I can make it work," she said, feeling uneasy. He did have a point.

"And there's water, sure, but no washing machine or dryer." He shook his head. "It's the kind of place someone totally down-and-out would live in, not a mother and kids. In fact, no doubt we'd have some drug squatters here if Papa didn't keep such a close eye on it."

His objections were valid, but... "I'm sure we can figure out something."

"You run the risk of Children and Youth stepping in. These are bad conditions."

And you'd like nothing better. You'd probably call them on me yourself.

"Look, the property is half yours, once the will goes through probate. If it's because you're angry at me, I can stay out here and you stay in the house." He frowned. "I'd only ask that you let Papa stay in the house with you. He shouldn't be climbing the ladder."

"Of course!" She'd never kick an old man out of his home. "No, you and your grandfather need to stay at the big house. I'm the interloper. I'll move out here."

He shook his head. "No, Erica. Listen, I...I'm rotten at friends and family. Anyone will tell you. I apologize for treating you badly. It's nothing about you. It's me."

He looked forlorn and bitter all at the same time. She steeled herself against the temptation to feel sorry for him.

"I really don't think you can get the place cleaned up yourself, but if you want to try, I'll help you."

Now, *that* would be a disaster. Working closely with the man who'd tricked her, but whom she still, to her chagrin, found attractive. The man she was starting to feel sorry for, at least a little. The man who looked so good in his lumberjack flannel and boots.

"I should get back to the twins," she said. And she needed to figure out whether living in the cabin was really viable. And most of all, she needed to figure out how to keep Jason and his grandfather at a distance—both so they didn't hurt her anymore, and so they didn't figure out the truth.

Four

By the time they got back to the main house, clouds had covered over the midday sun. And Jason had a feeling that, once they went inside, any chance of a private conversation would be avoided or lost.

The need to know about his sister's last days and why she'd bequeathed half the farm to Erica overpowered his politeness. If he was going to be a jerk, he'd really be a jerk. "We need to find a time to talk about Kimmie."

"You don't quit, do you?" She skirted him to walk ahead in the snow.

All of a sudden she stopped, looking toward the house.

Since the skies had darkened, the front room was illuminated like a theater. Papa stood there alone, holding some small object in his hand. As they watched, he put it down and picked up something else.

"What's he doing?" she asked.

"Those are my grandmother's crèches," he said, and the lump in his own throat wouldn't let him say any more.

What would it be like to have a relationship as close as his grandparents' had been?

He opened the front door, and Mistletoe barked excitedly. Between the dog and the noise Jason made taking off his boots and helping Erica with her coat, he hoped Papa had the chance to pull himself together.

But when Papa came to the doorway of the front room, he had to clear his throat and blow his nose. "The twins are upstairs napping," he said, his voice a little rough. "Ruth fed 'em some lunch and put them down, and she says they're out like lights. She had to take off."

Erica touched Papa's arm. "I'm curious about your decorations," she said. "After I check on the twins, will you show them to me?"

Maybe it was cowardly, but Jason couldn't cope with looking through the family treasures and dredging up a bunch of memories. "I'll make lunch," he said.

In the kitchen, he soon had tomato soup heating and cheese sandwiches grilling in plenty of butter. Comfort food. Even if he wasn't good at sharing feelings with his grandfather, he was a decent short-order cook.

He started to check and see what everyone wanted to drink, but stopped on the threshold of the front room.

Papa was pointing to the star atop the tree, one of Gran's prize possessions, and pulling out his bandanna to wipe his eyes.

And rather than backing away, Erica put an arm around him. "Do you have any photos of her?"

Was she crazy? Or was she trying to butter Papa up, to get something out of him the way she'd gotten something out of Kimmie?

Papa nodded, his face lighting up. "Would you like to see our family albums?"

Jason beat a hasty retreat. If Erica could get outside of herself enough to comfort an old man to whom she owed nothing, then he was impressed. But was anyone really that nice? Most likely, she had some selfish motive. Most people did.

Once he had the plates on the table, he couldn't delay any longer. Still, when he walked into the front room to see Erica and Papa sitting on the couch side by side, the gray head and the red one bent over an old photo album, he had to swallow hard to get his voice into cheerful mode. "Lunch is ready," he said with only a little hitch.

Funny, the twins didn't have red hair. They must take after their father. Erica hadn't mentioned one word about the man, and from her reaction to being asked about Kimmie, she probably wouldn't welcome Jason opening the discussion.

As they ate their lunch, Erica kept the conversation going with questions about Gran, which led to talk of Jason's and Kimmie's childhoods.

"Our daughter was a bust as a mother," Papa admitted, his spoonful of tomato soup halfway to his mouth. "She had her reasons. I'm glad we could step in."

"I heard about that, some," Erica said. "Kimmie spent a lot of time talking about her mom."

She did? Jason got up, ostensibly to get some extra napkins, but really to cover his own surprise. How much had Kimmie told Erica? What else did she know? If Kimmie had aired their mother's dirty laundry, it spoke to Erica's ability to get close to people and find out their secrets.

Papa obviously didn't have the same suspicions. "I just wish..." he said, and then broke off.

"What do you wish?" Erica asked.

"I just wish it had worked out better for Kimmie." He put down his spoon and shook his head, staring off out the window.

Enough of taking Papa down their family's unhappy memory lane. It was time to learn something about Erica. "You said your mom had issues, too. Did you have grandparents to step into the gap for your mother?"

"Estranged," she said. "So Christmas can be sort of sad for me, too." She looked from Jason back to Papa. "Did you know there's a movement called Blue Christmas for people who are mourning at Christmastime?"

"What won't they think of next?" Papa waved a dismissive hand. "People are oversensitive these days."

"Or maybe more in touch with their feelings?" She softened her disagreement with a smile. "I think it's a good idea. Pretending you're having a Currier and Ives Christmas when you're not can make you even more depressed."

Papa chuckled. "Got your own opinions, do you?" He took a big bite of grilled cheese.

"Yes, and sometimes I'm even right."

As they talked on, Jason took note of the fact that Erica had neatly evaded his effort to probe into her background. He tucked that bit of knowledge away.

Against his will, though, he got caught up in Erica's description of the special church services they'd had back in Arizona for people who had a hard time dealing with the holidays. He wanted, in the worst way, to ask whether Kimmie had attended any such services. Had his sister been sad, missed the family during the holidays? Had she maintained the strong values she'd had as a younger woman, the faith they'd shared with Papa and Gran?

Guilt washed over him. Why had he let Kimmie become alienated from the rest of the family? Why hadn't he tried harder to find her and mend their differences?

He studied the woman talking with animation to Papa.

No, she hadn't been Kimmie's drug friend. And yes, he was starting to care for her more and more.

But he still had questions. Okay, Erica had been lonely, had needed a surrogate sister in light of her own mother's absence. But what had Erica done for Kimmie in return that she'd gone so far as to leave her half the farm?

Later that afternoon, Erica got the twins strapped into their car seats and tried to back out of the space her little car had occupied since they'd arrived at Holly Creek Farm three days ago.

In the icy tracks, her wheels spun.

After a couple more attempts, she stopped and looked up "how to drive in snow" on her phone.

Go forward and back, get traction. She could do that. She put the car into Drive.

The wheels spun.

She clenched her jaw. She didn't even really want to attend the charitable clothing giveaway, but when she'd seen the flyer, she'd forced herself to copy the information in her planner, because the twins needed warm clothes. Now, to have this kind of obstacle getting there... She switched into Reverse and floored it.

The wheels made a loud spinning noise.

The car didn't move.

Teddy started to cry.

Why would anyone want to live in this snowy, obstinate state, when the blue skies and warm air and green palms of Arizona were just a few days' drive away?

A knock on her window made her jump. Jason. Great. She put the car into Park and lowered the window.

"Having problems?"

She clenched her jaw. "Obviously."

"Where are you headed?"

"I'm going to town," she said over Teddy's wails, "if I can get unstuck."

He squatted and studied her front tire, then stood. "Tires are almost bald," he said, "and this is a lightweight car. Why don't you let me drive you in my truck?"

"No!" The refusal was reflexive, automatic. Help usually came with strings. That, she'd learned at her mother's knee.

"I was planning to go in anyway. Give me five minutes to grab my things and pull the truck around."

"I don't need any help." Even though the evidence was blatantly to the contrary.

"My truck has a back seat. It's going to be a lot safer for the twins."

The one convincing argument. "Fine," she said, and then realized she sounded completely rude and ungrateful. "I mean, thank you. I would appreciate that."

Five minutes later, as they drove down a snowy, twisty, evergreen-lined road, she looked over at him. "Thank you for doing this. You're right. It wouldn't have been safe in my car."

Which meant she needed to get a new car, or new tires at least. Add that to the lengthening shopping list in her head.

"No problem. Where are we headed?"

"The church." Heat rose in her face, but she forced herself to continue, staring straight ahead. "They're having a clothing giveaway."

"Oh." He steered around a sharp curve and then asked, "So money's a problem right now?"

"Yeah."

"What were you doing for work, prior to coming here?"

Her stomach tightened. Not because of the probing—he'd earned that right, driving her to town—but because of what he might find out.

She hated lying, always had. But she didn't want to put the detective in Jason on high alert, and she couldn't dodge the feeling that any talk of the past might do that. "I worked as an aide in a nursing home." Which was true. "And I was taking classes at the community college."

"Studying what?" If he'd sounded skeptical, she would have cut him off, but he actually sounded interested, like he believed her.

"Human Services. It could lead to Social Work or Early Childhood Education, if I went on for a bachelor's degree." She looked at him quickly. A few acquaintances had laughed about someone of her background going to college. If Jason did...

"Makes sense. What all had you taken?"

Relieved, she shrugged. "College Writing. Intro to Psychology. I was actually in a class called Introduction to Gerontology when...when Kimmie got sick." She clenched her teeth. *Stop talking.*

"No wonder you get along well with Papa."

Good, he was going to let the past—*her* past—go. "I like old people," she said. "Old people and kids." She opened her mouth to say that it was the people in the middle who caused most of the problems in the world, but she snapped it shut again. The less information she volunteered, the better.

"So you were out of a home and you went to stay with Kimmie?" he asked abruptly. "Did she take care of your kids while you worked?" An undertone of censure ran beneath his words.

"It wasn't like that." She crossed her arms over her chest. *Think, think.*

"What *was* it like?"

She had to give him some information, the bare bones at least, or he'd never leave her alone. "She was too sick to care for herself. I left my apartment empty to live with her and care for her." *And her babies.* Which of course, she couldn't say.

"If she was too sick to care for herself...how'd you manage the babies and the job and the schooling?"

She blew out a sigh. "My class was online, and I finished it." She was still proud of that accomplishment. "My job... I didn't have the time off, so..."

"So you lost it?"

"Yeah." She'd actually given notice and quit, but to someone like Jason, the difference wouldn't signify.

He was pulling into the church parking lot, and he didn't respond. She glanced over at him, expecting contempt, but instead he just looked thoughtful.

Inside, the church basement was crowded with people of all ages looking through tables full of clothing, toys and small gifts. Large signs explained the rules: one item from each table, as needed.

The stale smell of used clothes and unwashed people brought back memories. A girl of ten or eleven flipped through a rack of girls' clothing, her face tense.

Erica's gut twisted with sympathy.

She'd been that girl, desperate to find used clothes that didn't look used. Once, she remembered, she'd been excited to find a beautiful shirt with lace around the neckline and sleeves. She'd worn it to school, proudly, only to be found out by the rich girl who'd donated it.

She's poor. Look, she's wearing my old shirt.

She's poor.

She's poor.

"Let me hold one of the boys so you can see what you're doing." Jason held out his arms, and when Teddy reached for him, Erica let him go, swallowing hard.

She was reduced to charity, for now, but it wasn't what she wanted for the twins. She wasn't going to make a practice of this. She *would* get a job. Right here in this area, because thanks to Kimmie's bequest, she had a rent-free place to stay. She'd find a way to manage a job and child care.

Her kids were *not* coming to events like this once they were old enough to understand what it meant.

"Aw, are they twins?" A woman about Erica's age, but much better dressed, came over and ran a long, polished fingernail down Mikey's cheek, tickling his chin. "Such cute boys! Let me see if I can get permission for you to take two things from the tables."

"Thank you." Erica swallowed and started searching through the jeans and sweaters, trying not to wrinkle her nose at the stained ones, putting aside a couple that would be wearable, even cute, with a good washing.

The woman came back. "I'm really sorry, but rules are rules. You see, if we let one person take more than one thing—" she brushed back her hair and waved an arm around "—everyone would want to, and it wouldn't be fair, because—"

"It's fine," Erica interrupted. "Thank you, anyway."

Jason coughed and she looked over to see him lift an eyebrow and point to his own chest, clearly offering to claim the additional item as his own. She just shook her head a little, picked up the little pair of elastic-waist jeans she'd found for one or the other of the twins and moved on to the next table.

"Nothing like treating other adults like kids," he muttered.

"Yeah. Annoying, isn't it?" Of course, Jason wasn't accustomed to being spoken to in a patronizing way; he had a good job and had never been reduced to accepting handouts from anyone.

"What all do you need? I'll have a look around."

"Pretty much anything warm. They're fifteen months, but we could go as high as eighteen to twenty-four months, sizewise."

"There are more boys' clothes over here." Another well-dressed woman about Erica's age approached, this one with hollows under her eyes. She gestured Erica over. "Your babies are..." She swallowed hard. "They're really sweet." Her voice got rough on the last words, and she excused herself and walked rapidly out of the hall.

There was some story there. And it was a good reminder to Erica: just because someone was pretty and dressed in designer clothes, that didn't mean her life was easy.

Most of the people working were incredibly kind, and Erica ended up with a useful little stack of clothing that would help the boys manage winter for now. As she was trying to figure out whether she was done and could escape, there was a small commotion at a table behind her.

"Mommy! That girl has my Princess Promise game," the little girl behind the table said, pointing at a bedraggled mother and daughter.

"Oh! Oh, no, ma'am, that's my daughter's. These are

the free toys." She indicated the much less shiny toys on the table.

"I'm sorry." The poor mother blushed as she handed the toy back and knelt to comfort her disappointed daughter.

"What'd she say, Chandie?" A scruffy-looking man with bloodshot eyes and the pinpoint pupils of an addict came to stand beside the woman and child. "She disrespecting you?"

"Nothing, it's fine." The young woman, Chandie, took the man's arm and steered him away, beckoning for her little girl to follow.

The little girl hurried after, looking frightened.

So there were drug problems even in the sweet little town of Holly Springs.

Erica made an internal vow. Once she got on her feet, she'd keep the twins miles away from anyplace people with those sorts of issues hung around.

She spent a few more minutes thanking the volunteers, then turned to locate Jason. She was done here. And from the look of things, he hadn't found anything for Teddy. She wanted to leave.

They came together near the door. "Do you want to stay for dinner?" he asked. "I usually do. It's a holiday-type meal and it's open to everyone."

So that was the source of the mouthwatering smells, of turkey and pie.

"If you're staying, we'll stay, too," she said, squaring her shoulders. "If the twins fuss, though, I'll probably have to take them out to the truck."

"There's child care in the church nursery. In fact, Ruth usually takes charge of it, so she'll know what to do with the twins."

"That's good, then." She reminded herself to be grateful for the church dinner, and for the kind people who had put this event together, rather than being ashamed that she had to participate.

"Here, I'll take the stuff to the truck, and then I have to run out on a quick errand. By the time you get the twins settled, it'll be about time for the dinner. Do you want to shop a little for yourself?"

"Is something wrong with my clothes?" She narrowed her eyes, daring him to say it. Kimmie had always been on her to wear things that showed her figure rather than hiding it.

He backed away, palms up. "Nope. Nothing at all. I just thought most women like to shop."

"Nice of you to call it shopping." *Get that chip off your shoulder, girl. You're poor.* She forced a smile. "I really do appreciate your help. Take as long as you need. I'll see if Ruth needs help in the nursery, and if she doesn't, I'll meet you wherever those great smells are coming from."

On the way out, she saw Sheila, the woman who'd already given her the snowsuit for the twins, beckoning her over.

"Hey, I'm going to say something, and if it makes you mad, just tell me and I'll shut right up." She smiled at the babies. "They are so cute."

"I doubt you'll make me mad. Shoot."

"There's this green winter dress here. It's great quality and it's only been worn a couple of times." She flipped through the rack. "Look. Pretty, isn't it?"

And it was, absolutely gorgeous. A sheath dress with a lace overlay of the same shade over the shoulders and sleeves, and a row of gold grommets around the neckline.

"It's gorgeous," Erica agreed, fingering the fabric.

"I donated it, and it hurt me to do it, but—" she gestured down at herself "—these hips are never fitting into that dress again. You should take it."

"Oh, I couldn't."

"Why not?" Sheila held the dress to her. "It would fit you perfectly. And you'd rock it, with your red hair and being so tiny."

"Someone else could use it more. I never go out."

"It's not super fancy. You could wear it to a Christmas party, or a church service."

"That's true…" Temptation overcame her. She'd feel like a queen in that dress.

"It's been hanging here all evening and nobody wanted it." She tickled Mikey's chin, making him laugh. "Go on, take it. Otherwise it'll just stare at me from my closet and make me think about how much weight I've gained."

So, feeling a little foolish and a little excited, Erica let the woman wrap it up for her.

Once the twins were settled in the nursery with plenty of attention—no help needed, as Ruth had two other assistants—Erica went to the door and looked out into the parking lot. If Jason's truck were here, she'd find him, get his key and put the silly dress in the truck before going to dinner.

He was just pulling in, as it happened, so she went out to meet him. Cold wind whipped through the icy parking lot, and she was grateful for the coat she'd borrowed from the front closet back at the farmhouse.

Jason emerged from the truck, and when he saw her, he looked almost guilty.

"I got something for myself, like you suggested," she said, holding up the bag. "Can I just stick it in the truck?"

"Um, sure."

When she did, she saw that the floor of the back seat was full of bags that hadn't been there before. A red snowsuit peeked out of one, a big plastic tool set from another.

Slowly, she backed out of the truck and looked at him. "You...have friends with babies?"

"I hope you consider me a friend."

She stared at him, then at the bags, then at him again. "You did *not* just go out and buy a bunch of stuff for the twins."

"I actually did. But I kept the receipts. I got the sizes you said, but we can exchange them if anything doesn't fit or if it's not what you like."

"Why are you doing this?" Inside, emotions churned. She didn't deserve for someone like Jason to treat her well. She'd never had that. People like her didn't get treated well.

And beyond that, she was deceiving him, so she *really* didn't deserve his help.

Not to mention that taking such big gifts—charity, really—from anyone made her uncomfortable.

"You lost your job to take care of my sister, okay?" His voice was rough. "It's the least I can do."

"I didn't do that to get something." Which she could see now was exactly how it looked. Did people think she'd bribed Kimmie? *I'll care for you if you give me half the farm?*

"I can afford it," he went on. "I have a good job and a good salary." He frowned. "At least, I think I'll go back to it."

That distracted her. So he might not return to Philadelphia? Did that mean he might stay here?

"You're a good mom, you're doing your best, you love

your kids." He said all those things flatly, as if they were facts, and the words buoyed her up. "We all need a hand sometimes. Kimmie did, and you gave it."

She opened her mouth to protest some more and then closed it. Looked up at the stars for guidance and didn't find any.

"Just accept someone doing something nice for you and your kids," he said, his voice persuasive now. He reached out to adjust her coat, pulling it higher on her neck against the cold wind. Then he cupped her chin in his work-roughened hand and looked into her eyes. For a breathless moment she thought he was going to kiss her.

And she thought she might let him.

But he pulled his hand away, his eyes dark and unreadable, and nodded toward the church. "Come on, we'd better get some of that good food while we can."

As they turned toward the church, she felt his hand at the small of her back, guiding her, gently caring for her.

It was appealing. Beguiling. Tempting.

And incredibly dangerous.

Because getting close to Jason—as her heart longed to do—meant betraying Kimmie's wishes for the twins.

Five

Normally, Jason loved church dinners. He'd eat massive amounts of fried chicken, marshmallow fluff salad and green beans cooked to within an inch of their lives and still save room for a couple of pieces of pie.

Today, sitting across the long table from Erica, he wasn't even hungry.

This thing with Erica was getting weird. Intense. Dangerous.

He hadn't dated anyone since Renea, and for good reason; she'd pegged him correctly as bad at relationships. Before her, he'd dated a lot, but it had all been shallow. His heart hadn't been involved in the least.

But against his will, he was connecting with Erica, feeling strangely close to her. To the point where, when he'd seen her tension at the clothing giveaway, he'd wanted to ease it.

He'd *wanted* to pull her into his arms, but he knew better. So he'd done something to help her sons, instead.

He hadn't even minded, because he liked Mikey and Teddy, which was weird because he was *not* a baby kind of guy. He'd bought them a couple of matching outfits, flannel shirts and jeans, rugged country winter clothing they could wear as they crawled around the floor of the house.

That was the thing, though: he wanted them in the house, not out at the cabin.

He could blame his desire for them to stay on Papa, but the truth was he wanted them there for himself.

Wanted Erica there for himself.

"Eyes bigger than your stomach, young man?" Mrs. Habler, an apron tied around her waist, scolded as she looked at his still-full plate. "I made that three-bean salad, you know."

"And it's delicious," Erica said, giving Jason a chance to shove some into his mouth and nod.

Mrs. Habler turned to focus on Erica. "Still staying out at Holly Creek Farm, are you? Tongues have been wagging, I'm afraid."

"Erica was a friend of Kimmie's," Jason interjected. "Having her and her boys there is making Papa happy."

"Then that's reason enough, and I'll try to quell the gossip."

"Wait a minute, Mrs. Habler." Erica put a hand on the woman's arm. "You seem like you know a lot of what's going on in town. Do you happen to know of any job openings?"

Now, *that* was interesting. Suggested that Erica would stay around, as did her desire to fix up the cabin, actually.

The thought put way too much joy into his heart.

"I might know of a couple of things." Mrs. Habler pulled out a chair and sat down beside Erica. "I just heard Cam Cameron is looking for help at the hardware store. And there's going to be an opening at Tiny Tykes Day Care, since Taylor McPherson got put on bed rest today."

Erica's eyes widened. "I love kids. And maybe the twins…" Her cheeks flushed with obvious excitement. "Does anyone from the day care happen to be here tonight?"

"Ruth Delacroix is in the nursery, I believe. She's the owner."

"I know her!" Erica clapped her hands together. "Maybe that's what God has in mind for me. Thank you so much, Mrs. Habler!" She leaned over and gave the woman a one-armed hug.

"You're surely welcome." Mrs. Habler bustled over toward a small group of women clustered near the kitchen, clearly delighted to have put her interfering skills to work.

Erica looked to be brimming with excitement, but before they could discuss the possibility of her working at Tiny Tykes, Pastor Wayne stood to offer a message.

"Keep it short, Pastor!" one of the men cleaning off tables called, grinning.

"That's not in my skill set, George," the pastor called back to general laughter.

As he launched into a message welcoming guests and focusing on coming home to Christ if you'd been astray, Jason finished his plate of food, listening to the pastor's remarks with half an ear.

He hadn't felt the presence of God in some time, even though he dutifully attended church with Papa when he came home. He'd gotten angry at God for letting Kimmie go downhill so badly. Which was wrong, of course.

He hadn't done things right, faithwise. It looked like Kimmie hadn't, either. It occurred to him that he didn't know whether Kimmie had been right with the Lord or not when she'd died.

As for himself—was he right with the Lord? He'd certainly strayed far away.

Appropriately enough, the pastor was sharing the story of the prodigal son. As he started to wrap it up, Ruth Delacroix came into the fellowship hall and approached Erica. For a moment Erica looked excited, but as Ruth whispered to her, she looked increasingly concerned. As soon as the pastor finished, Erica followed Ruth out of the fellowship hall.

Jason debated with himself. He shouldn't follow after Erica, should he? For one thing, as Mrs. Habler had said, tongues were already wagging. For another, Erica could handle things herself and didn't need him interfering.

But the worry on her face...

Before he half knew what he was doing, he was out of his chair and headed out the same door where Erica had gone.

When he reached the nursery, the twins looked to be fine—a relief.

But Erica didn't.

She was sitting on the floor next to Lori Samuelson, the local pediatrician and an active member of the church, while Ruth dealt with the twins and two other toddlers and listened in.

It wasn't his business, and it wasn't right to eavesdrop. The twins were fine. But as he turned to leave, he caught Erica's concerned question: "So you think it's serious?"

"They're quite delayed for fifteen months. The earlier you get help for them, the more likely they'll catch up by the time they're in school."

He forced himself to walk away, but he couldn't force away the look on Erica's face nor the worried tone of her voice.

The twins were in some kind of trouble. And for better or worse, he cared. He wanted to help.

"Can I take you to lunch as a thank-you?" Erica asked Jason the next morning as they drove away from Ruth Delacroix's big Victorian home, half of which operated as the Tiny Tykes Day Care.

She felt like she was about to burst—with anxiety, with gladness, with worry and anticipation.

She'd basically gotten the job. She could start right after the Christmas week closure, provided her paperwork turned out fine. Best of all, the twins could come. They'd be together in the infants and toddlers' room, and Erica would be alternating between that room and the preschoolers' room. It would give the twins a lot of time with her, and some time without her, too, to get more accustomed to other people and to get a different kind of stimulation.

Their life here was shaping up—except for the secret she had to keep and the worry of getting the twins the help they needed. She had an idea about how to handle the early intervention issue, but she had to talk Jason into it very carefully.

"You don't have to buy me lunch," he said as he steered the truck through the snowy streets of downtown Holly Springs.

"I want to. What's the best lunch place in town?"

He grinned over at her and her heart just about stopped. "Well, if you insist... I do love a good burger at Mandelina's."

"Let's do it." It was just a thank-you, she assured herself. Nothing more.

In the corner diner, overwhelming stimulation confronted them. The combined aroma of grease and coffee. Bright Christmas streamers, multicolored lights and three Christmas trees. "Grandma Got Run Over by a Reindeer" blaring from corner speakers.

"The best place, huh?" she murmured as the hostess took them to the only empty booth.

"You'll see."

When the menus came, Jason plucked hers out of her hand. "I know what you're going to do. You're going to order a salad. It would be a mistake."

"How'd you read my mind?" She lifted an eyebrow.

"You're a light eater most of the time. But when in Rome…"

"Don't make assumptions. I might surprise you."

"Oh, really?" He held her gaze for a second too long.

The man was way too good at flirting. He was even tutoring her, a remedial student, in the art.

A chubby, twentysomething waiter appeared, pencil and pad in hand. "And what can I offer you fine people today?"

"I'll have a burger and fries, please," she said, earning a nod of approval from Jason.

"Same for me," he said, and gave her a gentle fist bump. "Only trick is, Erica, you have to save room for pie."

"You absolutely do, because it's coconut cream today," the waiter said as he took their menus. "It's to die for. I had two pieces for breakfast, which was a mistake, but one for dessert will make you the happiest you've been in weeks."

Hmm, she wanted Jason to be happy when she floated her idea. Should she wait until after dessert to suggest it? No, better do it now while he was smiling at her.

"I have a proposal for you." She leaned forward.

He smiled and lifted an eyebrow. "I'm flattered, but we barely know each other."

Her face heated. "Stop it! I'm serious." And then she plowed into an explanation of her idea.

His face grew more disbelieving as she spoke. Not a good sign. "So you want to sell me your half of the farm, but let you live on it?"

"In exchange for my fixing up the cabin, yes. If you need me to pay a small amount of rent, I could do that."

"But why would you do that, when you already own the place?"

She blew out a breath. This was the tricky part. "I need cash." Which was true. "It's been an expensive time, moving the boys across the country."

"And losing your job," he said, frowning. "But the farm will bring you a steady income. Surely that'll be a plus for you as the boys grow up."

She nodded and swallowed. "It would be. But I need the cash now."

"Why?"

The waiter appeared with their drinks. "Don't argue, be happy," he said. "Hey, Jason, did you hear about what's happening with Chuck and Jeannine Henderson?" And he launched into a dramatic breakup story that Jason appeared to want to avoid, but couldn't cut off.

Their conversation gave Erica a minute to think. She'd anticipated that Jason wouldn't warm to the idea immediately, so she couldn't let that discourage her. She'd been pondering and praying all night, and this was the solution she'd come up with—especially now that she'd gotten a job.

Staying in the area would be good for the twins. Staying near their relatives.

But she had to get them early intervention. And she couldn't get public assistance without a lot of paperwork, including birth certificates, which she didn't have.

She knew that someday she'd have to go through the appropriate channels to get the twins their birth certificates and other paperwork. Probably, she'd need to hire a lawyer, maybe that one who'd been a friend of Kimmie's.

But for the time being, lawyers' fees were out of reach.

And the boys needed early intervention, now, and on an ongoing basis. A onetime trip to some clinic wasn't going to be enough.

So she had to get private help, which would be no questions asked. The fact that it cost money was okay— as long as Jason would buy her half of the farm.

A busboy brought out plates, and their waiter waved a hand. "Thanks, Ger. Sorry I got to talking." He put steaming plates down in front of them, and the aroma of burgers and fries wafted up.

"Here you go, Jason and...what did you say your name is?"

"I'm Erica." She held out her hand.

"Pleased to meet you. I'm Henry, but you can call me Hank. And I need to get it in gear." He turned and headed off.

The burger was enormous, so Erica sawed it in half with her butter knife.

Jason picked up his whole burger. "There are two kinds of people in the world," he said, grinning. "The ones who are dainty with a hamburger and the ones like me." He took a big bite.

Good. Let him eat up and get into a good mood. In

fact, this burger could put her in a good mood, too; it was delicious.

Hank returned to their table, coffeepot in hand. "How is everything? More coffee, Erica?"

She swallowed and held out her cup. "Yes, please."

She kept quiet during the rest of their lunch, letting Jason eat and thinking about what she needed to say or do to convince him. *Be strong, girl. It's for the twins.*

Jason finished his meal and Erica ate half of hers and asked Hank to wrap up the rest. After he brought Jason a piece of pie, she launched into her proposal again. "Will you at least think about making a deal with the farm? You wouldn't have to buy it all right away. We can do payments. Figure something out."

He held up a big bite of pie. "Sure you don't want to try it?"

"No, thanks. It's just that," she pushed on, "I need some of the money pretty soon, here."

He put down his fork. "For the twins?"

She bit her lip. The fewer details he knew, the better.

"Is the reason you're wanting to sell property so that you can pay for therapists and specialists?"

She looked away, trying to figure out how much to tell him.

"Look," he said, pushing the rest of his pie away, "I'd hate to see you sell. It's going to appreciate in value. You're thinking short-term."

"But they need help now," she protested, shredding a napkin with nervous fingers.

He put a hand over hers, stilling them. "There's a children's health insurance program for low income people. They should have good services. Pennsylvania usually does."

She pulled her hands away. "I don't want to get public insurance."

"I respect not wanting a handout, but programs for children's health are different. You've had a hard time here, and you have two little ones. That's exactly what those programs are for."

"I don't want it," she said. Let him think it was pride.

Around them, the noise of the diner went on: forks clattering, people talking, the bells jingling on the door as it opened and closed.

"Could their father help?" Jason asked.

"No."

"He should."

"He's in prison and he has no claim on them."

Jason looked startled, and for a moment, she could see him sifting through images in his mind, trying to figure her out. He'd thought she was a drug addict, but he seemed to have ruled that out now. However, having the father of her children imprisoned put her back in that same sketchy camp in his mind, she could tell.

What he didn't know, of course, was that the twins' imprisoned father was Kimmie's partner, not her own.

"I don't understand why you won't at least see a doctor and start the paperwork for CHIP. You could make a final decision later."

He was trying to be so reasonable, and it was killing her, because under normal circumstances he'd be right.

Oh, Kimmie, why'd you put me in this position? Why couldn't you have been up front with your family?

"Hey, Stephanidis." A man with a military haircut, about Jason's age and with similar muscles came over and shook Jason's hand, an encounter that ended in a slight test of strength. "How's the hard-line detective? Didn't expect to see you out of your mean streets. How's Philly going to stay safe without you?"

Jason introduced her but didn't try to draw her into the conversation, which was fine.

As the two men talked, Erica bit her lip and pondered. She'd prayed and she knew that God would be with her no matter what. And yes, Kimmie had been a flawed person, and maybe wrong about Jason, but he *would* be angry about the deception, right? Angry enough to take the twins.

And once he had them, he'd have no reason to keep her around.

A guy like Jason wouldn't *want* to keep someone like her around.

She loved the boys too much to let them go. Her desire to mother them grew every day.

As his friend left, Jason turned back to her, smiling. "Come on now, Erica. Won't you just try signing up for CHIP?"

"I'm not getting public insurance!"

"Don't you care about your kids?"

"It's because I care about them that I won't—"

"Hey, you two, I said no fighting." Hank was back with the check. "Look, I brought you kisses to make you feel all better." He put down the check with two foil-wrapped candies on top of it and spun away.

Erica reached for the check at the same time Jason did. She grabbed it, but his larger hand closed over hers. "Let me get this."

"I said I was taking you out to lunch."

"You need the money more than I do."

"I can afford a lunch!"

"Put the money into your fund to help the twins."

Deftly, he got the check out of her hand, but she closed her hand on his.

His dark skin and large hand contrasted with her own small, pale one. But as far as calluses, she had as many as he did. She'd worked hard in her life, as had he.

"Let me have my dignity," she said quietly, and immediately he let the check go. Understanding and sympathy shone in his eyes.

"Thank you for lunch. I appreciate it and it was really good."

She could see that it cost him to let a woman pay, especially when Hank came over and took the money from her and lifted an eyebrow at Jason. But he didn't protest any more.

"Look," he said while they waited for change, "we need to talk more about the farm and what should be done with it. That's not a discussion to finish in an hour, over lunch."

"What do you say we talk about it while we're working on the cabin?" she suggested. Because she *had* to get out of that house.

"Possible," he said, nodding. "I have tomorrow afternoon free. Would that work for you?"

"As long as I can get Ruth to watch the twins again, yes."

"It's a date, then." His words were light. But she could tell that his suspicions about her had been raised again.

Six

Jason pulled his truck in front of his friend Chuck's house, looked over at Erica and hoped this was all going to go okay.

They'd spent the afternoon working on the cabin, and *that* had been great. She'd opened up a little bit about Kimmie and their friendship, how they'd been in and out of touch, how Kimmie had been like a sister to Erica, albeit a flawed one.

It was what he'd done *after* working on the cabin that had him sweating a little. He was going to have to tell Erica about it tonight.

Instead, he told her the easier thing. "This could be a little awkward. They're both still living here."

As they headed up the sidewalk to Chuck's house, Erica touched his arm, stopping him. Almost stopping his heart. He was getting way too sensitive to casual contact with her.

"This is a nice house. I'm not going to be able to afford anything they have." Her voice was husky. Behind her, the sunset made her loose red curls glow like fire.

"I can afford it." As she started to protest, he lifted a hand. "It's an investment in the property."

"Does that mean you're buying it from me?" She raised her eyebrows.

He rang the doorbell. "I'm considering it."

Chuck opened the door, looking like he'd aged thirty years since they'd hung out together in high school. "Hey, come on in."

"This is Erica," Jason said once they were inside and taking off their coats. "She's going to move into the cabin on the property and she's looking for some furniture."

"Great—we could use the cash." Chuck ran a hand through his already-sticking-up hair and grabbed a roll of colored stickers. "Here, just put one of these on anything you want. Only not if it already has a sticker. I'm green and Jeannine's yellow. You can be orange."

Erica's eyes widened, and Jason felt his own gut twist a little. He'd never been this close to the sad details of a marital breakup before.

"Go on, walk through. She's out somewhere and I'm packing up the basement." Chuck sounded mechanical.

"If you're sure, man." Jason clapped his friend on the shoulder.

"*She's* sure." Chuck turned abruptly and strode out of the entryway.

When Jason and Erica walked into the front room, both of them stopped at the same moment.

The mantel was half decorated with evergreen garland and red bows, and a box containing more of the same sat on the hearth. A Scotch pine, unadorned, sent waves of Christmassy scent through the cozy room.

Erica looked over at him. "I don't feel right about this."

From the back of the house, a door opened. "Hey,

I'm…" called a woman's voice, trailing off into dejection. Like she'd forgotten for a moment that happy greetings to her husband weren't part of her life anymore.

There was the sound of a heavy tread climbing the basement stairs. Chuck.

Erica's brow furrowed. "What should we do? Should we leave?"

"No, he was serious about wanting to sell stuff, and he said they both knew we were coming tonight. Come on. Maybe we should start upstairs." They headed toward the staircase, and if Jason put his hand on the small of Erica's back, he was just guiding her. Right?

"Were you ever married?" she asked as they climbed the stairs.

"Nope. Just engaged."

"What happened?"

He shrugged, nodding toward one of the smaller bedrooms, guiding her toward it with a light touch. "She regained her sanity and dumped me."

"You don't sound very upset."

"I'm not. Saved me from going through *this*." He waved an arm to indicate the whole house, the breakup of a marriage.

But Erica pressed a hand to her mouth as she looked around the room. "Oh, wow."

It was a nursery, perfectly decorated but empty of the clothes and sheets and paraphernalia that indicated a baby. There were no stickers on any of the furniture.

"Do they have a baby? Or…is she pregnant?"

He shook his head, opening the little blue dresser's drawers to confirm that they were empty. "This might be nice for the twins, huh?"

"Yes, it would, but…" She trailed off. "Are they sure they want to get rid of all this?"

"They did years of infertility treatments." He explained in the same matter-of-fact way Chuck had explained it to him. "She finally got pregnant, but about six weeks ago, she lost the baby. I guess…that and all the doctor's bills…" He shrugged.

"That is so awful." Erica's eyes got shiny as she ran a finger along the railing of the brand-new crib.

"Should I put a sticker on it?" His hand hovered over the dresser.

"Yeah. I guess. If it'll help them."

He really, really wanted to wipe that sadness off her face. He even felt a strange urge to do it by kissing her, but that would be a mistake. "What are you doing tomorrow?" he asked instead, to distract her.

She considered, then shrugged. "I don't know. The twins are getting bored. I'd like to find somewhere new to take them."

Footsteps sounded on the stairs. Light. A woman's.

Jason didn't know Chuck's wife very well, but he recognized her when she looked in the door. "Hey, Jeannine, good to—"

"Just don't." Her face crumpled and she spun and hurried away from the room.

"Oh, wow, that's the woman who looked so upset at the clothing giveaway. I've got to see if I can do anything for her." Erica went after Jeannine.

So obviously, Erica had had a better instinct about this than he did, or than Chuck did, either, for that matter. *Christmas, a miscarriage… Duh.* Not the time to participate in dismantling a home.

He heard a low murmur of voices from what looked

like the master bedroom and headed downstairs to see what he could do for Chuck.

An hour later, he and Chuck were watching hockey when Jason heard the doorbell ring. It sounded like someone was singing outside. Maybe a lot of people.

Jason looked over at Chuck. The man was still staring at the TV, obviously trying to distance himself from what was happening in his life. "Want me to get that?"

"Sure." Chuck sat upright, elbows on knees, fists under his chin.

So Jason opened the door to a group of about ten carolers, adults and kids, singing one of his favorite Christmas carols: "O Little Town of Bethlehem." Behind them, in the light from a lamppost, he could see that snow had started to fall.

There was a sound on the stairs behind him, and he turned to see Jeannine descending, Erica right behind her. When she saw what was going on, Jeannine sat abruptly on a step about halfway down the stairs and started to cry. Or maybe she'd been crying all along.

Erica sat beside her and put an arm around her, murmuring quietly.

Chuck had come out to the entryway, too, and he stood listening as the carolers came to the last verse of the song: *Oh holy child of Bethlehem...cast out our sin and enter in...abide with us, our Lord Emmanuel.*

For sure, this household needed the Christ child to enter in. And Jason did, too. He was saved; he accepted Jesus as his redeemer, but he didn't always let Christ in. Too busy trying to control things himself, fix the world by himself.

He waved a thank-you to the carolers and closed the door.

Chuck turned and took a couple of steps toward the staircase where the two women still sat. Erica got up and came quietly downstairs.

"She needs you," Jason said to Chuck.

"She doesn't want anything to do with me." Chuck's expression, looking up at his crying wife, was full of frustration and yearning.

Jason put a hand on his friend's shoulder. "You've got so much here, man. You should fight for it."

And then his eyes met Erica's, and they turned as one toward the door, grabbed their coats off the banister railing and walked out of the house.

"Wow," Erica said once they were outside. "Pretty emotional."

"Very." It was natural to take her arm on the icy walkway. "I don't know if you'll get that dresser or not."

"I hope not. I hope they work things out and get the chance to be parents."

"Me, too." He held the truck door open for her and helped her to climb in. And meanwhile, he hadn't gotten the chance to talk to her about what he needed to, and this was his last chance. Once they got home, it would be craziness, Papa and Ruth and the twins. A full house and a lively one, and he liked that, but it didn't allow time for quiet discussion.

Quiet persuasion.

For that, he knew exactly where he needed to take her.

Erica was so lost in thought, worrying about Chuck and Jeannine, that she didn't notice the direction the truck was going until it stopped. In the middle of a parking lot full of cars, apparently in the middle of a field.

"Where are we... Oh, wow!" She stared down at a wonderland of colored and white lights. "What is it?"

"It's the Mistletoe Display. Will you walk through with me?"

Her breath seemed to leave her chest. Why had he brought her here?

Against her will, her heart was warming to Jason, and maybe, just maybe, he was feeling similarly toward her. Why else would he have brought her to such a romantic place?

"We don't have to. If you'd rather get home to the twins—"

"No, no. I...I'd love to."

They walked down the path to a ticket shed, and he insisted on buying her ticket. "My idea, my treat."

Definitely date-like.

They strolled through winding paths, stopping to admire the light-made scenes scattered along the way. Here was portrayed a group of children carrying gifts; there, a family building a snowman. A brass ensemble played "Angels We Have Heard on High," and no sooner had those sounds faded than a quartet of singers in old-fashioned costumes sang "God Rest Ye Merry Gentlemen." Pastor Wayne was at a wooden stand selling hot chocolate and passing out invitations to the church's Christmas Eve service. Jason stopped, assured the pastor he'd be there and bought them both cups of hot chocolate, complete with peppermint-stick stirrers.

It was lovely and romantic, especially when Jason draped his scarf around her neck to keep her warmer.

"So, you're probably wondering why I brought you here," he said, sounding nervous.

"I wasn't, but…is there a special reason?" Her heart leaped to her throat. Was he going to make some kind of declaration? They weren't dating, although the things they'd been through together had made her feel closer to him than to anyone she'd dated. Not that there had been a whole lot of boyfriends in her life.

"There's something I want to tell you. Ask you." He led her to a bench beside a snowy lane, a little off from where most people were walking. "I…I'm going to Philadelphia tomorrow."

Her heart sank a little. She had grown accustomed to having Jason around, and she'd miss him if he left. But of course, they weren't really accountable to each other. "How long will you be gone?"

"Just a couple of days, three at the outside. I have to testify in the case that put me on leave."

"Okay." He'd told her a little bit about why he was on administrative leave, something to do with a corrupt partner. "Will this fix the problem?"

"It's a start." He took her hand. "You might be upset with me for what I did, but…how would you and the twins like to come with me?"

Erica's head spun. "Come *with* you? But…why?"

Her mind spun with possibilities. Was this a romantic proposition? Did he think she was easy and that, away from Papa's watchful eye, they could have a fling? But if that were the case, why bring the twins?

"I made an appointment with a specialist," he said, looking hard at her as if to see her reaction.

"What kind?" She wasn't following.

"A pediatrician who's, like, world renowned for helping delayed babies catch up."

Her jaw about dropped as emotions warred within her, chief among them an absurd sense of disappointment. He didn't want anything romantic, and this wasn't a date. "I *told* you I wanted to do this my own way. And I can't afford a famous specialist. You know that." She stood up.

"No, no, sit down." He tugged her hand, pulling her back down to the bench. "I just thought... I was talking about my visit to my buddy who has a child with Down syndrome, and he was telling me about everything they're doing for his daughter...you know, Philly has world-class hospitals and so I thought..."

"You thought you'd go over my head and get medical treatment for my boys?"

"You don't understand. It's so hard to get an appointment with her, but she had a cancellation. So...I went ahead and did it." He paused. "It's the day after tomorrow."

She stared at him as her head spun. Partly from his high-handedness and partly from fear. If a specialist wanted to look at the twins' medical records, she didn't have them.

"I wasn't planning to do this, Erica, but when it came up, I couldn't help but think of the twins. I care about the little guys. And about you."

"No." She was shaking her head before having even formulated a response. "Just...no. I don't want to visit some strange doctor, all the way over in Philadelphia, only to hear about treatments I can't afford in a place I can't get to—"

"My friend says lots of people come and consult with her and then do treatment in their own towns. And as for insurance…when I made the appointment, I explained that you didn't have coverage or the money to pay privately, and they sent some paperwork. The receptionist said it's not complicated at all, and that Dr. Chen works with a lot of…of low income patients. Don't you see, Erica? This way, you won't have to sell me the farm to get help for the boys. You can keep it for them."

She squeezed her eyes shut and tried to think as the hot chocolate curdled in her stomach.

He hadn't brought her here for a date. He'd brought her here to butter her up so he could find out the truth.

"No." She shook her head. "No. I'm not ready to take that step."

"You won't even do it for the twins?" His voice held a touch of censure.

He thought she was a bad mother.

She stared down at her denim-clad knees as waves of confusion and shame passed over her. She *was* a bad mother. Not fit for the wonderful gift Kimmie had given her.

Jason reached an arm around her shoulders, gave her a quick couple of pats and then pulled his arm away. "Look, I'm sorry to spring this on you, and I know you'd rather have time to think about it. You're a great mother. You want to take time and figure out what's best for your kids. You like to plan things out, and here I'm just throwing this at you."

You're a great mother. She looked over to see if he was mocking her, but his face was serious, earnest.

"For all kinds of reasons, I'd like for you to go. Mostly for the twins and the specialist, of course, but there's a Christmas party…" He trailed off.

"A Christmas party?" She couldn't keep up with the way his mind was working.

"For my department. It's at the home of my good friends, who have little kids, so you could bring the twins. We could even stay with them." He paused. "I'd really like for you to meet them."

She felt her forehead wrinkle. What was he saying?

That he wanted her to meet his friends because he was serious about her? Or that he wanted her to come to Philly for a fling?

He seemed to read her mind. "They have a huge farmhouse. You and the twins would have a big room and your own bathroom. I'd bunk down on the couch in the den."

Now she was thoroughly confused. "Do you... Why are you asking me to come? Besides just being kind about the twins?"

He dug at the snowy ground with the toe of his boot. "Look," he said, "I'm bad at this stuff. I'm bad at talking to people, working things out. I'm bad at, well, relationships, but...I'm trying to improve. Especially now that I have a reason to." He propped his elbows on his knees and rested his cheek on his hand, facing her. "I really like you, Erica."

Her heart pounded like a drum.

He was holding out a chance, however small, at everything she wanted: connection, someone to value her, a good family.

She couldn't have even a chance at that if she didn't take him up on what he'd offered, the trip to Philadelphia and the appointment with a specialist for the twins.

She looked up at the stars, sparkling in the cold air. *Should I go, Lord?*

The very question reminded her how much in the Christmas story depended on following a star, on faith.

Jason had overstepped by making the appointment, for sure. And figuring out how to manage that appointment without revealing Kimmie's secret was going to be a challenge.

Not to mention that any kind of a relationship with Jason was out of the question, as long as she was withholding the truth about the twins. How could she judge him for being a little pushy, when she herself was lying to him?

She glanced up at the stars again, took a couple of breaths and then met Jason's eyes. "Thank you for the offer and for what you're doing for the twins and me. We…we'll go."

His eyes lit and he pulled her into a spontaneous hug. A hug that went on a little longer than something friendly.

She pulled back a little and looked at him, her heart fluttering like a startled bird in a cage.

His eyes went dark with some unreadable emotion. He cupped her chin in his hand and studied her face.

"You are so beautiful," he said. And then he pressed his lips to hers.

All logic slipped away, replaced by almost-complete feeling and warmth and care. Almost complete, not fully, because something nagged at the edge of her melting consciousness: *this isn't going to work, because he doesn't know the truth about the twins.*

Seven

The small box was sitting on the table beside the door, where Papa always tossed the mail he didn't have time to sort.

Jason spotted it as he came whistling down the stairs. Something compelled him to take a closer look.

He could hear Erica talking to Papa in the kitchen. "No, no phone calls about the dog yet," Papa was saying.

"I think his foot is getting better," Erica replied. "Look, he chewed the bandage off again."

"It looks okay, but I don't think that fur is growing back. He'll always have a scar." There was the homey sound of dishes clinking and water running.

The box was addressed to him, in Renea's handwriting.

He should probably just leave it there, get on with loading up the car. They needed to head out so they could get to Brian and Carla's house and settle Erica and the twins before he hustled to meet with the lawyers.

But it would nag at him; he knew it. So he set his suitcase down and carried the little box upstairs.

In his room, with the door closed, he opened the box

up, feeling as if a viper might jump out. Renea had been
furious about their breakup even though she'd instigated
it, and the sight of her handwriting brought her angry
feelings and words back to him. His sense of dread increased as he used a pocketknife to slit through the tape.

Inside was a small envelope and a wad of newspaper.
Cowardly, he opened the wad first.

There was the engagement ring he'd bought her.

Okay, that wasn't a problem, really. He hadn't wanted
it back, hadn't wanted the reminder of his failure, but he
was getting past that now. Things were new and promising in his life, he reminded himself.

The thought of kissing Erica made him sit down on
his bed and close his eyes, still clutching the ring and the
note in his hands. She'd been hesitant but then so sweet
and giving as he'd held her. And although he'd kept the
kiss short and respectful, he had seen the emotion in her
eyes and he knew it had been reflected in his own.

She didn't throw her kisses around and neither did he,
these days. It meant something.

She was beginning to care for him, and that thought
had filled him with way more happiness and joy than
he'd had any right to expect.

He heard Erica trotting up the stairs, and then a minute later, something heavy bumping down. Erica must
be dragging her suitcase down herself, and she shouldn't
be; he should be helping her. He ripped open the note.

I've lost weight and they want to put me in the clinic
again. Haven't been able to eat since we broke up.
Can you get this ring resized down? Call me.

He looked at the ring, already the size of a child's

ring. The sight of it brought back the short two months of his engagement.

How he'd looked up some formula of how much an engagement ring should cost based on his salary and saved up that amount. How he'd consulted with his friends—clueless guys all—about what type of ring to buy. How she'd said yes, and instead of feeling happy, his heart had gone cold with the feeling of a cage door slamming shut.

And from then on, the whole relationship had gone downhill. She'd been discontented with the ring and with how he expressed, or didn't express, his feelings for her. He'd tried to whip himself up into a proper type of enthusiasm for a groom-to-be, not helped by a few of his friends who viewed their wives as nags and marriage as a ball and chain. And others of his friends, the more serious ones, who thought he'd made the wrong choice of mate.

Most of all, there'd been the sinking realization that being involved with a man brought out Renea's severe eating disorder. Although she'd hidden it before their engagement, she hadn't been able to hide it after. Her parents had begged him to break it off with her so as not to complicate her recovery. He'd tried, but she was so fragile that it had never seemed like the right time.

When she'd gone into a rage one night and broken up with him, he'd taken it as a blessing, especially since his only feeling had been relief. And he'd held fast against Renea's multiple attempts to get back together, each one ending in accusations that he had ruined her life.

He guessed the breakup had been fortunate. But had he changed any since then?

He didn't want to ruin anyone else's life the way he'd ruined Renea's. And obviously, he knew nothing about choosing a mate; he'd gone solely for beauty with Renea, and he'd almost made a huge mistake.

Ruined his fiancée's life.

Didn't save his sister.

He stood and looked out the window. Erica and Papa were loading things into the back of the truck, talking and laughing.

It would be wrong to go forward and try to get something started with Erica. Yes, she was beautiful, but Renea had been, too.

Why on earth had he kissed Erica? More of the same poor choices?

She's different, his heart cried as he trotted down the stairs double time, intent on setting right the wrong he'd committed. *She's a good person. Stable. Not hiding things.*

Papa must have gone inside, but Erica was there beside the truck, her breath making steam in the air in front of her beautiful face, a cap on her head unable to tame her red curls. Her cheeks were pink, and when she saw him, her eyes lit up.

"Hey." He sounded abrupt and he knew it, but that was what he needed to be. Short. Abrupt. Not paying attention to how pretty she was or to the concern starting to appear in her green eyes.

"Listen," he said quickly, "I shouldn't have kissed you last night. I want to apologize."

She frowned, tilted her head. Opened her mouth to say something, and then closed it again.

"I...I didn't mean to give you the wrong idea. I'm not... I'm not..." He trailed off, then forced himself to say it. "I'm really not up for dating or anything."

She waved her hand, her eyes shuttered. "It's fine. It

was a romantic setting. Anyone could make a mistake like that." She turned to lift a bag of baby supplies into the truck. "Or... Did you still want us to come with you? Because we don't have to. Maybe it's best if we don't—"

"No, no. I want you to come. Gotta keep that appointment."

"Right, the appointment." Wrinkles appeared between her eyebrows and she frowned down at the ground. "But we could go another time. Get there another way. I don't want to impose—"

"No imposition," he said, trying to sound happy and hearty and like his heart wasn't aching. "I'd welcome the company and we're all set up."

She looked at him, confusion clouding her eyes.

"It's important for the twins. And that's what friends do for each other, right?"

She swallowed and bit her lip and looked away.

All the work he'd done to convince her to trust him, gone.

"I'm sorry," he said.

"I... Well, if you're sure you want us to come, I'll go get the twins."

"I'll help."

"No, it's okay. I'll bring them myself." And she turned and went back into the house.

Loser. He was such a loser. She'd been happy, excited about the trip, and then he'd come down with his hurtful announcement. Now she was sad. And this trip across the state was going to be extremely awkward.

I'm doing it for her. I don't want to ruin another woman's life.

Let alone the lives of a couple of sweet babies.

But the whole thing made his chest feel as heavy as if a three-hundred-pound barbell were resting on it.

Two hours later, Erica was just about to scream into the awkward silence when Jason spoke.

"You want to stop?" He indicated the road sign announcing a service plaza.

"Okay." Anything to get out of this truck. "I shouldn't let the boys sleep much longer or they'll never sleep tonight."

"Papa packed some lunch for us. Want to eat it now?"

"If that's all right with you, sure."

They were being painfully polite with each other. As if they hadn't gotten close over the past week and shared a kiss last night. A kiss she'd thought meant something.

Apparently not to Jason. Apparently he thought it was a big mistake, and that was fine. Just fine.

Say it often enough and you might even start to believe it.

She got Mikey out of his car seat, and when she turned, Jason was standing there, so she thrust the baby into his arms. Then she unlatched Teddy. The way he lifted his arms to her with a crooked smile made her heart melt. "Aren't you the happy little man?" she cooed as she pulled him out and grabbed the diaper bag.

Mikey and Teddy were her priorities. She couldn't forget that, couldn't get too sad or upset. She had to take care of herself so she could take care of them. Like they'd said the one time she'd taken a plane ride: put your own mask on before assisting others.

She'd thought that Jason might be a positive part of her life, but if he was going to be negative and hurtful, then she didn't want anything to do with him. She flipped back her hair and followed him into the service plaza, determinedly not noticing how handsome he was and how easily he carried Mikey and the picnic container.

Once they'd put their bags down, Jason handed Mikey to her and then went to grab high chairs. Before she could ask it, he found disinfecting wipes and scrubbed the chairs down.

He was pretty good with babies, for being a novice.

"Aw, they look just like their daddy," a woman said as she carried her tray to a nearby table.

Jason gave her a half smile as he got out plastic containers of food, but Erica's heart pumped a little harder. *Did* the boys look like Jason? They were his nephews, but she'd never noticed a resemblance. Sometimes you didn't see things that were right in front of your eyes.

They each fed a twin. "You're getting pretty good at that," she said as Jason used a plastic spoon to scrape some food off Mikey's mouth. Then she froze. He didn't want to pursue a relationship, so did that mean she wasn't even supposed to talk to him?

But he smiled. "I'm a quick learner. And I think he's getting neater, isn't he?"

"Let's hope so."

Teddy wasn't hungry. He yelled and squirmed to get down, but Erica didn't like the look of the floor. She glanced around, trying to figure out what to do with him.

Jason seemed to read her mind. "I'll put my coat down and he can sit on it."

"But your coat will get filthy!"

He shrugged. "It'll wash." He spread it on the floor, and after a moment's hesitation, Erica put Teddy down on it.

Mikey, neglected, started to make some noise. "Ma-ma!" he complained.

Jason looked over at her, grinning. "Now I see what people mean about traveling with kids." He lifted Mikey out of his chair and put him beside his brother, and Erica hurried to wipe both boys' faces.

"I couldn't do this without you. I'm really grateful."

"It's my pleasure." He met her eyes for a moment and then looked away.

But she needed to get the necessary words out now, all of them, while they were speaking to each other. "Mikey's getting more frustrated that he can't move around. And Teddy's fussing more, I think because he can't communicate. They really need the help, so…thanks for setting up this appointment and making me keep it." And please, God, let it not get them all in trouble.

"You're welcome. And, Erica…" He looked away and blew out a breath. "I'm sorry I was… This morning. I hurt your feelings."

Who *was* this man? He'd kissed her like he meant it, taken it back harshly like he meant *that*, acted as if he were the twins' loving father, and now he wanted to talk feelings?

"Look, there's something in my past. A broken engagement."

She blinked and nodded. So he'd been engaged and it had ended and that had somehow caused his seesawing behavior. "Okaaaayyy…"

"I didn't handle it well. The breakup."

"You mean you were upset about it, or you didn't do it right?" It seemed crucial to know whose idea the breakup had been.

"Mostly, I didn't do it right. I'm a perfectionist, hard

on people. And I'm not good at talking to a…a girlfriend, I guess. Communicating."

"You're talking now," she said before she could think better of it. More than that, he was admitting to the problem that Kimmie had accused him of: being a perfectionist, being rigid. So maybe he was changing. Maybe he wasn't the hard-core, hard-line guy Kimmie had thought he was. Look how he'd analyzed his broken engagement, how he was trying to share his feelings.

And if this, the past relationship gone bad, was his big secret…

She needed to tell him the truth about the twins. Sooner rather than later. But how did you begin to say something like that? And would it be better to do it before or after the doctor's appointment?

If she told him and he got outraged at her and the twins, where would they be? She'd better wait.

"I'm talking now because I don't want you to feel hurt. I don't suspect you of sharing Kimmie's bad habits anymore. And… It was fantastic to kiss you, Erica. I don't want to have any expectations out of it, or for you to, but I sure liked it."

He looked up and met her eyes, and she couldn't look away. Couldn't stop herself from saying, "I liked it, too."

In fact, she very badly wanted it to happen again. But Teddy crawled off the coat onto the dirty floor, and Mikey started to cry.

"We'd better get on the road. I've got to meet the lawyers at three, and we still have—" he checked his phone "—about two hours to Brian and Carla's place."

They rode in silence for a while, but it was friendlier, more relaxed. Jason found a radio station the twins seemed to like, and Erica even managed to doze off for a bit.

She sat up, refreshed, and looked around, and Jason glanced over at her. "Feel better?"

"A lot."

"I've been thinking," he said, "about Kimmie."

Her heart rate accelerated. "Yeah?"

"Did she talk about her family at all? About us?"

Erica considered how much to say. "She did a little."

"Was she angry at me? Did she see what I did as a betrayal?" The words seemed to burst out of him.

She blew out a breath. "It's water under the bridge."

"Yeah, but it's my bridge. I want to know."

"Why? So you can torture yourself some more, like you do with your ex-fiancée?"

He glanced over at her, looking startled. "Is that what I'm doing?"

"It seems like it. Blaming yourself for everything. Kimmie made her choices. She did what addicts do." *Like have kids and neglect them.*

"Wait a minute. You did Al-Anon, right?"

"Yeah, it was pretty much forced on me when I was a teenager. Why, does it show?"

"Uh-huh." He put on the truck's blinker. "And the other thing that shows is that you're good at being evasive."

She stared at him as sweat gathered on her neck and chest. "What's that supposed to mean?"

"I asked you about Kimmie, and all of a sudden we're talking about me. And this isn't the first time. Is there some reason you don't like talking about Kimmie or the past?"

Tell him. Tell him now.

Instead, she sidestepped the question. "I grew up having to keep a lot of secrets. It gets to be a habit." And it was one she should break. Look how Jason was trying to do better at communicating. "Kimmie talked about happy times when you guys were kids. She really seemed to love you."

He glanced over at her as if to see whether she was telling the truth. "Really?"

"Yes. And, Jason, she had good values in a lot of ways. It was just… Addiction is hard to break. Drugs nowadays are so strong…"

"Tell me about it." He shook his head slowly. "I remember when she was in high school, those chastity rings were the thing. She got one. Go figure." He looked over at her. "I don't suppose… I mean, she used to talk to me about how she wanted to wait for marriage."

Erica froze. Kimmie hadn't waited for marriage; not only that, but she'd had twins out of wedlock. Twins who were sleeping peacefully in the back seat right now.

"Is that pretty important to you?" she asked.

"It's the ideal, and I hope…" He trailed off and looked over at her. "I'm sorry, Erica. I don't mean to judge. I haven't been perfect myself by any means."

Erica almost laughed and then restrained it. No need to give in to hysteria. Jason thought he'd offended her because of her supposed impurity, as an unmarried mom. Little did he know that she *wasn't* actually a mom. And that she'd barely dated, let alone gotten close enough to someone to conceive a child. Waiting for marriage hadn't been a challenge for her.

But there was a desperate hopefulness in Jason's eyes. She felt for him and she wanted to provide comfort, as best she could. "If you're asking whether there were a lot of men in her life, I don't think so. Times when I was around her, she was mostly on her own."

She was saved from expanding on that by the sound of a siren. She looked back, and red and blue lights flashed. Her heart raced and she felt guilty, like the police had somehow guessed she wasn't being completely honest.

Jason let out an exclamation and pulled over. "Wonder what's up. I wasn't speeding."

"Police make me nervous."

"You gotta remember I'm a cop myself. And in fact..." He was looking in his rearview mirror, and suddenly he laughed and opened the driver's-side door.

"Don't get out!" She couldn't keep the panic out of her voice. Bad things happened when you confronted cops. "Just sit still and keep your hands visible!"

"It's fine. Old friend. He's just busting my chops." He jumped out of the truck and walked back to meet the uniformed police officer, and a moment later they were thumping each other on the back and laughing.

She couldn't take her eyes off him as he talked to his friend. That strong square jaw, dark with the beginnings of a beard. The messy-cut black hair that contrasted so sharply with his blue eyes. His athletic build, the confidence of his wide-legged stance.

Was she falling in love with him?

No sooner had she thought it than she shook her head and let her face sink onto one fist. No. Not that. She couldn't be in love.

Jason needed to hold on to a positive picture of his sister. It would help him heal.

But knowing Kimmie had had children out of wedlock would tarnish that image.

The web of lies kept getting trickier, more complex.

Now, if she revealed the truth, she wouldn't just be breaking a promise to Kimmie. She wouldn't just be risking that Jason would take the twins away from her.

She'd be risking his own happiness, the image he was trying to create of a sister who'd been an addict but otherwise, had stuck to the values she was raised with.

Male laughter rang out, Jason's, and despite her racing worries, she couldn't help smiling.

When Jason was happy, she was happy. When he tried awkwardly to explain things and apologize, truly attempting to do better at communicating, her heart warmed toward him. When he unquestioningly helped with the twins, she felt safe, protected.

Yes, for sure. She was hooked. Falling, falling, fallen.

With the one person it would be a complete disaster to love.

After they'd arrived at Brian and Carla's house, escorted by his old friend Diego, Jason knew it wouldn't take long for someone to grill him. Sure enough, the moment he'd helped to carry the twins and the luggage to the guest suite, Brian was on his case, dragging him out to the garage, ostensibly to look at his new motorcycle. "Why didn't you tell us? She's a knockout."

"She's a friend. That's all."

Brian made a skeptical sound as he went to the refrigerator in the garage and pulled out a couple of sodas. "I saw the way you were looking at each other."

He shrugged. "I like her, sure. But you know better than anyone how I am with women."

"So you've made some dumb mistakes." Brian tossed him a soda. "You can't judge everyone by Renea."

He wasn't; he was adding Kimmie into the mix, and Gran if it came to that. He'd let them all down.

"How are you doing with Erica's twins?" Brian took a long swig of soda and then squatted down by his bike. "Check out these straight pipes. I never thought I'd go for them, but they're cool."

Jason snorted. "And that makes you think *you're* cool. I like the twins, if you can believe it. I even feed 'em and put 'em in their car seats."

"You?" Brian shook his head as he swung a leg over his bike and sat on it, despite the fact that, even with the garage door closed, it was freezing. "I'm itching to ride this thing, man."

"Might be time for a trip south."

"Can't. Carla's expecting again."

"This soon? You better slow yourself down, boy."

Brian grinned and spread his hands wide. "What can I say, man. I look at her, she gets pregnant."

"And then you brag about it while she does all the work." He clapped Brian on the back. "Seriously, man. Happy for you."

Brian got off the bike and gave it a regretful pat. "I'm getting over my shock that you like a woman with kids. But family's everything, and if she's willing to put up with a loser like you, you better grab her."

"Thanks, pal." But as they walked back into the house to a cacophony of babies rolling on the floor, guarded by Carla's two teen daughters, he was surprised to find himself actually considering his friend's advice. Family life was looking surprisingly good to him.

"I appreciate your girls taking care of Mikey and Teddy," Erica said to Carla as she unpacked a few things in the guest suite. "In fact, I appreciate your letting all of us stay with you. Are you sure we're not putting anyone out?"

"Absolutely sure." Carla lounged back on the bed and waved an arm toward the rest of the house. "This place is huge. And as for the girls, they're kind of fascinated by baby twins, since they're twins themselves."

"They're sweethearts." Erica pulled out the changing supplies and diapers she'd packed for the twins and stacked them on the dresser top. "Did they have delays?"

"Not like yours," Carla said. "I mean, they were a month premature, but they caught up by age one."

"You could notice the twins' delays just from those few minutes?" Erica rubbed the back of her neck. "Are they really that obvious?"

Carla nodded. "I'm glad you're getting them checked out, and Dr. Chen is the best. Well, except for her bedside manner, from what I've heard."

"She's not nice?" Erica's heart sank. "How can a pediatrician have a poor bedside manner?"

"I know, right? It's not that she's not nice, it's just... I heard she's kind of awkward. But she's a genius researcher who knows everything babies need."

Maybe she'll be too preoccupied or oblivious to notice their lack of a medical history. Erica sat down on the room's other twin bed and looked around. "This is really nice."

Carla smiled. "I'm glad to have another adult woman around. Believe me, the fifteen-year-old girls can be a challenge, and other than that, it's just me and the baby when Brian's on duty." She patted her stomach. "And another on the way, so believe me, I grab every moment of girl talk I can get."

"You're expecting? Congratulations." Erica liked the openness of the woman already. It would be nice to be so relaxed and confident in your family life. Even though Erica was blessed, *so* blessed with the twins, she didn't anticipate ever being the kind of comfortable-in-her-own-skin wife and mother that Carla was.

"Maybe we can get the girls to make us tea." Carla leaned forward and listened at the door. "Nah. It's pretty loud out there. We should hide out in here for a few more minutes."

Erica stood, stretched and strolled around the room. "I like your samplers. Embroidery like that is getting to be a lost art." She leaned closer to read them. "Are they just for decoration or from your family?"

"Mine, my parents' and my grandparents'. And all of us are still around and still married."

Wow. What would it be like to come from that kind of legacy?

"So where's your family?" Carla asked, flopping back down on the bed.

Normally, that type of question made Erica self-conscious, but with Carla, she just felt a little sad. "I never knew my grandparents or my dad. My mom had a lot of issues." Then she broke off.

"Had? So you're alone in the world?"

"Pretty much. Except for the twins."

The sound of men's voices resounded through the house, contrasting with the girl and baby sounds. Jason came to the doorway and looked in. "This looks comfortable."

"It is. And it's Erica's. You get the couch, pal." Carla grinned at Jason with the familiarity that bespoke long friendship. She stood and slipped around Jason to exit the room. "I'm going to go manage the chaos."

"I'll be right out," Erica promised.

"Hey," Jason said to Erica, "we got a reminder call from the doctor. We're supposed to arrive fifteen minutes early and bring the babies' medical history."

Erica's stomach twisted with anxiety.

Tell him.

"Listen," he said, "I've got to run to that meeting with the lawyers. You okay here?"

She nodded. "Brian and Carla are really nice."

He walked a little into the room, hooked an arm around her neck and gave her a fast, hard kiss. Then he spun and left the room, and a moment later she heard the front door slam.

She put her hands to her lips, swallowed. This morning he'd apologized for kissing her, and now he'd kissed her again. She could smell his cologne on herself, just a trace of it.

She sank down onto the bed, needing just a moment before she went out to take care of the twins. Just a moment to think about and relish that kiss.

And a moment to try to calm her worries about tomorrow's appointment, the doctor with the poor bedside manner and the fact that she didn't have any medical history at all to show her.

Tomorrow would turn out okay. It was for the twins. She'd figure out an excuse. Wouldn't she?

Eight

As soon as Jason walked back into Brian and Carla's house, he noticed the smell of Christmas cookies and heard the sound of women's laughter.

The contrast with the hard-edged, seamy lawyer meeting he'd just come from couldn't have been greater. He loosened his tie.

He wanted to come home to this world.

Still, he had to remember that he wasn't ready. Screwing this up by acting too soon would be disaster. On some level, he knew that was what had happened with Renea; he'd been tired of the tomcatting life, had met Renea, thought she was something special, and had moved too fast. He couldn't make that mistake again.

Girded against his impulses, he walked into the kitchen.

"Where's Erica?" he asked immediately. So much for not focusing on her.

"We…we kind of made her go change," Carla said, laughing.

"Hey." Jason's protective instincts took over. "Don't be hard on her. She's new to how we all joke around."

"No, no, we were nice! It's just that…she didn't know this is an ugly sweater party. How could she?"

"And her sweater really was kind of ugly…" That was Lisa, Randall's wife. She had a good heart, but no filter. "But not ugly in the way it was supposed to be."

"Stop." Carla frowned at her. "I dug up one of my ugly sweaters for her and she's changing and getting the twins ready."

"So you really like her?" Lisa asked. "How'd you guys meet?"

He didn't want to contribute to the gossip train. "Long story. I gotta go get out of this monkey suit."

And on the way, as much as he'd intended not to do it, he found himself heading upstairs and knocking on the door of the guest suite.

When she called for him to come in, he had to stop and stare.

Normally, Erica wore loose, plain clothes. But now she was dressed in a snug-fitting sweater in a bright shade of pink with white fluffy fur on it. He supposed the sweater was a little silly, but it certainly wasn't ugly. She looked stunning, sitting on the floor with the twins while they played with a stack of blocks. He couldn't help but stare.

"What's wrong? I shouldn't have let them give me this sweater, should I?" She stood up and came over to him.

He reached out and took one of her hands. "You absolutely should have. You look gorgeous."

She looked down at herself. "It's a little tight. And it's supposed to be ugly, but…"

"Hey." He touched her chin so she had to look into his eyes. "You look really pretty, and it's not too tight. I say wear it. But…" He dropped his hand from her face because he was so extremely tempted to kiss her. And he'd decided he wasn't going to do that again. "You wear whatever's comfortable."

The hallway outside the guest suite was balcony style, with a direct view into the main family room, where the party would take place. Trying not to focus on Erica, Jason stepped outside and leaned over the balcony, looking down. Christmas lights twinkled on the tree, and a real fire glowed in the fireplace. Brian and Carla stood together, arm in arm, talking quietly.

Jason wanted what Brian had with a longing so intense that his chest hurt.

Erica came to stand beside him. Her wistful expression matched the way he felt.

"I hope they know what they've got," he said.

She nodded.

"Make you sad?"

"A little." She paused, watching as Brian tugged Carla into a hug and kiss. "But we have to remember that not everyone has it like that. For so many people, it's not like the commercials."

"Yeah. True."

"And," she added, putting an arm around his waist, "it's not what Christmas is really about."

The fact that she'd voluntarily touched him made him go still, every muscle controlled. He had to treat her like a bird that had landed on his arm, with gentleness, no sudden movements.

He turned to her and smiled, determinedly keeping his elbows propped on the balcony railing rather than letting them wrap around her as he wanted to do. "You're right," he said. "Joseph and Mary weren't living the dream when Jesus was born."

"Exactly." She smiled up at him and then looked down

at the cozy room below. "They're great, Carla and Brian. I like them."

There was a sound from the bedroom behind them, and they both turned back to see the babies. "I need to get them dressed for the party. Wish they had something cuter to wear."

She'd given him the perfect cue. "Hold that thought. I'll be right back."

When he returned to the guest suite, she was back on the floor with the twins, who were now stripped down to diapers. Teddy's scooting crawl was already a little more efficient, and Mikey seemed to be stage directing, waving his arms and babbling at his brother.

"Don't be mad," he said, holding out a bag to her. "I was walking from the car to the lawyer's office, and there was a kids' clothing store... I couldn't resist. Consider it my Christmas present to them."

She took the bag, looked at him with a wrinkled forehead and then opened it. He held his breath. Too silly? Not classy enough? He was opening his mouth to offer to return them when she let out a little squeal. "Oh, these are perfect!"

The joy on her face spread warmth through his whole body. He wanted to keep giving her joy, whatever the cost.

She laid the outfits on the floor beside each other. They were one-piecers with snaps on the bottom; he'd been with the twins enough now to know that was what you needed for the diaper set.

"Should Teddy be the elf and Mikey the Santa, or the other way around?" She studied them and then looked up at him.

He sank to his knees beside her. "I was thinking

Mikey's more the Santa type. Even though he doesn't move around much, he's kind of the boss. Teddy's like the sidekick who gets things done."

She turned and put her hand on his arm, and when he looked into her eyes, they were brimming with tears. "You already get that about them?"

"Hey." He reached out, and when a single tear rolled down, he brushed a thumb along her cheek. "I wanted this to make you happy."

She cleared her throat and nodded, her eyes never leaving his. "It does. You have no idea how much."

The sound of laughter from downstairs broke into their silence. "Come on, let's get them dressed."

As he dressed Teddy while Erica got the Santa suit on Mikey, something softened inside him. Not only did he care for Erica, but he was coming to care for her children, as well. He wanted with all his heart for Mikey to start crawling and walking and for Teddy to learn to talk. As he looked into Teddy's wide brown eyes, he felt like Teddy understood, because he offered a sweet smile before reaching out to grab for the button on Jason's shirt.

"Hey, quit that now." He batted Teddy's hand away and finished snapping the suit, then picked him up and stood him on his feet.

Teddy couldn't support himself or balance, but he was approximating a standing position, and when Erica looked up from putting on Mikey's hat, her eyes widened. "That's how he'll look when he's walking! Oh, Jason, I want so much for them to catch up."

"I want that, too." He sat Teddy down next to Mikey. "Listen, I need to run downstairs and see if I can borrow a sweater from Brian. But there's something I want to tell you."

He hadn't known he was going to say this until it came out of his mouth. He'd been thinking about how he'd given up his quest to find answers about Kimmie, but he hadn't lost track of the fact that he had some work and growing to do before he could hope to have a relationship.

The beautiful woman and adorable babies in front of him were making him want to speed up on that goal. Maybe he could learn it best by doing it. Strong, hot joy bloomed in his chest at the possibility that he and Erica might be able to build something together.

If there was any chance of that, he had to be honest. "I haven't always been the best… You know how we were talking about Kimmie's values? Well, mine haven't always been perfect."

"Whose have?" She watched him, her face accepting. "Are you worried about something tonight?"

"It's… There are some women." He hadn't been as bad as a lot of guys, but still, he didn't want Erica getting upset or hurt. "I dated quite a bit before I got engaged, and some of those women might be here."

"Trying to get you back?" she asked lightly, but there was concern underneath her light tone.

"No. But maybe not being the most… I mean, I wasn't…" He broke off and then started again. "What I'm trying to say, I guess, is that I care for you and I want to pursue something with you, if you're willing. But there's some baggage."

Her eyebrows rose a fraction of an inch. "That's not what you said this morning."

"I was fighting against what I felt inside," he admitted.

She looked at the floor and he thought he'd doomed himself with her. Then she started fussing with Mikey's outfit, adjusting his little white fur cuffs. "I…well, I have some baggage, too." She looked up at him. "Not the same kind, but it could hurt the chances that we could…"

He gripped her hand. "Whatever is in your past, I'm going to do my best to help you get over it and move on. And I hope you'll do the same for me."

She bit her lip and nodded, but this time, she didn't meet his eyes. She was shy. He had the sense that she was almost completely inexperienced with men.

He held out a hand and helped her to her feet, feeling the fragility of her slender fingers. She was vulnerable. Innocent.

He had to get this right. He couldn't ruin another woman's life, break another woman's heart. Especially when that woman was Erica.

As Erica walked down the stairs into the crowd of lively, laughing strangers, her stomach twisted with nerves. But she wanted to do this. Wanted to be a part of Jason's world. She tightened her grip on Teddy and Mikey and walked out into the party.

Immediately, she was surrounded by women, ooh-ing and aahing over the boys and their outfits. Everyone wanted to hold them, and Teddy and Mikey, being budding showmen, smiled and laughed and agreeably let themselves be passed from person to person.

"Those outfits," a woman named Lisa said. "Where did you get them?"

Erica hesitated, not sure whether Jason would want to admit to having given the boys such a gift.

"Seriously, was it around here?" someone else asked. "Those are adorable."

"I think the bag said Children's Cloud Creations." She

looked around for Jason, but he was nowhere to be seen. "Jason bought them."

"That place is expensive!" Lisa looked speculatively at Erica.

It was?

"Are you and Jason, like, together?" Lisa pressed.

Erica bit her lip and looked down, but that was bad because it made her notice that her borrowed sweater was a little more revealing than she would have liked it to be, especially now that the shield of the twins was gone. "I...uh...I don't really know."

Carla pushed between Lisa and Erica. "Don't mind her. She means well, but she's way too nosy."

"I didn't mean... Oh. I was overstepping, wasn't I?"

Carla nodded. "Yep. And you told me I should call you on it, so I am." She turned to Erica. "We're together all the time, the spouses, because our husbands work together. Well, and Delphine joins in, too, although she's the cop in the family." She nodded toward a tall, slender African American woman who was deep in conversation with Carla's husband, Brian, while a couple of toddlers played on the floor in front of them.

Carla and Lisa's ongoing conversation gave Erica a chance to regroup. She picked up Mikey and kept an eye on Teddy, who was scooting toward a bouncy toy.

She was overwhelmed with everything that was happening, so much so that she felt like her mind was on overload.

Worry about the doctor's appointment tomorrow bounced against excitement that Jason actually seemed to like her. Her! The one with the druggie mother and church-bin clothes, the perpetual new girl and sometime foster kid, was the choice of a handsome, successful, kind man like Jason. The way he was with the twins brought tears to her eyes.

What would happen, though, when he found out that he was related to them?

Jason came inside with another man, carrying armloads of wood, which they stashed by the fireplace. Immediately, Jason looked around the room, and when he saw her, he headed her way.

All the people here and he chose to talk to her. Of course, he was kind and was acting as a host, but still, she felt special and cherished, truly honored.

Why had Kimmie been so adamant that Jason shouldn't have the twins, shouldn't even know them? Was it to maintain her own perfect image in her brother's mind, to continue thinking of herself as the big sister role model?

If that was Kimmie's reason, it was starting to seem a little bit selfish. Jason could offer so much to the twins. It was *they* who needed a role model, and Jason would be an amazing one.

A pretty, dark-haired woman stepped into Jason's path and put a hand on his arm. Erica couldn't hear the exchange, but she could read the body language. The woman was definitely interested in Jason.

He made a couple of quiet comments and nodded toward Erica. The woman turned and looked at her, cocked her head to the side and shrugged. Then she swooshed her arm as if to gesture Jason over toward Erica. He did as she bid, laughing, and behind him, the brunette pointed and nodded as if to provide an endorsement.

That was a little embarrassing, especially considering how many people had seen. But it felt good, too. If Jason was choosing her, maybe she *did* have something to offer, not just as a friend or helper, but as a woman.

Jason approached, and Erica hoped for a little time alone with him to catch her breath. But before he could get through the crowd, another couple came up to Erica. "Hi!" the woman greeted her, a toddler on her hip. "How old are your little guys?"

Erica steeled herself for the inevitable comparisons. "Fifteen months," she said, hugging Mikey a little closer.

"Hey, that's how old our princess is, too!" The woman nodded toward the little girl she was holding, all dressed up in a red-and-pink-striped dress and tights.

With the features of a Down syndrome baby.

"She's beautiful," Erica said. "Look, Mikey, this is... what's her name?"

"Miranda. And I'm Corrine. Miranda, say hi to Mikey." The woman lowered her voice. "I think...Jason talked to Ralph, here, about Dr. Chen. We consulted with her about Miranda."

"Thank you for the reference. I appreciate it." Which was true, mostly.

Jason finally arrived at their little cluster. "I see you've met. Hey, Miranda, sweetie!" He held out his arms for the baby.

Corrine and Ralph looked at each other. "You sure you want to hold her?"

Jason laughed self-consciously. "I'm known as the worst with babies," he said to Erica. To the couple he added, "I've had a little practice lately."

"He's great with the twins," Erica said, and finally the mother released little Miranda into Jason's arms.

The dad whistled. "Man, have you changed. Are you the reason for this?" he asked Erica.

She shrugged. "I guess I am," she said shyly.

Jason put an arm around her. "She's been very patient. And I've learned that you don't feed a baby in a white shirt."

Suddenly, the door to the party opened with a bang, letting cold wind blow in from outside. Beside her, Erica heard Jason draw in a breath and then mutter something. The party noise of chattering voices died down.

A woman stalked in, shaky on extremely high heels that she didn't need—she had to be six feet tall in her socks. Carla hurried to close the door behind the new visitor.

The woman looked around, obviously searching for someone. When her eyes lit on Jason, she stopped still. "There you are," she said in a husky voice. She slid off her fur coat and Erica couldn't help but gasp. In the light, the woman was starkly gorgeous, with sharp cheekbones, enormous dark eyes and blond hair down to the middle of her back. The dress she wore was red lace and fitted her like she was a model.

"Don't suppose anyone has a drink for a lady?" the woman said.

Nine

As he stared at the woman he'd once thought he loved, Jason's gut churned with the same feelings that had nearly driven him to despair two years ago.

Renea was beautiful and intelligent, but hopelessly, endlessly mired in alcoholism interconnected with an eating disorder. After knowing her parents, he could pretty well guess her problems stemmed from her childhood.

He'd tried, he'd failed, and they'd broken up. After getting the ring package from her earlier today, he'd sent her a brief text reiterating that it was over between them.

So what was she doing here now?

"Aw, look at the babies!" She teetered over toward the small circle of women and children by the fire. It looked like she was going to fall down until someone helped her into a chair.

Erica was there to see it all. And judging from the way she glanced over at him before focusing her attention on the twins, she could tell that Renea had been important to him.

"I'm gonna get married someday!" Renea gushed in a loud voice. "I'm going to get me one of these little buggers, too!" She reached down as if she were going to pick up Teddy.

Smoothly, Erica sank to her knees and swept the baby out of Renea's grasp. "You know, he just ate, and I'm afraid he'll spit up on your pretty dress. Is that a Christoson?"

"No!" Renea looked insulted. "It's DeBrady."

"My mistake." Erica smiled a little and cuddled Mikey.

The comparison between the two women was striking. Renea was the more classically gorgeous, for sure, and there'd been a time when that had been important to him. Plenty of men had envied him having someone like Renea on his arm.

But Erica, with her wise-beyond-her-years green eyes, her natural hair and her comfortable, kneeling position on the floor, one baby in her arms and the other attempting to crawl into her lap, looked like everything he'd ever wanted—even if he doubted whether he'd get it.

Seeing that Erica and the twins were safe and that the other women had engaged Renea in conversation, Jason took the coward's route and stepped onto the back porch. He took breaths of clear, cold air and tried to think.

Now that he was learning what love was, he knew he hadn't had it with Renea. But the question was, had he mended himself enough from the mistakes of the past that he could dare to pursue something with Erica?

You don't have a choice. You're already pursuing it.

But he could put on the brakes, stop it now before anyone got hurt.

He thought of how hurt Erica had looked when he'd told her their kiss wasn't real. *Too late.*

He looked up at the stars. Sometimes God seemed that

far away, too cold and distant to help Jason with what seemed like a fairly impossible situation.

Even the thought brought back the minister's words from last Sunday's sermon: nothing is impossible with God.

He needed God's help to fix an impossible situation, to get to where he could manage to head a family like his friends did. Somewhere in the neglect from his careless parents, or maybe in his own horribly mistaken tough love for his sister, he'd gotten broken.

He hoped God could fix him. "Will You try?" he whispered to the stars. "I'm a sinner, but You took care of that. Help me do better."

There was a bang behind him and Brian came out onto the porch. "You okay?"

"Just getting a soda." Jason bent down to retrieve a can from the cooler full of ice. "Want one?"

"Sure. Um…you've got a situation in there, huh?"

"Renea?" Jason shook his head. "For real."

"She's all over Kameer." Brian laughed a little. "And she's really lit."

Jason looked past Brian into the living room. He couldn't see Renea—nor Erica, which was probably for the best—but he saw three of his friends, all guys, talking and laughing as they looked in the direction of Renea's shrill voice.

She wasn't his responsibility, but then again… "I'll be back in just a minute," he said to Brian and went out into the backyard.

A minute later, he had Renea's mother on the phone. "No, I'm not coming to get her," the woman said. "She's made her bed and she can lie in it."

"Can I talk to Monty?"

"He's washed his hands of her, as well. And he's away on business, anyway." There was a pause. "She's a lost cause. We've given up on her for the sake of our own sanity."

When he didn't answer, the phone clicked off.

A lost cause. Jason pocketed his phone and shook his head. Despite all the tough cases he'd seen on the streets of Philadelphia, he didn't believe in those.

When he walked back inside, a couple more guys had joined the crowd watching Renea. Most of the women seemed to be in the kitchen, or in the playroom with the kids. He could hear their talk, mingled with the sound of kids playing. He hoped Erica was there with the other women, enjoying herself.

He looked over at Renea and saw that a strap of her dress had fallen down. She was leaning on the much-shorter Kameer, who looked like he didn't know what had hit him.

Jason could identify. He used to feel that way about Renea, himself. And Kameer was young, a new officer on the force.

Jason crossed the room and approached the couple. "Hey, Renea. It's time to get out of here."

"I found somebody else," she said, slurring her words. "He's a *very* nice man."

"Yes, and maybe you can get to know him better another time. Right now, it's time to go home."

"You don't get to have a say over me."

"The lady's right," Kameer said, getting a little in Jason's face. "It's her choice."

Jason stared down the younger man. "Sometimes a lady isn't in any condition to make a choice. And at that point, a gentleman steps away from the game."

"You just don't want anyone else to have me. You ruined my life, made a mess of me." Renea's words were loud in the room that had suddenly gone quiet. "Or maybe it's just that you want me back?" She teetered a couple of steps to Jason and draped herself over him.

She felt like deadweight.

"Let's get you home." He looked at Kameer. "Get her coat, would you?"

Kameer gave an indignant snort, looked again at Jason's face and headed to the front closet.

Renea leaned over and vomited into a wastebasket with an alcoholic's quick, practiced move, still clinging to Jason's arm for balance. Then she stepped away from him and opened the door.

Some of the women had come back out—it looked like their husbands had summoned them, probably because they didn't want to deal with a sick woman themselves.

Erica was among them.

He shot her a quick, apologetic glance. This sort of display was just what she wouldn't want, and between Renea hanging on him and talking trash about him, he couldn't blame Erica if she decided to back off.

All the same, he couldn't leave Renea to freeze to death alone. Even though he hadn't invited her, she was here because of him.

He grabbed her coat and shrugged into his own.

"You need some help, man?" Brian asked.

"No, I've got it. Sorry for the disruption," he called back into the party crowd. "Carry on."

"Come back after you get her home."

"Sure. I'll be back."

He looked at Erica when he said that, wanting her to know that, despite this scene, he wasn't abandoning her.

But she was talking to another of the women with some intensity. He could just imagine their topic.

He headed out, caught Renea and draped her coat around her. He was trying to talk her into getting into his truck when the house door opened again.

Erica emerged and walked down toward the two of them, her hands in her jacket pockets. "Do you want me to go with you?" she asked him. "I know how..." She gave a shrug. "I know how to deal with someone who's impaired."

"Who you calling impaired?" Renea slurred, but without much energy.

"But the twins..." Jason said.

"Carla's going to put them to bed, or try to. It's fine." She frowned. "Unless you don't want me here. If you'd rather handle it alone..."

"So *you're* his new squeeze." Renea patted Erica on the head. "You've gone down in the world, Jason."

Erica looked up at the woman, at least a foot taller than she was. "Yep, I'm a pipsqueak," she said. "Want to get in the car? I'm freezing."

"I don't have anywhere to go." Renea looked at Jason. "My mom told me if I went out, I couldn't come back. Can we go to your place?"

"It's sublet," he said.

"You living with her now?"

"Nope." He took Renea's arm and urged her into the truck, with a manhandling move he knew from years on the narc squad. Not rough, but not particularly gentle, either.

He could smell Renea's trademark scent of alcohol covered by perfume and breath mints. And he was still a little stunned by Erica's matter-of-fact willingness to help.

After Renea was in, Erica climbed in after her.

"You're sure about this? It might not be pretty."

She gave him a little smile. "I know. I'm fine."

He jogged around to the driver's side and started the truck. They hadn't driven two blocks before Renea made a sound like she was going to be sick. Jason skidded to a stop and she leaned over Erica, who simply opened the passenger door and scooted Renea's upper body a little bit farther out of the truck, pulling back her hair and holding her head while she vomited into the street.

When Renea was done, Jason held out a bandanna and Erica wiped off Renea's face.

And then Renea settled down with her head in Erica's lap and went to sleep.

Jason reached out and touched Erica's face. "You're made of steel, you know that?"

She shook her head, looking down. "I'm really not. Where are you headed with her? Does she live with anyone?"

"Her mom won't take her in." Even as he said it, his gut twisted tight. He couldn't judge Renea's mom, because he'd basically done the same to his sister. Oh, he'd offered Kimmie a place to stay, but he'd set strict rules on it and refused to send her money, only an airline ticket.

She'd never come home.

"Does she have a purse?"

Jason indicated the sparkling thing he'd found with her coat.

Erica opened it and riffled through. "Let's see, there's—"

"You're going through her purse?"

She shrugged. "What else are we going to do? She kind of gave up her right to privacy when she threw up on me." She pulled a couple of cards out of Renea's small bag, and a crisp hundred-dollar bill. "The way I see it," she said, "we can either take her to this Welcome Home shelter for women, or we can check her into some safe hotel, or we can call this woman, her AA sponsor."

Jason nodded, stopping the truck at a red light. "You're good. And I'd say..." He plucked the shelter's card out of Erica's hand.

"The Welcome Home shelter. Me, too." She nodded decisively. "Because even in a safe hotel, she could get taken advantage of. And sponsors aren't supposed to take the people they sponsor into their homes."

"How do you know so much about addicts? Is it all from your mom? Or Al-Anon?" He turned the truck in the direction of the Welcome Home shelter.

She didn't answer.

He glanced over at her. "Kimmie?"

She hesitated, then nodded. "Mom, Kimmie...that's part of it. I also volunteered some after Mom died. And, well..." She shrugged and spread her hands. "I just... That's the people I grew up with. You get accustomed to finding ways to help." Before he could say more, she said, "Your turn to answer. How'd you get involved with Renea?"

As if hearing her name, Renea shifted restlessly, and Jason slowed. But then she sighed and settled back into sleep, her face childlike.

"She got caught up in a sting, but she was never convicted. We liked each other, so after a while, I gave her a call." Like an idiot.

Erica nodded but didn't speak.

"I guess I like to help people," he said. "Or maybe I was on a power trip. That's what Kimmie always said."

"Maybe you were trying to replace Kimmie in your life," Erica suggested quietly.

He frowned. "I don't think so, but..." He pulled into the shelter's parking lot.

"It's a Christian place?" She was looking at the blinking cross on the side of the building.

"Big-time."

"That's the only thing that'll help her. You feel okay about leaving her here?"

"She'll be as safe as she can be."

"Then go ahead on in and do whatever paperwork you need to. I'll wait here with her. Better to wait and wake her up when we have a place she can crash."

He shook his head, amazed at Erica's generosity and kindness. "If you're sure."

"It's no problem."

He nodded and got out of the truck. "You know all my dirt," he said, "but you still can tolerate me?"

A strange expression crossed her face. "Of course."

He walked into the shelter quickly, smiling.

The next morning, when her quiet phone alarm went off, Erica hit Snooze and buried her head under her pillow.

They were going to see the specialist today, and she didn't know if she could face it.

She was excited, of course she was. Maybe the famous doctor would have ideas of what Mikey and Teddy needed, some particular combination of physical therapy and nutrition that could move them along toward where they should be developmentally.

Being with the other women and children last night

had just confirmed how far behind they were. She needed to get them help, the sooner, the better.

But she'd be walking through the doors of the prestigious research hospital with zero paperwork on these babies and a police detective at her side. That combination could mean disaster.

Upping the ante was the fact that she truly cared about Jason. He'd been nothing but kind to his drunken ex last night. And after they'd gotten Renea into the shelter, he'd had tender words for Erica as they'd driven back to Brian and Carla's house.

She hugged her pillow, happy butterflies dancing in her stomach, thinking of the tender moments they'd shared after coming back into the quiet house and checking on the twins.

He thinks I'm an amazing woman. Who had ever said such a thing about her, unless it was someone wanting to get something out of her?

But Jason hadn't had anything on his mind except helping her find towels for a shower and a snack because she hadn't managed to eat anything at the party.

He was truly a good and kind man. And the way he looked at her gave her the insane hope that maybe, just maybe, they could have a future together.

Except you couldn't build a future on a lie.

More than ever, she wondered why Kimmie had painted Jason in such negative colors, why she'd refused to let him, or her mother or grandparents, know about Mikey and Teddy.

Had Kimmie kept the secret to cover her own sins? Though she'd put on a party face for much of the time Erica had known her, the contrast between her and the rest of her family made Erica suspect that Kimmie had carried a deep sense of shame inside herself.

Teddy stirred, then rolled over in the crib. His round eyes met hers and he smiled, and Erica's heart gave a painful little twist. How was it possible to love a tiny little being so much? To want his good more than her own?

She reached a hand in for Teddy to play with and sank to her knees beside the crib. She couldn't control what happened today, and she knew she'd probably done some things wrong. But it hadn't been for bad intent.

I put it into Your hands, Father, she whispered. *If it's Your will, let this doctor help the boys. And let me raise them or at least help to raise them.*

Praying for something to work out with Jason was just way too much to ask, so she didn't. She just remained there, focused on her Lord and Savior, trying to rest in Him, until the clock and the babies forced her to stand up and face the day.

Ten

Jason pulled the truck into the Early Development Center's parking lot and looked over at Erica. "Ready?"

"This place is huge!"

"That's the university hospital over there," he said, waving a hand toward the big block of buildings to the left. "The Center is just this part, here." But he could see why she was impressed, or maybe intimidated. The two-story brick building looked brand-new and everything, from the signage to the landscaping, spelled *tasteful* and *exclusive* and *expensive*. His big, late-model truck was probably the cheapest vehicle in the lot. "This is the kind of facility you get when you're the best in the country. Dr. Chen has published lots of books and articles and done all kinds of studies. It was a good thing we had strings to pull and that she had a cancellation."

"Yes, and I appreciate what you've done. Really." She put a hand on his arm, squeezed and let go. Despite her tension, she was still appreciative. That was Erica.

He came around to her side of the truck, where she was leaning into the back seat to get Mikey out. As had become routine for them now, she handed him to Jason and climbed in to free Teddy.

He noticed the fine sheen of sweat on her upper lip as she emerged from the back seat with Teddy, and he extended a hand to help her down. Teddy dropped a toy, and when she bent to get it, the diaper bag on her shoulder spilled out half its contents.

"Oh, man," she said, "I'm a walking disaster today."

"Slow down." He squatted to pick up a diaper, a container of wipes and a plastic key chain toy and handed them to her. "I'm sure this parking lot is cleaner than some people's tabletops."

The day was cloudy, but the temperature was above freezing and the piles of snow were starting to melt, making the streets sloppy. Here, though, the parking lot was clear and dry.

"You know," she said as they carried the boys inside, "I'm still not sure this is such a good idea. I won't be able to come back here to get them any treatment."

"Dr. Chen does consultations for people from all over," he reminded her, wondering why she still seemed resistant. "She can refer you to local practitioners and therapists."

"And I don't have any of their medical records."

He held the door for her. "Why not?"

She hesitated. "They're back in Arizona." She didn't look at him, intent on studying the wall listing of offices. "It was a spur-of-the-moment decision to move. I have some stuff in storage. Oh, there's Dr. Chen. I guess we go to office 140."

"Did something happen in Arizona that made you decide to move?" She never talked about the twins' father, except to mention that he was in prison and had no claim on the twins. But a breakup would explain why her decision to move had been sudden, and also why she was so skittish with men. At least, with him.

Although her skittishness seemed to be fading, which was very, very nice.

Still, his detective instincts were aroused, just a little, by the way she avoided answering his questions. But then Mikey dropped his pacifier and started to cry, and Teddy let out a few sympathy wails, and it didn't seem to be the moment to probe.

Inside, the waiting room was plush and quiet. Despite the small box of toys and the shelf of children's books, it didn't look much like a pediatrician's office. One other couple was waiting, and a mother had a sleeping baby in a carrier. Diplomas and awards lined the walls.

When they approached the receptionist, she greeted them cordially and smiled at the twins. "You must be Erica Lindholm. With Mikey and Teddy?"

"That's right," Erica said.

"I'll just need your insurance card."

Erica bit her lip. "We're paying privately. Do I need to prepay?" She fumbled in her purse.

"It'll be taken care of." Jason slid the woman a credit card. "I'll handle whatever needs to be paid for today, and you can send the bill to the address I'm going to write down for you, if you have a piece of paper."

The receptionist lifted an eyebrow as she handed him a notepad and pen. "Here you go."

"Jason!" Erica hissed. "What are you doing?"

He finished writing down the address, handed the woman his credit card and turned to her. "Don't worry about it. The officers in my precinct always pick a Christmas charity for children, and this year…"

"We're your Christmas charity?" she interrupted. "Are you serious?"

She walked over to a seating area near the toys and sat, putting Teddy down to crawl.

Jason finished his transaction and brought Mikey over. "I thought you might be happy. Did I do something wrong?" Even as he said it, he knew where she was coming from; independent as she was, she wouldn't necessarily be thrilled at accepting the gift.

"I don't feel right about accepting charity. I mean, I'm going to own half that farm. I won't need that kind of help, and it should go to someone who does."

"You need it now, and the guys were looking for an opportunity." He touched her hand. "Accept it in the spirit it's given. It'll help the babies."

She looked down at Mikey, then Teddy, and then she nodded. "You're right. Thank you."

"Mrs. Lindholm?" a nurse called at the door.

Erica stood, hoisted Mikey and the diaper bag, and squared her shoulders. When she didn't turn to get Teddy, Jason took it as an invitation to join the appointment. He picked up Teddy and followed her in.

"Let's weigh and measure them right here." The nurse was a broad-faced, no-nonsense-looking person in scrubs. "They're fifteen months? Were they preemies?"

"Only by three weeks."

The nurse made a notation and then passed a tape measure around Teddy's head, then measured him from heel to the top of his head. "Just a few questions before you see the doctor. Let's talk food. Breastfed, bottle fed?" She looked inquiringly at Erica.

"Ummmm...breast?"

Odd that her answer sounded like a question.

"How long?"

"Just a couple of months."

"Okay. And when did they start on solids?"

Erica opened her mouth and then closed it again.

The nurse turned from the computer to face her. "I asked about solid food. Is there a problem?"

Erica closed her eyes for just a moment. Then she opened them. "Look," she said, "there's a whole period of their lives that I don't know much about."

Jason tilted his head, wondering if he'd heard that right.

The nurse's lips flattened. "And why's that?"

Erica sat up straight and gave the nurse a level stare. "I'd rather hold the rest of my discussion for the doctor."

"But our protocol is for me to—"

"Can the doctor see me even if I don't answer all of your questions?"

"Ye-es…"

Jason felt like his world was spinning off somewhere he didn't understand. He'd never seen gentle Erica act quite like this.

Well, actually, he had. When she was defending her kids.

"Then I'd rather save the rest of the interview for the doctor herself." Erica didn't look his way.

Something was *definitely* going on here.

The nurse looked at him as if to say, can't you control your wife? But he didn't rise to the bait. If he admitted he wasn't any relation to Erica and the kids, he'd probably be sent out into the waiting room. And despite her huffy attitude, he had the feeling Erica needed support.

"Fine." The nurse stood. "Follow me." She stormed down the hall and flung open the door of an exam room.

"The doctor will be in shortly." She slammed Erica's folder into the plastic holder beside the door and stomped off.

Erica went into the exam room and he followed behind, Teddy in his arms. "So what was that about, how there's a period you don't know about? Did you just not like her attitude, or…" He didn't want to contemplate the other alternative. That she didn't remember because she'd been in some way out of it, in trouble personally or with the law.

He'd known people with big blackouts in their pasts, but drugs or alcohol were usually involved.

She'd set Mikey down on the carpeted floor, and now she lifted Teddy from his arms. "Jason."

There was a funny tone to her voice. "Yeah?"

"I'd like to speak to the doctor alone."

"Of course, I can leave after—"

"No, I mean now." She lifted her chin. "I don't want you here."

The words shocked him. He'd thought they were getting closer, thought that she liked and needed him. He wanted to hear what the doctor said about Mikey and Teddy.

And why would she—

"So could you leave?"

She was standing there with her shoulders squared, facing him, but she wasn't meeting his eyes.

"You want me to leave."

"Yes, please." She glanced up then, and he saw that her eyes were a little shiny. "If you don't want to wait around for me, it's okay. I can call for a ride. A taxi or something."

"Car seats?" He shook his head, backing out of the

room. "No. I'll be outside." He turned and spun out of the room.

He walked right through the waiting room and outside. *Goodbye, softhearted nice guy. Welcome back, Detective Stephanidis.*

In the windy parking lot, he pulled out his phone and scrolled through his contacts. "Hey, Brian," he said a moment later. "Could you do a little bit of investigating for me?"

An hour later, Erica sat in the examining room with the two babies cuddled on her lap. "I realize that you might have to report me," she said to the white-coat-clad doctor in front of her, "but I hope you won't."

Dr. Chen tapped a pencil on the table. "There's such a thing as doctor-patient confidentiality, and I believe in it. On the other hand, I'm *required* to report any situation where a child is at risk."

Erica nodded, dismayed. She was making one move at a time here. She'd only thought of kicking Jason out of the pediatrician's office this morning. If he wasn't there, she'd realized, she would be able to be completely honest with the pediatrician.

And she had been. She'd spilled the entire story: what she knew of Kimmie's pregnancy, of the early months with the twins, of their father and of Kimmie's relapse.

And she'd explained all the things she *didn't* know.

Dr. Chen had listened and watched the twins on the floor. She'd asked questions, held out toys for them to grasp, listened to their babble. Her forehead wrinkled with focus, her questions for Erica pointed. Erica didn't find her awkward at all, as Carla had said; she was just very, very intense.

Finally, after about twenty minutes of observation, Dr. Chen had nodded briskly. "Teddy's just about to crawl, and that mobility will help his mind develop," she'd said. "But he'll come along faster with some physical therapy. Speech, too. Mikey..." She'd studied Mikey's feet again, bent his legs at the knees, rotated his ankles. "He may just go directly to walking. His muscle tone is pretty good."

"I'm so relieved that you think they'll be okay," Erica said. "Look, I know there are probably a million ways I could have done better with the twins. Maybe I should have stayed with Kimmie, let them be taken into foster care. I just..." She shook her head. "I've *been* in foster care, and I know how wrong it can go. I know how siblings can be separated. And Kimmie didn't want that for them. So...I did what she told me to. I brought them here."

"Do you think she was trying to get them back together with her family?"

Erica shook her head. "For whatever reason, she didn't want her brother to find out. She thought he was hostile, judgmental. And... I realize now, she was ashamed of having them out of wedlock, and she didn't want him to know. He idealized her, you see."

"Why did you bring the twins here," Dr. Chen asked, "knowing you might be reported?"

Erica shrugged, her arms still around the boys. "Once they were able to get me the appointment and I thought about it and prayed about it, I knew I had to do what was right for the twins." She met the woman's steady brown eyes. "I know you're the best, and I want the best for them. They need to get started on early intervention, like you said. If I didn't tell a specialist—tell you—everything I knew about their past, they could suffer for it."

The doctor held her gaze, then nodded. "From what I see at this moment, the twins are loved and well cared for."

Erica's breath went out in a sigh of relief.

Dr. Chen held up a hand. "However, if you decide not to get them the help they need, now that you know more about it, I would consider that to be neglect." She leaned forward. "You're going to have to come clean about all of this, you know. Their need for medical attention will be ongoing. Nothing in medicine is inexpensive." She glanced at the chart. "Even without seeing test results and writing it up, I know they'll need therapy. Speech and physical, at a minimum. That's not cheap."

Erica nodded. "I know, and I mean to go through their mother's things and contact the hospital where they were born, do a little digging. I need to... I need to let their other relatives know about them."

"Is the man who accompanied you one of those other relatives? Or is he just a boyfriend?"

"He's a relative."

"The courts might leave them with you, even once your lack of formal guardianship comes out. Unless there's another relative claiming them. Just keep doing what you're doing and after the holidays, when you can get all the testing done and I can analyze it, we'll figure out a program of treatment."

As they exited the turnpike and headed toward Holly Creek Farm, Erica breathed a sigh of relief that this hard day was almost over.

It had been an uncomfortable ride home. Jason had rushed them back to the house after the doctor's appointment with literally not a word, his face set and angry.

Then he'd headed off to testify while she got the twins ready to go home.

He hadn't spoken except for short, efficient communications since they'd gotten in the car.

He'd taken off his overcoat but was still in his dark suit, white shirt and thin tie, and he looked so handsome he took her breath away.

And she'd ruined any chance of being with him.

The moon made a path on the snowy fields and stars sparkled above. A clear, cold night. As they rounded a corner on the country road, she couldn't help drawing in a breath. "This is where I went off the road, right?"

"Yep." He didn't volunteer more.

But emotions flooded Erica. She'd been desperate then, worried about Kimmie, not knowing where she'd land with the twins, not knowing if she could manage them.

Now she was half owner of a farm and she'd started to become part of a community. Sad, because she'd lost Kimmie, but stable.

A big part of why was Jason.

They were almost home. There wasn't time for a full discussion and she recognized her own cowardliness in that. But she had to say something. "Look, Jason, I'm sorry."

He didn't speak, didn't look over. Just steered the truck.

She looked back and saw that the twins were still sound asleep. "I'm sorry about shutting you out. You've been nothing but kind to us and… I'm sorry I had to do that."

He was silent a moment more, and then he glanced

over. "I'm trying to be an adult about this, but I don't understand."

"I just... There are some things about the twins' early months that are private."

"You said you didn't remember. Was that true?"

She thought. Should she just tell him now? But no, they were only a few minutes away from home and Papa would be there, and the twins would wake up...

"Is it their father? You've never really talked about him and I've respected your privacy, but did he do something to you or them? Because that can be prosecuted. He should have to pay. Let alone pay child support, but to cause a blank out of months or to cause delays..."

"No, it's not that."

He fell silent. A waiting silence.

She couldn't form the words.

"I thought we were building something together!" He hit the steering wheel and stepped down on the gas.

She cringed. "Be careful! The twins!"

Immediately, he let up on the gas. "Sorry. I'm angry and upset, but that's no way to act."

He was going to be *really* angry when he found out the truth. "I'll talk to you about it tonight," she said. "There *is* something you need to know about their background, and I... I promise, I'll tell you."

She was promising herself, too.

Jason pulled into the parking place at the rail fence in front of the farm.

The house was dark.

Jason frowned. "Wonder if Papa had something to do. He didn't mention it."

He turned off the truck, opened the door. She opened hers, too.

And looked at him. "Wouldn't the dog…"

"I have a bad feeling. Let me go in first," he said.

Protective to the core, and why should that surprise her?

He went inside, and from the way his hand moved under his suit jacket, she knew he carried a gun. But she also knew he was safe. She trusted him with that gun. She watched as he disappeared inside. He flipped on lights, and she saw him moving from room to room.

Papa must have gone somewhere. They were being overcautious. Surely that was all it was.

Still, she felt lonely and vulnerable, just her and the twins in the cold truck. She slipped out and into the back seat between their car seats. Cramped, but she wanted to be there when they woke up.

Father God, she prayed, *help me to tell Jason the truth.* And then she prayed what she hadn't dared to this morning. *And if it be Your will, let me be with him, Lord. I love him. Keep him safe.*

He wasn't coming back out. Her prayers got more fervent. *Keep him safe.*

The twins were stirring.

She loved them so much.

Jason didn't emerge. Should she go to him?

She opened the door, torn as to what to do.

Then, suddenly, she heard an explosive sound, not from the house but from somewhere off beyond the barn.

A gunshot.

Eleven

The sound of the gunshot crashed into Jason's consciousness. He ran out of the house, and Erica met him beside the truck.

Papa. If Papa were hurt...

"It came from the barn area, maybe beyond," he told her. "I'm going out. Take the twins inside and lock the doors."

"Should I call the police?"

"Call and tell them we heard a shot and Papa's missing. He could be out in the barn, and the shot could be hunters, but..."

"I'll do it. And my phone's on." She gave him a fierce, fast hug, but she didn't offer to go along. She needed to stay with the babies and he needed to move. Fast.

He saw lights in the barn and walked toward it on the path worn through the snow, now icy. When he glanced back, he saw Erica framed in the doorway of the house, waving to let him know they were safely inside.

His breath froze in his nose and his mouth. Was Papa out here somewhere, in the cold, freezing? Why had he left Papa alone?

Of course Papa didn't want protection or babysitting, but maybe he needed it.

His phone pinged and he glanced at it. Brian from Philly. He turned it off.

When he got to the barn, the door stood open and the lights were on. "Papa? Hey, Papa."

There was no answer, and disappointment pushed in. He checked out the whole place, though. Maybe Papa had fallen or even fainted.

But the barn was empty.

Back outside, he noticed there were tracks leading away from the barn. Human and animal. Why would Papa have gone that way? Unless…it was the direction of the cabin, but why…

Another shot rang out, close this time.

He gripped his own weapon tighter and sent up a prayer. *If You let Papa be all right, I'll stay here with him. I'll take care of him.* You weren't supposed to bargain with God, Jason knew that, but he was desperate.

He moved forward. Heard a faint sound. Then barking that sounded like… Mistletoe?

He ran toward the sound, and a moment later an excited snow-covered dog leaped up at him, bounced off and turned toward the woods, looking back over his shoulder, his tongue lolling out.

"Where's Papa, Mistletoe?"

Mistletoe gave one short bark and trotted toward a small stand of bushes. Jason followed.

There was a rustle and a grunt. Then: "About time you got here."

Jason had never been so glad to hear Papa's crotchety voice in his life. He rushed forward, nearly slipping on icy ground, and sank to his knees beside his grandfather.

"What happened? Did you break a bone? Where does it hurt?"

"It doesn't hurt, but I'm cold. I can't seem to get myself up."

Mistletoe romped in a circle around them, kicking up snow and barking.

"Hit an icy patch and my legs went out from under me." Papa propped himself on an elbow and grimaced. "Every time I try to stand up I fall back down. And that's not good at my age, so I figured I'd call for help this way." He patted his rifle. "Might scare out the squatters in the cabin, too."

"You came out here alone because you thought there were squatters in the cabin? You could've been killed!"

"You're not going to be in town forever. I have to be independent." Papa was breathing heavily as he got himself into a sitting position. "Except that crazy dog wouldn't leave me alone. Curled up right beside me. Kept me warm for close to an hour." He rubbed Mistletoe's head. "Didn't like me shooting off the gun, though."

Jason ran a hand over the dog. "Steak bones for you tonight, buddy." Then he braced himself and lifted Papa's not-insubstantial weight, getting a shoulder under him, almost falling himself. "We'll talk more once you're inside and warm." He clicked on Erica's name and dictated a text. "Papa's fine but cold. Turn up heat."

And then, as he and Papa made their way toward the house, he sent up a prayer to God. *Thank You. I'll keep my promise.*

Erica couldn't stop looking at Papa's dear, tired face. She fussed over him, bandaged a scrape on his hand and brought stacks of blankets downstairs. The front room was toasty, and they soon had Papa ensconced by the fire.

"Tell us what happened." Erica sat down at Papa's feet.

"All of it," Jason added.

Papa pulled up the blanket Erica had put over his legs, settled back in his chair and smiled from Erica to Jason, almost as if he were enjoying the attention. "I missed you two and those babies," he said. "Aside from Ruth Delacroix calling to check on me, I didn't speak to a soul while you were gone. Got to feeling blue, and the cure for that is work, so I went out to do some extra chores in the barn."

"Papa!" Jason sounded exasperated. "You could've let it go until I got home."

"I told you, son, I was feeling blue. So I was out there mending that broken board on the front stall, and I thought I heard noises. When I went outside, I saw a light bobbing up and down out toward the cabin."

Erica glanced at Jason, who was studying his grandfather, and wondered if they were both thinking the same thing. Had he really seen something, or was his mind wandering? Papa seemed sharper than she was, most days, but he was definitely old.

"A light like…a lantern? Headlights?" She adjusted Papa's blankets again.

"I couldn't tell. So," he said righteously, "I got my shotgun and headed down there."

Jason let his head sink into his hand. "Papa. What were you going to do if you found a crowd of drug squatters out there?"

"Why do you think I brought the shotgun? And the dog?"

Jason shook his head. "You should have just called the police."

"I'm a farmer. Independent. We don't call the police unless we really need 'em." He looked suddenly concerned. "Did you call them when you didn't find me here?"

"Of course I did," Erica said.

Papa made a disgusted sound.

"We were worried! Anyway, I didn't tell them to come right out. I just wanted to have them on alert. I called them back as soon as Jason let me know you were okay."

Papa sat up. "I'll never live this down. They'll be busting my chops at the diner for weeks."

"Those guys!" Jason snorted. "If anything, they'll be impressed."

"Wait, so you headed toward the cabin," Erica said. "Then what happened? You didn't see anybody suspicious, did you?"

Papa gestured toward his leg. "What happened next is that my bad knee went out. I fell and I couldn't get up."

The image of Papa struggling alone in the dark and cold twisted Erica's heart. "You could have frozen to death! Papa Andy, promise me you won't go out without one of us anymore."

Papa Andy looked at her as if she'd lost her mind. "I'm not making a promise like that, young lady. I'm fine ninety-five percent of the time. It's just, that path to the cabin turned into an ice rink, what with the thawing and freezing. I couldn't get a grip on anything."

Jason shook his head and added another log to the fire.

"I didn't want to break a bone," Papa said matter-of-factly, "so I shot off my gun. Figured somebody would hear me."

"That was smart… I guess," Erica said. "Where I grew up, shooting off a gun was an invitation for someone else to open fire on you, but you country folks are different."

"It would have been smarter to call someone on your cell phone. You took a couple years off my life!" Jason actually still looked shaken.

Papa looked at the phone on the end table with obvious irritation. "That cell phone is a nuisance. Keeps going off, and by the time I find it and answer, there's no one there."

"I don't care if you don't like it." Jason glared at his grandfather. "I don't want you anywhere without a phone in your pocket from now on."

"One little mishap," Papa grumbled, "and every young person thinks they can tell you what to do. I have more knowledge in my little finger than you—"

"Would you like some more tea?" Erica said to interrupt their argument.

"Tell you what I'd like," Papa said, "is to take a look at those babies, and then get in bed. I know it's early, but lying out there in the cold took a lot out of me. I'm just going to listen to the radio and stay warm."

And that way, he wouldn't get into more of an argument with Jason. Men. When they felt emotional, they fought.

After they'd taken Papa upstairs to peek at the babies, they got him settled in his bed, propped up with pillows, TV remote in hand.

"One more thing," he said as Jason and Erica were leaving. "I want you to check the cabin."

"Papa…"

"I saw lights," he insisted. "I'd check it out myself, but I've had enough for one night."

"I don't think it's anything," Jason said. "Just moonlight or an animal."

"If that's the case," Papa said, "then why was that path worn to an icy gully instead of just snowed over?"

Erica and Jason looked at each other. "Good point," Erica said, suddenly uneasy.

Jason's phone went off for the second time that evening. He looked at the lock screen and shoved it back in his pocket. "You stay with the twins," he told Erica, "and I'll go look over the cabin."

"I'll keep an eye on the twins," Papa said, sounding irritable. "I'm good for something at least. She should go with you. Not to confront anyone, mind you, but to call for help if needed."

Erica looked at Jason. "He's right." And she wanted to help. Wanted to build a closer bond with Jason before she told him the difficult truth about the twins.

Jason turned to Papa. "I'll only consider you staying here if you have that cell phone out and on. If anything goes wrong, with you or the twins, you call me and then the police."

Mistletoe jumped onto Papa's bed, seeming to smirk at Jason and Erica.

"You're not supposed to be there, boy, but we'll let it slide tonight," Jason said, thumping the dog's side.

"You and Papa watch out for each other, okay, Mistletoe?" Erica massaged the dog's large head and then punched her own number into Papa's phone. Quickly, she enlarged the text, just as she'd used to do for the seniors where she'd worked. "See? One click. I made myself and Jason your favorites."

"You *are* my favorites," Papa said gruffly. "Thank you for getting an old man out of a tight spot."

Erica felt tears rising to her eyes. She was growing so fond of Papa, almost like he was her own grandfather.

Out in the hall, Jason turned to her. "You've done nursing work, right? Do you think he's really okay?"

"He's fine. Probably needs a little time to himself to regroup." She turned toward the twins' room. "I just want to check on them once more, and then we can go out together."

"As long as you agree to stay well back, out of any trouble we might find."

She held up her hands. "I'm not aiming to be a hero."

In the twins' room, she listened to their even breathing. Then she leaned over the crib railing and touched a kiss to each beloved forehead. "We're going to get you the help you need, little ones," she whispered. "I promise I'll take care of you."

Outside, the sky had cleared, leaving a mass of bright stars. Heaven seemed close enough to touch.

She followed Jason, and when he got to the icy section where Papa had fallen, he broke new trail so they wouldn't have to walk on the same precarious path Papa had.

The aroma of wood smoke grew stronger. "Do you smell that?" she asked. "Is it coming from the main house or the cabin?"

"I think maybe Papa was right," he said. "Look."

Sure enough, in the direction of the cabin she saw lights. Jason turned slightly and held out a hand. "Stay back."

"Okay." Her heart pounded, hard and rapid as a drumbeat.

He crept forward, his body naturally graceful, practiced in the moves of surveillance and detection. He approached the window cautiously and peeked in.

Then he stepped back, rubbed the window with the sleeve of his jacket and cupped his hands to his face as if making sure of what he saw. Why wasn't he being more careful to avoid getting caught?

Then he turned in her direction. "We need an ambulance!" he yelled. "Somebody just had a baby!"

Jason experienced the next ten minutes as a crazy blur. Erica, staggering through the deep snow toward him as she shouted into the phone. Himself, giving the dispatcher exact directions, and then pounding on the cabin door. A pale-faced young husband answering, acting protective— and then, when he realized Jason and Erica wanted to help, looking relieved.

Inside the cabin, on a sleeping bag with a blanket over her, was an exhausted-looking, smiling woman and a squalling newborn.

Jason was afraid to even approach the damp, fragile little being. He'd gotten confident with babies of the twins' sturdy size, but not this tiny thing. Erica, though, waded right in. "Is she...he...okay?" She knelt beside the blanket-covered woman, who was propped on one elbow, wrapping the baby in a towel that at least looked clean. "Here, let me help you. Oh, he's precious!"

"We didn't cut the cord yet." The man stood beside Jason, sounding shaky and worried. "I was afraid...none of this is sanitary." He waved an arm around the cabin.

"How'd you even know what to do?" Jason nodded at the mother and child. "I mean...the baby looks fine."

"Truth?" the young man said. "YouTube videos. My phone's running out of juice and it's super old, but I got enough to know how to help her, and what to do right after the baby was born."

Jason was impressed to see, now, that the area in front of the fireplace had been scrubbed clean. An old cast-iron pot sat beside the blazing fire, and a bucket of snow was nearby. "You melted snow for water."

"We found some dishes here. I didn't expect the baby to be born so soon. We don't even have a name yet." He rubbed his hand through his hair. "This is our hometown, and I thought we'd find someone to take us in, but everyone's busy at Christmas."

Erica glanced up from her position beside the mother and child. "We want to help, right, Jason? Although I think a hospital is the first place for you. All three of you."

"Absolutely." The young man sat down on a large cut log as if it were a stool. "Man, look at this. I'm shaking." He held out his hands to illustrate.

"You did a good job," Jason told him.

"He did," the young woman said.

"And so did you." Erica smoothed the young woman's hair back and found a backpack to tuck under her head as a pillow. "You made an amazing baby." Her voice was soft.

Jason's phone buzzed. Brian, again. When would his friend get the message that Jason was way too busy for a chat?

"Come down here?" The woman was looking at her husband, and he immediately got down on the floor beside her, slipping an arm underneath her neck and touching the baby's hand. "I love you, babe. And I love him, too."

Erica found another sleeping bag in their stack of gear

and put it over the two of them, leaving the baby free. Then she scooted back, stood and looked at Jason. "Can the ambulance even get back here?"

"It's four-wheel drive. They'll be fine."

"Then let's give them privacy." She walked over to the cabin's kitchen area and leaned against the counter, and Jason came to lean beside her.

"Is it okay that they didn't cut the cord, do you think?" Jason was still processing the fact that a kid under twenty had just helped his equally young girlfriend have a baby.

"Smart, I would guess. The paramedics will know what to do."

"Where'd you have the twins?"

"What?" She looked at him blankly.

"The twins. Did you have them at a regular hospital, or at a birthing center or something?"

She hesitated. "They were born in a regular hospital."

There was something odd, off, about the way she said it. "Does this bring back memories?"

She shook her head. "These guys seem loving and happy, even though they're basically homeless. It's so sweet."

Their disagreement of earlier that day, the fact that she'd kept him out of the doctor's office, seemed trivial in the face of what this young couple had just experienced and of the scare about Papa Andy. He put an arm around Erica's shoulders, and after a moment, she cuddled in, slipping her own arm around his waist.

It wasn't romantic, not this time. It was comfort, a desire for human closeness, and she seemed to feel it to the exact same degree that he did. As the couple lay together, bonding with their baby, so he and Erica, two people alone in the world, bonded, as well. It was a Christmas moment.

Soon enough, though, the ambulance pulled up, right to the cabin's back door, and all the tranquility was lost. The paramedics asked questions of the mother and father, did tests on the baby and loaded them all into an ambulance in a matter of minutes. Jason and Erica gave their names and numbers, and the ambulance pulled out.

And then they were gone, and it was just Erica and Jason at the cabin. They made short work of putting out the fire and locking up.

"You know," she said, "you were right about something."

"You're kidding," he joked.

She swatted his arm. "I can admit when I'm wrong. And I was wrong to think I could have lived here with the twins. It would never have worked. It's too primitive."

"You're welcome," he said. "Just ask me anytime you need advice."

"You're impossible," she said, and then yawned hugely. "We'd better get back to Papa Andy and the twins. I'm beat."

Jason felt the same, only with a bit of an edge of adrenaline still hanging on. He wanted to hold her in the worst way, but he also knew they had differences to resolve. And they were both exhausted. "Let's head back."

Halfway down the new broken path, his phone buzzed yet again. He looked at it and rolled his eyes. What did Brian want? Impatient, he clicked into the phone call. "I'm kinda busy here, and it's late. What's up?"

"I have some news," Brian said, his voice stiff, guarded. "About that matter you asked me to investigate."

Erica. Kimmie. Arizona. "Oh, man, it's been crazy here. I forgot all about that."

Erica glanced back at him, questioning. He waved her ahead. "I've got to take this," he said to her. "Go get warm. I'll be right there."

She nodded and headed toward the house. Jason walked slowly behind. "What's up?" he asked Brian.

"You're going to want to be sitting down to hear this," Brian said.

Twelve

Jason stood outside the house and listened to Brian's incomprehensible words. Surely his friend had gotten it wrong. "You didn't find this out for sure, right? It's just a theory."

"It's true." Brian's voice was flat. "Those twins are your nephews. Your sister was their mother."

"But why—" He broke off. "What could Erica..."

"Can't say. She trying to get something out of you? Money? Land?"

He thought of the will, how Kimmie had left Erica half the farm. But his head was spinning too much to understand.

While he and Brian had been talking, Erica had gone into the house. Now lights came on in the front room, and he watched as she moved around there, picking up a cup from the coffee table, adjusting an ornament, bending down to pat Mistletoe.

From where he stood, it was like watching a Christmas movie. The perfect setting, the beautiful woman. A happy home.

And it was all a lie. "Was she married?"

"What do you mean?"

His hand was sweating on the phone. "Kimmie. Was she married to the father of the twins?"

"No." There was a dim sound of papers rustling. "She didn't name a father on the birth certificates, but my contact out there did a little digging, looked up her past addresses and other public records. Apparently she was cohabitating with a man around the time they must have been conceived, but he went to prison before the babies were born."

Cohabitating with a man.

People did that all the time. Who was he to judge?

All the same, the image he'd always carried of his sister—beautiful, laughing, pure—seemed to shatter into a million jagged fragments.

"You still there?" Brian asked. "Listen, I wouldn't worry about the father having any claim on those kids."

"Yeah. Thanks, man. I'll... We'll talk."

"One more thing," Brian said. "When I spoke with Kimmie's landlord—piece of work, that guy—he said there was a box of your sister's personal effects that was sent to your grandfather's address. Should have arrived by now."

Maybe it had, and Erica had hidden it. Suddenly, he wouldn't put anything past her.

"I guess there could be a note, some kind of explanation."

He closed his eyes for just a second, then opened them again. "Yeah. Thanks, buddy." He clicked off the phone.

And then he just stood still and looked up at the starry sky. The twins were Kimmie's. His, now. He'd been getting to know them, coming to care for them, never even realizing—

The front door opened. "Jason? Everything okay?"

Erica was framed in the doorway. The soft light behind her made her skin and hair glow.

A little bit like Kimmie had always glowed in his mind.

In truth, Erica, like Kimmie, had lost her luster, if she'd ever even had it.

He strode up the front steps and brushed past her into the entryway. Sitting down on the bench, he took off his snowy boots and tossed them into the pile of shoes by the door. They made a satisfying crash.

"Shh! The twins!"

He looked at her, and it was like she was a different person from the woman he'd been getting close to. "Yeah," he said. "We should talk about the twins."

Her eyes widened. "What was the phone call about?"

"Let's take this discussion into the front room." He watched her face. "We wouldn't want to wake up Kimmie's babies."

Her hand flew to her mouth and her eyes went impossibly wide. "You know."

Until that moment, in a corner of his mind, he'd thought Brian might have gotten it wrong. Or that maybe, Erica hadn't known the babies were Kimmie's. Which didn't make any sense, but was easier to believe than that sweet, gentle Erica—the woman he'd fallen in love with—had been lying since the moment they'd met.

"Jason..."

He jerked his head sideways toward the front room. "In here."

She walked in ahead of him, shoulders slumping, and perched on the edge of the couch. He sat in the chair that was kitty-corner. Mistletoe lifted his head from his bed in front of the fire and whined softly.

They both stared at the floor.

Finally, she spoke. "Jason, I've been wanting to tell you about the twins practically since the first day I knew you. It's just… It's been complicated."

Understanding dawned. "That's why you didn't want me in the doctor's office."

"Yes. I knew I had to tell the doctor the whole truth, and—"

"You owed more honesty to the doctor than to me?" He knew dimly that his remark wasn't fair, but he couldn't make himself stifle it.

"It was for the twins." She leaned forward, elbows on knees. "The doctor needed to know everything so she could give them the best help possible."

A log crackled and fell in the fireplace. Mistletoe stood, turned in a circle and flopped back down with a sigh.

"All this time," he said. "Knowing it, being what I thought was close, and you didn't see fit to tell me those boys are my own *nephews*?" His voice was too loud, but he couldn't seem to control it. "What does that say about you?"

"I… Jason, I'm so sorry. I wanted to tell you."

He pressed his lips together so he wouldn't say the immediate, awful things he wanted to say.

She'd lied to him. That was one thing to focus on.

The fact that the twins were his sister's, were his blood—that was too big to take in right now.

His body felt like it was going to explode. He jumped up and paced the room, picking things up and putting them down. "Why'd you do it, Erica? What are you trying to get out of me and Papa?"

"Nothing. I don't want anything from you."

"Why, because you already got everything you need from Kimmie? What was that will about? Blackmail? Did you steal the twins from her?"

"No! I—"

"Because I'll prosecute. If you in any way made my sister's last days harder, if you..." He nearly choked as all the possibilities whirled in his thoughts. "If you caused her death, taking away her kids and stressing her out—"

"No, no!" She held up a hand, looking up at him, her eyes filling with tears. "Jason, it wasn't like that at all."

"Child abduction," he recited, his voice flat because he'd said it so many times before, though never in such a personal context. "Wrongfully removing a child by persuasion, fraud, open force or violence. I don't doubt that you'll see prison time over this."

"She gave them to me." Erica's face was white. "She asked me to take them, because she couldn't care for them herself anymore, and she didn't want them to go into foster care."

"You expect me to believe that? Why would they have been put into foster care when they had a perfectly loving family back here and a mother there?"

"Because..." She stopped, shook her head, looked away.

"Can't think of an answer, can you?"

She hesitated, then met his eyes. "I don't know if you want to know the answer."

He clenched his fists. "I want to know. Not that I'll believe one thing you say."

"She was using," Erica said quietly, "and the police were coming."

Jason pounded a fist into his hand as bitterness spread through his chest. "With her babies there, she was using?" All this time he'd been trying to maintain an image of Kimmie, and it had been false. For that matter, the same was true of Erica.

He shook his head. "So she asked you to bring them to me and Papa, and instead you—"

"No." Erica shook her head. "You have to understand, it was all hectic and hurried. She thought I could live in the cabin until I got on my feet. It was all she had to offer me for...for raising her children. But, Jason, I love them like they're my own and I want what's best for them. I'm not trying to pull something over on you. I did this—I've been taking care of them since leaving Arizona and even before—because I cared for Kimmie and I've come to love her boys." Her voice choked up on the last words.

"You can do better than that. You're a great liar."

"She didn't want you to have them." She was staring at the carpet, her voice low.

He wasn't sure he'd heard her right. "What did you say?"

She looked up at him. "Kimmie didn't want you to have the twins. She asked me to raise them and not to let you know."

Jason grabbed a plastic snow globe he'd loved since childhood and threw it against the wall.

Erica flinched as it shattered, water and little plastic pieces flying everywhere. Her shoulders hunched in, like he was going to hit her.

"That can't be true. Kimmie would have trusted me

before someone like you. A liar with nothing. No connection to the family, no experience, no resources…"

She was looking at him now, her face set and serious, except that tears were running down her cheeks.

"Kimmie was smart," he continued, trying to work it out in his mind. "She knew the babies would need help—"

"They need help now," she said, standing up.

"What?"

"I heard one of them crying. Coughing. Something." She hurried toward the stairs.

He followed her. "You're faking this to get away from me. But I'm watching you. I'm not letting you take the babies again—"

"Or maybe you woke them up, throwing things like a little boy because you're mad at your sister." The words, tossed over her shoulder, cut into him.

Still, he followed her into the room she shared with them. Her nightgown hung on the bedpost, slippers at the foot of the bed. Her Bible and a little devotional book on the bedside table.

He swallowed the bile that rose in his throat and approached the crib.

The twins lay in striped Christmas pajamas, Mikey with his head toward one end of the crib, Teddy with his head toward the other. Their legs were intertwined, and as he watched, Mikey tossed back and forth, coughed and let out a fussy little cry.

They were Kimmie's babies. His nephews.

Jason's throat tightened.

Erica's breathing sounded choked and she brushed the backs of her hands over her cheeks. The flowery smell of her hair rose to his nose.

He ignored the tiny shred of sympathy and caring that pushed at him. He'd been about to fall for this liar.

He always picked the wrong person—as witness Renea and now Erica. He had a knack for it, choosing those who were already on the way to some kind of emotional ruin, and then nudging that train along to full speed.

Mikey fussed some more, kicking his legs restlessly, and Erica picked him up carefully, trying not to disturb Teddy. She jostled Mikey gently in her arms. "You've picked up a cold, haven't you?" she said in a quiet, bouncy voice. "Let's wipe your nose, huh?" She carried him over and got a tissue from a box on the dresser, wiped the baby's nose. Then she grabbed another tissue and blotted her own eyes.

Teddy thrashed in the crib as if looking for his twin and then let out a wail.

Before he could think about it, Jason had Teddy in his arms. He gently bounced him, stroking his soft hair.

This was his nephew. His blood.

The babies Kimmie had borne and hadn't told him about.

"Did she try to get in touch with me?" The question burst out of him. "Or Mom, or Gran and Papa?"

Erica shook her head. "She didn't want any of you to know."

"But the safety of her own children, their health!"

Teddy started to cry again and Jason swayed with him. Erica had found a little medicine bottle and a dropper and was filling it, blocking Mikey from rolling off the bed with her body. "Here you go, sweetie, this'll help your cold," she said, propping Mikey up and popping the syringe into his mouth.

Mikey turned his head away and spit out some of the

bright red medicine. "There, but some got inside, huh?" she crooned, using another tissue to wipe Mikey's chin. "There, that'll help you feel better and sleep. Rock with Mama."

"You're not their mother."

She drew in a little gasp and her eyes flashed up to Jason's, and then she looked back down at Mikey again and rocked, back and forth.

"So when the nurse asked you if they were breastfed..."

She shook her head, still rocking the baby. "I don't know. Kimmie said she was able to stay clean while she was pregnant and for a while after. I'd assume she at least tried."

"You weren't around her then?" His hunger for more information made him keep talking to the woman who'd betrayed his sister and lied to him.

She shook her head. "I wish I had been. I wish it so much. But that was when my mom was having so much trouble and I could barely... Anyway, I lost touch with Kimmie."

"Lost touch until when?"

"Until she called me two months ago and told me she was dying and she needed help."

He bit down the pain those words roused in him. "Why wouldn't she call us? Why would she call a young woman, a stranger with who-knows-what intentions..."

"We were friends, Jason, and I didn't judge her."

His mouth had been open to ask more questions, to vent more feelings, but her words made him stop. *Would* he have judged Kimmie, had he known what had happened in her life?

"Hey, what's going on in here?" Papa pushed through

the half-open door, clad in flannel pajamas with a plaid robe tied on over them.

"I'm sorry we woke you up," Erica said.

He waved a hand. "Old folks don't sleep well. Are the babies sick?"

She glanced over at Jason. "I think they picked up a cold or something. They were at the doctor's and around other kids so much, it's inevitable."

"Why don't you tell him what else has come out tonight," Jason said to Erica.

She narrowed her eyes at him. "Is this the right time?"

"No," he said, "that would've been when you met us for the first time. But you didn't choose the right time, did you?"

She sighed. "No, I didn't."

"What's going on between you two?" Papa Andy sat down on the bed beside Erica.

"I... Papa, I'm really sorry," she said, "but there's a secret I've been keeping since I came to Pennsylvania. Jason just found out about it, and he's angry. Understandably. You'll probably be angry, too."

"Oh, now," Papa said, patting her back, "what could a sweet young woman like you do that would make an old man angry?"

She swallowed hard. "I... You know how Kimmie and I were friends, right?"

Papa nodded, tickling Mikey's foot.

"Well, one reason she and I spent a lot of time together, toward the end, was that..." She trailed off and looked at Jason.

"What she's trying to say, Papa, is that the babies aren't hers. They're Kimmie's."

Papa's mouth opened in an O. He stared from Erica to Mikey to Teddy.

Erica thrust the baby into his arms and fled from the room.

Erica ran down the steps and into the front room, gasping with sobs.

Why, oh why, hadn't she told them on her own terms rather than letting the truth be discovered? And what would happen now?

Would the twins be taken from her? Was her dream of motherhood already at an end?

"I'm sorry, Kimmie," she whispered. She picked up a photograph of Jason and Kimmie as kids with Santa. It was one of Papa's favorites, and she often saw him looking at it.

What had gone so wrong in this family that huge, painful secrets were needed?

She saw a tiny plastic Christmas tree on the floor in a little puddle of water. The nearby shards of plastic looked sharp.

She walked into the kitchen and got paper towels, feeling stiff in every part of her body, exhausted, old. She came back into the room and started cleaning up the mess.

Jason had been so furious. Of course he had. No one liked being lied to, and this was the lie to end all lies, a lie of major proportions.

She inhaled the piney scent of the Christmas tree as she searched out all the little pieces of a broken Christmas scene. For a moment she thought about saving them. Maybe the snow globe could be put back together.

She studied the bits in her hand. *No. Hopeless.*

She carried the pieces to the trash can and threw them in. Upstairs, she could hear Jason's and Papa's low voices, but no sound of crying babies. The boys had probably gone back to sleep. They were exhausted from their big day.

Loss, a huge hole in her chest, opened with such an ache that she sat down on the couch and hunched over, clutching her elbows.

She was a horrible person, not deserving of a family.

That little moment in the cabin, when Jason had put his arm around her like she was his longtime wife, when she'd cuddled into him, was the last time she'd have the opportunity to touch him.

And they'd take the babies from her—she was sure of it. Why wouldn't they? Papa and Jason were kind, loving men who could raise Mikey and Teddy to adulthood. If Kimmie had stayed in touch with her family, she would have known that, and Erica would never have even been in the picture.

Her heart felt broken into three distinct pieces. Four, actually: one for Mikey, one for Teddy, one for Papa and one for Jason.

The fun, happy moments they'd spent together played through her mind. How they'd decorated the tree, how Teddy had scooted toward it. The capable way Papa held a baby on his lap like he was born to it. The sleigh ride to church, bells jingling, the twins laughing.

There wasn't going to be any more of that for her.

Unbidden, a memory from childhood spread into her mind. She'd rushed home from school to the motel where they'd been living, excited to have a Christmas gift for her mother. A clay dish, fired in the school kiln. Now, as an adult, she knew it had been a lopsided, ugly thing.

And indeed, her mother had laughed when she'd seen it, given Erica a quick pat on the head and gone back to partying with her friends.

Erica got up, walked over to the Christmas tree and looked at the little lump ornament Jason and Papa had laughed about. In a family like theirs, children's humble efforts at art were treasured and kept.

She'd always longed to be in such a family. And she'd had a brief moment there. But now that time was over.

Heavy footsteps sounded on the stairs. Jason came to the doorway and looked in at her, his expression a perfect storm of hurt and anger and mistrust.

He spun away. A moment later, the front door slammed.

It's over. She sank to her knees and pressed her hands to her mouth. *Help me, Lord.*

Thirteen

The next morning, at dawn, Jason was awakened by a rhythmic scraping sound. He looked around and blinked at the interior of his truck and the pink-and-gold glowing world outside. What was he doing here? And why was he so cold, despite the down coat stretched over him and his big boots and warm socks?

He turned on the car and cranked up the heat. Slowly, the night before came back to him. The revelation about the twins. The fighting with Erica. Storming out.

He'd driven aimlessly and then realized it wasn't so aimless; he was headed to the suburban Pittsburgh home where his family had lived during his elementary school years, after they'd moved back from Arizona. He'd sat in his truck in front of their old house, thinking about his sister, until he'd fallen asleep.

Now, as the defroster cleared the windows, he looked out to see that the Michaelson place next door was decorated with the same blue icicle lights and big blue-lit deer that the older couple had always argued about: he'd loved them, and she'd thought they were tacky.

As a kid, Jason had found the blue lights to be much

cooler than his family's plain old white lights, and he'd loved the way the blue deer had raised and lowered their heads. He remembered the year that Kimmie had taken him over to pretend-feed the deer with burned, broken-up Christmas cookies they'd made. He'd been young, first or second grade. Probably, he realized now, she'd thought of the scheme to make him feel better after their cookies had turned out inedible.

Years later, she'd covered for him, taking the blame herself, when he and his friends had dragged one of the deer over to their bonfire and accidentally burned part of its back leg. He squinted through the dim morning light. Sure enough, one of the deer had a hind leg half the length of the other three.

How had he and Kimmie gotten so far apart that she'd died alone, not even telling him she'd borne two sons? That she didn't want him, the little brother who'd idolized her, to get to know her children?

Tap-tap-tap. He lowered his driver's-side window to see a bundled-up woman, white hair peeking out from beneath a stocking cap. "You're going to freeze out here, sir. What's your business in this neighborhood?"

The voice was familiar, if a little raspier than when he'd last heard it. "Mrs. Michaelson? I'm Jason Stephanidis. I used to live next door."

The old woman cocked her head to one side and studied Jason. "You're the little kid who once decorated my front bushes with those tinsel icicles?"

Another memory Jason had forgotten about until just now. "The very same," he said, turning off the truck, climbing out and shaking her hand. "I'm sorry about that. I'd guess you were picking those things up out of your yard for weeks."

Mrs. Michaelson chuckled, leaning on her snow shovel. "That we were, but we didn't mind. We always enjoyed the kids in the neighborhood, since we didn't have any of our own."

"I see you're still putting up the blue lights," Jason said, gesturing to the Michelsons' house.

"Sure do, every year, and sometimes I leave 'em on all night. The mister has been gone these past eight years, but it doesn't seem like Christmas otherwise."

So Mr. Michaelson had passed away. And Mrs. Michaelson, although she looked spry enough, had to be well up into her eighties. She'd seemed ancient even when Jason was a kid.

"Can I help you shovel your driveway?"

"No need. I just do the walkways, and they're done. I don't drive anymore." She sighed and gestured at her thick glasses. "Vision problems. I turned in my license before they could take it away from me."

"Sensible decision." He looked around the neighborhood. "I have good memories of living here."

"You look like you could use a cup of coffee," she said. "If you'd like to come in, I could fix you some breakfast, as well."

There was the tiniest undertone of eagerness in the old woman's voice. "I would appreciate that," he said, and followed Mrs. Michaelson inside.

After breakfast and promises to stay in touch, Jason drove back to the farm. He felt ashamed of having left Papa alone to deal with Erica and the twins, but when he arrived, Erica's car was gone and the house was quiet. He had a moment of panic. "Papa?"

"Up here," his grandfather called.

Papa was putting on a Christmas sweater-vest that

had to be as old as Jason was, his hair wet from a recent shower, his face freshly shaved.

"Where are Erica and the twins?"

"She took 'em to the Santa Claus breakfast at the church."

After the bomb that had exploded here last night, she'd gone to a Santa Claus breakfast? "You let her go? What if she abducts them?"

Papa waved a hand. "If she were going to abduct them, she'd have done it already. She'd never have come here at all." He leaned closer to the mirror to straighten his bow tie. "She said she'd promised to help with the breakfast, and she didn't want to let Mrs. Habler and the ladies' crew down."

"Oh." Jason stepped next door to her room. The bed was neatly made, but all her and the twins things were still there. A weight seemed to lift off his chest, even though he *thought* he wanted her to leave, to get out of their lives.

"Where are you going?" he asked his grandfather.

"Christmas Eve ham delivery," Papa explained. "Remember? The Men's Group has been doing it since I don't know when."

Jason did remember, how Papa went to a Christmas Eve luncheon with other men, out at some restaurant, and then did a surprise ham delivery to some of the poorer members of the congregation.

He didn't want to ask, but the words burst out of him. "How was Erica?"

Papa shook his head, pressing his lips together. "We didn't talk much. She was broken up, though. Red eyes. Kept apologizing." He eyed Jason. "I don't know what to think or do about this whole situation, except to make sure those babies are cared for and loved."

"What's she going to do?"

Papa picked up a comb and ran it through his hair. "I doubt if she's gotten that far in her thinking."

"I just can't understand what she did. Kimmie, either."

"Some things don't make a whole lot of logical sense." Papa put on his dress shoes and checked himself in the mirror again. "Tell you what you need to do, though. Get a shower. Get yourself cleaned up. You'll feel better."

Jason gave Papa a half smile he didn't feel inside. "Sure. Will do."

As he left Papa's bedroom, he heard a car approach and a door slam. His heart leaped. He hurried to his bedroom window to look out.

It was only Papa's ride.

Jason didn't want to see Erica, anyway.

After he'd showered and put on clean clothes, he didn't know what to do with himself. Erica and the twins hadn't come back yet, not that he was waiting for them. Once again, he got into his truck.

As he started to turn out of the farm's long driveway, a brown delivery truck appeared and stopped in front of the drive, brakes squeaking. When Jason saw that the driver was a high school acquaintance, he waved.

"Got a package for you and your grandfather," Elmer called, hopping down and carrying a two-foot square box to the truck's window. "Want me to throw it in the back of your truck, or should I take it up to the house?"

"Throw it in the back. Thanks."

"Merry Christmas!" Elmer waved and the brown truck chugged off.

Jason stopped at the hospital to check on the young

couple who'd given birth in the cabin. He found them in good health, just waiting for the doctor to release them. He admired their new son and envied the loving smiles on their faces. Exhibit A that you didn't need material things to be happy.

Since it seemed they had no idea where they'd go once they left the hospital, Jason found the hospital's social worker and made an anonymous donation for a month's rent for them.

But it didn't make him feel a bit better.

Aimless, he drove around and finally ended up at the mall two towns over, thinking to pick up a little something more for Papa. He wandered until he found a bookstore and picked up a copy of Papa's favorite author's new hardcover spy novel. The thought of Papa's reaction— "I could have gotten this at the library for free"—gave Jason a minute's pleasure. Secretly, Papa would be glad he didn't have to join the long waiting list to get the book.

He looked at his watch and realized he'd killed only half an hour. Package in hand, Jason sat down on a bench.

Repetitive Christmas music played, audible over the sounds of people's voices, some irritable but most happy and excited. People crowded through the mall and into the stores, and he heard snippets of conversation.

From a man in a wheelchair, talking to the young nurse pushing him: "Figures my disability check would be late this month. But I know, I know, I should stop complaining and be grateful I can still get something for the grandkids."

From one frazzled-looking young mom to another: "Did you see the Dino Dasher is finally on sale?"

From a pretty teenage girl: "If I get Aunt Helen an

extra large, she'll be insulted, but if I get her anything smaller it won't fit."

Families. None of them having perfect Christmases, but the holiday spirit shone through the complaints and the crowding.

The smell of candied nuts tickled his nose, and he looked around, spotting the source in a kiosk in the middle of the mall. His mother had always loved those nuts. He should call her.

He turned away from the crowds and covered one ear and put in the call, but there was no answer. Either she was out or maybe all the circuits were overloaded, it being Christmastime. Did wireless circuits get overloaded?

He strolled over to the kiosk and bought a paper cone of candied nuts, then wandered through the mall, nibbling them.

"There's the most handsome detective in Holly Springs." The voice behind him was merry and loud, and he turned to see Ruth, as always with a baby in her arms. "Doing some last-minute shopping, are ya?"

He held up his bag. "You, too?"

"Sure am. Do you know the Glenns from church?" She introduced him to a bedraggled-looking man who didn't smell any too good and his much younger, stressed-out-looking wife. Then she held up the baby for him to see. "And this is little Maria. We're out doing some shopping for her. Gotta make her Christmas bright!"

"Nice to meet you," he said, and watched the small group head into a baby store. He could guess who'd be footing the bill there. Ruth was widowed, and she wasn't wealthy herself, but she had a generous heart. She must have taken it upon herself to play Santa for the Glenn family.

On his way out to his truck he spotted Chuck and Jeannine, walking arm in arm through the parking lot. He was happy they were back together, but he didn't want to intrude on their holiday.

But Chuck called out a greeting. "Jason! Come hear our good news!"

Standing in the cold parking lot, they explained that they'd decided to keep all the baby furniture because they were planning to adopt.

"I finally figured out it doesn't matter how kids come into a family," Chuck said. "I was on some kind of male ego trip, wanting my descendants to be my own blood."

"But he finally realized that was ridiculous." Jeannine squeezed her husband's arm. "What's important is how much love is there."

How much love is there. Jason wasn't feeling any excess of love, himself. He had Papa, of course, but even Papa had plans today, long-standing friends in the community. Everyone in Holly Springs, single or married, seemed to be rooted and connected. Everyone except him.

Maybe he ought to think about staying here, settling down. The pace of life, the way people cared for each other, was starting to appeal to him. Maybe, like Papa and Ruth, he could build a life here even though he was single.

He drove by the Mistletoe Display and, on impulse, turned in. Twilight was gathering, and he figured he might see a cheerful crowd. He didn't feel like being alone.

But as he drove up to the gates and parked in an almost-empty lot, the display's lights clicked off. A worker came out and hung a sign. "Sorry, buddy, we're closing down."

"No problem. Merry Christmas." Jason waited until the guy had gone back in to lock up the office and then read the sign. "Closing early so our workers can spend Christmas Eve and Day with their families."

Jason wandered along the fence, looking into the now-dark display. In the rapidly deepening twilight, he spotted the bench where he and Erica had shared their first kiss.

The emotions from that evening washed over him, and this time, he didn't even try to push them away.

He'd cared so much for Erica. He could admit it to himself now: he'd fallen in love with her.

But in the end, she'd betrayed him. Just like Kimmie had, and Renea, and even his own mother.

A nagging, honest voice inside his head said: Who's the common element here?

I know. It's me! I make bad choices!

Honesty compelled him to push further. Was it really just about choices?

Renea had been his own bad choice. But he hadn't chosen his mother or Kimmie. They'd been his family, and while his mother had definitely been the one to distance herself from her children, he'd followed up on that by judging Kimmie, pushing her away.

It was a decision he regretted, and would regret his whole life.

Erica had come into his life as a result of that decision; in all probability, she'd have never been involved with Kimmie if he had taken the proper responsibility for his sister.

Or maybe not; Kimmie had been her own person, and she might have still chosen to run away.

God works all things to good.

Even bad things, like Kimmie's death, God had worked to good by bringing him, Erica and the twins together.

Except that, last night, he'd judged Erica harshly, yelled at her, pushed her away. Just like he'd done with Kimmie.

But she lied to me! He banged back into his truck and drove too fast to the diner. That empty feeling inside him was hunger. He hadn't eaten anything since Mrs. Michaelson's breakfast and a few of those candied nuts.

He had a moment's fear that the diner would be closed, too, but it was brightly lit. When he pushed the door open, bells jingled and steamy warmth hit him, along with the homey scent of turkey and stuffing.

He'd have Christmas Eve dinner here and then go to church services. He'd done holidays alone plenty of times, back in Philly. And there were other solo diners here, too.

Hank came out to take his order, dressed in a Christmas apron atop his black slacks and shirt. "Where's your friend?" he asked.

"What friend? I have a lot of 'em." Which wasn't true, at least not here.

Hank lifted his hands like stop signs and took a step back. "Whoa, I meant the cute redhead. But I *didn't* mean to touch a nerve. What can I get for you? Coffee first?"

Just to prove he wasn't pathetic, Jason ordered the full Christmas Eve platter—turkey, stuffing, potatoes and vegetables. "Give me pie, too."

But when the food came, he could barely stuff down a quarter of it.

He sat back and waited for the check and thought about

the day. Thoughts about Kimmie, and then about Erica, edged their way into his mind and wouldn't leave.

He'd gotten so rigid lately, judged people harshly. Partly it came with the police work, but he knew himself well enough to understand that he was trying to keep control.

He'd condemned Kimmie harshly when he'd learned she was using. He'd gotten all strict and judgmental, and that had pushed her away.

Would he do the same to Erica?

But how could he forgive what she'd done to him and Papa?

He gave Hank a credit card for the check, leaving an oversize tip as befitted the occasion and the fact that Hank had to work on Christmas Eve.

And then he ended up at church, even though he was an hour early for services.

It was where he probably should have been all along.

Erica carried the twins upstairs, her muscles aching, her mind and heart calling for rest. She'd stayed out all day on purpose, and it looked like her plan had worked; Jason's truck wasn't here. She wouldn't have to see him, to say goodbye.

Saying goodbye to Papa and the twins would be hard enough.

She set Mikey down on the floor and placed a basket of colorful blocks in front of him. Then she fastened Teddy in the bouncy swing she'd found at the thrift store a few days ago, and right away, he began to babble and jump. His legs were getting stronger by the day.

"Ma-ma, Ma-ma," he chortled, waving his arms.

She did a double take. *Teddy* had said a word. He'd called her Mama.

It was the first time. She knelt in front of him, laughing and crying at the same time. "Oh, honey, I'm not your mama. But what a big boy you are for saying it."

"You *are* his mama, or the closest thing he's got to one." Papa Andy stood in the doorway.

She looked up at the old man who'd become so dear to her, and her heart twisted in her chest. "I guess I am. But that's all going to change now."

"Does it have to?"

She sat back and wrapped her arms around her upraised knees. "Jason's going to report me to the local police. He said last night that I'd probably do jail time." Which was terrifying, but even worse was the prospect of losing the twins forever.

"What a man says when he's angry and what's true can be two different things."

Papa hadn't heard the icy determination in Jason's voice. "I hope you're right about the jail time, but no one will disagree that he has more right to raise the twins. Along with you. You're their closest relatives, whereas I..." She was a nobody.

"Something you need to know about Jason. He's always seen things in black-and-white. I think he's growing out of that, but..."

"I don't." Erica hugged her knees tighter. "He sees me as evil now. I'm on his bad list, and I don't think there's any chance of a change."

"Huh." Papa gestured toward Mikey. "That one might walk before he crawls. You'd best keep an eye on him."

Erica turned to see Mikey next to Mistletoe, both little hands buried in the dog's fur. He was trying to pull himself up to his feet, and it had to hurt poor Mistletoe, but the dog didn't seem to mind. In fact, he tugged to the side a little as if he were trying to help Mikey to stand.

Erica pulled in a breath, her hand going to her heart. Was it possible to die of love?

"They grow fast," Papa said, and paused. "Mind if I come in a minute?"

She gestured toward the rocking chair in the corner of the bedroom. "I'm going to start packing, but I'd love some company."

"Where are you headed?"

She shook her head. "For the moment, to town. I lined up a room at the Evergreen Hotel." She sat down on the edge of the bed, facing Papa. "I'll say goodbye as soon as I've packed. I'll leave…" She stopped, swallowed hard. "If you can handle them, I'll leave the twins here tonight."

Papa leaned forward, elbows on knees. "You're a pretty strong woman."

"How do you figure?" So she wouldn't have to focus solely on her misery, she knelt to pull her suitcase out from under the bed and opened it.

Inside were all her shorts and T-shirts. Arizona clothes. It seemed like a lifetime ago that they'd been what she put on every day she wasn't working.

Maybe she'd end up going back there, get away from the cold. But the thought didn't give her the least iota of happiness.

Restraining a sigh, she opened her drawerful of cold-weather clothes and started refolding them and placing them, carefully, on top of the summer things. If she focused, maybe she wouldn't cry in front of Papa.

Mistletoe trotted over, toenails clicking on the wood floor, and nudged his shaggy head under her hand, whining faintly. Automatically, she tugged the dog against her leg, rubbing his back.

"It took a strong woman to care for your friend, sick with cancer. And then you drove her kids across the country, which couldn't have been easy. You got them early intervention. You've made yourself a place in a brand-new community, even though you've got barely two nickels to rub together."

"I had your help with that," she said. "Thanks to you, I've had a place to stay and food to eat." Honesty compelled her to add, "And it's thanks to Jason that I got in to see the developmental specialist. I could never have done that on my own."

Papa ignored her remarks. "It just surprises me, that's all."

"What surprises you?"

"That you'd give up so easily."

She stared at him. "Give up? What do you…"

"You love those boys, don't you?" In the midst of his wrinkled face, blue eyes shone out, bold and challenging.

"Like they were my own." As if to illustrate, Mikey held out his arms, and she scooped him up and hugged him fiercely.

"And I suspect you have some feelings for my grandson, as well."

Erica set Mikey down in the crib and went back to folding clothes, avoiding Papa's eyes. "You see too much."

"I see what's there. And I see what's there on his side, too. He's a hard one, that Jason, but you've helped him to soften up. You and the twins. That's worth something."

"Thank you, I…" She didn't know what to say, how to respond, but she stumbled to put some words together. "I hope there was something good he got from knowing me. It's been..." Her throat was too tight to go on. She took a sweater out of the suitcase and refolded it, blinking away tears.

"You also did something that hurt him. Hurt me, too, but—"

"I'm so sorry, Papa." She dropped the sweater and hurried across the room to kneel at his side. "You've been so good to me. It was unforgivable of me to deceive you."

He took her hand in his own hard, leathery one. "I'm also old enough to know that nobody's perfect and everybody makes mistakes. Yours wasn't for a bad cause." He tipped her chin up to look at him as her tears spilled over. "Seems to me our Kimmie put you in a mighty confusing dilemma. You tried to do the right thing for her and for the twins. How can we fault you for that?"

She swallowed and wiped at the tears rolling down her cheeks. "Thank you, Papa Andy. That means a lot to me."

"You mean a lot to me, sweetheart. You and these boys have helped me more than you know." He squeezed her hand. "Now, why don't you go find yourself a corner and do a little praying? I'll watch the twins."

"But I need to pack—"

"You in too big of a hurry to listen to God?" He lifted a bushy eyebrow, his sharp eyes pinning her.

"I... No. Thank you. I'd appreciate a few minutes." She grabbed her Bible from her nightstand and hurried downstairs to sit beside the Christmas tree and the nativity scene.

Half an hour later, she knew what she needed to do. Something terrifying, something unlikely to work, something against her whole shy nature.

And she needed to get started right away.

Fourteen

"I'd love to stay and talk more, but I have a sermon to preach." Pastor Wayne pounded Jason on the shoulder. "I think between you and the Lord, you can figure out what to do. You're welcome to my office, if you need a place to think."

"Thanks." Jason watched the pastor gather his Bible and leave, confident, ready for his next challenge.

That was how Jason had used to feel about his detective work, too. Now he wasn't sure of anything.

He needed to stay in Holly Springs with Papa. And he needed to take care of his sister's children.

But the big question was Erica.

Could he forgive her? Could she forgive him?

The church bells rang, announcing that services would start soon. Jason closed his eyes and slumped forward, elbows on knees, his forehead on his folded hands.

Ten minutes later, he still wasn't certain what to do, but he'd gained a measure of peace. The Lord didn't leave His sheep without a shepherd.

He stood and looked out the window into the twilight-darkened parking lot. People were starting to arrive for services.

And it hit him like a missile.

The box the postman had delivered.

Brian had mentioned that a box of Kimmie's belongings should be on its way.

Was it possible…?

He strode out of the pastor's office and into the parking lot, almost running to his truck. He grabbed the box from the back and brought it up into the cab, turning on the vehicle for warmth, clicking on the interior light.

He studied the package. An Arizona return address.

Hands shaking, he used his pocketknife to slit the tape and opened the flaps. Inside, there was a stack of envelopes held together with a rubber band and about four or five newspaper-wrapped items.

He set the letters aside and was opening the first packet when there was a knock on the window.

He lowered it.

Outside was Darien, the father from the couple who had given birth in the cabin. "Dude, mind if I get in for a minute?"

Yes. "No. Come around." He clicked open the locks and moved the box from the passenger seat to the middle.

"I got a ride here," Darien told him. "Hoping I'd see you. Thanks for setting us up with rent, man!"

Jason nodded. "Glad to do it. How're Caylene and the baby?"

"They're great. We're gonna live in a carriage house that belongs to one of my aunts. Now that we can pay rent, the relatives are being a little nicer."

"Good." Jason's eyes strayed to the box on the gear area between them.

"What's that?"

He picked up the packet he'd been opening, too curious to wait for Darien to leave. "Stuff from my sister." He cleared his throat. "She passed away recently."

"Sorry, man."

Inside the packet, metal clanked together. He got it open. "Gran's cookie cutters." He cocked his head to one side. "Wonder why she kept these."

"Must've been important to her."

"Yeah." Jason thought back. "At Christmas, as soon as us kids got there, Gran and Kimmie would always bake a bunch of cookies." He remembered it like yesterday, them laughing and talking, bringing out the final results for him and Papa to rave over and eat. Under Gran's watchful eye, the cookies had always turned out well. Good memories.

"What're these?" Darien was holding the stack of envelopes. "They all have your name on them, man." He held them out to Jason.

"I don't…" Jason shook his head. "I don't think I can deal with these right now."

Darien flipped through and whistled. "Some of these look pretty beat-up. But this top one here looks new. Maybe it's recent." He handed it to Jason.

Jason couldn't deal with it, but he couldn't resist it, either. He opened it up and read the first line:

I'm sorry I'm not what you think I am, but please don't hold it against my sons.

His throat tightened and he couldn't speak. He kept reading and learned that the reason Kimmie had relapsed into drugs was her terminal diagnosis. And that she'd strayed away from her faith, but with Erica's help, she'd read her Bible and discussed Jesus and prayed in the last days.

Erica is really a special woman. If you're reading this, give her a chance.

Words of wisdom from beyond the grave.

At first, I wanted Erica to keep the twins away from you. But now, I keep remembering the good times. I love you, Jason, and I know you love me. I hope you'll give that love to my sons.

Jason's chest hurt. He closed his eyes.

"Check this out." Darien nudged him, reached into the box and pulled out a plastic sleeve with official-looking papers inside.

Darien pointed to the top document, visible through the plastic. "That's a keepsake birth certificate," he said. "Just got one of those for our boy today. See the footprint? And then you order the official one online."

"What's the Post-it say?" Jason heard the hoarseness in his own voice.

"For Erica Lindholm." Darien held the packet closer to the dome light. "Looks like there's medical records in here, too."

So Kimmie *had* meant for Erica to have the babies.

Jason didn't trust his voice, but he pulled the one remaining packet from the box, hard and flat. With trembling hands, he opened it.

Inside was an old picture frame he recognized as one Papa had made, years back, from barn siding. The photo in the frame was of the twins. He studied it, trying to figure out what looked familiar.

It was their clothes. They were just a little out-of-date.

They were Jason's own baby clothes. He'd seen them in photographs. In fact, Teddy's outfit was the one in the Santa picture back at the house.

How had Kimmie managed to keep those clothes for all these years, for all her moves through the gutter?

A whole wave of memories came back to him then. How Kimmie had loved dolls, had collected them when she got too old to actually play with them. How she'd showed him outfits that had belonged to him as a baby, outfits she'd saved from the trash or donation bin.

She'd told him how she'd played with him like a doll when he was a baby, and though Jason had no memory of it, he suspected that a good portion of the mother love he'd gotten had come from Kimmie rather than their mother.

And she'd kept his baby clothes, put them on her own sons.

He stared up at the ceiling of the truck to keep the tears in his eyes from falling.

"What's up with the picture?"

Jason drew in a deep breath. Let it out slowly, and then repeated the process. Cleared his throat. "My sister helped raise me and I guess she kept my baby clothes. She put them on her twins for this picture."

"Wow, heavy."

It *was* heavy, but Jason felt like a huge weight was lifting off his shoulders.

Kimmie had kept these things. She'd loved him and had remembered Gran and Papa warmly. She'd wanted

Erica to have the twins, and she'd wanted Jason to give Erica a chance.

Kimmie hadn't been perfect. And that was okay.

Erica wasn't perfect. Also okay.

And that meant Jason didn't have to be perfect, either.

A strange warmth came over him. He looked out at the parking lot, where more and more people were heading into the church, to celebrate the birth of the Christ child.

He grabbed Darien's hand and pumped it. "Thanks."

"Anytime, dude. I gotta get back to Caylene and the baby. You hang in there, hear? Let me know if there's anything I can do for you."

After Darien left, Jason put the precious items back into the box and set it on the seat behind him. Then he dropped his head into his hands. *I'll do what You tell me, Lord. Not my will but Thine.* He left the truck and walked into the church foyer.

As soon as he got inside, he saw Erica. Her back was to him, and she wore a green dress that hugged her slender silhouette and showed off her clouds of red hair. She had Mikey on her hip, and Papa walked beside her, holding a squirming Teddy.

His impulse was to go to them, but he was trying to follow God, not his impulses. So he leaned against the church wall and just watched and thought.

He loved her—he knew that. His feelings for any woman in his past paled in comparison.

But love was tricky and messy and people didn't live up to his standards. More important, he himself didn't live up to his own standards. The question was, did he want to hold back and judge, or did he want to wade in? And if he made the latter choice, was he healed enough to do it right this time?

She turned and looked over and saw him. He saw her mouth drop open a little, her posture tighten. Then she lifted her chin and held out her arms, low, palms facing him. As if she were offering him an embrace.

In front of all these people. He felt a wave of love for her that she would try.

But people surged around her, between them. Partly, of course, because the twins were so adorable. Partly because Papa was such a popular figure.

And partly because Erica was so incredibly appealing that all the males between fifteen and fifty were drawn to her like bees to a colorful flower.

Organ music rose up from the sanctuary, the signal for people to stop milling around and come in to worship. There was a general movement toward the sanctuary.

Jason had lost sight of Erica, but he was going to find her, no matter what.

Erica followed Papa into what was apparently his usual front-and-center seat in church. She probably would've chosen a seat in back, given that she had two wiggly babies to contend with, but she treasured that Papa had forgiven her, had wanted to come to church together.

When she'd seen Jason across the foyer, leaning against the wall, her heart had swelled with love for him.

Had she made a fool of herself, reaching out to him in that obvious way? He hadn't jumped into her arms, that was for sure.

On the other hand, maybe her gesture hadn't been clear enough. Maybe she should have run across the room to him and begged forgiveness. There would have been no ambiguity in that gesture, but it was totally against her nature.

People stood for the opening hymn, and she and Papa each scooped up a twin and joined their voices in "It Came Upon a Midnight Clear." The dimly lit sanctuary, smelling of fresh pine and spruce, the advent wreath at the front of the church, the greenery and red bows decorating the pews and railings—all of it brought her calm. Not joy, not yet, but calm.

It was a time of new life, new birth. She wanted so badly for that new life to be right here, raising the twins with their great-grandfather and their uncle.

And her prayers this afternoon had reminded her that she was forgiven, ultimately forgiven by God. That she had value and was worthy simply in Him, regardless of her own significant mistakes.

Feeling like she deserved love and good treatment and a chance—that would take a little more time. God had a lot of work to do in her, but she was starting on the path.

When it was time to share the peace, Papa tapped her shoulder and gestured toward a gray-haired man in a wheelchair, alone in the back of the church. "Need to go sit with Tommy. He's a Vietnam vet and this is his first time at church in years. He shouldn't be alone."

"Of course."

She cuddled the twins, one on either side of her, giving Mikey a board book to look at and Teddy a couple of colorful blocks. Surprisingly, they played quietly while the Bible passages and carols continued on.

They were so dear to her. How could she possibly say goodbye to them?

And what was in store for her afterward? A prison of loneliness? A real prison?

"Fear not, for behold, I bring you good news of great joy that will be for all the people."

Fear not. Erica repeated it to herself, over and over.

They were half an hour into the service when Teddy got restless. He slid down from the pew and tried to scoot along it, which was awesome—he'd walk soon—but he kept falling, and the effort to pull himself up again, the frustration of it, made him cry. Mikey, as was his way, babbled instructions, which got progressively louder.

Erica scooped Teddy up and put him on the seat beside her, but he wasn't having it. He cried harder.

Erica was starting to gather her things to leave when someone behind her picked Teddy up. She expected more crying, but instead he quieted down immediately.

She turned partway around.

It was Jason. "I'll hold him," he said, and his slight smile made her heart soar.

That hadn't been an "I hate you" smile.

With only Mikey to contend with, she was able to keep him entertained and even to listen and sing a little more. But she was hyperaware of the man behind her, singing in his deep bass voice, whispering to Teddy.

The lights dimmed for the candlelight part of the service, and as "Silent Night" echoed out from the choir and organ, Erica's heart filled to the brim.

Christ had been born for all of them. In this fallen world, how badly they all needed Him, and He had come.

God had seen fit to send His son to save sinners like her.

The candles were lit, person to person. She was struggling to keep hold of Mikey and sidle to the nearest person when Jason came around from his pew to hers. He lit her candle and met her eyes. "I'm sorry," he whispered.

"I'm sorry, too," she said.

And then she turned away to light her neighbor's candle and the twins babbled and everyone sang. But she was still unsure about the man next to her. What could it mean, his kindness, in contrast to the outrage he'd shown her yesterday?

Soon enough, the lights came back on. Joyous music rang out and people greeted each other, stopped to chat. Children shouted and ran with the excitement of staying up late and presents to come.

Ruth and Papa Andy approached as the crowd thinned out. Without a word, each took a twin, and they headed toward the reception in the foyer of the church.

That left Erica and Jason alone together, side by side.

His arm was draped along the back of the pew, behind her but not touching. "I've been thinking—"

"So have I, and, Jason, I'm so sorry."

He opened his mouth to speak again and she held up a hand. "Let me say this. I was wrong to pretend the twins were mine. Especially as you and I got closer. It was deceptive and that's a horrible thing to do. I was trying to do the right thing, but that's no excuse. I just... I really care for you, Jason, and I apologize for the wrong I did to you."

He looked at the floor, then met her eyes. "Thank you for that."

And then there was no sound but the organ music and a little distant chatter as people left the sanctuary.

Was that all? Erica wondered. Now that she'd apologized, were they done?

And then he took her hand and held it. "I've made a lot of mistakes in my life. One of them was saying some pretty harsh things to you, things that came out of my sadness about Kimmie and my anger at myself, more than being about you." He shook his head, looking away, then looked back at her. "I can be judgmental. A perfectionist. I've been like that all my life, but I'm trying to improve. I was hurt by what you did, but I shouldn't have said those things to you." He paused, cleared his throat. "To the woman I love."

"To the woman you…" Erica's heart pounded so quickly she couldn't catch her breath. "You *love* me?"

He nodded and smiled, touching her cheek. "Is that so hard to believe?"

She laughed a little as tears rose to her eyes. Jason wasn't angry anymore. He wasn't expecting her to be perfect.

He *loved* her.

A lifetime of feeling inadequate seemed to rise up in her like a wave, and then crash and dissipate. "Yes, it's hard to believe," she whispered. "You might have to tell me more than once."

"Then you'll…" He broke off. "We should be practical."

"Practical?" She lifted her eyebrows and clutched his hand. She'd never had an experience like this and didn't know how it was supposed to go. But *practical*?

"I want to stay in Holly Springs, at Holly Creek Farm. Papa needs me, and I…I owe it to him to be here, like he was here for me and Kimmie."

"Of course," she said, hardly breathing.

"I can find work here. Probably police work, but there's so much to do on the farm, as well. I need to figure all that out."

She nodded. Inside, she was thinking, *He wants career counseling? Really?*

"Look, I'm making a mess of this because I don't

know… How do you feel about me, Erica? Would you want to…"

She closed her eyes for a moment. *You have value. And you're strong.* "My dream would be to stay here, too, and to raise the twins with you."

There. She'd said it and it was out on the table.

"Like, coparenting?" He shook his head. "No. Erica, that's not going to be enough for me. I know it might take you a while to have the feelings, but I'd like to try to move toward a true, permanent partnership. Toward…" He swallowed. "Toward marriage."

"You want to *marry* me?"

"Kimmie knew what she was doing when she left us each half of the farm, I think," he stumbled on.

Was that true? Would Kimmie have left her part of the farm because she was *matchmaking*? Erica's head spun and her heart pounded. Jason loved her. He wanted to marry her.

"I know it's soon and we haven't known each other long, but—"

"But sometimes you just know," she interrupted, her eyes pinned on his face. "I love you, Jason. And my answer is yes. Yes, let's move toward marriage but I…I'm pretty sure that my answer is yes, forever."

He pulled her into his strong arms, and Erica knew she had found the home and the family—and the Christmas— she'd always dreamed of.

Epilogue

Twelve months later

Erica tucked the blanket tighter around Teddy and Mikey, nestled in back of the old sleigh.

"Ready, everyone?" Up front, Papa made a clicking sound with his tongue, and the horses started to move.

"Ready as we'll ever be." Jason held Mistletoe by the collar and reached across the twins to squeeze Erica's shoulder.

As they approached the covered bridge, white with a simple Christmas wreath, Erica couldn't help but remember the first time she'd ridden in the sleigh, one year ago. Her life had undergone a radical change she never could have envisioned, and she was loving it.

Sunlight caught her wedding ring, making it sparkle like fire.

Papa cleared his throat. "Thought I'd stop and pick up Ruth," he said over his shoulder.

Erica looked at Jason, raising her eyebrows.

He leaned over. "Maybe Papa has some news to share, too," he whispered.

As they approached Ruth's house, Mistletoe spotted a rabbit and started barking, straining to escape Jason's strong grip.

"No, Miss-toe!" Mikey scolded.

"No, Miss-toe," Teddy echoed.

"Are you sure it's okay to bring the dog along?" Erica asked as Papa jumped spryly out of the sleigh and strode up the sidewalk to Ruth's front door, sporting its Tiny Tykes sign—a spot very familiar to Erica, since she'd spent a lot of time working there in the past year.

"Mrs. Habler wants to try him out as a camel in the pageant, and Hank promised to watch him during the service. He and his friend are running the hot chocolate and cider stand for Sleigh Bell Sunday." Jason shrugged. "Could be a disaster, but they insisted."

Ruth came out, dressed all in red, and Papa helped her into the front of the sleigh.

She twisted around to see the twins, laughing at them and pinching their rosy cheeks.

"Roof, Roof!" they said in rapturous voices, their adoration obvious.

"And don't you both look handsome in your new snowsuits," she said. "New boots, too!"

"Boots," Teddy agreed, holding a leg out.

Ruth looked over at Erica. "Honey, do you think you can sub for a few hours tomorrow? I know you want part-time, but—"

"Of course, no problem. You know I love the center." Erica gave Jason and the boys a mock-stern glare. "Just as long as these three let me study for my test tonight. You're not on duty, are you?" she asked Jason.

"No more evenings, remember? That was my condition for the promotion." Jason was enjoying small-town police work, but he was clear about making time for family. "And it's hard for me to let you study, but I'll do my best."

Erica blushed. "Leave your hat on, Teddy," she ordered as the sleigh drove on.

"No!" He looked up at her to see what she thought of his opinion.

"Told you he'd started his terrible twos," Ruth sang out from the front seat. "He's late, but you're not going to escape them."

"I know." But she relished every stage the twins went through. And now she could look forward to sharing every future stage with Jason. She snuggled down under the blanket, Teddy on her lap now, Jason at her side with Mikey on his lap, the dog at her feet. Papa and Ruth in the front seat.

Glorious stuff, for a girl who'd never had a real family.

At the church, they tied up and the twins were immediately off, shouting and running in the snow under Ruth's watchful eye. Papa started to follow them, but Jason put a hand on his grandfather's arm. "Papa," he said, "we have some news."

Papa stood still and looked from Jason to Erica. "Is it what I think it is?"

Jason nodded. "A little girl."

Papa folded them into his arms. "I was already happy, but you two young people just made me even happier."

Erica pulled back so she could look up at both of them. "I've been thinking about names," she said. "If it's okay with the two of you…I'd like to call her Kimmie."

It was just as well the church bells rang at that moment, because none of them could speak. They just stood, holding on to each other as the twins came back to grab legs and Mistletoe barked to be let out of the sleigh.

Full circle. Erica lifted her face to heaven with a prayer of gratitude and joy. And it seemed to her that her old friend Kimmie, all sins forgotten, must be smiling down at the entire family.

* * * * *

New York Times **bestselling authors**
Debbie Macomber, Brenda Novak and Sherryl Woods
deliver three holiday favorites in one stunning collection!

Silver Bells **by Debbie Macomber**
A single dad's rambunctious teenage daughter hatches a plot to find her father a wife, and she has just the woman in mind. He may claim he's not interested in remarriage, but perhaps the magic of the holiday season will help him change his mind.

On a Snowy Christmas **by Brenda Novak**
When their private plane crashes in the Sierra Nevada mountains shortly before Christmas, two political enemies discover that survival means more than just staying alive. In their case, it also means falling in love...

The Perfect Holiday **by Sherryl Woods**
What's a holiday without a handsome husband? To a matchmaking aunt, it isn't very festive at all! So she sends the perfect man to her single niece. But will he become the perfect groom-to-be by Christmastime?

Available now, wherever books are sold!

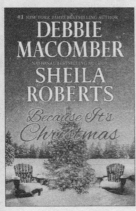

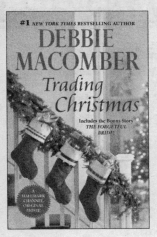

Turn your love of reading into rewards you'll love with
Harlequin My Rewards